I0622374

Nymphomania Bloodlust

Jack E. Dunning

2D4 Press

Cave Creek, Arizona

This book is a work of fiction. Names, characters, places, and incidents come from the author's imagination or are used fictitiously. Any resemblance to actual events, locales, or persons living or dead, is coincidental.

Copyright © 2016 Jack E. Dunning

All rights reserved. No part of this book may be used or reproduced in any manner whatsoever without the written permission of the author or the publisher. 2D4 Press, P.O. Box 347, Cave Creek, AZ 85327. Email author: bjpost@cox.net.

First edition printing
ISBN-13:978-0692608586

This book is lovingly dedicated to my wife, Barbara, who has been my inspiration and the cornerstone for my writing from the beginning.

PROLOGUE...

The animal, or whatever it was, kept ripping at the flesh on her right arm. She screamed hysterically but Deke wasn't there. Where was he? It was in the middle of the night. Lani looked at her other arm, which was bleeding profusely. Then it took another swipe at her, ripping off the top of her nightgown and leaving deep, gushing scratches on her chest. At this rate, she thought, she would bleed to death. She could feel fur rubbing against her skin, and she cringed at the thought of what this might be.

The beast stood back as if it wanted to taunt her, making Lani wonder just what part of the body it would attack next. Even in the darkness of their bedroom, she could see fierce yellow eyes trained on her, and behind them must be some kind of sick brain that was deliberating its next move. There were snarls mixed with deep growls that scared the life out of her, causing her legs to weaken.

She began to buckle. The demon caught her and decided to take the opportunity to sink its fangs into her shoulder.

Lani shrieked in pain again but after this latest attack her strength returned, which she used to push away from her attacker. She didn't remember getting out of bed, but she was standing on her side, which meant that the bathroom was just behind her. She turned and vaulted through the door, almost falling into the shower. The curtains were open, drying from when she and Deke had showered together earlier. She hurried to lock the door.

Complete quiet. Maybe it had given up but she doubted that. Lani took inventory of her wounds and determined she wasn't bleeding as much as she thought at first, but the night-light wasn't very bright so she couldn't really see that well. The pain was agonizing, and she knew she was still losing blood and could lose consciousness if this continued. God, where was Deke? At that moment, the door shattered.

The wood splintered like it was nothing, hitting Lani in the face and upper torso. She had been holding up what was left of her nightgown but let it go in the turmoil of being buffeted by the door's destruction. She was completely nude now and the thing stood in front of her and…gawked? "What do you want from me?" she blurted out, connecting directly with the animal's eyes. There was a moment of hesitation, almost as if it wanted to answer her.

But there was no answer, just more ululation.

Lani backed away, trying to put space between her and this savage that didn't seem in any big hurry to finish the job. It gave her the opportunity to chance a quick look behind her and she saw the open closet. But what the hell good would that do, she thought? It would just smash through the door again. She had boxed herself in with nowhere to go. "I'm naked and I don't want to die this way," she was sobbing uncontrollably now, something she rarely did.

And then it moved closer.

Standing her ground, the creature suddenly lunged forward with claws extended, fangs bared and glowing eyes that seemed to anesthetize her for what it was going to do. Temporarily bridled by fright, in a second she snapped out of her stupor and bolted sideways toward the toilet. Lani's nemesis plunged through the open closet door, letting out a high-pitched wail that curdled her blood. Then it let out a roar and she slammed the door.

Lani headed back into the bedroom to try and find out why Deke wasn't coming to her rescue. She flipped on the lamp on his side of the bed and screamed as she saw him lying there, saturated with blood. Both of his arms had been ripped off at the shoulder and there was a huge gape in his chest exposing the cavity where his heart had been. He was missing a head. The animal had artfully mounted it on the top of the bedside lamp.

"Oh God, oh God," she repeated over and over.

That's when she heard the closet door being demolished as the slasher started for the bedroom. It moved through the bathroom, gnashing its canines in a fury that petrified Lani to the point she was unable to move, literally pinned against the wall. Moving around the bed, the beast grabbed one of Deke's arms and flung it across the room. She squealed in terror as she realized what was about to happen to her.

And then it grabbed her with claws that sunk into her body with more excruciating pain and she realized she was being attacked by a werewolf.

Lani felt a jolt to her body as she was finally jerked back to reality, trembling as she took her hand off the Death card from the Tarot deck in front of her. "That was too real," she said out loud, when the bell on the shop door signaled her scheduled client was here for a reading. That was a werewolf, she confirmed in her thoughts, but what does it have to do with me?

ONE…

Deke McKenna is a modern day cowboy who uses his cunning and ingenuity to catch criminals in Arizona. Folklore has it that he is descended from a family that lived in Roswell, New Mexico, who was temporarily taken up into an extraterrestrial spacecraft that had landed in the desert. The McKennas returned to earth unharmed, but supposedly with a newly acquired ability to see and understand the abnormal. They weren't necessarily psychic, just very insightful.

Deke didn't know if the story was true but never denied it either. A guy needs some mystery in his life, and this was his.

McKenna had broad shoulders like most swimmers with corresponding strength that he had developed on the swimming team at the University of Southern California. He was there on scholarship from Ventura High School, located in a small beach city just north of Los Angeles. Also a track star, he walked around in a well-rounded physique. His dark brown hair was thinning but to Deke this was just a sign of maturity.

At thirty-three he was solid as a rock. McKenna rarely went to the gym but had a treadmill at home he worked out on. The man was way too busy to let his body get flabby, which was a carry-over from his days on the Navy Shore Patrol. A boatswain's mate second class petty officer, he had spent the last two years of his four-year hitch as an SP working out of the Pentagon. And yes, contacts had been made, many of which were out of the service now and back in civilian life.

* * * * *

There is an Arizona mystery in the Phoenix metro area, the Superstitions, a range of mountains southeast of the city where the Lost Dutchman's Mine is supposed to be located. Jacob Walzer was a German who ended up in Arizona via New York's Ellis Island. He was nicknamed "Dutchie," thus the mine was given his name. Legend has it he discovered gold there in the 19th century that has been the source of over-zealous greed and mysterious deaths ever since.

1

The earlier mention of, "where the Lost Dutchman's Mine is supposed to be located," comes from the fact that there are so many stories about where you will find this treasure that it takes several chroniclers to keep up with them. And these are in abundance, since it seems that just about every journalist that has ever come to Arizona has taken the time to record his or her theory of where the gold is and where it came from.

It fascinates tourists and locals alike, while at the same time compels many to make their way into the Superstitions.

But some never come out of the mountains or are forever changed when they do. Arnold Barber, a snow bird, said goodbye to his wife, Agnes, one morning and then joined the clique of those succumbing to the lure of gold. Agnes warned Arnie, as she called him, but with strong shoulders and being one of those healthy mid-westerners, he was sure he still had enough vim and vigor to watch out for himself. And he didn't think he looked sixty-seven.

Arnie had a Hispanic friend from the Navy and one day the two of them were sitting having coffee in the crew's mess. His friend Luis was very superstitious and regularly talked to Arnie about Día de Los Muertos, the Mexican Day of the Dead. Luis eventually moved to Florida, but on that day aboard ship he told Arnie about a map that had been passed down through generations of his family, showing a gold mine in the Superstition Mountains.

When Arnie became an Arizona snowbird, the two reached an agreement that they would share half and half of anything found through using the map, and it was decided that on his next trip to Arizona in the fall of that year, Arnie would make his first trek into the Superstitions. Luis wasn't sure just how accurate the map was but said that it had been handed down with great care.

Barber traveled down the 101 Interstate from Cave Creek toward Apache Junction, turned east on U.S. 60 and headed into the Superstitions, finally arriving at Weavers Needle. He took the Peralta Trail and headed deeper into the mountains but stayed on the assigned passageway. Arnie finally reached a designated area on the map, where he was directed to venture off the trail.

As Barber headed into denser vegetation, one couple looked like they might follow him but apparently thought twice about it and continued on their way. Arnie began to perspire and wondered if it was due to the weather or the unknown in front of him. Was he all of a sudden beginning to believe the stories of how people got lost in these mountains, never finding their way out, or worse?

All of a sudden, he realized he had gone far enough off the trail that the other hikers were completely out of sight. Arnie turned to his map to study some of that expert advice that was supposed to lead him to the gold. He had followed the directions explicitly so far and didn't want to make the mistake of missing something critical that Luis' family had carefully documented on the paper. He became more confident by the minute and prodded ahead.

"Crack," a sound from the brush ahead. Arnie said "damn," and stopped in his tracks. "Who's there?" No answer. Nothing was visible, but the feeling that he wasn't alone grabbed his psyche and held on for several seconds. Then he looked up and caught sight of Weavers Needle, and the adventurer's blood began to surge through his veins. It was one of the major landmarks on his map. His mind was made up; this would be Arnold Barber's day.

Meanwhile, back on the Peralta trail, two seasoned prospectors talked about stories they had heard about something called a portal here in the Superstitions. One guy remarked, "There's supposed to be some kind of opening into another world where mysterious creatures come from. Sorta like those vortexes over in Sedona."

The other one asked, "Anyone ever seen these suckers do their act?"

The reply, "You believe in the supernatural?"

Surprised, the friend responded, "Come on, Luke, you don't really think there are hob goblins running around up here, do you?" They stopped on the trail looking straight at each other.

"Didn't say I did, just relating what I heard from Josh Beaumont, and he's about as skeptical as they get when it comes to the weird stuff."

Barber had started out at around nine AM and his watch now told him it was almost noon. He stopped and sat on the part rock, part vegetation that covered the ground in what he figured was a sandy wash. Looking at his map, Arnie spied an old dead tree right in front of him that was a carbon copy of a landmark on the map.

Arnie remembered reading about the Spaniards from as early as the 1540s, when Arizona was still part of Mexico, using the Superstitions as a storehouse for their treasures. They carefully sealed and camouflaged the entrance to their hoard, not knowing they had entered sacred Apache territory. The Apaches were very territorial and considered the gold an omen from their gods.

But in 1748 the land, which is now Arizona, was given to Mexican cattle-baron, Don Miguel Peralta of Sonora, in a land grant. The Peralta family would make infrequent trips to retrieve the gold left by the Spaniards that they had discovered, but stopped short of exhausting the supply. This was yet another of those stories that had been passed down through the years, and no doubt had something to do with the Apache attacks.

TWO…

But Barber would be more careful, more so than the people lost in the Superstitions, never seen again or found murdered in the mountains. Bodies found, skeletons seen in caves or unearthed in shallow graves by animals. These people were killed by guns, knives and even blunt instruments like a rock. One hiker reported being shot at by a sniper. He wouldn't succumb to this.

It was time to head around to the other side of Weavers Needle as the map directed. By the time Arnie reached the area, daylight was waning, and it would be getting dark in a few hours, so he had to work fast. The map was guiding him to the cave where the gold was supposed to be located and he started looking but couldn't find an opening. As twilight began to shroud the Superstitions, he searched fiercely for the cave.

Back to the map, Barber retraced his steps to make sure there was no mistake and that he was in the right area. But the landmarks matched, and he regularly checked his pedometer to insure the right number of steps. There was a small stretch of hills where he had been guided with instructions that weren't completely clear on the direction of the cave, but indicated the opening could be found if you stood in front and were looking straight at Weavers Needle.

He moved sideways along the small range but was never looking directly at the Needle. Daylight was growing dimmer and dimmer, and a semi-sense of panic was beginning to come over Arnie. Although he had a map to lead him, it would be all but useless at night and he wasn't prepared for an overnight stay. While he was contemplating turning around and heading for home, he noticed a part of the hill jutting out, facing in a different direction.

Walking around the bank there was just more overgrowth like there had been along the rest of the hill's wall. But Barber decided to take the standing position anyway, which he did, and found that he was looking right at Weavers Needle. The time of day forgotten, he eagerly started to clear away what didn't look like years of underbrush, but more like someone had just covered it as temporary camouflage.

5

As he worked to clear the opening to the cave, he suddenly stopped. The sun had gone down some time ago, with shadows forming all around him, and he had to decide what to do about a night in the mountains. First, he would call Agnes on his cell phone and explain, which he really didn't look forward to. He had picked up a couple of candy bars on the way in and still had plenty of water. What more could you ask for to celebrate what must be millions in gold bullion?

Barber took the phone out of his pocket and dialed Agnes. He hadn't noticed that he had no bars showing, but realized the problem when the message came up, "No Service Available." Panic returned, but he thought his wife would understand when she heard what he had found. Back at work, he was clearing loose branches covering one thin piece of rock that sat flat against the side of the hill. It was easy to move, and he let it slide to the ground.

Voila! A small opening, just three-foot square. All of a sudden he realized he would be entering ... sacred ground? He decided to conduct a quick search of the area to make sure no one was observing him. It wasn't easy to see his surroundings because it was almost dusk now, and once again he felt something evil nearby, which made him shudder. He looked even harder in the looming darkness. Nothing.

Barber took out his flashlight and shone it on the opening. He flashed it around the area to make sure there were no cracks in the surface of the hillside. All he needed now was to enter the cavern and have the roof or sides cave in on him. Everything looked secure, but he didn't really believe that ruled out any danger. It had been well disguised, but our amateur prospector had finally found the entrance and carefully went inside. It turned out to be well worth the effort.

His six foot height required that he bend over to enter, and a swing of the flashlight around the room showed there was definitely something ahead in the tunnel. Venturing further, now on high alert, he tried to penetrate the shadows but found the darkness was just too thick. Moving slowly with caution, Barber stopped to listen for sounds that could be human or an animal but heard nothing. Hoping it was safe, he continued to move ahead.

There were several tunnels off the main cave he checked. Nothing. But along the cave walls were markings that were undoubtedly left by the Indians, petroglyphs. Along with all the artwork, there was what looked like writing symbols. A warning?

He walked into a large circular room. Suddenly the flashlight exposed what looked like gold bricks stacked in the middle of the opening. Arnie thought he would explode with ecstasy and had to literally cover his mouth to keep from screaming for joy! The bullion was assembled in orderly rows about eight feet long and three feet wide. And then suddenly the reality of the discovery began to register.

After this initial shock subsided, OK, now that I've found the gold, how the hell do I get it out of here, he thought, obviously something he hadn't made arrangements for when planning this trip. Well, he had the map, so he could always return but would obviously need help. However, there was no one other than Agnes and Luis that he would trust. "Things are beginning to get complicated," he said out loud.

And then it occurred to him, there was a treasure of gold in the cave, but was it being protected by someone? The Apaches had considered the Superstitions sacred land and had killed all intruders in the stories he had read. Although he had examined the surroundings, that didn't insure there was nothing out there. And he still had that feeling of something ominous in the area. Maybe there was an Apache warrior that still held a grudge.

It was time for Barber to leave, reset the entrance to the way it was, and find a safe place to spend the night. He took out the Glock 9mm that he had in his waistband and checked it to make sure it was ready.

Arnie looked around; hadn't really disturbed anything, being careful to place the gold brick exactly in the same position he had taken it from. He was also careful to use a branch he had gotten from outside to sweep his footprints from the floor of the cave.

Were there any wild Indians left in the Superstitions? he thought to himself. If it actually was an Apache, he would have to confront him and maybe even have to kill him to protect his discovery. "Damn, I'm acting like a savage myself," Barber said. But he might have to use his 9mm at least for self-defense if he was threatened.

7

Now it was time to decide how he was going to spend the night. If he found a cave, he would have to build a fire to protect himself from animals. The fire might very well attract other prospectors or those from the trail. And of course there was always the possibility the owners or at least the guardian of the gold could return, or maybe even they were watching the cave entrance right now.

Arnie knew he had to come up with something fast, and it was then he decided he should get as close to Weavers Needle as he could, not really knowing why, but just that it seemed he might be more secure there. He would still need the fire but he would just have to take his chances. Fortunately, he had brought along a jacket just in case; Agnes had insisted. That and the fact that he was now a millionaire would get him through the night.

THREE…

Arnie took one last look at the gold, then turned and headed toward the mouth of the cave. Recovering the entrance, he exited and was glad there was still enough light available to get him to Weavers Needle. Then Arnie saw a round white light about two or three feet from the ground that was getting brighter and brighter. Images appeared in the circle that looked like a Rorschach design expanding into a kaleidoscope that went on for several seconds.

At that instant the circle changed to an opening resembling a black tunnel through which appeared a specter walking out and straight toward him. The orb began to close as the apparition strode ahead with a ring of light around the body, and what he saw stunned Barber beyond belief. It sure wasn't human and as it moved closer the abnormality let out a howl that almost panicked Arnie to the point of paralysis: "AAAAOOOOWWWW."

Barber could see exposed fangs from its maw, and it was then that he noticed the creature's blazing yellow eyes and furry body. The beast snarled as it moved even closer, walking on two feet; this was definitely some kind of animal. Arnie was petrified as he focused on…a werewolf?

There were more growls just as the attacker sunk its canines into Barber's shoulder. He fought with all his might but whatever it was, it had superhuman strength and there was no way he could match it. He started to pray and screamed with terror and pain as the slasher took off much of the front of Arnie's shirt and more skin with it.

The assault continued as it hacked at his right arm, ripping off his shirt sleeve. Barber heard slurping sounds in between more howling that resembled like someone or something eating their favorite meal. Was it not through with him yet? But it was then that he felt a puzzling sensation surge through his body, as if all of a sudden he was more than just Arnold Barber, very other-worldly.

And then everything stopped. As Arnie looked around for the abomination he noticed the white circle of light again, less than ten feet from him, just hovering above ground as it had before. The brute moved toward the light and stepped through as if entering another world, and in a second it was all gone. Barber stood there dazed but knew he had to get out of here and back to the Peralta trail if possible. He started his hike barely in a conscious state.

*   *   *   *   *

The Keeper of the Demons looked on with satisfaction as the first of the two beasts needed to complete its mission was spawned and was ready to do its bidding. All the planning necessary had been worthwhile and there was the feeling of great accomplishment. The Keeper had been there when Arnold Barber had been transformed into a werewolf and would be controlling his every move. But first, a test to determine the discipline of its creation.

*   *   *   *   *

Arnie woke up lying on his back, with the sun beating down, and several people standing around him. He quickly sat up and looked at his audience. "We thought you were dead," one guy said. Another added, "Your clothes are in such bad shape. Brad, here, has a change in his backpack if you want them." He thanked them but said he could manage OK, even though his shirt hung on him in torn ribbons.

But first he had to check his arm, shoulder, and his chest to see just how bad the gash wounds were from the beast that had attacked him. This was certainly no human being he had been confronted with, and he was concerned with the damage it might have done. Astonishment gripped him when a careful inspection of the areas concerned appeared to be as normal as the rest of his body.

But the memory of the night before was etched in his mind and he could still see his revolting adversary. A werewolf? "What the hell is going on?" Barber blurted out, and heads quickly turned as he tried to recover from his unexpected utterance. "Not to worry," he added.

Arnie declined any explanation to the group and rechecked directions on how to get back to his car. While on the way, he surveyed his body again, but it seemed to be fine. How do you explain wounds healing that fast?

As he hit the 101, headed back to Cave Creek, Barber began to wonder what Agnes would say. Should he come clean about what had really happened, or just say that he had stayed too late and realized he couldn't find his way out of the Superstitions at night? But how could he explain the condition of his clothes? He began to take an inventory in his head of what he had lost. Just the flashlight, his cellphone and…the map.

Horrified, he wondered if he could find his way back to the gold without it.

Of course, did he really want to find his way back? The mental image he had was fixed in his mind and was as vivid as if it had happened moments ago. He remembered every detail that took place, experiencing the terror and agony as if it were real again. Claws slashing into his skin from what looked like a supernatural animal that had also taken a bite out of his shoulder, but didn't kill him? Why? Was he losing his mind?

But when he got home there would have to be a complete explanation, putting himself at his wife's mercy. She was understanding, but coming home with his clothes in this condition would certainly look suspicious. Not to mention traveling down the freeway looking like he did. But somehow he thought, things would fall into place.

It was when Arnie was leaving the freeway on his way north that he had his first weird feeling. His bones began to ache and there was a tremor in his jaw, both only momentary, and then he felt normal again. This whole episode had been creepy, no, it had actually been bizarre, and by the time he got home he'd better have his story straight. Agnes had been beside herself when he called her using the phone of one of the hikers. She pressed him for details but he begged off saying anything in front of the others.

The closer he got to his house, the more jangled his nerves became. And for the first time he noticed there was more hair on his arms than usual, extending to the palms of his hands. "I've never had hair in the palm of my hand," he barked to no one. Observing his fingers on the steering wheel, they felt somewhat sore, with his fingernails looking different to him, more pointed than square.

11

And then he was pulling into his driveway and there was Agnes, looking through the front window as he got out of the car. She rushed out the door and grabbed and hugged him with a ferocity he had never experienced before. His wife wouldn't let go, and Arnie realized how traumatized she must be, so he just held on until both seemed satisfied. Then she stood back and surprise flashed over her face as she noticed the ragged shape his clothes were in.

"Let's go in the house," he said.

After over an hour of explanation where Agnes raised her hand to an open mouth in alarm no less than ten times, Barber sat back, satisfied that he had related his tale of horror as accurately as possible, replacing the werewolf with just some animal. Agnes sat there stunned. Minutes passed without either of them saying anything when he said, "There's more." Agnes bolted forward in her chair expecting the worst, as if she hadn't already heard it.

Arnie stood up and took off the remnants of his shirt as his wife gasped, expecting to see terrible scratch marks on his arm and chest, and puncture wounds on his shoulder. She gulped even harder when there was no damage to her husband's body at all. He was about to mention the hair on his arms and palms when he noticed it was no longer there. Better left for later, he thought, but feared these phenomena would definitely come back.

Agnes suddenly came out of her daze, jumping to her feet exclaiming excitedly, "We have to get you to emergency right away. What if that animal was rabid? You'll have to get shots." She made a move to their bedroom when Barber stood up and grabbed her arm in a quieting way. "What do you think an ER doctor would do if I told him the same story I just told you? He'd put me in the psycho ward and I would probably be under observation for months."

He let that sink in and before his wife could protest said, "I'm going to get out of these clothes and take a shower," then added, "I can get a tetanus booster from doc Bainbridge." Arnie hurried off before Agnes could react and headed for the bathroom. He kicked off the tennis shoes, when it hit him like a bombshell. His feet were disfigured, covered with hair, and had toenails forming that looked like claws.

FOUR…

Barber hadn't mentioned anything to his wife about his feet but had had a tough time getting his slippers on over the freakish change. As he sat on his side of the bed now, he nervously hoped that the aberration had gone away, or that he would be quick enough to get his feet under the covers before Agnes noticed. The slippers were easy to remove, thus, providing optimism that he would be normal again.

The two said good night and Arnie kissed his wife, more passionately, she thought, than usual. Agnes knew something was going on, but she was totally confused between her husband's story and the way he had been acting since he returned home from…those mountains. She readied herself for a sleepless night.

He lay there as quiet as possible, hoping not to disturb his wife. She always had a hard time falling asleep, but he would know when she did because of the snoring that always followed her dropping off. Tonight would be even harder with all that had happened since he had gotten home. He thought back that Agnes had prepared dinner and after they had progressed in the meal, all of a sudden she had this startled look on her face. Arnie stopped abruptly and then realized he had been eating with his hands, his silverware untouched.

As he continued to lie quietly, he began to consider the episode in the mountains and all that had happened since he was back home. Was his nemesis some kind of supernatural animal that had made its home in the Superstitions? It did have superhuman strength, which he had experienced, and it definitely looked unearthly, but how many animals walk on two legs? It wasn't an ape. Barber didn't want to even think it, but he did…was it really a werewolf?

Arnie waited patiently for the snoring but apparently the dismay over what had happened to him was keeping her awake. Up until now he thought he could wait this out but strong urges were gnawing at his psyche, ripping into his inner soul, demanding to be acknowledged and satiated. What the hell was happening to him, he thought, where is this going? The feeling was so overpowering that he was afraid to go to sleep until it was gone.

13

Agnes had a sudden inner quake, fearing that something was going on in the bed that she had no control over. The feeling escalated until she thought she might scream, but she held it when she felt her husband shudder next to her.

The sensation continued to consume Barber as he began to twist and turn in the bed uncontrollably to the point that he was afraid of disturbing Agnes. Something was out of control, and he had to do something about it now.

He got out of bed and headed for the bathroom. There was a night light bright enough so he didn't have to turn on the overhead fixture. He could see himself in the mirror, and the minute his reflection rebounded from the glass and reentered his inner mind, he felt something take complete control over his body.

And then another shudder convulsed his body as he began to tremble frenziedly. He already had an agonizing headache as he watched normal fingernails turn into pointed claws, while dark grey hair covered his arms and chest in a heavy mantle of fur.

The pain was becoming unbearable as Barber watched his hands turn into paws, and when he looked into the mirror again, noticed his canines mutating into fangs. His nose began to take the form of a protruding snout and his ears were growing longer and pointed. Normal shoulders reshaped into contorted masses of muscular revulsion, making him look like a…wild animal.

He hadn't worn his slippers into the bathroom and Arnie observed his feet make another switch into horrific shapes, with toes sprouting into claws and dark hair and fur replacing the skin. His legs were taking on the configuration of the beast he had confronted last evening, as his pajama bottoms were ripped through from the transformation and fell to the floor. He stood there nude, at least in the sense of a human, which he suddenly realized he no more was.

The bathroom door began to open slowly and then Agnes was standing there in her nightgown looking at him, at first not recognizing what had happened to her husband. Then she turned on the overhead light and let out a scream that could only be fathomed by someone who had experienced the supernatural. And then she fainted. Arnie was

14

slowly evolving from human reasoning into that of an animal but still had the judgment to pick up his wife and lay her on the bed.

He knew he had to get out of the house before he did something terrible, so he headed into the great room, unlocking the front door. He snarled in a way that Barber felt sure would be the last thing he would remember tonight as Arnold Barber. And then there were more retractions in his body. He opened the door and headed outside as he started growling ferociously. The changeover was complete.

*   *   *   *   *

On the street, the beast, now with the full instincts of an animal, knew it had to beware of humans until it was ready to spring and do what it had been sent here to do. Crouching low but still on two feet, it sped down the street, giving off regular snarls as it passed homes that were blacked out for the night. Predators can smell their prey, but the demon caught no scent nearby. It continued on, picking up speed as it examined the empty intersection ahead, contemplating its next move.

Barber lived in one of those neighborhoods in Cave Creek that was medium class with houses that snowbirds were attracted to. Passing over Cave Creek Road, there was a newly built apartment complex. Two young girls had just gotten out of their car and were crossing the parking lot to the apartment entrance.

The fiend moved faster toward the girls and at the edge of the tarmac let out a brutish growl; the girls stopped in their tracks. When they saw where the noise had come from, both let out a blood curdling scream that must have reverberated throughout all the apartments. One girl took off running toward the building, yelling at her friend to run. But the other girl was frozen in her tracks and simply stood there waiting, as if she had been summoned to.

The mutant was still moving and reached its target in seconds. The woman was frightened out of her mind and suddenly she stopped any sound, paralyzed by fear as she was grabbed with claws that ripped off her left sleeve, then the arm. The pain was excruciating, and she was bleeding profusely as she was swung around, and the attacker from behind dug its claws across her chest leaving almost nothing left of either breast.

It wasn't finished. When she fell to the ground, the demon tore into the already slashed chest and ripped her heart out while the woman was still alive. The devil-murderer stood back as if to marvel over what it had done and then seemed to admire the organ for a split second. Suddenly it began to consume the heart with the ravenous appetite of… an animal. Then a transformation began to take place, back to Arnold Barber.

By now the few people who lived there were looking out their windows, and the friend who got away had called Phoenix police. In the darkness, all the apartment dwellers could see was a form but couldn't even tell if it was a man or a woman. Certainly not that it was completely nude, and was changing from animal to human.

Arnie heard the sirens and knew he had to leave now, and he had to take a route home that would lead him around the cops. He crossed the side street and walked south through some underbrush that kept him from being seen. Then, when he was sure all the police cars that were coming had arrived, he darted across Cave Creek Road and headed toward his development. He was lucky it was late and there was almost no traffic.

* * * * *

The Keeper was happy. Arnold Barber had passed his test and was primed for the task his fiendish metamorphosis had been created for. He was ready, and the next attack was already planned that would make Phoenix and Arizona politicians pay for what they had done. Revenge was the Keeper's, and it planned to make those responsible accountable.

* * * * *

Barber arrived at his locked front door and quickly rang the bell several times but Agnes answered almost immediately. The light was on in the great room, where she had been waiting for him. But seeing him

16

naked was more than she expected, although the manifestation she had seen him in earlier was certainly worse. She managed a, "Where have you been?" as he quickly entered the house, slamming the door.

"Can we talk about this tomorrow?" he pronounced as a decree, not a question, and went to bed.

FIVE...

Reporters had the entrance to Phoenix Police headquarters surrounded waiting for the press conference that was scheduled by Chief Ruben McIntyre. He promised not only information on the brutal murder of Cynthia Haskins, the young Cave Creek woman allegedly attacked by a monster, but also to name a special investigator to examine the facts and get to the bottom of this terrible atrocity. Chief McIntyre walked out the door accompanied by another man.

"Hello and welcome to a briefing that I would have preferred not to give." He looked tired as if he had been up all night. "First of all, let me introduce you to Deke McKenna, who will be assisting me in the probe to learn who or what perpetrated the heinous crime on Ms. Haskins."

The Chief continued. "We have looked at the details of the assault on this young lady, interviewed her neighbors at the apartment building, and have taken a statement from her roommate, who will remain anonymous for obvious reasons. As far as I know and according to all my investigative officers, nothing like this has ever happened in the city of Phoenix, or even Arizona." Hands went up from reporters but McIntyre waved them off saying, "Questions later."

Continuing, "Because the description by Cynthia Haskins' friend was so inconceivable," he paused, "representing something perhaps...not of this world, I decided to bring in my friend Deke McKenna. As some of you may know, Deke dabbles in the supernatural and has become something of an expert in preternatural beings. I really am not convinced our perp is from another world, but just to be sure I've asked my friend to assist us in this investigation. Deke?"

The man who was already familiar to most of the reporters stepped forward, clean shaven for a change, sporting a six foot two inch frame that mirrored the Marlboro Man. Wearing his familiar black t-shirt with jeans and black sneakers, he was not the kind of guy anyone would expect to be into the abnormal. He was so well-versed on the subject that he taught classes in the local community colleges. His students loved him and his sessions overflowed.

"From what I can tell," McKenna started, "there is more to this than the evidence we have seen so far, even more than what the murdered girl's friend told us about what she had seen. I don't want to say supernatural, but I already have, haven't I?" Grin. "I know you like a juicy story, but so far I'm not sure that's what this is. Right now my gut wonders if some maniac might have dressed up in an animal suit and killed this girl."

"How about the fact that the girl's breasts were ripped off and her heart removed?" one reporter asked.

"The attacker could have used artificial claws to do his damage," McKenna decided to take questions.

"How about the ripped off arm and what happened to her heart?" was another question.

"We're not positive it was ripped off. Could've been severed by a very sharp knife."

Deke looked at Chief McIntyre, then back at his inquirer, "The heart being gone has us stumped so far," was the answer.

"Which means you really aren't sure about anything except that she is dead?"

"Well, you might say that…" when McKenna was interrupted.

"What special action do you plan to take on this, Chief McIntyre, I mean since it is so out of the ordinary?"

"I've assigned two detectives to work on this full time until they find the monster that did this. We're checking bits of evidence found at the scene and when that is evaluated we'll know more."

"What kind of evidence, Chief?"

"Looks like bits of hair, and there may be pieces of flesh under the woman's fingernails." A pause while he looked at McKenna. "Forensics is checking everything we collected and will get back to us shortly."

"How about clothing? Did our butcher leave anything that could be checked?"

"Nothing we found." Then the Chief said, "That's all I can tell you right now until we hear from forensics. Thank you all." And with that Ruben McIntyre and Deke McKenna turned around and walked into the building.

Most of the reporters loaded up their gear and headed for their cars except for Miriam Maloney with KBED-TV in Phoenix, who hung back and sidled up to her producer/cameraman, Marty. "What do you make of the side glances between those two guys?" she asked. Not waiting for an answer, "The first one was by McKenna when he was talking about Haskin's heart. The second by McIntyre when he was talking about the evidence."

Miriam thought about all this for a couple of minutes, then took out her notepad and started making notes. "I took some classes on the paranormal at Northern Arizona U. but I always thought the professor was creepy. Guess where we're headed next?"

* * * * *

The two men walked quietly to the Chief's office; Deke was the first to speak. "Hope I didn't screw up using the word supernatural."

"Hell, I thought you did it just to throw them off after what I said," was McIntyre's reply. "Anyway you probably satisfied their curiosity when you allowed as how it was some kind of dress up costume."

"I don't know. Did you see the look on Miriam Maloney's face from Channel 16? That looked like an inquiring mind if I've ever seen one. Don't think we've seen the last of her."

"You may be right but don't you agree this is all coming down awful strange and these guys have a right to be curious? I placed a rush on getting the evidence analyzed so we can put this preternatural speculation to rest."

As they walked into the office and closed the door, McKenna said, "I wouldn't be so sure about ruling out something unconventional. We both know that arm wasn't severed by a knife; the stump looked like it had been ripped loose with nerves and tendons just left dangling. But the other thing, it is the custom of the werewolf to use its super-human strength to hunt down humans and eat their hearts."

McIntyre was absorbing what he really didn't want to believe. He had a creature on the streets of his city committing murders he didn't understand. He expected a call from the Mayor, maybe even the

Governor, any time now, and he'd better have more answers than he had at the present time. "What do we do, man?" he said. "Are we really talking about something from another world?"

"I think there is a distinct possibility there is something out there that ordinary police work cannot explain." The two had worked together before, although not with a case this extraordinary, but the confidence was there to know the man knew what he was talking about. "The flesh under the fingernails won't prove anything without DNA. Animal and human flesh are basically the same."

The Chief nodded, as if overwhelmed with everything that he was hearing. "Guess I'd better order the extra DNA test," he said. "Will it tell us what kind of animal?" He asked.

"Yup. Humans have 46 chromosomes and animals have different numbers, which is how they determine what kind. Once we know what we're dealing with here, we can chart an approach to the investigation. Until then, there's not much more we can do."

McIntyre pondered the last statement and just hoped they found an answer before another grisly event occurred.

* * * * *

The Keeper was not happy that Deke McKenna was going to be meddling in its affairs. It could handle the Phoenix Police Department because they were not schooled in the ways of the supernatural but McKenna posed a problem with his fluency in the subject. There were ways to handle this but if this person so closely connected with law enforcement was eliminated, especially so early in its master plan, there could be real repercussions. Not now but maybe later.

But it was satisfied the first of its creatures' tests had been successful.

21

SIX…

Sometimes a fella just had to go rejuvenate his energy, he thought to himself, as the two of them got ready to head up to Sedona. Deke McKenna made it a habit to visit one of the vortexes there at least once a month to enrich his endowment for the abnormal; he liked the one at the airport best. Elaine Baker (Lani) finished packing her suitcase for the trip and set it by the door next to Deke's.

Lani also regularly went to Sedona to compare notes with other metaphysical and spiritual professionals.

McKenna had a small cabin in Oak Creek, and after they had taken care of business, they would head back to the serenity of the cabin and let it all sink in. Sedona was known for its vortexes and there were four that were considered the strongest: Bell Rock, actually in Oak Creek, Cathedral Rock, Boynton Canyon and the one at the airport. A vortex is like a funnel created by the motion of spiraling energy. They could look like a whirlwind, a tornado, or water flowing down a drain. Or not visual at all.

Lani liked to renew friendships with other metaphysical practitioners and hone her craft in the holistic environment. She specialized in reading tarot cards. She was disturbed when people reacted to the reading of them as witchcraft and voodoo. When interpreted correctly, the cards were a means of divination, self-visualization and understanding, plus fortune-telling to help others make decisions for themselves.

Deke pulled the Hummer H1 Alpha around to the front of the house and opened the back for their luggage. It was a 2006 diesel fully equipped with oversized tires and a protected powertrain for navigating the desert.

McKenna went down Schoolhouse Road to Cave Creek Road, headed west and then curved south to Carefree Highway where he turned west again. The Hummer sped past several small communities until it came to Intestate 17 and then took a right onto the freeway. They would travel north until reaching state route 179 heading north and into Oak Creek. In the village of Oak Creek, Deke turned right on Desert Sky Trail and followed this until reaching the cabin.

It was positioned about fifty yards off the road in a clump of tall juniper shrubs as well as Arizona cypress and pinyon pine trees. Lani always had a feeling of tranquility when they arrived here. Together they hauled in their stuff and placed it in the bedroom. She went back out and picked up some groceries while Deke went about bringing the place back to life after hibernating for a month.

"Wanna head over to Casa de Habas for dinner?" It was their favorite Mexican restaurant in Arizona.

"Why not, but let me call Gwendolyn first and set something up for tomorrow." She pulled out her cellphone and made the call. "OK, everything is set up for me. How about you? Making your regular trek up to the Airport vortex?" She had been there once with McKenna, but had had the weirdest sensation that she could not explain and had not been back since. Her friends in Sedona explained it as her spirituality challenging the energy of the vortex. Lani wasn't sure.

At the restaurant they sat across from each other in a booth, munching on chips and salsa. "What're you thinking about?" she asked, already knowing the answer.

"This damn case," he answered, adding, "don't you think it's curious that we have a werewolf invading Phoenix, all of a sudden?" The question wasn't rhetorical since McKenna valued Lani's opinion.

"Wanna talk about it?"

"Not now, maybe after I've had time to think about it."

The food came and they pushed aside the chips for the main course, chile relleno for Lani and a cheese burrito for Deke, which they both ate quietly with very little conversation. They never did talk much while eating but this was a particularly quiet meal. "Guess we've both got a lot on our minds," McKenna concluded.

Lani had had weird dreams before, some about McKenna mixed with the supernatural and they never ended well. She hoped to get some answers in Sedona. "I'm anxious for Gwendolyn to read my tarot cards and see if she can interpret my bad dreams," she said. They had flan for dessert with coffee and headed back to the cabin.

McKenna puttered with things that needed attention from their month of absence. He found evidence that a snake had made its way into the kitchen, leaving its skin after molting, apparently using the side of the table leg to help the shedding process. He picked up the discarded covering and threw it in the trash. Next it was time for his favorite book, which he left at the cabin, and read over and over. It was Jack London's *Martin Eden.*

Lani took out the card table and put it up not far from where Deke was reading and pulled a chair over. "Do you mind if I read my tarot cards? It takes a lot of concentration."

"No problem, once I pick up London, I can't put it down. We'll both do our own thing."

They had the kind of relationship where they could do this without neglecting each other, a kind of comradery where silence between two people was OK, even when they were going in different directions. But they always reconnected with a refreshed feeling and the sense of self accomplishment.

Lani spread the tarot cards out on the table and began to shuffle them. She used a combination of the card player's method along with scrambling the cards, which she felt produced better readings. And she was good at what she did helping many of her clients and friends solve their problems. Finishing the shuffling, she started placing the cards in the Celtic Cross layout. It consisted of ten cards in an arrangement that resembled a sideways cross.

Number one, representing the present, revealed the Devil card, indicating violence. Two, the challenge position, was the Death card, symbolizing death when accompanied by other specific cards. Three, signifying the past, disclosed the Ten of Swords, one of the cards that supported death. Four, the future, proclaimed the Nine of Swords, also a partner with Death with the Ten. Lani was almost afraid of number five but it was insignificant.

The six card, denoting what was in the reader's subconscious, was The Tower card, which meant a sudden change with unexpected events. She really didn't need to see more with the six cards pointing clearly to violence and death. But she completed the ten cards, the last four of no consequence, and just sat there looking at the display. Should she tell Deke or not? It would just add to his problems. Maybe she could shake it off; at least she could try.

Lani reassembled the Tarot cards into a deck and returned them to their container. She was a professional Tarot card reader and had done this sort of thing on countless occasions, both for others and herself. This had been a general reading with no direct relation to any person or event. She just let the cards fall to see what was going on in their sphere of intimacy around the cabin. But with an obvious outcome she worried about what would happen next.

What if I don't tell him and something real bad happens? she thought. Tarot isn't absolute, and a lot depends on the reader's interpretation. Maybe I'm just down in the dumps today and seeing things that aren't there. But when you mix the Devil card with Death, and supported by the others, it's hard to question those results. She had never once interrogated her conclusions like this but she had a feeling this was too close to home.

"How about listening to some music?" and Lani almost jumped out of her skin.

"Oh hell, I'm sorry I startled you. Deep in thought about something?"

"No problem, yes I was but I would much rather listen to music with you and cuddle, unless you don't feel romantic?"

"Are you kidding?" and he turned on the stereo inserting several discs, turned the lights down low, and beckoned her over to the couch.

As she sat down with McKenna there was a very creepy feeling in the pit of her stomach and she had a terrible premonition.

SEVEN…

They looked like zombies congregated around something just
outside the cabin. She could see them clearly with the outdoor lights that
came on automatically when there was motion. But she couldn't see
what their focus of attention was on. Lani had heard the sounds and
turned over to wake up McKenna and found that he was gone. When
she couldn't find him in the cabin she rushed to the front windows and
saw the commotion.

"Good God, is he outside?" she began to choke on the words.

"Deke, Deke, where the hell are you?" she screamed. No answer.
From room to room, a complete search of the cabin produced nothing.
The only thing she could find missing was his pants. Had he put them
on to go out to investigate what the noise was all about? He wouldn't
walk right out the front door into their hands. She checked the back door
and it was unlocked. Had he discovered these…whatever they were, and
crept into the woods to investigate?

But what were they, and then it occurred to her they looked like
the vampires McKenna had described in his paranormal class she had
attended. One decided to move up to the window where she was
standing and she was afraid it would attempt to get in. It stopped about
two feet away and it was then that Lani saw the cold black iris in its
eyes, which meant it, was hyperdilated, she knew, so it could see in the
night.

The whites of its eyes were a flaming red. They were definitely
vampires.

She ducked down, hoping it had missed her, assuming it could
see inside. The question was whether they would try to enter the cabin
and she began to think what she could do to repel them. It was then that
she thought of her laptop, on the table in the kitchen. Lani crawled on
her hands and knees to the dinette table where she had left her computer.
Her hands shook so frenziedly she almost toppled over.

She powered it up and immediately went to Google. In the
search line she typed, "what repels vampires?"

The very first site that came up was, "Weaknesses of the
Vampire," and it listed a total of twelve. She started through the list and

garlic was at the top followed by a new edition, silver. She had neither. Her vision blurred from the fear. There was the cross and the mirror plus others listed, most of which she either didn't have or couldn't create the necessary setting. And then she hit upon the one that had kept them out.

Vampires cannot enter your house without first being verbally invited inside. But safe for how long?

And why hadn't Deke come back into the cabin? The creatures were all out front and were concentrating on something they had encircled and he must know this. So why didn't he slip back in through the back door since he must know of the invitation weakness? Now she was really worried, but McKenna could take care of himself and he must be trying to figure out a way to get rid of them.

She tried to contain herself but when your emotions are running out of control it's hard to think clearly. She shook until she thought she would come unglued not knowing how long she could handle the stress. She hated guns but for once wished she had an AK-47. But bullets were useless against vampires unless they were silver. Lani sobbed at the thought of what these monstrosities would do to her. Or maybe what they had already done to Deke.

She headed to the front and heard shouts coming from the demons. They all had fixed their attention on the cabin, huddling around like a monster brigade readying for the attack. But they all held their positions about five feet away, and she still couldn't see what they had been converged on earlier. This was beginning to feel like another nightmare, but her attention was averted as she heard one of the fiends cry out, "Come out Lani, come out and join us."

"How do they know my name?" she said with alarm, as if hoping these things would answer. Again, "Come out Lani, come out and join us." It reverberated in her ears like a chant, with the expectation that Lani would obey. They were messin' with her mind, she thought, and stood on her tip toes to see over the hoard of shapes that confronted her. It looked like a body.

The incantation went on in regular cadence, getting louder by the minute until she realized there would be no way she could ignore the vampire's wailing. Afraid she would weaken, Lani decided to turn on the stereo and drown out their calls. She hit the switch and the blue light didn't come on, meaning there was no power. "Oh God, they've cut the electricity." Thankfully the motion lights on the front of the house were solar. Again, "Come out Lani, come out and join us."

After an hour of listening to their droning on and on with "Come out Lani, come out and join us," getting louder and louder, she was afraid she might break. She tried stuffing her fingers in her ears to try and cut off the sounds. It worked partially but the clamoring still came through enough to grate on her nerves. Would it eventually weaken her senses so she would actually want them to come in and get it over with? Lani shuddered.

Once again she thought of Deke, hoping he was safe, and wishing he would burst in at any minute with a plan. He always had a plan. She felt sure he was working on one and they would be rescued from this predicament any moment. But it was more than just a predicament, it was a full-blown crisis. She couldn't call him on his cell phone for fear the vampires would hear the ring. But she could call 911 and report what was going on. But would they believe her?

Lani headed to the bedroom where her phone was located in her purse. Yanking it out she hit 911 and waited for the call to go through. Nothing. Panic. She started to try again and noticed there were no bars on the top. No reception. This had happened before but not now, "God why did it have to happen now?" she screamed. Another attempt produced the same results. She rushed back to the front of the house to see if the reception was any better. It wasn't.

When she looked out the window she squealed with the pain of someone who had seen a living hell that meant the end of her world. She blinked. They were still there and she let out another terrifying cry that seemed to ricochet all around the room and reenter her body like a horrifying projectile of doom. She was looking at Deke McKenna being held by two vampires. Another monster walked up behind him and sunk its fangs into his left shoulder.

Blood spurted everywhere and Lani collapsed.

Hanging in limbo, her senses slowly returned from the atrocity she had just witnessed. Maybe I was imagining it, she thought and she pulled herself back up to the window and looked out. "Oh God," another of the vampires was on the other shoulder now with blood running down the front of Deke's bare chest from both attacks. It looked like there was a line for each to take their turn that would drain McKenna's body of all its blood.

"OK, why don't you just come and get me too," she said it before she thought.

Lani had just invited these freaks into her house, and they were quick to do her bidding by first dropping Deke and then crashing through the front door as she turned and ran for the bedroom. They could smell new blood. Slamming the bedroom door and locking it wouldn't stop them so she had to figure out how to save herself. When the beasts smashed through the bedroom door, the bathroom was all that was left but it was then that they grabbed her.

The only way Lani could see was from a side table clock that was lit up and what she saw was hideous. The eyes with black centers and red rims so bright and penetrating in the darkness that they seemed to dismiss any thoughts she might have of saving herself. Their mouths drooling McKenna's blood from fangs that were obviously ready to consume their next victim. And then the mutants threw her on the bed and carnivorously began to drink her blood.

Lani screamed and she kept screaming.

"Wake up, wake up," Deke was shaking her, "you're having another nightmare." She couldn't believe it was a dream so she continued to thrash around until she felt strong arms grab her and hold her in a vise grip. Finally she began to relax. "Oh God McKenna, it was so real. I thought you were dead." He ruffled her hair and said calmly, "Well, I'm not, and you're just fine. We fell asleep on the couch listening to music and then I heard your screams."

Later they were sitting at the kitchen table drinking coffee. Lani had insisted on going out front to convince herself there were no vampires. After she told McKenna the whole story, they talked about the significance of her dreams and just what they meant in relation to her metaphysical abilities. She decided to tell Deke about the Tarot card reading and that just added more fuel to an already conflicting dilemma. They both sat in silence for a long time.

He got up and walked around the kitchen clearly in deep thought. Then he spoke, "Lani, a supposed werewolf has already viciously killed a woman in Phoenix. And now you have an out-of-this-world dream. Dear God, are we now supposed to expect a vampire attack?" She had no answer.

*   *   *   *   *

In her dream Elaine Baker had anticipated the Keeper's next move. Was this just luck? it thought. This was another one that bears watching. But, again, moving too fast on Deke McKenna's girlfriend could create more backlash that would put obstacles in the way of the Keeper's blueprint to wipe out the anti-Apache politicians in Arizona's state government. For the time being it would just continue with the plan and keep a close watch on Elaine Baker.

EIGHT...

   The Arizona Cardinals were playing the San Francisco Forty-
Niners on Sunday and Jerry O'Ryan and his wife Bernice had season
tickets. Even with the rotten record of the team, along with constant
meddling by the owners, the two were loyal fans. They would attend
Sunday's game with Jerry wearing his number eleven Larry Fitzgerald
jersey, and Bernie, as he called her, would wear Jay Feely's number
three. Both the white versions.
   There was a storm rolling through Phoenix so the roof of the
University of Phoenix stadium would be closed. "I don't care if the
stadium is open, do you?" Jerry asked Bernice.
   "Nope," she replied, "football is football, no matter where it's
played." Her husband was so glad she loved the game as much as he did
because it gave them something to do together. "Why don't we just plan
to eat at the game," she added, to which Jerry gave a thumbs up.
   They always got there early to watch all the festivities. Bernice
knew Jerry liked to watch the cheerleaders—he even carried
binoculars—but he wouldn't admit it. They were both in their thirties,
her a couple years older than he. She was a very attractive woman with
a full figure, and as her husband bragged, really filled out her sweaters.
Jerry was nice looking, balding early, but a buff guy as the younger set
defined it.
   Bernice looked at her watch and it was just before eleven AM
when she called to her husband in the bedroom to get moving. The
game started at one-fifteen and they had to drive from Mesa to Glendale
on the west side. "The weather's going to make for slow driving so
we'd better get started if you want to see the girls in action." Coming
around the corner, Jerry smiled and said, "Why would I want to look at
them when I have you?" The right thing to say.
   They arrived at the stadium around eleven forty-five, and ran
inside as fast as they could under a large umbrella with rain pouring
down. They headed directly for their seats needing no help from the
attendants. Once seated, Bernie looked around for the regulars that were
usually there but many of them were missing. Then there was a huge

clap of thunder, quite unusual for Arizona, and the storm seemed to be escalating.

"Where're the girls?" Jerry shouted over the music, and received a side glance from his wife. About that time the cheerleaders, as if reacting to his question, marched onto the field and began one of their routines in time with the music.

"Are you happy now?" she asked, knowing the answer. Her husband smiled without taking his eyes off the show.

Walter Rogers sat with his wife, Amy, in a section adjacent to Jerry and Bernice. They were not season ticket holders and neither was really a sports fan, nor did either know much about or even support the Cardinals. On Monday, Amy had awakened and said to Walter, "We're going to the football game this weekend." Walter was surprised but agreed since, at least, it would get them out of the house. Amy even took care of the tickets.

"Why are we here, Amy?" he asked her, with a look on his face that said he was definitely serious. "To see a football game, what else?" she responded, and she too looked perfectly sincere. But there was a certain amount of trepidation in her answer and her husband noticed it.

Amy began to perspire, more than usual she thought, when she asked her husband, "Are you warm?" She noticed most people were sitting around in sweaters or light jackets so why was she feeling flushed? Amy was a gorgeous brunette with a great body sporting breasts that looked like they were chomping at the bit to get free from her T-shirt. She shifted in her seat nervously and looked at her husband.

Walter, who had on a vest, said, "I'm fine, seems a little cool in here to me." He observed his wife again and noticed perspiration break out on her neck and forehead. "Are you okay, Amy? You've been acting strange since your overnight trip into the Superstition Mountains. Walter's wife was very adventurous and enjoyed the out of doors, where he preferred to sit at home and read a book. Sometime she just had to get out and let it go.

The question triggered thoughts of the recent mountain excursion where Amy had strayed from her two fellow hikers and spent the night alone in the mountains. When they eventually found each other, she told them, later Walter, about the strange thing that had happened.

It was too dark to look for her two partners so she found a shallow cave to get her out of the elements and built a small fire in its entrance to keep away the animals. She laid out her sleeping bag in the limited space and was soon asleep. Awakened, she noticed the fire was ebbing and got up to add more wood. Startled, she saw a figure approaching out of a white halo that turned out to be a beautiful Indian girl dressed only in moccasins, a brief cloth covering her privates, and braided hair.

Amy had had an attraction to other good looking women in the past and she and Walter had discussed this on several occasions. With her husband's general nature of passivity about sex, he didn't seem concerned, and she had had a couple of affairs on the side. Nothing serious but enough to convince her she was a switch-hitter. Amy looked at the Indian maiden with interest and she definitely noticed a positive response. But was this safe?

As she moved out of the cave, welcoming arms were raised as an indication of friendship, and when coming together the two of them embraced in a way that felt to Amy like deep passion and she responded. The Indian girl started to remove Amy's shirt and bra and slowly turned her around. While massaging Amy's breasts and pressing hardened nipples into her back, she began to kiss Amy's neck from one side to the other, back and forth, sending her playmate into ecstasy.

She began to breathe hard with short breaths that matched her sexual euphoria but when trying to turn around to face her partner she was restrained with a strength that was far greater than normal. All of a sudden Amy was frightened and struggled to free herself. But it was no use as her constraints only grew tighter. It was then that the Indian girl brushed Amy's neck with her lips, like another kiss.

Then she felt what seemed to be two pin pricks, almost painless, and at that point she passed out.

It was the next morning when she woke up, still out in front of the cave, with her mind reeling from the memory of the night before. While not recalling everything, yet enough to scare her all over again, she looked around to make sure she was alone. It was then that her two friends found her and both immediately put their hands up to their mouth in surprise. Amy put her hand on her neck, defensively, but they couldn't have seen the marks.

"What?" she exclaimed, thinking her adversary might have done more damage to her somewhere else. Again, "What?" no answer. Then one friend said, "Amy, where is your shirt and bra?" She looked down and suddenly realized she had nothing on from the waist up. "Oh my God," while covering her breasts with her arms. "Here they are," the other friend said coming out from behind her. "OK, what the hell were you doing last night?" and both friends laughed.

It was then that Amy related her story, repeating the same account of the incident to Walter when she got home. She tried to show the prick marks to all but the general consensus was that if there were any marks on her neck, they were probably scratches. When she went to bed that night, she wondered if the friends or her husband believed her story. Was she losing her mind? Had this all been a nightmare? "No," she said to herself, "it was too damn real."

"I think they're kicking off," Walter brought her out of her reverie and back to the Cardinal game. About that time the kicker Feely's foot hit the ball and it was in the air on its way down the field. At the moment the San Francisco player caught the ball, there was a huge clap of thunder, and the crowd was startled but quickly returned to the game. That was followed by another strike preceded by an enormous flash of lightning, clearly seen through the transparent closed roof.

Amy was becoming more restless by the minute, fidgeting in her seat so much that the fan next to her became suspicious and seemed to be eyeing her. Walter apparently wasn't paying much attention to the game and was looking around as if admiring the stadium. He didn't even notice his wife leave her seat and head for an exit to the restrooms and refreshment stands. She headed for one of the fifty public toilets.

Amy felt changes taking place in her face and thought she sensed a change in her heartbeat. Her jaw began to spasm and then she realized it was centered around her eyeteeth. She pushed open the restroom door and had the place all to herself since the kickoff had just occurred and nobody else dared leave their seats. A quick glance in the mirror showed a feral expression on her face with a darker tinge to the skin and very dark eyes.

And then it was evident, she was sprouting fangs that were growing longer and sharper.

Bernice had already killed one sixty-four once beer before the game, starting on another after kickoff. Drinking beer always made her pee and all of a sudden she had the urge. She told Jerry where she was going and headed out the exit and looked for the nearest restroom. As she proceeded to her destination there was more thunder, and as she opened the door to the restroom, there was a thunderous roar that shook the building and all the lights went out.

"What the hell do I do now?" She said out loud. "Is anybody else in here?" It was then that Bernice, still in the dark, heard a snarl. She thought maybe it was someone pissed because the electricity had gone out, but then she heard it again, and it sounded…animal-like. "Who…is…it?" she said, her voice trembling, while she tried to find the door. But Bernice never made it out as a hand grabbed her with strength beyond her defenses, and whipped her around.

Another hand grabbed her other side, and she felt a tongue brush against her body followed by very sharp teeth sinking into her right shoulder in a vice-like grip that she knew she couldn't get away from. Moments later she was experiencing ecstasy, realizing she didn't want it to stop. Bernice was in a state of sheer bliss as she started to moan with pleasure, when the teeth, no, they were fangs, began to rip at her skin and blood began to pour out.

The last thing Jerry's wife heard was a passionate sucking sound.

NINE…

    It was Sunday afternoon and Deke McKenna had other things to do but his pager told him that he was needed at Cardinal Stadium PDQ. That's exactly the way Chief Ruben McIntyre had put it and Deke knew it was going to be bad. Lani looked less happy than he was, still in a pose that indicated something more than sleep.

    Deke tooled down Cave Creek Road until he hit the 101 and turned west picking up speed to over 75 mph. As the 101 turned south he watched for Glendale Avenue and when he was there, exited and turned east to reach the stadium.

    The parking lot was still full and McKenna wondered if the game was still going. He had wanted to go but it was his first free day in a long time and his lady companion had lobbied for an afternoon together, an appeal that he couldn't resist. Elaine Baker was his latest flame and they had been together for over two months. Lani, as he called her, was a redhead, with great breasts and a body that would attract monks in a monastery.

    So what the hell was he doing here at the University of Phoenix stadium?

    It wasn't long until Deke McKenna learned the grisly facts. He was ushered right inside to one of the restrooms where McIntyre met him still shaking his head. "Jesus Christ, Deke. It looks like the woman doesn't have any fucking blood in her body. What the hell is going on?" McKenna hoped that was a rhetorical question but it really wasn't because the Chief was desperate for an answer and he knew his friend was the only one who could fill the bill.

    "I'm telling you, I'm pretty sure there's not a drop of blood in her body.

    "The only lead we have is a guy in the stands that says a woman sitting next to him was acting very strange as the game was beginning and then just after kickoff, and just before the lights went out, she bolted from her seat and took off for an exit. She returned right after the lights went back on and had blood on her mouth and her T shirt. The guy just thought she cut her lip and was dribbling blood, and then she left the stadium within seconds."

36

McIntyre turned around and leaned up against the wall with both hands as Deke examined the body. "Obviously forensics has been here," not looking away from the chalky looking torso. That's what it is now, he thought, just some anatomy minus its main ingredient. When the Chief told him what forensics had said, he turned the body over and saw the gashes in the shoulder. "Just what I thought," he said. "Why don't you shut the door."

"I need to give you a quick education in the world of the supernatural," he said with McIntyre still facing the wall. As Deke McKenna started his exhortation, he was interrupted by a surge of cold air that shot across the room but was gone in seconds. Both men looked at each other with the same thoughts in their minds: there are no windows in this restroom. Deke started again. "When you deal with something out of this world, you want to know where it came from."

"In many cases they enter through what are called portals or openings in the universe where supernatural beings just breeze through to do their evil. Once done, the portal opens again and the celestial phantom leaves our world. Make no mistake, these phenomena are dangerous and not something to be taken lightly. As an example, Ouija Boards are portals where inexperienced people often try to entertain ghosts.

"There are known portals in Sedona, Arizona, sometimes referred to as vortexes.

"I'm thinking our perpetrators entered through recently discovered portals in the Superstition Mountains, created by the tellers of tall tales to explain the strange deaths associated with the Lost Dutchman's gold. One of these portals is supposed to be located around Weavers Needle and I now believe the theory just might be valid. What comes from these portals, called Harbingers, can create other supernatural beings to do the work of a higher being.

"This higher being will always have its own mission, in most cases one that is meant to avenge some wrong it presupposes."

The Chief had turned around now paying strict attention. "But I can't categorically tie the two murders to this premise…yet," McKenna added.

"Should I send a group of officers up to the Superstitions to investigate?"

"Naa, wouldn't do any good because these apparitions only come out when they're ready to commit an act of evil, mostly at night. You don't want your people in those mountains at night, trust me."

"This is sounding more weird every minute."

"And my gut tells me it's gonna get worse," McKenna said.

The Chief was mulling all this over, then said, "Something tells me there's more."

"Oh yeah," was the quick reply.

Deke McKenna leaned against the wall and readied himself for what he was about to say, which he wasn't at all sure he could convince McIntyre to believe.

"Over the years folklore has led the way in developing new beliefs about werewolves and vampires, which have been turned into movies and TV shows. It's all believed to be fiction but in many cases fact has actually mirrored these fables and the horror writers were actually describing what really existed.

Cynthia Haskins' friend characterized the attacker as something not from this world and based on the destruction of the body, it was a brutal attack that required cunning and uncanny strength. I would bet that when you get the DNA report on the hair and flesh it won't be human and it won't be a normal animal. It took an unearthly monster to turn Haskins' body into that kind of carnage.

"And now you have a body that has been drained of all its blood, a feat that either requires a medical technician or something inhuman. I go with the latter since the fan indicated he was sitting next to a very restless woman who jumped up just after the kickoff and ran through one of the exits. Moments later, the lights go out and when they go back on the woman returns with blood on her mouth and clothes, then immediately leaves the stadium."

The two men stood quietly for a minute looking at the body of Bernice O'Ryan. Neither said anything since one knew what had to come next and the other dreaded it being said. "Chief, it looks like we're dealing with a werewolf and a vampire."

There was a knock on the door and McKenna had to answer it because the Chief seemed dazed to the point of being in another world himself. Officer Gouyen said, "We think we've identified the victim. A man who says his wife never returned from a bathroom break is just outside the door. Want him to identify the body?"

The word 'body' shook him loose and McKenna looked at McIntyre who said, "Bring him in," and he headed toward the door.

She opened it and he stood in the doorway to prevent any view of the body. "Mr…?" as the man just stood there waiting.

"Jerry O'Ryan, and who are you?"

"I'm Chief Ruben McIntyre of the Phoenix Police Department. Mr. O'Ryan, I have to warn you that if this is your wife inside you must be prepared for the worst." O'Ryan entered the room.

"Oh my God," said the husband, "What happened to my wife?" And then the Chief let him proceed.

"Jesus Christ, she's as white as a sheet. What the hell is going on here?"

"Please try to stay calm, Mr. O'Ryan. We need you to identity your wife."

O'Ryan dropped to his knees beside his wife and looked directly into her eyes that were still open at Deke's request for further investigation. "Why is she so pale, like a ghost?" Tears came to his eyes as the reality hit him and shock began to set in.

"Mr. O'Ryan, I'm Deke McKenna, a special investigator working with the Phoenix PD. There is a deep bite along with slashes in the skin on your wife's right shoulder, and all of the blood has been drained from her body."

"Are you telling me a vampire killed my wife and drank her blood?"

"Not really since we haven't had time yet to analyze the evidence and do an autopsy on the body. I know it looks…unusual," he paused, "but we mustn't jump to any conclusions without corroboration."

Jerry O'Ryan was still kneeling by Bernice, trying to wipe tears from his eyes and now breathing heavier in short gasps, with a look on his face so lost and confused that both men felt sorry for him but worried he might be going into deeper shock. The Chief called the medics in who were still outside the door as the husband collapsed over his wife's body.

Bernice O'Ryan was removed on a stretcher and taken to the morgue, her husband to the hospital. McKenna asked, "Guess you'll take his reaction as an identification of his wife."

"Hell yes. I would not put that man through anything else after what he's seen."

It felt completely confident now with the success of the second part to its planned cataclysm in place, the vampire having passed its test with the killing of Bernice O'Ryan. The Keeper had been there when Amy was taken by the Indian maiden in the Superstitions, and knew from her reaction that the woman would be pliable to its wishes. In the scheme of things, and assuming its two major players continued to facilitate the commands given them, it would be easy to bring Arizona to its knees.

"We have a real mystery to solve and it definitely is not of this world," Deke theorized. "But even worse, we have something else that also needs explaining."

"What?" McIntyre responded.

"Our vampire was walking around in the daylight. According to tradition, they can't do that."

TEN...

A reporter spoke out as the two walked up to the microphones, "It's time for the Deke and Ruben Show," and the crowd laughed as the Chief cleared his throat and started to speak in a serious tone. "Excuse me if I don't join in the levity and it's not because I don't have a sense of humor as all of you know." "If it is possible that any of you don't already know," he stopped for any confirmation but received none, "we have had another murder and it is so cockamamie that only Deke McKenna can explain it."

Deke was standing next to McIntyre and took the cue with an equally serious inflection. "A woman was found dead in one of the restrooms at the Cardinals' game yesterday. Her body had been drained of all its blood." Hands shot up everywhere. "Know you have questions but that will come in time." The hands went down. "But first, let me tell you what we know."

"There were gashes in the victim's right shoulder and that was the only sign of violence. Forensics is working on what little evidence was found, and the medical examiner is performing an autopsy."

With no hands, a salvo of the reporters asked the same question almost in sync, "Was it a vampire?"

"Don't you know vampires can't come out in the daytime? This was during early afternoon." The crowd waited, anticipating more. "The reason our perp ventured out on a Sunday afternoon was that this vampire is a hybrid. I had to confirm it from my background material but it's true"

Another barrage of questions and Deke decided it was time to respond. "OK, but let me decide who talks. You first," pointing to a male.

"What the hell is a hybrid?"

Not really sure if they were ready for this, Deke McKenna launched into an explanation he feared he might be sorry for later. "Hybrids are a crossbreed between two different species. It could be plants, it could be cultures, it could be animals. Let's just take a hypothetical example and say we are talking about the supernatural." It sounded as if the assemblage all took a deep breath at once.

41

"We have the DNA results back on the Cynthia Haskins murder and it tells us that the hair found at the scene and the flesh under Haskins nails was a mutation between a wolf and a human. It was a mish-mosh of 46 chromosomes, human, and 78 chromosomes, wolf. But not present were three more mysterious chromosomes that cannot be identified with modern day technology found in our vampire but not in the werewolf.

"Many studies have taken place in the last few years by scientists in Romania, which is the source for most werewolf and vampire behavior. Along with mutation DNA such as the above, these scientists have concluded that when that brand of credentials is found, it is an affirmation of a hybrid mixture.

"Hypothetically again, if we were dealing with a werewolf, being a hybrid would give it certain added advantages such as being able to turn into the wolf form at will, without the influence of the moon, along with added strength and agility. I said 'if' because I won't be convinced that's what we're dealing with until we get more corroboration of what it looks like, someone takes a picture of it, or I see it myself.

"Yesterday's murder was a demon of a different color." Guffaws you would expect after a bad joke. "We obviously don't have the DNA back yet but I fully expect the same results indicating that we are dealing with a hybrid, but of a different form. A hybrid vampire, which is the reason why our villain was able to walk around in the daytime. There is also the added strength and agility present in hybrid werewolves.

"You will notice that I am openly referring to both of these killings now as being committed by something supernatural. The reason for that is, while we are being perfectly honest with our facts, at the same time we are asking you to temper your coverage until we have more evidence. The last thing we want to do is panic the people of Phoenix and our surrounding suburbs. You will note that you are a select group of the press and that we are inside in closed quarters.

"Where were we?" Deke asked, continuing without an answer. "There is more but you all have to agree it is off the record until the Chief gives you the go-ahead." There was general agreement.

"You think you've heard things from the abnormal up to now," he said. "You ain't heard nothin' yet."

And then McKenna dove into another realm that he knew would literally blow their minds. "The supernatural is known to have been harnessed by people who seek power, along with enriching themselves in any way they can. They are normal human beings that have nothing else to do with the 'other world' than to take control of its events and guide them in the direction they want. That direction so far has mostly been for evil." The room was decisively quiet.

"I only have time for one example so I'll use the best, or worst; you can decide when I'm finished. Louisiana is known for its paranormal events, mostly vampires, but there are also legends of werewolves running around in Plaquemines Parish just south of New Orleans. Anne Rice confined herself to the Big Easy with her vampire novels, and that is where we will reside with our story. But some of the narrative has to take place in Baton Rouge, Louisiana's capitol.

"Politicians in this state are known for their corruption. They actually thrive on it, all the way from Huey Long, the Kingfish, a name he gave to himself, to Jimmy Guilbeau, who served as the governor in the 1970s and 80s. James Carville, a Democratic political consultant and native of Louisiana, once said, "I'm not saying that we don't have corruption in Louisiana, but at least our corrupt politicians have the good graces to entertain us."

Long certainly did but Guilbeau's administration was more sober.

"A preternatural episode occurred during Guilbeau's time in office, also involving state government officials and legislators. 'Someone' in a high level position in Baton Rouge unleashed a scenario of terror in the New Orleans' Vieux Carre, the French Quarter, designed to disrupt its tourist trade while instilling fear in the merchants for their safety as well. It worked. The shop and bar owners all got together to work out a plan to address the problem. Here is the story."

John Comish, who owned a praline shop on Royal Street, described his encounter. "I was closing my store a little after 10PM on Saturday when I heard someone scream out front followed by a series of snarls and growls and then more shrieks of horror. By the time I got to

43

the street, the…thing was ripping this guy apart piece by piece, with an arm laying on the sidewalk and a leg in the monster's hand, and the man was still alive wailing.

"People were rushing toward all the commotion but stopped short the minute they spied the…werewolf. There was no doubt in anyone's mind that this was what it was. The light in front of my shop is bright enough that I could see its fangs digging into this person and the gleaming yellow eyes, and the long ears and the claws it used to rip out the heart and eat it. It was hideous." Comish realized he had almost flipped out, but from what happened, why not?

"Fortunately, the crowd on the street scared the beast away, and it took off toward Chartres. But as it did, parts of the heart fell from its mouth. People not only let out howls of revulsion but some vomited as they looked at the grotesqueness of what was once parts of a living person." John Comish had finished. The meeting ended as all the participants decided to band together and seek protection for their businesses and their customers.

ELEVEN...

Deke McKenna looked around and figured the group was not going to interrupt him because they knew there was more to the story. They had become used to his style of briefing, accustomed to the fact they would always get the whole story. He glanced at the Chief who gave him the nod to go ahead.

"Like I said, Louisiana is known for its stories of the supernatural and the corruption of its politicians. There are other incidents but we don't have time to go into that now. Anybody wants to hear the story, catch me later. Right now it's about why and how these creatures are running around on our streets. But we have to return to the Pelican State to finish my story so you can better understand where the werewolves and vampires can come from.

"In the 19th century, voodoo queens were very popular in much of Louisiana, particularly in New Orleans, conducting private rituals that New Orleanians and tourists would flock to. Queen of the queens was Marie Laveau, who dispensed her powers from a house on St. Ann Street in the French Quarter. Marie died on June 16, 1881, at age 86, but left a legacy and descendants rich with a history of mysticism.

"One of those offsprings was Lola Brion, a great-granddaughter who still lived in the French Quarter, but in an elegant courtyard home behind one of the bars. Lola, who was a beautiful Creole girl, knew her powers from an early age and used them to seduce politicians to get what she wanted. Brion was surprised one day by a visit from one of Gov. Guilbeau's cronies with whom she was very familiar.

"For certain favors in her bedroom, Ernie Masterson would make sure Lola was *really* taken care of. But today Ernie was there primarily to represent the Governor and with a request that chilled even Brion. This is what happened."

"Jimmy wants you to conjure up a supernatural gang to do his biddin,' you know, make one of them magic holes they can come from," Masterson said.

"I don' conjure Ernie. My work is the result of ceremonial rites I perform to achieve the wishes of my patrons," she said. Masterson was illiterate but he was useful to her so she humored him. "Explain Jimmy's needs."

"He wants to scare hell out of the bar and shop owners so he can set up his own protection business. You know, like them Mafia guys did all over the country."

"Why does it have to be supernatural, why can't he just hire some tough guys to threaten them with violence?"

"Cuz New Orleans is known for this weird shit and Jimmy wants to take advantage of the notoriety and the fact that he was able to fix things. You don't question the boss when he sends you on an errand, and don't think you want to either."

Lola thought about what he was asking. There were no portals she knew of in New Orleans; Jimmy had been reading too much science fiction. If she was able to create what Guilbeau wanted, it would have to be her best incantation ever. Brion wasn't sure she could do it but she had to try.

"OK Ernie, but I need time." Nodding, he understood. With that she dropped the chemise, which was all she was wearing, and headed to the bedroom followed by her loyal benefactor.

Deke McKenna jerked his listeners back from The Big Easy to the room in Phoenix where they were. He said, "New Orleans Voodoo is a hybrid voodoo having been imported from West Africa, Haiti and Jamaica through slavery, and combined into the spiritual folkways of Voodoo Queens like Marie Laveau and her ancestor Lola Brion.

"Because the slaves were pressured to convert to Catholicism, there is a major connection between voodoo and the Catholic Church, which also practices exorcism.

"With its many rites, voodoo has the ability to both heal and destroy. It can combine sorcery with the occult to accomplish its goal of either good or evil. To perform these rituals, the practitioners must have a background in the paranormal, hopefully be a descendant of a priestess like Marie Laveau. A ceremony such as this could quickly get

46

out of hand when conducted by an amateur and end up deadly. With that I return you to the French Quarter."

Lola was sitting in her courtyard. This was where she held most of her private rituals, moving inside when the ceremony became too intense and the neighbors might suspect something. And then an idea came to her that brightened her outlook on what she had been commanded to do. "I'll use voodoo dolls," she said out loud. "But I'll have to invoke a completely different kind of spirits, create my own spell to supplicate the kind of fiends Jimmy wants."

This Lola could not do in the courtyard so she headed into her house and moved toward the room that had mystic powers. The windows were blackened over and the only light available was from candles. She began to light them in a protocol that would help produce the results she wanted. "It's been a while," she was talking out loud again, "and I must be careful to make the transition in the spell acceptable to the Voodoo God Bondye."

And then she sat in a straight back chair that faced a cabinet with glass doors rimmed by a special wood with figures of a snake coiled around the frame and bleeding over onto the glass. Lola opened the left side and then the right. "It's time to beget another one of my babies," she said, eyeing all the paraphernalia before her. "But this time it must be more special than ever. It's for Jimmy and his plans to unleash my demons on the French Quarter."

She carefully selected four sticks from the cabinet and placed them in her lap. Next was the Spanish moss she had freshly secured from an area in the New Orleans garden district. She removed it and placed it beside the four sticks. Then she looked at the bright colored fabrics, cut in two inch strips between two and three feet long. "It will be yellow for the werewolf, representing his eyes, and red for the vampire, as a symbol of her blood." Each had accompanying yarn.

She picked out a waxed thread from one of the shelves, along with four black buttons to serve as the eyes. Black thread was taken to attach the eyes and then she rummaged around for the glue that would secure the doll. She wouldn't need the pins since the idea was not for

47

the dolls to do harm. Instead, they would be an aberration to bring something from the other world. And then Lola heard the sound behind her and she quickly turned to see an eerie form in the room.

Alibi Bon Dieu," she muttered, obviously shaken, as the ingredients for her dolls fell to the floor. What was going on? This had never happened before and for once in her life she showed fear for the unknown she was supposed to have complete control of. "Who are you?" and the image began to mutate into demon form with an orange-red mist behind it. The fiend had wings that seemed to be in tatters unlike anything Lola had seen before. Then it spoke.

In a voice that sounded like it was in an echo chamber, it said, "You are entering into areas of the unknown that are highly capricious and could bring you untold misery and distress. I was sent by your grandmother, Marie Laveau, to warn you of the jeopardy you are entering. You must cease your rituals now to prevent future infliction of harm to yourself." And in an instant it was gone. The wall behind her where the apparition had been was empty.

Brion sat there for a moment before she began to pick up the components for her two dolls. Then, "Well, Ma Ma Marie is watching over me but I know what I'm doing and Jimmy always comes first." She began to assemble the first doll securing the two sticks together like a cross. Next came the Spanish moss she wrapped carefully around the sticks followed by the addition of the yellow fabric, allowing the moss to stick through representing the hair of the werewolf.

Sewing on the black buttons with the black thread created two devilish eyes for the head and then it was time to use the glue to make sure everything was firmly bound together. Lola looked at her creation and marveled that it would be the first voodoo doll that she didn't invade with the consummate pins. And now for the other doll, which she completed with the same acuity as the first. It was time for the spell.

First she must prepare the pentagram that would be used to create the Black Magick she hoped would bring her two dolls to life. Since Brion had never even experimented in forging the spirit of a malevolent being, the pentacle or pentagram must be perfect, leading only to the two subjects of her motives. The runes she used would help direct this energy. Runes were the emblems of her conception of the werewolf and the vampire.

Still in the same room, she looked with satisfaction at her masterpiece on the floor in front of her. The inverted star was filled with symbols of the occult and those meant to resurrect the reality of her evil beings. The pentagram was inverted because to turn its "divine" point on the top down was to represent evil and Satan. Finally she documented the spell in her grimoire, Lola's textbook of Magick.

Everything was in place. All she had to do was step inside the circle of power with a doll in each hand.

As she entered the unknown, a rush of cold air engulfed the room, and she shivered slightly as she allowed the spirits entry to her body that would beseech the Voodoo God Bondye to grant her wishes. She began to chant in a language known only to Voodoo Queens, focusing first on the Werewolf image. Suddenly there was primal screaming in a cacophonous rhythm that shook the room and seemed to send Brion to a higher level of ecstasy.

And then she began to dance in the circle, still holding the dolls.

Effigies of the miscreant vampires and wolves cavorted around her outside the pentagram, in an attempt to enter and take possession of Lola but she was protected by the pentacle. As she continued her ritual, there was a thunderous roar of snarling and howling when the wolf doll literally crumbled in her hand and the real thing materialized in the circle with such force that it threw Brion from the pentagram against the wall.

But the werewolf could not venture out without her permission.

The Voodoo Queen was prepared and summoned her creation out of its confinement and over to the corner of the room where she performed another incantation that immediately turned the beast into a manageable human being. This way she could house her handiwork until the Governor was ready. She would let Jimmy know of her success, but first she must petition the vampire succubus.

Lola went through the same machinations and was once again rewarded with her goal. She looked at the vampire and was a bit uneasy over the likeness to herself but nevertheless proceeded with her plan. The male and female were arranged in the corner and hidden by a room divider, although no one entered this room but her. Next she had to formulate the gris-gris bags that would keep Jimmy and his people safe from the freaks she had created.

Unfortunately, they would prove to be fatally ineffective.

TWELVE…

Deke McKenna surveyed the group for anyone whose interest might be waning and saw no notice. How could anyone resist a werewolf/vampire story? "Now you know how it's done. Next I'm going to tell you why it was done and what eventually happened to the cast of characters. What is important to understand here is that we believe that there is some transcendental being that is the overseer of *our* demons. The problem, we don't know what or who."

"In cases like this there is a blueprint for the bureaucracy from the hierarchy down to the grunts. The Harbinger is at the top, which would include Lola Brion. Under that, in our case, is whatever is in the Superstitions that has graced the Phoenix metro area with our very own werewolf and its vampire companion. This is the source of our problem and until dealt with could continue to produce their harvest of abnormalities.

"Moving down the ladder, the Harbinger fosters what is called the Enforcer to carry out its violence and that would be Lola Brion's two minions in the corner, and whatever manner of monstrosities that we have running around on Phoenix streets. In Brion's case, she stopped with only two. In the case of our Harbinger in the Superstitions, since we don't have a hand on just who or what the werewolf or the vampire came from, there is no way to know what's coming next."

Except…more violence.

"Louisiana Governor Jimmy Guilbeau was happy with Lola Brion's work which resulted in werewolf incidents like the one Comish described earlier, and then there were vampire attacks in the French Quarter where blood drained bodies were found on the streets. This put the fear of the supernatural in the merchants. Guilbeau's guerrillas quickly whipped shop owners into line and protection money started flowing.

"Unfortunately, Ernie Masterson couldn't keep his mouth shut and bragged about how he was a big shot, something like the consigliere of the Mafia Don, Governor Guilbeau, running a big time protection business. The media got it and both Jimmy and Ernie ended up in jail. Neither revealed the fact that they had both been involved in the

51

creation of the two mutants preying on New Orleans. They figured if they did, they would be committed to Mandeille, the local nut house.

"Lola Brion didn't fare so well. On a Sunday afternoon following Jimmy's and Ernie's arrests, Lola was sitting in her courtyard wondering where she would find her new patronization. She didn't wonder long, when her two unearthly procreations, in their full paranormal form, charged from her front door and attacked Brion. There was blood curdling screaming, which brought people off the street.

"Her fate matched the violence she had created. They found Lola in eight pieces: the head, the body, two arms, two hands and two legs. In creating the Voodoo Doll to do harm to someone, there are eight pins with colors from red for power to pink for death. There was a pink pin in each part of the Voodoo Queen's body. It had not a drop of blood and she had no heart. Her Voodoo God, Bondye, had extracted its redemption."

The reporters remained quiet, contented, like what you might find when the librarian had finished telling the tale of *Gulliver's Travels* to a bunch of kids. But Deke McKenna's spell quickly ended and the questions came pouring out, primarily centered around how this related directly to the Phoenix killings. Like, "What the hell does this trip to New Orleans really have to do with what's happening here?"

Chief Ruben McIntyre stepped forward. He looked at McKenna with the satisfied expression that he agreed with what he had said and appreciated the background.

"Like Deke said, you know how and why they did it in New Orleans, so how does this have anything to do with what's going on in the Superstitions? Since this is completely new to all of us, we thought it important that we have some frame of reference to use for what may be going on here. Deke's narrative serves as a guideline on how the Phoenix events might evolve." Hands went up again but the Chief intervened.

"That's all folks. Press conference is over. We're waiting for the coroner's report and DNA results for Bernice O'Ryan, and then we'll call another meeting."

McIntyre and McKenna left the room, heading to his office and the reporters grabbed their cell phones, rushing to auto dial their editors and file a story. The room erupted into pandemonium as the collection of journalists all began to talk at the same time. The killings had gone nationwide and many out-of-staters had been invited to the briefing. This concerned the Chief since it brought bad publicity to the state and Phoenix and more higher-ups breathing down his neck.

Ruben McIntyre was a good cop who had come up through the ranks and kept his record spotless, one of the reasons Phoenix Mayor, Clarence Talbot, had chosen him to lead the city's police department. At age fifty-two McIntyre wasn't married and there were rumors he was gay, which had riled a bunch of old boy bubbas, but, then, that was just a part of the Arizona tradition. Anything out of the norm and you stood out like a sore thumb.

The Chief didn't care, conducting himself like he hadn't even heard the gossip. He was a native Zoni and had grown up in Apache Junction, which sits right at the foot of the Superstitions. Ruben McIntyre was a hands-on Chief who had a great deal of respect and confidence in his police officers but liked to be on the line himself. What he enjoyed most was working with specialists like Deke McKenna who brought in a completely different angle to police work.

McKenna spoke first, "The question now is how the media will treat it after you cautioned them not to alarm the community. Probably get more attention from those people who live out-of-state since they have nothing to lose."

"Any odds how long it'll take the Governor's office to call the mayor when they hear all this?"

"Probably nano-seconds, but think of this. This is a state thing as much as it is local. Anita Butts is also going to have to answer to the rest of the country. Another thing, you'll get some feeling for where it's going by how the Governor replies. If it's everything as usual—her mouth in forward gear and her mind in reverse—she could even draw much of the attention to her office."

Together they thought all this over until the Chief said, "Will your source at the state still be able to update us?"

"Absolutely. She's pissed at the way the Governor has shut down so many programs for the poor, and she's really ticked off over the gun legislation. Plus, she's covered herself so that if the hammer does fall, it won't hit her."

"Another of your bed buddies?"

Deke grinned, "A 'used to be' bed buddy." He thought for a moment and then added, "I'm kinda serious about Lani."

The Chief didn't look real surprised but knowing Deke McKenna for several years, he was at least caught off guard by the guy who had always professed to be a confirmed bachelor.

Bly Gouyen knocked and opened the door into the Chief's office with a dour look on her face, then shut the door behind her. "Afraid we've got another one, Ruben."

THIRTEEN...

"Give me the details," McIntyre spoke.

Officer Gouyen was a seasoned cop and she knew how to handle most any situation, including the bizarre. "Chief, this one was ripped apart with arms and legs everywhere," showing almost no emotion. Gouyen had been on the scene and she said the people who discovered the body, uh, body parts, were heaving all over the place." She paused, "That's not the worst part. The victim is Clarence Talbot, the Phoenix Mayor."

"Holy shit. Where did it happen?"

"Just out back of that bikin' restaurant in Cave Creek. You know, where all the motorcycles hang out. The C.C. mayor has already requested that Phoenix PD handle the investigation."

"Just great," McIntyre said out loud. "Now we have two jurisdictions and the victim is the Mayor of one of them." It had been less than a week since the first werewolf strike and the Mayor had already been on the Chief's back since the admission that they were dealing with the abnormal. Won't have to worry about that anymore.

"Okay, it's time," McIntyre said. "Officer Gouyen, set up a task force, assemble the officers available to investigate this new spate of killings." The werewolf murders would take precedence since there had been two, only one vampire. They would meet soon to go over the evidence.

* * * * *

The Keeper was ecstatic, with the first real trial of one of its preternatural slaves a complete success. The Phoenix Mayor was the first trophy in a long line of city, county and state officials that must be dealt with to satisfy the rancor in the Keeper and its people. But now the game plan was in place with proof that it could be executed, and it must maintain the momentum and put the next move in motion. Everything was working out perfectly.

* * * * *

55

The City and the State Capitol were frantic following the grisly death of Phoenix Mayor, Clarence Talbot. All offices were in lock down mode to determine how to offset this latest blot on Arizona's reputation. National headlines were emblazoned with the fact that Talbot had been killed by some supernatural creature.

Sam Parks, the Governor's Communications Director, was in Butts' office and they were talking about a recent conversation with Chief McIntyre. "What kind of crap does that whatnot think he's pulling not keeping me in the loop? He's gay, isn't he?" the Governor asked.

Although Parks considered Butts downright dull-witted, he played her game willingly, expecting to be rewarded with a high-paying private sector job when she had finished her term. "Everybody thinks he is. I mean he's in his fifties and has never been married. But that doesn't mean he isn't capable of running the police force."

"I know," she said, condescendingly. "So why hasn't he done something about all this supernatural stuff? And what about Talbot's murder now? I just heard it on the news and, hell, even though he's a Democrat, this kind of publicity is bad for my state. We have to do something, Sam, to steer all the bad publicity away from my administration, particularly me."

"I'll start distancing you and the staff as much as I can and point the finger at the city. Meanwhile, you need to show your sympathy for former Mayor Talbot. I'll arrange a news conference."

Butts wasn't satisfied Parks had the iron fist he thought he did but she didn't have any choice. No one else was close enough to take into her confidence. "Just make sure you keep *me* out of the bad news loop," she charged.

"You can count on it," was the reply.

*   *   *   *   *

Chief McIntyre and Deke McKenna were just leaving the office when a small group of reporters asked them about the latest killing. "Since you already know about it you must know it's in Cave Creek, but they've asked Phoenix PD to handle the investigation. Suggest you just

56

head up north and join your other buddies." With that the two hopped in his patrol car and headed east across Washington to the I-10, then Hwy. 51 north to Cave Creek Road.

When the two got out of the cruiser in front of Biker's Throne, several customers spotted the Chief and rushed over to say hello. It wasn't long before Deacon Ballew came out of the building to greet McIntyre and McKenna. He owned the place.

"Ruben, how about keepin' your freakin' monsters in Phoenix. I got enough up here for customers." Everyone laughed and the Chief introduced Deke around.

"The Deacon and I are old buddies," McKenna related, goin' back to when he first opened this place."

"Didn't know you were a biker," McIntyre looked surprised.

"I'm not. Used to drive one of those tourist jeeps and this was one of my main stops. You know everyone's interested in motorcycles. Most just afraid to ride one."

"Seriously, Ruben," Deacon started, "What the hell is going on? This body's been here all night. The Cave Creek Mayor has done nothing but bug the hell out of me since this happened. This dufus thinks a biker was responsible for the killing."

"Well, if he does, he hasn't been paying attention to the news. But Deacon this time we're talking about the Mayor of Phoenix as the victim. That means the pressure is more intense. It's obvious the killers aren't normal people. Has he got a hard on for you?"

"Yeah, and with all the business we bring to this little burg, I mean from all over the world."

"Don't worry, Deacon, I'll be talking to the Mayor real soon to explain just what happened in his town. Now let's get to the crime scene."

They started moving to the back of the building and were swarmed by a bank of reporters being restrained outside the official yellow tape. In a chorus of shouting, they turned to the Chief and McKenna, "tell us what happened."

"Hey, you guys know the shtick, you don't get to look until I do." McIntyre looked around and asked, "Where is Gouyen?"

"Over here, Chief," from behind some desert brush where he headed with Deke. She had preceded them to the crime scene. Bly Gouyen was a full-breed Chiricahua Apache and a descendant of one of Arizona's famous female Apache warriors of the same name. Her ancestor's husband had been killed and scalped in a Comanche raid and the forebear Gouyen had avenged his death by sneaking into their camp then seducing a drunken Comanche Chief, stabbing him to death with his own knife then scalping him.

The victim's body, obviously the Mayor's, was splayed across a large rock where blood had run down the sides in hideous ribbons that looked like it had been decorated for a party. They were looking at body parts strewn around the torso. And then the cavity in the chest revealed that the heart was missing. This all had occurred the night before. Gouyen filled them in.

The two went to face the gaggle of reporters who were flinging questions as fast as a Gatling gun. The Chief waved his hand and shouted, "Hold it!" When things were normal McIntyre and McKenna covered all the facts in the latest killing. The Assistant Chief had already notified next-of-kin from headquarters. Then they told the reporters who the victim was followed by a flurry of cell phone calls. The Chief noted many TV network reporters in the crowd.

FOURTEEN...

Agnes Barber wasn't sure what was going on. Arnie had been
out on one of his "tears" again with his night out followed by news that
the Phoenix Mayor had been brutally killed in Cave Creek. She didn't
read the entire article because it sounded so barbaric. Besides, she
thought, Arnie could never do something like that. He wouldn't even
kill a bug. It must have been just another coincidence like the other
killing.

They were talking about werewolves and vampires, and Agnes
didn't want to hear any more.

But why wouldn't her husband tell her where he'd been? She
was sure he wasn't being unfaithful after all these years so what was the
answer? They had always done things together, yet now he wanted to
take a night out without her. Yes, it was suspicious. They would just
have to have a talk and Arnie would level with her and tell her what was
bothering him. Satisfied with her decision, she turned around and
jumped as she saw Arnie standing there staring at her.

"You startled me," she said. No reply from her husband. Agnes
turned further in her chair as he continued to stare with a look of
uncertainty in his eyes. It was disquieting because his demeanor wasn't
the Arnold Barber she knew. His eyes had a yellowish tint whereas they
were normally a hazel color. "Arnie, why are you staring at me like
that?" Nothing. "Arnie, you're frightening me. Please stop it." She
watched as he slowly seemed to return to himself.

"Guess I was in another world," he said, adding nothing more
and with none of his normal enthusiasm.

"Honey, we have to talk. You've been acting very strange
lately."

"Don't know what you're talking about," and he walked out of
the room.

* * * * *

Lani was sitting in her shop in Cave Creek trying to put all the
pieces together. Deke had told her about the latest killing which was

59

another werewolf attack and she wondered when the next vampire incident would occur. Should she ask the cards again? They had predicted the first happening and she wasn't sure she wanted to broadcast the next one. And there was something that bothered her. The vampire had killed rather than just drinking the blood it needed.

These demons usually sucked just enough blood from their victims for subsistence. This one drained the body dry, nothing left. Nada. McKenna's paranormal class had revealed so many facts about the abnormal and supernatural beings like werewolves and vampires. She was normally able to combine this with her knowledge of metaphysics and come up with her own conclusions, but these details only he could clarify.

Lani pulled out her cellphone and called Deke. He answered on the second ring. "Hi love," he had her on his speed dial, "what's going on?"

"Where are you? Am I interrupting something?"

"I'm at the latest crime scene, not too far from your place. We could use your input on this one."

"Why, did our monster decide to change its MO?"

"No, but it's another vicious killing, and this time it's Mayor Talbot."

"Holy crap," she exclaimed, "why do you need me?"

"This is so weird, Lani, we need all the help we can get. McIntyre is beside himself and I hate to think what will happen when the public gets this."

"Good, where do you want me?"

"Your place in an hour. We need the atmosphere."

"I'll be waiting."

Elaine Baker's shop was small and she liked it that way. The closeness gave it a coziness necessary for her work doing Tarot readings. You had to get next to the person you were working with, relate to them and them to you. Lani also sold crystals and books on metaphysics and carried a good supply of Tarot cards. She was originally from Mississippi and had picked up her esoteric strengths from an old Negro mammy that was into voodoo and other crafts of the abnormal.

Lani migrated west, first to California and then over to Arizona where she could be closer to the Sedona events. It had helped enrich her knowledge and really brought insight into her Tarot card readings which she had picked up on a trip to New Orleans several years ago. She was hooked right from the beginning, able to put the cunning of Tarot together with the divination of voodoo. It helped her understand Deke's field and she liked helping with his police work.

Lani was sitting in one of the chairs in the outer area of her office. Her reading room was located in the rear separated by a sliding plastic partition for complete privacy. The two walked in looking about as grim as anyone could look, considering it was one of those perfect fall days in Arizona. She motioned them to sit on the sofa. McIntyre spoke first.

"It's not good, Lani," he started, "and it just seems to be getting worse. Here's where we stand." The Chief related the facts of what had happened behind the Cave Creek eatery. They waited for Lani's reaction. What they were really hoping for was for her to do a reading but knowing how that drained her psyche, nobody asked.

"Let's do a reading," like she read their minds; "Deke, put the closed sign on the door and pulled down the curtain." Sometimes she had walk-ins for readings. "Thanks."

Lani pushed her chair in front of the coffee table in the middle of the room and sat facing the two on the couch. She pulled out the Tarot cards and did a quick shuffle. Then she laid them on the table, scrambling vigorously until she was satisfied they had been put in random order. And then she dealt the Mystic Cross layout she had done that night in the cabin. Everyone focused on the cards, caught up by the mysterious rhythm in the presentation of the Tarot cards.

One by one Lani placed the cards on the coffee table until all ten were down. Just after the last card hit the table, she jerked back as if she'd been hit by a double whammy. Her eyes rolled back in her head and she began to shake violently.

Two fully trained professionals sat there momentarily dumbstruck by what was going on. McKenna was the first to react and grabbed Lani before she thrust forward and banged her head on the coffee table. "Lani, Lani, look at me." She didn't.

McIntyre was up and at her side, Deke on his knees in front of her. Lani's head was gyrating around in a circle as strange sounds erupted from her mouth in a voice that was not hers but from somewhere out of this world. "They're all doomed," she croaked, stopping the motions of her head and concentrating now on the Tarot cards in front of her.

With bestial strength she pushed McKenna aside, leaning over the table and scrabbling all the cards as if she were trying to destroy what was besieging her.

The two stepped back, deciding to let her complete the obvious trance she was in, but staying close enough to be able to come to her aid if she looked like she would harm herself. The machinations continued for another minute or so and then Lani's two arms went straight out to her sides and started rotating in a circle, one arm in one direction, the other in the other direction. Her eyes were back to normal and she appeared to be staring straight ahead, at nothing.

The Chief looked at Deke as if he felt they should be doing something to help Lani. But McKenna had a look on his face that signified everything was under control. He's probably been through this before, he thought.

Nobody moved until Lani seemed to crumple in the chair and they rushed to her side again. McKenna was in front of her and all of a sudden she looked into his eyes and screamed. He grabbed her and held on tight as she began a slow sobbing accompanied by shivers running throughout her body. The look of despair on her face was so real that he wanted to quiz her right now about what happened but he didn't.

Instead, "Everything's OK," McKenna consoled her.

"No it's not," she said.

FIFTEEN...

Upton Sinclair spent a short time in Buckeye, Arizona before moving to New Jersey. Walter Rogers was a big reader and one of his favorite authors was Sinclair and his novel, "The Jungle," which exposed the conditions in the U.S. meat packing industry. Walter's wife, Amy, wasn't impressed with the literary significance of Buckeye, where the two of them lived in an upscale section, but her husband was and he had whined until they moved there from California.

Amy sat on the backyard patio staring at their pool, thinking about the fact she wanted to go bar-hopping with her friends. But her mojo was giving birth to another command from the Keeper and this time it wasn't random. The focus was on a specific person, and, although she wasn't into politics, she knew who her target was and she was surprised. At the same time it was clear that she should make arrangements for that night out on the town with her chum.

In retrospect, Amy wasn't sorry the Indian maiden had turned her into a vampire. She was a swinger at heart and this gave her a wide range of possibilities to sate her appetite. And although she had taken someone's life at the ballgame, it wasn't out of malice or the desire to kill; it was a simple matter of survival and pleasure. It was her or me, she thought, which helped keep the remorse from her door. But now she had that gnawing feeling again for blood .

The craving was growing stronger, much like a drug addict looking for a fix. Sometimes she thought about trying out Walter's blood. But that would tip her hand, although he was so comatose most of the time, he might not even notice. Then she began to concentrate on the vibes she was receiving. Walter was going to be at work until at least six-thirty and she knew he would come home exhausted as usual. Amy would make her plans and then spring it on him.

On the phone she said, "Hi Karen, what are you doing tonight?" Karen was an old friend and one of her closest drinking buddies.

"Nothing. Just trying to figure out how to get out of this house and have some fun. Got any ideas?" Her husband Robert was a slug like Walter.

"Have you heard of The Big Place in downtown Phoenix? On Camelback, just off Central Avenue. I've heard it swings and there's a show and dance floor. They say everyone who's anyone goes there and that includes us."

"Sounds delicious." Karen was always willing and if they both didn't connect with a guy, they would just go to a cheap motel and do each other. They had an unwritten agreement with their spouses; each could do what they wanted to do and so could their husbands without letting it damage the marriage. Amy and Karen did fine but they both doubted if Walter or Robert got lucky that often, if ever. Tonight Amy felt lucky and the Keeper's mental transmissions told her she would be.

"I'll pick you up and we can go together. About six-thirty?" Karen lived in Glendale which was east of Amy and on the way.

"Fine. I'll be ready."

Amy went into her walk-in closet, which she monopolized with her clothes, and looked for the sexiest thing she could find to wear. She selected a double-strap bra top dress that barely covered the lower essentials with a plunging V-neck in a candy coral color with matching high heels. No one will be able to resist this, she thought. She knew she was going to connect with someone special tonight and she must be dressed as glamorous as she could be.

Shortly after six-thirty Amy pulled up in front of Karen's house and honked. She had no desire to talk to Robert whom she was sure was convinced she was leading his wife astray. Who cares. If he didn't service his wife, someone had to. Karen rushed right out and when she got in the car and looked at her partner for the evening she said, "Wow, somebody has some serious plans for tonight." She made the statement while sitting down in an outfit that was designed to arouse a room full of Jesuit priests.

"Wow, again at you, hon, and how in the world did you get past Robert with that?"

"He was working on a puzzle and never even looked up. Just said goodbye and waved."

"Walter wasn't home when I left but if he had been his head would have been in a book and he probably wouldn't even have noticed."

"Are we lucky or not?" Karen said, "so let's go get the party started now."

The Big Place's parking lot was full as she had expected but they eventually found a spot and she pulled in

There were two rooms to the place. The front had an oval bar with stools around it and tables scattered. In the back was a small dance floor with more tables and a stage in the corner for the shows that would start at eight PM. It was seven o'clock. Amy and Karen stopped in the front room for now and moved up to the bar. No stools were available until two gals, who had just been hustled by two guys, headed with them to a table. They sat down and ordered a drink.

The drinks came, a martini for Amy, a cosmopolitan for Karen. The bartender asked and they confirmed that they wanted to run a tab so a credit card would be necessary, which Amy provided. They would split the bill later, assuming they were still together. If not, tomorrow. They toasted to a successful evening and began to survey the crowd for prospects.

Karen's dress was as short as her partner's and her cleavage was obvious but when she leaned over to talk to Amy, it looked like everything might pour out in her friend's lap. The two of them had turned toward each other on the stools so their knees were touching, which made it clear they were there for something other than just drinking.

"Do you see anyone who's anyone?" Karen asked.

"Not yet, but I'm looking. Lots of guys have gazed our way but no one's making a move. Don't tell me this is family night."

"Maybe we should come on to each other and see if that gets somebody's attention." They thought about it and decided not since it was their first time in this place and didn't know what they could get away with.

And then it happened. First one appeared, then the second, acting like two male dogs sniffing out their mates in heat. They had come to the right place and both hormone raging females immediately turned to accommodate the two huntsmen as they heard, "Hello ladies," in unison, "can we buy you a drink?"

God, Amy thought, nobody's original anymore. Just once, she wished the guy would approach her with, "You wanna fuck?" It's what's on his mind. Why not say it?

Instead she said, "I'd love it, how about you, Karen?"

They were both good looking and seemed to be okay guys, at least as far as she could tell. "Sure, I'm game if you are."

The two hit men gestured to a table in the middle of the room and asked their prey to join them, waiting for both to descend their stools, where Amy first took care of their bill.

She clicked across the hardwood floor with her heels in a walk that would, well, bring down the house in vaudeville. But this was another show and she would play it to the hilt. Then she did her Sharon Stone impression, sitting down in a chair and crossing her legs very slowly. She had on no panties. It did not go unnoticed, both with the guys and Karen who almost broke up. Unfortunately she couldn't beat Amy's act so she just sat down as sexy as possible.

"Hi, I'm Dan Thornton and this is my friend Rudy Brown, and you are?"

"Amy Rogers and Karen Briggs," Amy replied, noting no new wedding rings in the foursome. "And don't I recognize that name from somewhere," she was looking at Thornton.

"Probably, I'm the aide to Cyrus Dean, the Governor's Chief of Staff." No mention was made of his friend.

"Wow, we're in the company of royalty," Karen said. "Do we salute?" which got a laugh from everyone.

"Naa, have my 'night out on the town' hat on tonight and Rudy's a good friend who decided to join me. Left the State business at the Capitol. Are you two ladies here for the same reason?"

"Pretty much," as Amy zeroed in on Dan Thornton as the objective of her mission for the Keeper. It was an omen that the two had come here tonight and had met in a precarious rendezvous that only the devil would understand. "We've never been here before so fill us in."

"Dan's only been here a couple times before but I'm a regular," Rudy finally spoke up. Then he told them about the show that would start at eight, which was generally a group of Mexican dancers and singers. Who cared? By then everyone was at least half-smashed.

The evening progressed until it was time to go to the back room where they could already hear the music. Rudy had pull so he was able to get a table and they sat down and ordered another round of drinks. "Would you like to dance, Amy?" Dan asked.

"Of course," the reply as Rudy started to ask Karen to dance, yet he couldn't keep his eyes off Amy's butt.

"Nice, huh" Karen kidded him and he nodded while still looking.

Then, "Hey, believe me you are equally equipped. Let's dance."

After several dance numbers it was clear what the intentions were of all four so Dan finally said, "Let's cut to the chase here. Why don't we split up and do our own thing?" It was unanimous and after goodbyes were finished, Karen and Rudy headed for his car and Amy and Dan for his.

SIXTEEN…

"Wait," Amy said when they got to Dan's car, a BMW she noted, "can't afford to leave my car here but I know I can't leave it in front of your place so is there some secluded area where I can park it close to your house?"

"Sure, there's a wooded area around the corner from my street we can actually drive into where you can leave your car."

"Great, so I'll just follow you," and they both got into their cars.

She had to think fast. How am I going to get him into a doable position before it's too late? His place is definitely a no-no since two other people know I left with him. Has to look like we got separated and I went home. Rudy would take Karen home. Have to make my move in the woods. She had a plan. She would call Karen and tell her they split up just to be sure. Amy just hoped Rudy would not call Dan but she was pretty sure her partner had him occupied.

On the way she called Karen and got her voice mail. Perfect! "Just wanted to tell you Dan and I split and I'm almost home. Hope you have fun."

Dan drove into a small grove of trees and Amy followed until she was sure the car was sheltered from the outside and parked next to his car. They both got out of their cars and Amy said, "Where's your house from here?"

"Remember where we turned left into here?" Without waiting for an answer, "My house is the one on the corner, the left side. Walking distance but we can drive in my car."

Satisfied she had just received the last piece of her puzzle, she said, "Don't know about you but I don't think I can wait for us to get to your house."

That stopped Dan cold but it didn't prevent him from immediately unzipping his pants and making his tool available. Amy got on her knees and began to pleasure him until she heard moans and that was her cue to ramp up the action. She pushed her dress down until her boobs were exposed and in the car lights he could see her nipples were hard. Caressing them, his attention was averted just long enough for her to sink her fangs into his member.

It was the slightest of stings that sent the essence of her vampire elixir throughout his body, paralyzing his senses for anything other than the rapture she was giving him that felt like a joyride to the moon. Thornton leaned back against the car not able to maintain his balance with what he was going through. Where had this woman been, he thought, and what is she like in bed?

Dan groaned with ecstasy and she knew that meant he wanted more. Amy dug her fangs in deeper and started sucking, but not just for his gratification this time. She planned to drain Dan Thornton of all his blood through his penis. Wasn't that remarkable? All the blood rushing to his dick. Most guys would love to have this problem. He was experiencing euphoria and couldn't get enough as he looked down and Amy looked up at him with a demonic smile on her face

It was then that her victim suddenly realized something was wrong as he became steadily weaker, finally crying out "What're you doing to me?" That made Amy work even faster as the blood rushed from his gorged organ into the vampire's mouth with an urgency that meant new life on one end and death on the other. Dan couldn't decide whether to praise the woman for the intoxication of the sex or…and then he crumbled to the ground where she finished the job.

Amy stood up, brushed off her knees and pulled up her dress. She checked and there was no blood on the dress. She took out a toilette from her purse, wiped her mouth and chest, and returned it to a plastic bag in her purse. At the peak of her strength now with the new infusion, she easily picked up Thornton's body and put it in the passenger side of his car. As she backed her car into the street, there was no one around and the area seemed isolated.

She returned to Dan and his car, starting it, and then driving back and forth over the tire tracks to erase them as much as possible. After backing the car into the street, she carefully scanned the area for anyone that might see what was going on but it was as dead as the body next to her. Carefully, Amy pulled around the corner to Dan's driveway and checked the number; she had looked at his driver's license for the address. She sat there for several minutes.

Then she hit his garage door opener on the sun visor and pulled inside. Turning off the engine and shutting the garage door, Amy hoisted Thornton over, moving him to the driver's seat. She wiped clean all the surfaces she had touched, including the garage door opener and license. With the same handkerchief she opened the door into the house and made her way to the front door. She couldn't take the chance there was an animal in the backyard.

Opening the door using the same protection, she exited, cautiously moving in short steps so that she could check for anyone who might see her. Hopefully, he didn't have any nosy neighbors, but if there were, it was a woman leaving the house and Dan probably had many. No, she felt secure and continued around the alcove that partially enclosed the entrance

Reaching the gravel road where her car was parked, Amy repeatedly looked behind her to insure there were no possible witnesses. She got in and started the engine but didn't turn the lights on. The streetlight was enough to get her out of the neighborhood but she was still very careful, stopping at the corner to confirm her anonymity. Everything looked okay so she slowly pulled out into the street.

On the way home she asked herself whether she had forgotten anything and carefully went over every move she had made from the bar to Thornton's home. The fresh blood breathed new life into all her senses so she was able to remember everything that had happened and she could think of nothing she had forgotten.

Amy drove home slowly as she laid out her blueprint for the cover that she had so carefully thought out earlier. Fortunately, no one could connect her with Bernice O'Ryan's murder at the Cardinals' game, but with another similar death, they were certain to put the two together. That could be explained. She didn't have to worry about the DNA since her genes were so closely entwined with the vampire, any results would be inconclusive.

And, of course, Walter would give her the perfect alibi for tonight.

Before leaving home Amy had set the clock back one hour in the family room where Walter read until late on a weekend night. Her timing had been perfect all evening from nudging Dan Thornton to get out of the bar to completing her mission in the wooded area beside his house, which had occurred at the actual hour of ten thirty PM. She was home by ten twenty, bogus time, which meant she was in her house ten minutes before the murder happened.

"Hi honey," she said to Walter as she walked past him on her way to the bathroom. Shutting the door then opening it again, "What time is it Hon?" Walter looked at the clock and replied, "Ten twenty." He returned to his book immediately with no indication of suspicion.

She flushed the toilette down the john, looked at herself, and was satisfied with what was in the mirror, even though she had just offed the aide to the Governor's Chief of Staff.

"I'm going to bed, want to join me? she said in her most seductive way.

"Yeah, let me finish this chapter and I'll be right in."

With what's waiting for you, she thought, most men would drop the book and run. Sex with Walter was, well, sex with Walter. He never got her off. Just jumped on and pumped away for a minute or two and blew his wad. She did lie there and moan for him, which soothed his ego, and the whole effort gave her complete freedom to pursue her sexual fantasies, until the next time. But she got terribly frustrated and very cranky going too long without an orgasm.

SEVENTEEN...

"I'm here," he said, as if it was George Clooney entering her boudoir. Walter moved toward the bed with a look on his face that indicated the excitement of a man about to do his taxes. He had on a pair of cargo shorts and a T-shirt, both of which he discarded beside the bed with his under shorts. The man was ready, and perked up slightly when he saw Amy lying there nude massaging herself.

"Hold on," she said, "I forgot to turn off my cell phone," and she headed to the other room where Walter had been. Amy quickly corrected the clock, saying as she finished, "Hold on, I'm comin' Hon," knowing full well that wouldn't happen. But now the alibi was established and Walter would provide a perfect excuse for her whereabouts tonight with his precise thinking. He was a CPA and would remember the time she arrived home with explicit accuracy.

He was already getting an erection but it needed help so she used her tongue and then started a sucking motion that created more ecstasy as his love muscle began to grow. Although Walter wasn't real big, he was well enough endowed to knead her lips and throat in such a way that gave Amy the sensation she always got when giving head. Now he was moving it in and out and if he kept this up she would surely cum. But then he moved between her legs.

She waited until he entered her, which came in a burst of energy that rammed it home on the first try. None of that slow, sexy stuff for her man. He jabbed away like a first-timer not really sure that he would ever get any more the rest of his life. Walter hammered Amy like he was mad at something, not passionate, but with ferocious lunges that she didn't understand. He was usually non-committal and removed, but this time it seemed Walter was on a mission.

He continued his assault until he lost it inside her and with a jerk, backed off and fell on his back. They both lay there for a few minutes until Amy said, "Is everything okay Walter?"

"Yeah, why not? Guess you're not satisfied though."

"No, it's not that, just that you never make love to me in such a frenzy, like you were pissed or something. Anything wrong at work?"

"No, everything's fine. Guess I just don't measure up."

"What's that supposed to mean?" she asked.

"Oh nothing, I'm going to sleep."

What the hell is going on? she thought.

* * * * *

Monday morning in Phoenix and the state legislature was in session doing the dumb things it did on a regular basis. In the Senate, Rob Gum was lobbying for his gun bill with Republican colleagues and a handful of Democrats who would listen. In the House, Representative Chew Quanah, a full-breed Comanche, was introducing his legislation that would further restrict the benefits to the San Carlos Apache Indian Reservation.

* * * * *

It was ten o'clock on the same Monday and Agnes still couldn't get Arnie to open up to her. He was close-mouthed and not making eye contact, just staring off in the distance. It looked like he definitely had something on his mind, but what? How could someone change this much overnight? What in the world had happened in the Superstitions that would turn her husband into such a different person?

I mean, Arnie was no Don Juan by any means but he had always been affectionate, telling her repeatedly that he adored her. It couldn't be another woman unless his trip to the mountains had been for something other than gold. No, she was sure something had happened there to him that had radically changed his personality and his behavior habits. They hadn't been out anywhere since he came back from his trip and that wasn't like them. Agnes was getting desperate.

"Arnie, would you agree to some counseling?" she asked.

"For what?" he shot back with a look that chilled his wife and pretty much indicated he would have none of that.

"Then would you at least see a doctor? I mean, I can't go on like this."

"What the hell is wrong with you woman? I'm perfectly fine. Maybe you should see a doctor, like a shrink, the way you've been acting."

Agnes teared up and covered her mouth with astonishment. Arnie never talked to her like this and he rarely swore, certainly not at her. She couldn't help it, she broke down and ran to the bedroom hoping her husband would follow and they could work this out. If something didn't happen soon to explain her husband's behavior, she felt she would crack. He didn't follow and she cried herself to sleep on the bed.

Sleeping until after noon, she went back to check on Arnie and he was gone.

*   *   *   *   *

The Comanche would suffer for this as will all the other leaders in state government. The Keeper was furious over what Chew Quanah was doing to its people. Quanah was like the coyote, it thought, representing greed and dishonesty in his Indian folklore and true to form now in the Arizona legislature. But this Comanche savage will endure the wrath of all the demons I can summon to ravage his body in such a way that no one else dares such a move.

The supernatural power of the Superstitions had offered the Keeper a Pandora's Box of potential horror. Her two enforcers were in place and functional. And so far it had been very careful to anticipate the moves of McIntyre and McKenna but had to be careful not to allow them to get too close to its modus operandi, as it was called in law enforcement. But that girl, Lani, was also a big threat to its goals and might have to be dealt with.

*   *   *   *   *

"He was a fine man and a credit to my staff and we will all miss him," Cyrus Dean was saying in a quickly called press conference. McIntyre and McKenna were watching TV coverage at the crime scene on Deke's tablet from a local independent TV station broadcasting the mysterious killings. "What I don't understand," Dean continued, "is why the police still don't have any leads on these unorthodox murders. This is the fourth and the second of local and state political figures. What's going on?"

"Should we tell him we don't know?" Deke asked the Chief.

"Might as well, cause we don't," was the reply.

They were standing in Thornton's garage after forensics had finished but left the body for the Medical Examiner who hadn't arrived yet. Both men shared the complete look of bewilderment and it was obvious that this case had them by the balls. Officer Gouyen was also there and had been checking out the house for any evidence of a confrontation. She walked into the garage shaking her head.

"I'm not seeing anything that would indicate there was anyone here with him. When the ME gives us a TOD we can start backtracking and see where he was before he was killed. The guy is apparently single since there are very few female clothes in his closet. What's there probably belongs to girlfriends. Maybe a place to start." Gouyen was guessing with the rest of them.

"Thanks, Bly, why don't you go back to the office and write up a report. We'll hang around for the Medical Examiner." She left but noted mentally that the Chief usually wanted her to hang around until they closed the crime scene

"I'm on the way," she said, and made a mental note to follow up on the ME's report.

"We've got to start keeping the evidence we collect limited to as few people as possible to prevent leaks in the department. Bly is loyal but she is a full-blooded Apache and the tribe still considers the Superstitions sacred ground so she must have some concern about what is going on here. What do you think?"

"My gut tells me she's first an Apache and second a cop. That's just natural, Ruben, but I don't see how she'd ever figure into this mess, except investigating it. We're dealing with something from a world most people don't understand and, although she may see it from an Indian's point of view, she is a trained professional."

The Chief's cell rang and it was Gouyen. When he had finished listening, he hung up and said, "We have a witness."

EIGHTEEN…

Walter Rogers sat in his fifteenth floor Mesa office looking out the window at distant mountains he was pretty sure were the Superstitions. What the hell had really happened up there when Amy was with her friends? She supposedly made out with some female Indian, something that she hadn't fully explained. Walter didn't necessarily approve of his wife having sex with other women but at least it kept her off his back. Apparently he'd married a nympho.

It wasn't that he didn't enjoy sex, but it just wasn't a priority with him like it obviously was with Amy. God, she was beautiful, though, and he had long ago realized what an asset a woman like her could be in business to her husband. She was the hit of his office parties and he was pretty sure at the last Christmas event she had snuck away with his boss and they had made out in his office. When they came back, he looked like he had been put through a ringer.

Right after that Walter got a big raise.

But what he still couldn't explain was the incident at the Cardinals' game where she returned from the rest room with blood on her mouth and T-shirt. He still didn't know what happened at the game. Amy said she cut her mouth and they needed to go home so she could attend to it. And then the news reported someone was killed that same day in one of the restrooms at the University of Phoenix stadium. It was all so weird since Amy had been so fidgety at the game.

Walter thought of the outfit she had worn when she went out recently with her friend, Karen. Most guys would consider that a real come-on. And there was also another creepy murder that same evening where someone was drained of their blood like that woman at the Cardinal's game. But Amy was home before that happened. And there is no way Amy could do something like that anyway, so what was he thinking?

* * * * *

Officer Gouyen had Rudy Brown in the interrogation room and when the Chief and McKenna arrived she filled them in on who he was and what connection he had with the deceased. "He's pretty broken up, Ruben, like they were real good friends. I told him to be ready to answer all your questions so he could help you find out who did this to his buddy."

"Thanks, Bly, let's go Deke." The three of them filed in to the room where there were only two chairs left. Officer Gouyen stood by the door.

"Mr. Brown, thank you for voluntarily coming to us with your information. I understand you were one of the last people to see Dan Thornton before his death?"

"Call me Rudy, yes, probably next to last. His, uh, date would have been the last as far as I know. Her name is Amy...ah...something, can't remember. However, the woman I was with should know, they were good friends. Her name is Karen Briggs. But you have to be careful, they are both married." Brown looked at Officer Gouyen for her disapproval but saw none.

"Do you know how to get in touch with this Karen Briggs?" McIntyre asked.

"Yes, have her cell phone number but you can only call during the day while her husband is at work." He took out his phone and read off the number; Gouyen wrote it down.

"Now, start at the beginning where you guys met these two ladies and take me through the evening to where you obviously parted with Thornton. In the meantime, Bly, could you make a quick call to Karen Briggs and ask her to come in for questioning? Tell her we'll send a squad car if she needs it."

"Right, Chief," and she left the room.

Rudy Brown started with the meeting of the four at the bar in The Big Place and continued until he and Karen went their way and assumed Amy went home with Dan. Deke questioned him extensively about the woman Thornton was with; was there a misunderstanding that had gotten out of hand? Brown could think of nothing suspicious about Amy. All he remembered was what a good-looking woman she was, sexy enough to bring down the Southern Baptist convention.

"But what you need to know, Chief, is the fact that Amy called Karen right after we left the bar and left word on her voicemail that she was in her car and headed home. I don't know what happened but maybe Karen can tell you."

"What time was that?" McIntyre asked.

"Well, we left before ten PM, so I would judge that it would have been just after ten when she called."

"I assume Ms. Briggs went home with you, and did she stay all night?" McKenna asked.

"She came with me but didn't stay. I took her home at three in the morning." He had a sheepish grin on his face.

"Let me get this right, you meet this married woman in a bar, take her to your house, keep her out until three AM, and then deliver her home to her doorstep. Am I right?" the Chief said.

"Not exactly, you see, I kind of dropped her off on the corner around the block from her house. It was her idea." Said in a contrite but bordering on braggadocio way.

McIntyre looked at Deke to see if he had any more questions but got a negative reaction.

"Okay, Mr. Brown, that's all for now, but here's my card if you think of anything else." They all got up and started out the door.

"Chief, I really want to keep Karen out of trouble, so could you go as easy as possible, please."

"We'll do what we can but can't make any promises."

McIntyre and McKenna headed for the Chief's office and ran into Bly Gouyen. "Karen Briggs is on the way down here and she sounds scared to death. Don't think it's the murder as much as the fact she's afraid her husband will find out about this. She begged me to keep her name out of the news and I told her it all depended on how much she cooperated. Don't think you'll have a problem. She should be here any minute."

"Thanks, Bly, good work."

* * * * *

Karen Briggs was perspiring profusely. Distracted, she almost pulled in front of another car while making a right on red. She gripped the leather steering wheel so tight her knuckles were bloodless. She had

78

left a note for Robert who was due home soon. Karen didn't know how long this would take but she was concerned over being involved in a murder and if it would get back to her husband. Jesus, Amy must be going through pure hell right now.

She decided to call her friend and give her a heads up on what was going on. Karen didn't know how much the police knew and she had only talked to Amy once the morning after their night out. She explained then that Dan Thornton had come on too strong for her, leaving the bar, trying to seduce her on the hood of his car, and when she rejected his advances he called her names.

After that she had said that she left him in the parking lot and had gone right home. That's when she called Karen.

Karen pulled out her cell phone and speed dialed Amy. "Hi you," her friend said, "what's going on?"

'I'm on my way to the police station about Dan Thornton's murder. Rudy Brown told the police I was with him Saturday night and that you were with Dan Thornton. Rudy didn't know how to get in touch with you but I gave him my telephone number so they called me." Pause. "Amy, I'm scared. This is murder we're talking about and Thornton is, was, a big deal in state government so it's bound to hit the newspapers. How do we explain it to our husbands?"

"Calm down Karen, we'll figure this out. Just a couple of girls out on the town who met a couple of guys who bought them a drink. Unfortunately, one of them was killed. Nobody was in the parking lot when we left so there are no witnesses. Dan sure as hell can't say anything."

Karen thought that last comment was a little callous but they were both under severe pressure so she overlooked Amy's remark. "What're you going to do?"

"I've been thinking about it all morning, and I'm going to call the police and offer to come in and give them a statement. It's the least I can do."

"Good idea. I'm here so I've got to hang up now."

"Oh Karen, don't tell the cops you talked to me."

"Don't worry. Got enough to worry about on my own. Good luck."

"Yeah, good luck to you." Amy smiled.

The noose tightens but the web keeps getting wider and stickier.

NINETEEN...

Lani still couldn't get over that last reading with Deke and Chief McIntyre when Phoenix Mayor Clarence Talbot had been brutally murdered. She and McKenna had talked about it and he had spoken with the Chief but she still couldn't get it out of her mind. She had finished placing all ten cards down and then there was the Death card with the Devil, then the Tower and the Fool cards.

And when she began to put it all together and do her interpretation of the cards, that was when the contortions in her body started and she went into convulsions that sent Deke and McIntyre into a panic. Lani would never forget what she saw. There was a great montage of Arizona politicians lined up against a mountain. There was blood gushing over the precipice and dripping down the side of the cliff onto the people who were there.

She thought, was it just a coincidence about the recent supernatural murders?

*   *   *   *   *

Rudy Brown tried to backtrack in his mind to this past weekend to figure out if there was anything he had failed to tell police about the events of Saturday night. His best friend was demonically murdered by some blood sucking fiend that was terrorizing Phoenix. And why had it picked Dan Thornton for a victim? Why not himself? Was it because Dan was in government, and if that was the reason, did that mean these demons were going after politicos?

"Let's see," talking out loud to himself as he was driving back to work, "there was nothing unusual about the way they had met Karen and Amy, didn't look like they were setups or anything like that. Both said they were married and Karen had sounded more scared about her husband finding out than if she had been involved in a murder when they talked today. No, don't believe they were involved in this.

"So if there's no connection between their two dates and the murder, maybe it was just coincidence."

Brown was stopped at an intersection with a red light and when he looked over at the car next to him, a woman was staring at him curiously, until he realized he had been talking to himself. He smiled. The woman took off. Maybe I'm losing my touch, he thought, but back to his friend, there was still something very suspicious about this whole thing that was bothering him and he couldn't figure out just what it was.

Something about Amy Rogers wasn't right and it had to do with her face, her smile maybe?

*　*　*　*　*

"You think Rudy Brown is telling us the whole story Ruben?"

McKenna and the Chief were at Phoenix PD in another session to decide what to say to reporters. "Yeah, probably innocent but what do you think about those two married women, especially Amy Rogers? I think we should bring her in right away for an interview. Sounds like she has an alibi but it also appears like it could be concocted and I think we should firm it up. Besides, she's the last one to see Thornton alive. I'll have Gouyen contact her to come in."

"I agree that we should talk to her but unless she's our vampire, it's not likely Amy Rogers was involved."

"I know, but," and there was a knock on the door. "Come in."

It was Phoenix PD's Director of Forensics, Randy Clovis, who had been with the department for over fifteen years. He had the Dan Thornton crime scene results. He started right out. "The man had not one drop of blood left in his body. I think we all agree at this point, you either have to be a medical technician or a vampire to do this. Know it sounds crazy when we have that kind of alternative but there is simply no other answer.

"Nobody in the neighborhood saw anything and we checked the surroundings but nothing of significance. There is a wooded area next to Thornton's house that we went over, and there were tire tracks but they had been driven over so many times that identification was impossible. There was no blood and if there were footprints, the car tracks obliterated them. I can't imagine why Thornton might have been in those woods unless he was lured there."

"He probably wouldn't go in there willingly," McIntyre offered.

"Unless it was a vampire and she was human…and a good looking woman," McKenna added, and everyone stared right at him for more. "For years the males had a corner on the vampire thing, starting even before Bram Stoker's Dracula. But the modern-day scenario includes gorgeous females with large breasts and red lips with fangs protruding and a trickle of blood on her chin. They are not only deadly these days, they are sexy as hell."

"Well, the gorgeous part would apparently fit Amy Rogers but she has a good alibi," the Chief remarked. "Anyway," he was still chewing over the whole thing, "how could you suspect a typical housewife to be a vampire? No way, right?"

"But here's an even bigger shocker, Ruben," Clovis spoke up again, "I can't find any marks, teeth or otherwise, where Thornton's blood was drained from. He appears absolutely clean all over."

* * * * *

Amy picked up the phone and called Phoenix police headquarters connecting with the desk sergeant. "Phoenix Police Department, how can I help you?"

"My name is Amy Rogers and I think you might want to talk to me about the Dan Thornton killing." God, she should've been an actor.

"Hold on Ms. Rogers while I put you through to someone."

"Chief Ruben McIntyre. I understand this is Amy Rogers, the person who was at The Big Place last Saturday with the murder victim, Dan Thornton?"

"One and the same," jeez I am cool, "figured you might want to talk to me."

"Yes, Ms. Rogers, one of my officers has been trying to get in touch with you."

"Sorry about that. Let my cell's battery run down and it's been charging. When would you like to talk to me?"

"As soon as possible. Would you like me to send an unmarked car for you?"

"No, have my own car and I'll come on down now if you'd like."

"Yes, please do, we'll be waiting."

"Fine, I'm on the way." They both hung up.

Okay, Amy thought, this will be the performance of your life. She had been rehearsing her statement all the time someone from the police department had been trying to reach her and had just let her phone ring. Although her call to Karen did give her an alibi, it was close, but with Walter's confirmation of when she got home, that should cinch it. Once again she went to the closet and selected a semi-sexy outfit, including panties; mustn't shock the Phoenix PD.

She would leave a note for Walter, not exactly where she was going, of course, but to let him know she might be late for dinner. When she was back home, they would have a conversation about all that had happened, including the fact she had a drink with the guy on the Governor's staff that had been killed. Depending on what happened in the police interview, she would tell Walter some of the facts, leaving out anything that might drive him over the edge.

"Please sit down Ms. Rogers." Officer Gouyen had escorted her to one of the interview rooms with a one-way mirror. Deke McKenna was on the other side. "I'll let Chief McIntyre know you're here." She left the room.

Amy looked at the glass and wondered if they had some kind of profiler there to pick her facial expressions apart. Karen hadn't mentioned this when they talked but maybe she was so scared she didn't notice. Good, just another witness for my Oscar performance. Break a leg Amy.

"Hello Ms. Rogers. Thank you for coming in for this interview. I believe you have already met Officer Gouyen." They both sat down.

Who was on the other side of the glass? Interesting, and her mind did a hundred computations to try and determine what that meant, but there was a slight twinge of fear that they might really suspect her of something. All the more reason for my stunning soliloquy. Amy was in the big leagues now and had a mission to accomplish. There was no way she would let the Phoenix Police Department stand in her way.

TWENTY...

"Now, we have talked with your friend, Karen Briggs, and she explained to us that you and Ms. Briggs met two men at The Big Place, Rudy Brown and Dan Thornton. Mr. Thornton is since deceased and we are trying to determine what happened to him after the two of you allegedly separated in the parking lot of the bar." He stopped. Amy figured he wanted the mirror person to record her expression from behind the glass. She had the stone-face ready.

Continuing, "Could you go over the events of the evening for the record?"

"So far you are correct in what you have said except I don't understand the word "alleged" that you used, unless Karen didn't confirm my story."

"No, Ms. Briggs did say you called her sometime after ten PM on your way home alone and Mr. Thornton's time of death hasn't been absolutely confirmed due to the way in which he died, but we think it was around ten-thirty. You do know we're dealing with a supernatural event since the victim's blood was completely drained from his body?"

Bingo. Amy didn't know for sure but thought the exact time of death would be a problem for the police. So maybe that great act she had planned wouldn't be necessary. Or, at least save it for later. Now, the coup de grâce. "Chief McIntyre, if you need further corroboration, please feel free to contact my husband to confirm the time I arrived home. Although I would prefer that you do it in the evening when he's home from work.

"You see, we have this, uh, arrangement."

McKenna walked in. "Ms. Rogers, this is my special assistant Deke McKenna. Deke specializes in the paranormal and has been with the department from the beginning on this case. He has some questions for you."

Amy looked at this hulk of a man and immediately decided she had rather be in bed with him than sitting here answering his questions. God, she was turning into a nymphomaniac since her conversion. She wondered if he could sense her emotions.

86

The Chief broke the tension, "You have a question for Ms. Rogers?"

McKenna was so smooth no one realized the tenseness between them. "You are married, right?"

"Yes I am."

"Does your husband know what's going on? I understand this was a chance meeting between you and Thornton, and the first time you had met the deceased, so there was no reason to believe your husband could have retaliated?" It was a question.

"God no, Walter wouldn't hurt anyone. Anyway, we have this arrangement that each of us can do our own thing sexually and not let it affect our marriage. We are both very happy in that kind of situation." Where was McKenna going with this?

"Have you ever been to The Big Place before?"

"Nope, never."

"What made you decide to go there last Saturday?"

"Not sure, just looking for a fun night out and I had heard about the place."

"It attracts the well-connected in Phoenix and a lot of the crowd goes there to meet people in important positions. Of course, that was what Dan Thornton was. From what Ms. Briggs told us Thornton and Brown asked you to have drinks with them. Is that right?"

"Yes they did."

"And you and your friend just followed them to a table, no questions asked?"

Now Amy could see his intent, like maybe she went to the bar just to meet Thornton, a set-up, which in a way she had. But they couldn't possibly know that and she could easily call his bluff. She shocked them all, "They were good looking and we were horny so we let nature take its course. I've done it before but fortunately the guy wasn't murdered. You're single aren't you? You should understand."

The Chief almost grinned. Gouyen was non-committal. McIntyre spoke up first, "Ms. Rogers, would you take us through your meeting with Mr. Thornton until you left him at…what time did you say?"

Obviously a trick question but she was on top of it, "Sometime before ten PM."

"And why did the two of you split up instead of you accompanying Mr. Thornton home?"

"Because he tried to seduce me in the bar's parking lot on the hood of his car. Wouldn't call it rape, but almost had to kick him in the crotch to get him off me. I mean, I like sex but not that way." She now had their attention. "He was obviously pissed and by then I was completely out of the mood. He went his way and I went mine. That's when I called Karen." There, she could bring the curtain down and just wait for the applause.

McIntyre said, "Deke, you have anything else?"

"No, believe I've heard enough."

"Officer Gouyen?"

"No Chief, nothing."

Amy looked at Bly Gouyen and had a strange feeling she had met her somewhere. Karen had described her as having a manikin type personality with Marine-like posture and speaking rarely. Her demeanor bothered Karen and maybe Amy was just reacting from that. But Gouyen looked to her like she knew something none of the others did.

"Ms. Rogers, guess that's all for now but we might want to call you back again if things change. In the meantime here's my card if you think of anything else. We're not going to call your husband, at least not now, but might sometime in the future so please leave your home phone number with Officer Gouyen." Amy did.

Thank God she had been able to hold that smirk of, *Amy-1, Phoenix PD-0,* until she got to the parking lot. "Girl you aced it," she said out loud, and looked around immediately to make sure she wasn't overheard. No one else there. The more she thought about this the more confident she became in her mission. But she knew she mustn't be too cocky. Amy headed home.

Following the Amy Rogers interview, Chief McIntyre had brought the task force together to discuss what they had for the four crimes. Basically nothing if you were talking about conclusive evidence. No fingerprints, the DNA didn't match, no eyewitnesses, only the two women connected to the Thornton death. And there was absolutely nothing anywhere that would lead them to the identity of the werewolf. It was as if it just killed and then disappeared.

*　*　*　*　*

She screamed as he walked in from the garage. "Arnie, what is wrong with you? There is hair all over your body and your ears and hands are grotesque, you look like an animal. What have you been doing? Oh mercy no, you aren't mixed up in these beastly killings, are you?" And she started to cry out again, this time headed for the front door. He had just returned after the Clarence Talbot murder.

He put a hand over her mouth and with eyes still yellow with rage he shoved her up against the wall and put his other hand around her throat and began to squeeze. "If you make any more noise about this, Agnes, I promise I will kill you." He released the pressure around her neck but gave her a look that he meant what he said. "I'm going to take a shower."

She stood there gridlocked with fear and not understanding anything that was going on. Arnie had some kind of issue, and they could work that out, but he wouldn't kill her, would he? He had always been the most loving husband and now he was in trouble and she must help him. Who should she call? Not 911; that could result in several police cars in front of the house. She would just call the police station and explain that her husband had a problem.

She walked to the hall phone.

Agnes didn't know the number for Phoenix PD so she grabbed the phone book under the table and turned on the light so she could see. Arnie would thank her later for what she was doing, although she felt like a traitor to her husband. In the section for the city of Phoenix she turned the pages until she reached the police department. Agnes settled on a number but was having second thoughts when she heard Arnie come up behind her.

"I told you to drop this but, no, you had to keep pushing me and now I have to take care of you, Agnes." There was fire in his eyes when he swung his wife around and looked straight at her with a determination that she knew was real, but it couldn't be coming from *her* Arnie.

Somehow she had to reach through this…thing…and find her husband. She said, "Please, hon, sit down with me and talk about this…" when he pushed his hand in her face and slammed her against the wall again, almost knocking her out. Brilliant light bursts covered the hallway and she thought she might pass out. Then she could see her husband and was able to get off a weak shriek before his furry hands closed around her neck.

Arnie looked like he was morphing from a human being to some kind of freakish demon. She could see his eyebrows begin to connect to each other and his body was shaking as he began to snarl and growl. Agnes could see canine teeth actually growing and wondered if he would use them on her. The hair on his body was becoming more like fur now and she noticed pointed fingernails growing rapidly from once normal hands.

These same hands were evolving into paws that still clung to her neck.

Her husband had stripped to his underwear shorts for the shower and with the body bulging all over they were soon ripped apart and fell to the floor. All of this she saw out of her peripheral vision because Arnie still had a firm grip around her throat. Looking straight ahead Agnes was staring into two fiery yellow eyes when the creature let out a blood curdling roar.

Then its paws tightened around her neck.

Agnes felt her life ebbing away and she no longer saw her Arnie, just a monster where he had been.

TWENTY-ONE…

Amy Rogers was driving home when she began to have mixed emotions about her interrogation at Phoenix PD. Oh hell, she was going to call Karen for a drink. It was late afternoon and Amy had left Walter a note. The two met at a bar in Glendale that Karen selected. "Well, well, well," Karen said as she walked in. "So they grilled you under the lights but you didn't break."

"You don't know the half of it. They're dying to connect me to Dan Thornton's murder but I have no idea why, when I have an alibi that puts me at home when it happened," Amy half asked. And then she told Karen about all the cross-examination she had gone through.

"You really think they suspect you when I told them what time you called me?"

"They may think I was doing that to set up an alibi. But I do remember asking Walter what time it was when I got home and he confirmed it was 10:20." They had finished their drink and Amy said, "Gotta go and explain this to Walter." She didn't look happy.

Walter looked at the note Amy had left when he got home. At that very moment Amy pulled into the garage and came into the house. "Hi hon," she said, with a solemn look that meant something was going on. "Walter, we have to talk," and she walked into their family room.

"I have a problem that I hope you'll understand," she started, "and I want to tell you all about it before you hear it from someone else." And then she unloaded the whole Dan Thornton scenario on him and watched as he looked at her with the eyes of someone that analyzes figures. Maybe that's what she needed, she thought, an analysis by someone who did this sort of thing for a living.

"Are you saying you are under suspicion for murder?"

"No, just that I was involved with this man on the night of his murder. Well not really involved, he tried to seduce me in the parking lot of The Big Place and I had to fight him off. The guy worked for the Governor's office and when someone killed him later that night, apparently I was the next to last person to see him."

91

"What the hell is The Big Place?"

That's his concern right now? she thought, "It's a bar in Phoenix and Karen and I went there for a drink last Saturday. Remember? That's the night I came home early and we made love," like it was a normal thing for them when in fact it was really irregular at best. But she hoped he hadn't forgotten the time she arrived home.

Walter started to comment then all of a sudden it hit him. Cardinal's game. Woman dies when drained of her blood. Amy came back with blood on her mouth and shirt. Last Saturday, she's with some guy at a bar and he ends up dead. Was he married to the Black Widow?

"I'm not sure how to react to this, Amy. My analytical mind tells me there is a lot of coincidence here. First the Cardinals' game, the vampire killing there, blood all over your mouth and clothes, and now some guy you met in a bar dies the same way and once again you are involved. Is there something you want to tell me?" He was eye to eye with his wife and he noticed a tinge of pink in the iris and pupils of her eyes.

"Walter, I explained the Cardinals game when I told you that I had hit my mouth on the door of the restroom and that made it bleed. Then it got on my shirt so I thought we should go home."

Walter thought again about that cut and didn't remember actually seeing a laceration, only blood. He looked at her suspiciously and said nothing.

"What? You think I'm a vampire? God, my husband thinks I'm a monster." And now there were tears in her eyes but they continued to redden, and when she realized the change taking place she turned away as if hurt.

Walter wasn't a sensitive guy but he put his hand on her shoulder and said, "Of course I don't think you're a vampire. This is all so strange and I'm so used to a well ordered environment, so please forgive me, Amy, if I'm overacting."

Well done, she thought. I've still got it, and her emotions quickly subsided, including the color of her eyes, as she turned around and faced her husband. "I don't like fighting with you," and she gently kissed him.

Walter let it go at that and he did look relieved, but Amy wasn't at all sure that diagnostic mind of his wasn't still doing machinations over this whole thing. However, she was pretty sure that Walter wouldn't screw up a good thing by bringing the police in on this. As long as she kept his boss satisfied, Walter would continue to move up the ladder and that would keep him happy.

Maybe she should initiate another tryst with John Roberts just to seal the deal. Maybe even tomorrow.

Walter had left for work and Amy was rethinking last evening's talk and the more she thought about calling Walter's boss the more she thought it made sense. If something did get tense with the cops she would like to have this guy solidly on her side. She dialed his direct line that he had given her. He answered, "John Roberts here."

"Hi John, this is Amy Rogers," with each word bathed in erotica. "I feel so lonesome this afternoon and was wondering if you had the time to get together?" The phone was dripping at her end.

"Well, Amy, wasn't expecting your call but it's good to hear from you. I'm going into a meeting in ten minutes, out right after noon. Let me check my schedule and call you back." He had two appointments and talked to his secretary about canceling them. She confirmed that neither was urgent and she would take care of it. "I'll be out the rest of the afternoon," he told her.

Then he called Amy. "I'm free for the afternoon. You know the Wrangler Motel on Camelback Road east of Scottsdale Fashion Square?"

"I've passed it before, think I know where it is."

"Pull into the parking lot and park somewhere out of the way. I'll call you at one o'clock and give you the room number and instructions how to get there. Okay?"

"Great, I'll be there," and they both hung up. One PM, she thought; should be able to squeeze the last drop out of John Roberts by four and be home before Walter gets there.

Amy pulled into the motel parking lot at just past one and stopped in a spot off to the side of the main building. In a couple of minutes her phone rang and John Roberts said, "Room 185 on the left side of the motel, all the way to the back on the end, the last room."

"I'm on the way," and she started the car and pulled around to the area he described and drove until she found the room.

The door was ajar but as she approached, he opened it and was already down to his undershorts. 'Let's get down to business,' was the look on his face. "Well, hello John," and he swept her into his arms as he pushed the door closed and kissed her hard and passionately.

She had dressed in a short skirt and tight fitting blouse that buttoned down the front and high heels. She knew men liked heels on women, even when they were having sex. He started unbuttoning her blouse and kissed her around the neck down to her breasts and she conveniently removed her bra so he could get to the real thing. Then Amy unhooked and unzipped her skirt and let it drop. She was wearing no panties.

John Roberts moved her over to the bed and together they inched up toward the headboard until he could wait no longer as he spread Amy's legs and entered her. Since this was more duty-driven than for pleasure, she let Roberts do his thing until he finished, occasionally gasping with an ego-building moan. They took a quick nap and since he wasn't able to get it up again, they both dressed and went on their way.

TWENTY-TWO...

Barber was sitting in his living room looking at his wife on the floor in their hallway. It was obvious he had killed her. It would be easy to tell her few friends in Phoenix that Agnes had to return to Chicago unexpectedly for a family matter and since they had no children, no one else would be checking on them.

But how do you get rid of a body leaving no trace? Barber wasn't that adept on the Internet but he knew enough to do a simple search. He booted up their laptop and searched "how to dispose of a human body." He hit several sites and looked at the results but most of them not what he was looking for.

And then he noticed one with a teaser line that read "Mexican drug lord eliminates all remains of hundreds of victims using acid." That's it, he thought, and punched into the site. It seems that this drug kingpin had enlisted the services of a man located in Nogales, Mexico to dispose of several bodies using sulfuric acid. He simply dumped them into a grave and poured the acid in covering the bodies, then shoveled dirt over the carcasses and let the acid do the rest.

Perfect, Barber thought.

So where do you get enough sulfuric acid in Phoenix without raising suspicions? A rhetorical question, of course. But also answerable online, no doubt, so he searched for "high crime sections in Phoenix, AZ," and up popped a map of both safe and unsafe areas of the city. He had to do this incognito so they wouldn't be able to trace a large purchase back to him later that he couldn't explain. He figured this area would be best to find the right supplier.

There was a rectangle of Phoenix located just south of the Interstate-10 freeway, east of Interstate 17, bordered on the east where 10 turns south toward Tucson and on the south was Buckeye Road. Lots of violent and property crime that Barber felt sure would indicate hustlers would be around that could procure what he wanted, no matter what it was. And he wasn't worried about safety with his alter-ego available on command.

But first, he had to place Agnes in something to slow down decomposition.

There were thirty-three gallon garbage bags in the garage. If he combined three or four and placed them around the top of her body, did the same thing around her lower body and feet, and sealed it in the middle with duct tape, Agnes would at least keep until he could get her in the ground. By sealing her body tightly, denying it oxygen, which bacteria feed on, he could delay decay, giving him time to do what he had to.

The man had done his homework. But now he must obtain the acid.

Arnold Barber headed south on Cave Creek Road and took the 101 Loop east, moving south on highway 51. It turned into Interstate 10 and he got off on Washington Street and headed west, entering right into one of Phoenix's worst crime areas. Nothing looked promising until he passed Seventh Avenue, when he noticed three Hispanic guys standing on the corner. It seemed like one guy was in control and the other two were there for something.

Barber pulled over and parked halfway down the block. It was still day and people were all around so he felt reasonably secure in approaching them. He had been careful to dress as a tourist would, Hawaiian shirt with shorts and sandals. The hood was finishing his business as Barber walked up the street nonchalantly looking around as if he was lost.

The guy in control had quickly pegged him for something other than a cop but was still careful to keep his eye on the approaching man.

When they were almost side by side, Barber turned to the young man and said, "Can you tell me where I might obtain some, uh, questionable merchandise?"

"Zactly what you talkin about?" he was more suspicious now.

"I need twenty-five gallons of ninety-eight percent sulfuric acid, as soon as possible."

The dealer grinned as if he was in on the whole thing. "You done offed someone and now you need to waste the body," he was still grinning but turned serious. "How much you willin' to pay?"

"How about two-hundred dollars?"

"How about five hundred?" and there didn't appear to be any room for negotiation.

"Okay, deal. Don't have the money with me but when you get my merchandise, I'll have the cash." Barber had made the decision to get it early on, just in case.

"You come back here in one hour with yo money and I'll have yo stuff. Go up this street right here," pointing to the one behind him, "and stop in front of the fourth house on the right. First the cash, then someone will bring the acid and put it in yo trunk."

"Fine, I'll be back in an hour."

Barber walked back to his car with the feeling of having just made a deal with Satan. This guy knew why I wanted the acid, he thought, but what difference did that make right now? As he looked behind him when entering his car, his contact was on the cell phone. Next on the agenda was to select the spot to bury his wife. He drove west on Washington to get out of this neighborhood and stopped just on the other side of Interstate 17.

He had several maps but his favorite was The Thomas Guide. He found that leaving his house, he could drive straight up Cave Creek Road, through Spur Cross Ranch and into Maricopa County, which was pretty desolate desert and likely to provide a perfect resting place for Agnes. He would pick a place and drive right into the sand until he found the right spot.

Satisfied with his calculations, Barber pulled away from where he was parked, turned into the next street, angling into a driveway then turning around. Hooking a left back onto Washington, he headed back to the pusher's street and made a left stopping at the fourth house. He was five minutes early but he could see activity behind the front window. Then the door opened and someone stuck his head out the door and focused on Arnold Barber in the SUV.

When the lookout was satisfied he had the right person, he waved his hand out the door and went back inside. Barber took that as a cue to open the rear of the truck but first the dealer came out and collected the five hundred dollars. It was in an envelope and after checking it carefully, he waved to the house and three guys walked out with twenty-five gallons of sulfuric acid. The contact looked at him and said, "Don't ya wanna check it man?"

He walked around to the back and one of the handlers opened the plastic container and said, "It don't smell but you can stick yo finger in and test it."

"Don't think I need to, I trust you guys," to which there were several snorts but nothing that made him doubt his merchandise. Barber headed to the driver's door when the head man walked up to him with a half-smile on his face.

"Good doin' business with you man. Need anything else, you know where I am. Just ask for Marvin if I ain't on my corner." Barber nodded, did a U-turn, and headed back to Washington. Soon he was back on Interstate 10 and headed for Cave Creek. First he would go home and get Agnes' body, then wait until later in the afternoon to continue the burial. I don't have a shovel, he suddenly realized and decided to find a Home Depot.

He found what he was looking for on the corner of Bell and Tatum, pulled into the parking lot and went inside the store. Directed to the outdoor section, there was a long line of digging equipment on the wall. Arnold Barber was no outdoorsman but he knew the sand in the desert would be relatively easy to dig in and that the shovel should be pointed. He found what he wanted, paid for it in cash, and was soon on his way north again.

In just two to three days Agnes would be seeping into the bowels of the Sonoran Desert.

TWENTY-THREE...

McIntyre decided it couldn't be put off any longer. He called Bly Gouyen in to his office and they sat down to prepare a release on the Dan Thornton murder. The actual killing had been reported to the press without the details of how it happened so now they had to fill in the spaces. The question was how do you tell the press, again, that someone had just waltzed into the house of the aide of the Governor's Chief of Staff, murdering him and not leaving a trace?

"Okay," the Chief started, "you have Thornton killed in his garage, no sign of a struggle, only his prints on the steering wheel so he was apparently driving. And there wasn't a drop of blood in his body, and none on the seat. You also have the crime scene report and forensics. Go with it and bring me a draft that we can go over."

"Got it, Chief," and she walked back to her desk.

When she had completed the release, she took it into the Chief's office and they made some corrections. Then he picked up the phone and called McKenna and read it to him. Deke seemed to agree with everything and with only a couple of additions of his own, they decided to go with it. And then Bly fed it into the computer, did a spell-check, and set it up to be sent to all the media outlets plus major political offices like the Governor.

It was only minutes and Bly Gouyen's phone was ringing, and it was the Governor who had decided to make her own call this time. "Who is this?" she snapped.

"Officer Gouyen, may I ask who is calling?"

"Let me speak to McIntyre."

"You mean Chief McIntyre?" Without waiting for an answer, "I'll be glad to see if he is available if you will tell me who is calling."

She sputtered, then said, "He damn well better be available, this is the Governor."

"I'll see," and she hit the hold button, knowing it would leave Butts seething.

Gouyen took her time getting up and walking into Ruben McIntyre's office. She knocked and even waited for an answer this time.

"Come in."

99

"She's on the phone again," and he knew exactly who she meant. "I might have riled her a bit. By the way, I took my time getting here."

The Chief smiled, sat back in his chair obviously not in a hurry to answer and waved her into the room. "Sit down," he said. Finally he answered.

"Yes, Governor," as he looked at Gouyen.

"Who the hell is this Gouyen woman? I want her reprimanded for discourtesy to the Governor. And I want it in her record."

"She is one of my best officers, Governor. Just what was this discourtesy you're talking about?" He grinned at Bly.

"She just didn't treat me with the respect due my office and I want something done about it."

"I'll talk to Officer Gouyen but I doubt seriously if she did anything she should be reprimanded for. And let me remind you, Governor, I don't work for you. I work for the city of Phoenix and that's where I take my orders from." He was surprised but glad he had said it. Butts had some friends on Phoenix's City Council but so did he.

For a few moments there was no answer from Butts and then, "McIntyre, one of my people has been viciously murdered. We've had other killings of this kind and you have come up with nothing. Either find out who killed Dan Thornton or I'll have your job."

The Chief was about to answer when he thought he heard the Governor slamming the receiver down. It was only a click but he knew what had happened. "How to win friends and influence people at the highest levels of state government. Butts says she's going after my job."

"Wouldn't worry if I were you. She has a few problems on her plate and who knows what might happen."

* * * * *

Arnold Barber dragged his wife's body to the door of the garage and then picked it up, throwing his wife over his shoulder. Even as Barber was fulfilling his objective, there was a feeling that the Keeper was communicating with him for a new rendezvous with death but it wasn't clear yet just who. First Agnes had to be put to rest so there would never be any trace.

The body was loaded into the back along with the sulfuric acid and then he opened the garage door. He backed out and headed toward Cave Creek Road, turning north. It was now late afternoon and according to his map it could take him around an hour to arrive at a location desolate enough to bury his wife's body. Arnold Barber was only slightly concerned over what he had had to do to Agnes and it was somewhat surprising to him that it didn't bother him more.

Was he losing his capacity for remorse?

It was a little over an hour before Barber found a suitable place. There had been no traffic for some time and then he spied a rock and boulder formation about a half mile off the road. He put the SUV into four-wheel drive and made his way toward the stone mass, driving behind it to hide the truck. This was a perfect location for providing cover and the soil felt soft, so it should be easy to dig in. Grabbing the shovel, he began excavating Agnes' last resting place.

After an hour Barber had made enough progress that he determined the hole was between three and four feet deep. Didn't they say it should be at least six feet when burying a body? Yes, but that was to keep animals from digging it up and he thought there was no way anything would dig into sulfuric acid so he was satisfied with the current depth. It was twilight and soon it would be dusk and starting to get dark so he had to hurry. Back to the SUV for Agnes' body.

He lifted it out of the back and laid it on the ground to remove the plastic covering. Placing his wife on the edge of the grave, he climbed down into the opening laying down the plastic. Placing the plastic under the body should keep the sulfuric acid from being absorbed into the ground too quickly. Reaching up with both arms, he gently pulled her body down until it was lying on the bottom. Climbing out, he decided she was ready for her acid bath.

Barber opened the first acid container and started pouring. Sulfuric acid acts very quickly and it began to burn through Agnes' skin the minute the two came in contact. Within three to four days there should be little or nothing left, even teeth. To allow the acid to take its course, it would be necessary to wait a while before replacing the earth so as not to dilute the solution.

Finally it was time to cover his wife and let science and nature do its thing. Arnold Barber began to shovel dirt into the grave and it was already obvious that the acid was doing its job. Her eyes were beginning to dissolve and her nose looked like one of those wax museum movies when the body tissue, or in that case wax, began to melt and slide down the cheek.

Her flesh was turning a greenish brown and after a few minutes Agnes had cooked enough that her body was no longer recognizable. Barber filled in all the dirt finally and stood back to look at his work.

There was a little hump there that would help in the settling of the ground and he would do what he could to cover his footprints. And the car tracks should be covered over with time.

On his way home now, Arnold Barber was satisfied that he had conducted a clandestine operation, as they would say in the CIA. There were no lights on the highway when he left and there had been none the entire time he was there, as far as he knew. Hopefully that meant there wasn't much traffic here in the desert, thus, a small chance of someone discovering the gravesite. Now he was getting that attraction from the Keeper again.

TWENTY-FOUR...

The Keeper was in the process of deciding who the next victim would be when the decision was made for it. The Governor was responsible for much of the repression of the Apache people in this state. This was not acceptable and must be dealt with quickly to thwart any plans she might have to do further harm. There were others in state government but eliminating the Governor would put all the others in chaos. The werewolf would be assigned to carry out the mission.

It would direct Arnold Barber to leave all body parts intact except for one, to not only show the power of the Keeper's supernatural strength, but also leave a metaphor that would illustrate the level of dispassion Anita Butts could stoop to. One by one they would be taken care of. Revenge was finally within reach.

*   *   *   *   *

Deke McKenna was just walking into the entrance to the Phoenix Police Department when the desk sergeant looked up and said, "Think the Chief tried to call you."

"Yeah, talked to him, was already on the way. Is he in his office?"

"Yep," and he was buzzed in.

McIntyre had mentioned the DNA results from Dan Thornton and they already had Bernice O'Ryan's. Now they had a comparison and Deke knew almost for sure what it would be. The door was open and he said, "Hi Ruben."

McIntyre was deeply engrossed in paperwork on his desk and without looking up said, "Come in and close the door. Well we pretty much got what we thought we would, like you said it would be."

When he had shut the door, Deke said, "The same DNA and there are no matches anywhere in the system."

"Exactly, didn't even run it through channels again 'cause I knew what we would get."

"Ruben, I wish my mother was here to give us her insight into this case. Sometimes when you're dealing with the paranormal it is

103

good to have someone who is way out there to talk to. When you're on the fringe of reality your ideas are uninhibited, therefore they translate into solutions that are equal to the logics of the dilemma at hand. She would easily relate to our vampire and werewolf."

His parents moved from California to Roswell, New Mexico thirty years ago and within the same year moved to Phoenix. "You know the story about us being taken up in a spaceship. Well, I was too young to know what was going on but my mother took me aside one day and described our interlude with space aliens. It was so freaky but realistic, and she was so descriptive that to this day I do not know whether the story is true or my mother was crazy.

"I moved back to Phoenix to look after her until she died."

McIntyre was quiet as McKenna looked like he was deep in thought, no doubt thinking of his mother. The Chief didn't believe Ms. McKenna was crazy, and he didn't think Deke thought so either. But what was more bizarre than a werewolf and a vampire working the streets of Phoenix? That made spaceship landings at Phoenix Sky Harbor Airport sound not only reasonable but a good possibility.

Ruben McIntyre began to wonder if he would keep his job long enough to solve this case.

* * * * *

Walter Rogers sat in his office thinking again about what Amy had told him about her tryst with this Dan Thornton. It had been all over the newspapers and TV but most heavily on talk radio where they were looking for a mystery woman that was supposed to be with Thornton the night of the murder. He wasn't worried about what his superiors would think about his wife sleeping around. No problem after that last office party. He called his boss on the phone.

"Mr. Roberts's office," his secretary chimed.

"This is Walter Rogers, could I speak to John."

"Just a minute Mr. Rogers." Formal to the end.

"Hello Walter, what can I do for you?"

What you can do is stop screwing my wife, unsaid but on his mind as he said, "John, I have a personal problem and would like to come to your office and discuss it."

"Sure, come on over."

As he hung up John Roberts wondered if Walter had found out that he was banging his wife. They were discreet enough, he thought, but the man could be a problem if he turned into a reprising husband. God, Amy seemed starved for sex so she mustn't be getting any at home. John normally wouldn't do this but she was so beautiful and stacked, and she came on to him first. Walter knocked.

"Come in."

The door opened and Walter had a sheepish look on his face that Roberts didn't like. All he needed was for this guy to get physical and have his wife find out what had happened. The office grapevine was unstoppable and he worried…"John, I have to tell you something I don't want you to see on the news."

Definite relief there. "Go on Walter."

"Amy's been involved in something that may be blown completely out of proportion in the media. You read about the Dan Thornton murder, the guy from the Governor's staff; well she was having a drink with him the night he was killed. They weren't actually involved. I don't think Amy would do anything like that." He paused for effect and knew he had caught his boss off guard. "They were just having a drink together at a bar. Amy's best friend was there."

Roberts had a blank look on his face until he realized Walter had stopped talking and was staring at him. Well, at least he didn't know about him and Amy, or did he?

"I don't think they actually suspect her of anything, but it's bound to hit the papers and the air waves eventually and I don't want the firm embarrassed over this."

"I think we can deal with this, Walter. Just a simple matter of two gals out having an innocent drink and some guy comes up and hits on her." What bullshit, he thought. Amy was out on the town to get laid and she was probably lucky he wasn't on top of her when it happened or she could be dead too.

"They're saying a vampire killed Thornton just like the woman at the Cardinals' game," Rogers said.

"Holy shit. What is this, serial werewolf and vampire murders? Some woman up north and the Phoenix Mayor were killed by some kind of wolf-like beast. What the hell is going on?"

"Don't know but I'm just glad Amy is okay."

So am I, John Roberts thought. He had considered calling her at home during the day while Walter was at work. A regular afternoon rendezvous would be a good workout, especially with this sexy woman, and it could replace one of his exercise days. "Hey, so am I Rogers, so am I."

I'll bet, Walter thought, and walked out the door. On the way back to his office he thought, how many more sexual encounters would it take before he got another raise?

TWENTY-FIVE...

Chief McIntyre and Deke McKenna were on their way to the cafeteria to get coffee, both remaining quiet, both ways. Deke was thinking that with the special-forces unit the Chief had on this investigation numbering ten officers and two detectives, what else would it take to solve the case? McIntyre was thinking if one of the top men in the country who specializes in the paranormal can't figure out what's going on, what would it take for them to get a break?

As they got back to the Chief's office, McKenna closed the door and stood as McIntyre sat down behind his desk. "Ruben, there's something I haven't told you about our two other-world suspects that could escalate violence even more in the future."

"Good God, how much worse could it get?"

"Plenty, if this comes about. One of the significant factors about anything that is a hybrid is that the mutation, which occurred to create the crossbreed, may continue to produce more evolution that is extremely unpredictable. This can be controlled in the breeding of animals and plants but when you enter the realm of the supernatural, the genome is much less stable and these chromosomes, thus the DNA, can engender a freak within a freak.

"In mythology, and in several Romanian accounts of werewolves and vampires, if the transformation continues unabated, one of the first things that can happen is they change into their demon forms permanently. But if there is a family member involved where the vampire or werewolf lives, then there is certain to be some serious suspicion, certainly when the permanent transformation takes place.

"Along with all this new alteration, there is also a record of werewolves mating with vampires and producing an offspring so aberrant that nothing can control it. With a gestation period of around two months and their output of four or five to the litter, it wouldn't take long to build a legion of monsters. This reportedly happened in a small village in the county of Sibiu in Romania, and the result was these preternatural creatures viciously slaughtered all its inhabitants."

"And that's what the portal in the Superstitions gave us?"

107

McIntyre looked dazed. More information than he could handle right now and even with all they knew, they didn't have one single solitary lead. Zilch. Nada. "We have all this technology working for us but so far it's doing us no good," he said. He looked at Deke McKenna for some kind of support but wasn't sure what. He was doing all he could but when would things start to fall into place? "Maybe it's time to start at the beginning again," he wondered out loud.

Then McKenna's cell phone rang.

"Hi hon, get my message?" He had called Lani earlier.

Apparently she did as he looked at the Chief and said, "Lani can make the Sedona call anytime. Wanna go over there now?"

"Hell yes," he said and they headed up to Cave Creek.

"We're here," Deke called out as they entered her outer office. Within a few minutes Lani came to the door from her reading room and waved them in.

I was meditating," she said, "and kept seeing these strange shapes play around in my head and sometimes they were making love and then they were trying to kill each other. Does that mean anything to you?"

The two guys looked at each other then looked back at Lani and said "no," almost in unison. But this set McKenna to thinking about what he and McIntyre had just been discussing regarding werewolves and vampires mating. However, what did the violence part represent? Was it to be in Phoenix or is her vision just generalized? He immediately thought of the people in the county in Romania.

"You're sure now you feel comfortable calling your psychic friend in Sedona?" Deke asked.

"Sure," Lani answered, and she took out her cell phone and dialed.

"Hello, remember to take care of your body. It's the only place you have to live. This is Loretta Popescu speaking."

"Hi Lo, this is Lani in Cave Creek with a problem for you but first, how are you?"

108

"Honey, I couldn't be better. I just met this gorgeous woman and I think I'm in love. And how are you and the big guy doing?"

"We're doing great personally, coming up on three months together soon. But we have a problem here in Phoenix that you must have heard about by now." Popescu was one-hundred percent Romanian coming to the U.S. with her parents some seventeen years ago. She was also gay and made no beans about it. There had never been any closet for this girl and she stood up for her rights.

"Of course I've heard about it and when I read your McKenna was involved, I was beginning to feel neglected when you didn't call me right away."

"You know you're always on my mind, but I had to wait until Phoenix PD said the word, and Chief McIntyre and Deke are sitting here with me right now. We're desperate, Lo." And then Lani took several minutes to bring her friend up to date on all the background and the latest developments of the vampire and werewolf murders.

There was silence from the other end and Lani knew that Loretta was absorbing all of what she had told her; after all, this was a story for the museum of the weird. Even someone who is into holism and has a general understanding of the supernatural would have a problem with these recent events. Everyone waited. Then…

"Let me spend some time deliberating over this and I'll call you back. I don't suppose you have any photos of the culprits you can email me?"

"Sorry, no, but I personally had an experience doing a Tarot reading recently where I thought I was seeing the end of the world and I know it was connected to this case."

"Okay, I'll keep that in mind. Call you back in no more than an hour."

"Thanks, Lo. We'll be waiting."

The three of them drove up the street to a coffee shop and gathered around an outside table to discuss what Loretta Popescu might come up with. Deke went for the coffee. Lani looked at the Chief and returning her glance he said, "Don't think I've ever seen this troubling a look on your face before. Is this whole thing too much, Lani, because it's really not your problem? If you'd rather not participate any longer I'll understand and am sure McKenna will too."

"No, please, I want to stay with this and do anything I can to help. It's just that whenever I think about that reading that took me off the edge, I get the terrible feeling again that the chaos I saw was right here in Phoenix. Until I get that explained, I guess I'm going to agonize over what I saw." She looked down and the coffee arrived.

"What're all the glum looks about? I thought we were encouraged that we might get some insight into the investigation from Loretta. Something happen I don't know about?" Deke asked.

"Lani is still reflecting on her Tarot reading of the apocalypse she saw, and I agree with her that we need to get that explained in order to know more about this case," McIntyre said.

McKenna sat down and no one said anything until Lani's phone rang. "Hello Lo." After listening a few seconds she said, "Can't do that. We're in a coffee shop." More listening, "We're on our way."

They both had the "that was that all about" look on their faces.

"We have to go back to my shop. Lo has come up with something and she wants me to call her back and put the phone on speaker so everyone can hear at once." They left. In the car ride back Lani said, "Lo also said to expect the worst, and in this case it would probably come to pass."

TWENTY-SIX...

They headed in the door to Lani's shop, she put the closed sign up, and they all went to the back room. Lani called Loretta Popescu and put the phone on speaker. "We're all here, Lo."

She jumped right in. "My initial deduction is that you have an internal force going on with the intention of disrupting the state and local governments. I can see momentum building to do away with certain political and law enforcement individuals. The common dominator of this heinous scheme is someone all of you know, but all I get is a blurry picture of a person with an owl in the background."

Nobody said anything for a few minutes until the Chief finally asked, "Any chance you could revisit that blurry figure and come up with an identification?"

"Sorry. Believe me, I've racked my brain for recognition but if it's someone from down there, I just might not know them."

Deke said, "Not even any identifying characteristics like height, color, male or female, anything like that?"

"All I could tell was that this person's hair must have been long because it was in braids that were at least to the middle of the chest."

All three said it at the same time, "Indian."

"I thought so too but wanted you guys to come to your own conclusions. If that means something, tell me and I'll do another session and see what I can come up with."

McKenna spoke up again, "We all think this originated from a portal in the Superstitions and of course, history tells us that the Apache consider that sacred ground and have been known to protect it with their life. We have it second and third hand that two people went into the mountain recently and are supposed to have gone through some kind of transformation. We don't know who they are and what the metamorphosis was but this all did happen before our recent killings."

"I heard about the portal and rumors of strange events going on in the Superstitions but nothing specific. Just wrote it off to Dutchman's Mine gossip."

"Well, you can believe it, Loretta," McIntyre said. "Not only is it real but it looks like we've got ourselves some supernatural serial killers."

*   *   *   *   *

It was just past dusk outside and Arnold Barber needed gas for the car. Once it was dark enough he would go where he knew he could get to the pumps without being seen by anyone. Now that Agnes was gone he still had to maintain the essentials but it was becoming harder as his shift back to human form became less complete. Fortunately, he had been able to order food online from Walmart.

As he was being prepped by the Keeper for his next task, Barber hurriedly went to his car and headed for the remote gas station he had thought of earlier. It was down Cave Creek Road and then onto Tatum. He turned in with only one car at the pumps, a young lady who certainly wouldn't pay any attention to an old guy like him. He still went to the farthest pump from her.

And then his body shuddered with throbbing in his forehead while he could see the hair growing on his arms. He touched his face and felt bristles there. He'd have to hurry and get this done. Thankfully the girl filling her tank was leaving. Barber broke out in a cold sweat and knew he had to get out of here now. He shut the pump down and got back into the car. Suddenly he had to get to the Desert Ridge shopping center, only a short distance south on Tatum.

As Barber turned left into the shopping center the canines were pushing through his gums and his fingers were turning into paws with claws ripping out. It was hard to control the car as he was losing his ability to think like a human and rapidly turning into an animal. But it was still clear in his mind where he had to go, and then he was almost at the end where large Klieg lights were glaring at a small stage. He parked behind several cars.

His clothes were expanding with the increased body size and would soon be shreds on the seat of his car. Barber's feet had evolved through his shoes and socks to twice the normal size. He quickly shut off the engine as the transformation became complete and a furry body threw open the car door as it snarled and contemplated about what it had to do. It dropped to the ground in a crouch as a man came down the row of cars, turning to see the beast.

"Holy shit," he said.

But it only took seconds for the creature to advance on the man and in an instant snapped his neck as the victim crumpled to the ground. The demon sensed he must carry the body over to Barber's car and threw it in the front seat and slammed the door. Then it headed toward the lights to complete its mission. Crouching again, it threaded its way through the parked cars until it was right behind the platform. Governor Anita Butts was speaking to a crowd.

"I want to thank the residents of Phoenix and the state of Arizona for supporting my PAC to fight the President and the federal government in their efforts to bring the kind of immigration reform to our state that we know the majority of the people don't want." There were a few cheers but a lot more boos as a Hispanic group that had heard about this rally had gathered to protest. Butts seemed flustered as usual whenever someone disagreed with her.

She ignored the dissidents.

"The time has come to take Arizona back to its roots and reclaim the individuality that brought our great state to where it is today." And then there was another cry from the Latinos, "Yeah, we're the most racist state in the country, even worse than Mississippi." And then there was applause from that group. Sam Parks, the Governor's Communications Director, was getting antsy. If the Gov looked bad, he looked bad.

But you couldn't tell her anything, so she would blunder right on, and she did.

"Some disagree with my policies," there was an uproar of laughter from the Hispanic group followed by, "You're right about that. Three-quarters of this state supports immigration reform, and you know it." That did it. Parks whispered in Butts ear to close it down now. She looked at him with extreme hostility, pushed him away by the shoulder and started to speak but nothing came out. She looked at the audience and those heckling her and completely drew a blank.

"Mexican got your tongue?" one Latino blurted out and the whole crowd broke out with a raucous howling that was obviously a sign of ridicule. Even some of Butts' followers who were at the rally were joining in the frivolity. The Governor looked at Parks, pleading again to save her, as he had done so many other times. He stepped forward. "The Governor has nothing else to say and thanks you for your attention."

More guffaws from the crowd but at the same time it began to disperse.

The official limousine pulled up by the platform and Butts hurried to get in. Parks was right behind but she looked at him derisively and slammed the door in his face. She told the driver to roll up the window between them and take off, which he did, and at that point discovered she wasn't alone in the dark backseat. Then she heard the growl, and her attacker grabbed the Governor by the neck and squeezed until the vocal cords cracked and were of no more use to her.

As the limo slowly made its way through the crowd, the fiend began to savagely rip open Butts' chest and tear at her heart. Barely alive and unable to make a sound, she flailed her arms frantically trying to stop this thing. The large sedan stopped abruptly, throwing the werewolf against the front seat. Thinking it was the Governor, the driver briefly rolled down the window and said, "Sorry, but traffic is backed up and we may be here awhile," without looking back.

Surprised and not really knowing what was going on, the animal started to react but then the limo jerked ahead and threw it back again. Returning to Butts, it began to pull the heart loose from her body and she took one last gasp before dying and falling limp on the seat. In the meantime the driver had taken the back road behind the shopping center around the traffic to get out and was headed north when the monster decided it must get out.

It banged on the glass partition that had been re-closed.

Knowing the Governor's nasty demeanor, the chauffer dreaded her ire but slowed down and opened the glass. "Yes ma'am…" and then there was something around his forehead that jerked back ferociously and broke the man's neck instantly. The limo veered right and collided with a fence and came to a stop. The thing kicked the door off its hinges and grabbed the heart and ran into the brush that bordered the shopping center.

Then in a kind of ritual it devoured the heart while blood still dripped from it.

TWENTY-SEVEN…

When the beast saw people headed in its direction the natural inclination was to flee but then the alteration back to Arnold Barber commenced. Slowly the conversion began to take place, then more rapidly, until he was standing in the field stark naked but still not completely back to himself. There were even more signs this time that the unearthly being would not completely go away. But he was thinking normally and knew he had to get back to his car.

He had parked it at the very end of the parking lot and away from where the Governor had been speaking. All the attention was toward that area and in a burst of speed he didn't know he had, Barber dashed from the brush area to his vehicle without being seen. Inside, pushing the man's body aside, he started the engine and turned left to exit the parking area. Luckily all the activity was still around the rally platform and the police were just beginning to work their way out.

Carefully he turned left again on Deer Valley Road and continued up to Tatum. He turned right and merged into traffic as innocently as someone could who was sitting in their car nude. Of course no one could see below the window line, except maybe a large truck driver, which he didn't expect to encounter on Tatum this time of night. Otherwise, it wasn't unusual to drive around in Arizona shirtless. He continued north on Tatum.

And then he looked over, confused. Wasn't sure why but he had a body to dispose of. But where? Barber was coming up on Pinnacle Peak Road and he turned right. Just before you got to Scottsdale Road there was a dumping area for dirt and rock, which should provide the right temporary cover and it, should be deserted in the evening. When he pulled up it was, and he quickly grabbed the body and lugged it around to the back of the dirt pile.

Finding a shovel next to a close-by shed, he dug into the mound. The dirt was stable enough that he was able to carve out a cavity big enough for the carcass, which he cautiously placed in the hole. Then he began to replace the dirt, filling in the opening, but painstakingly tamping it down to prevent a shift in the dune that would expose the carcass too soon. Although he wasn't sure why, for some reason he needed to keep this body from the police.

After removing his fingerprints from the shovel, he noticed leftovers from his werewolf state, like the hair and fur that hadn't gone away. Finally home, Barber pulled into his driveway and inside the garage quickly closed the door. He got out, gathering the shredded clothing first and took it in the house. At this rate, he would soon be ordering more apparel online.

Entering the family room, he turned on the TV, but before switching on any lights made sure the blinds were closed. Then he sat down, still in the nude, and watched the breaking news. It was being reported that Anita Butts and her driver were both killed in the parking lot of the Desert Ridge shopping center. The governor had been there for a rally for one of her PACs and somehow the murderer had slipped into her limousine unnoticed.

He knew he was just in a field at Desert Ridge and was naked and had buried a body on the way home. And then the news was showing pictures of the Governor's limousine where you could clearly see the driver slumped against the steering wheel but not Butts in the backseat. You could also see the police spread out over the field and Barber became more confused than ever. And why was he sitting home now watching TV without his clothes?

* * * * *

The Keeper had put away one of the biggest enemies of the Apache people. The Governor had gotten what she deserved and the Enforcer had followed instructions to rip out Anita Butts' heart. Now there would be no trouble in completing the mission. It thought of the next target, which had been delayed in the drive to create chaos by getting the head of state out of the way. Now, it would concentrate on Chew Quanah, the Comanche legislator.

* * * * *

Barber could see on the television that the Phoenix Police Chief was about to hold a quick press conference.

117

"This is going to be short. I'm going to lay out the facts and there won't be any questions. Governor Anita Butts has been murdered, or assassinated, take your pick, along with her limo driver whose name we are not releasing yet. It looks like another paranormal event, with the werewolf most likely our perp. Her heart was extracted from the body and is missing.

"As has been the case with all similar deaths, there were no witnesses. There's little or no evidence that we have found other than what looks like animal hairs again, similar to what we found at the crime scenes of Cynthia Haskins and Clarence Talbot. You're wanting to know if the creature ate the Governor's heart but we don't know and will release this when we do. Butts' cause of death is obvious, her driver's neck was broken. And that's all I have to say."

Suddenly there was a shout from the field that something had been found. They walked to where the cop had his flashlight shining on the ground. There was what looked like a large splotch of blood in an area where it appeared someone, or something, had been standing, compressing the grass. Officer Gouyen called for forensics.

The Chief seemed riveted to the ground with the look of a man that knew he had done the best he could in this investigation, but it still wasn't enough. He scanned the area where a supernatural being had likely just eaten the Arizona Governor's heart. They didn't know that for sure but it seemed unanimous among the group, considering past events. This was so bizarre, he thought, but how is it with all the technology available to them they had made no progress?

Deke McKenna could see the burden he was carrying written all over his face and felt deeply for his old friend. The killing of Anita Butts would bring in the Department of Public Safety, the state's police force, and probably mean the FBI might get involved. He was pretty sure that Phoenix would maintain jurisdiction since everything had occurred within its borders, but maybe the outsiders could shed some light on the case. God knows, they could use the help.

*   *   *   *   *

As Arnold Barber viewed the coverage, he marveled over the fact that, even though he suspected himself, there wasn't a shred of

118

evidence tying him to the murders. No one had identified him and once the transformation took place there were no fingerprints. The police had said the DNA couldn't be matched, so as long as they didn't find Agnes, he was safe.

Again at Desert Ridge, the Chief's cell phone rang. "Yes, Chief McIntyre here."

"This is Sven Eriksen here and I would like for you to brief me on the Governor's death as soon as possible." Eriksen was Secretary of State, who was next in line for Governor.

"Of course, Governor," which he would be in the succession of command. Might as well start getting in his brownie points. "I'll be here most of the evening but how about early tomorrow morning?"

"Sounds good. Can you come to my office?"

"Of course. What time? Eight-thirty okay?"

"Perfect, see you then." They both hung up.

"Can you believe that, McKenna? He *asked* me to come to his office. The reign of the wicked witch is over."

TWENTY-EIGHT...

Amy Rogers and her husband had enjoyed their dinner. She fixed his favorite dessert, banana pudding, and had surprised him after the main course of steak and eggs, another favorite of his. This idea of the way to a man's heart was through his stomach had its advantages. Walter loved to eat but at the same time he limited himself to reasonable portions and apparently his metabolism was good so he was always svelte.

The man was obsessed with his career and would do anything to further it, including allowing his wife to sleep with the boss. And she would do it willingly if it kept Walter happy and allowed her to do her own thing as she pleased. Amy knew she was gorgeous and was an asset to her husband at work where he was part of the largest accounting firm in the state, perhaps even the Southwest. His moving up the ladder would make sure they enjoyed the better life.

The evening was non-eventful, as usual, with him reading a book and her trying to keep herself from going bonkers with all the boredom. She wished Karen would call so at least she could get out of the house and was trying to send her vibes when the phone rang. It was Karen. First her friend wanted to know if Amy thought it wise to see Thornton's friend, Rudy Brown. Then she wanted to know if anything else had developed in the murder.

"I'm going nuts around here," Amy started, "why don't we meet for coffee and talk for a while?"

"Sounds good to me, where?"

"There's a Starbucks on Northern just east of the Wildlife World Zoo that stays open late. Meet you there in twenty minutes."

"You're on," and they both hung up.

Karen was waiting out front for her friend. They went inside and ordered.

Every man in the place had stared when they had ordered. Amy knew they were looking at her. Karen too, but it was obvious who the center of attention was on. Herself. There was a good reason for this. Amy was a man killer. She stood five feet, six inches, weighed one-hundred twenty pounds, had auburn hair and green eyes. Her measurements were 38-23-36, her legs were perfectly shaped, and in high heels they were absolutely luscious to look at.

"We need another big night out but this time without all the drama," Karen said. "Honey, you didn't even get the pleasure of sleeping with your fellow. At least I was able to clean out the cobwebs between my legs. I feel sorry for you. Maybe I should go inside and poll the place and find out who would like to do you. Probably be a stampede." They looked at each other for a couple minutes and allowed as how that might not be such a bad idea.

Outside again, Amy pushed her chair back and crossed her legs just as one of the men from the inside came out, sitting down at a nearby table. "I did it with Walter the other night," she said, "he jumped on top of me like a maniac with thrusts so harsh that I was sure he was pissed and was taking it out on my pussy. I asked him but he answered me like he had no idea what I was talking about."

She paused and felt a twitch in her gums, her eyes were burning and all of a sudden she was famished.

Even under the dim outside lighting, but still with a full moon, Karen could see there was something going on and said, "Are you feeling okay? You look pale and your eyes are bloodshot."

Amy shrugged, then said, "I'm starved. You want anything?" But by the time Karen answered she was already back inside at the order counter. She returned with two scones. "God, I had a big dinner and I'm still ravenous," as she looked right at Karen.

"Well don't look at me, at least not right here," and they both laughed. Then, "Hon, we need to get you laid and I mean right now," as she looked at the guy at the next table. While Amy was inside she had been staring, occasionally smiling, at the guy who had been reading a newspaper but paying more attention to the two of them than the news. He was alone. Finally he couldn't stand it anymore and he dropped the papers on the chair and headed for their table.

He was nice looking, about six/one with blond wavy hair and had a T-shirt on. His jeans were very snug and there was already a bulge around his fly. Maybe he was advertising too. "Hello ladies, and I would offer to buy you some coffee but all of us know what this is all about."

121

At last, Amy thought, a man who knows what he wants and comes right out and says it. But Karen had to play innocent.

"Not sure what you mean pardner, but sit down and let's talk about it." He sat with a grin that labeled him a man that was on a mission and hoped to do something about it.

Amy had stared at him too, so he directed his attention toward her since the friend was playing hard to get. "I am unbelievably attracted to you and I sense that perhaps you might have similar feelings." He didn't mention the fact that she was wearing an outfit that screamed going to bed with someone. "But I see the ring and I hope that I am not insulting you."

Wow, a gentleman on the make and it's all happening at Starbucks. She hoped he was as well-endowed as he was good looking. "You don't beat around the bush do you?" Amy said, "and you're right, I am attracted to you, but don't worry about the ring. The question is what do we do about it?"

"I don't live too far away and we could take a trip there and bring you right back here to your friend, unless we're interested in a ménage a trois?" It was definitely a question.

"Don't think so," said Karen, "my time of the month."

"Then it's the two of us, and my name is Stan."

"I'm Amy and this is Karen."

"Nice to meet you both."

"But Stan, I don't have the time to go anywhere. I'm just out for a while and my husband gets suspicious if I get home too late." Sure, Walter wouldn't care if I stayed out all night.

"I have an idea," Karen spoke up, "do you have a car here Stan?"

"Yeah, that's my Lincoln MKS parked over there by itself. Don't have my first ding yet."

Great taste and the man *is* particular. Excellent traits for a sexual encounter, Amy thought. But she had to get this moving quickly to keep from blowing her cover right here in a coffee house. "Good enough for me," and she stood up.

Stan stood also and took her arm like the gentleman he was and they were off to his back seat and what Amy hoped would be her chance to satisfy her imminent need and also the erotic fantasy she was having about this unusually sexy man.

He remotely unlocked the car and opened the back door for her to get in. She quickly canvassed the parking lot to be sure there were no witnesses around. No one. Amy got in and Stan followed. First the lovemaking, then, she would take care of her need. It really didn't make sense to kill such a hunk but her craving had grown so enormous for fresh blood that when an opportunity like this presented itself, well, she just couldn't help herself. But first the sex.

She put her hand on his crotch and decided that he was much more excited than he had been earlier when they noticed the bulge. After unzipping his fly and taking out his shaft, Amy said, "You sure run with the big boys, don't you," and thanked her lucky stars for answering her earlier wish. All the time she had her eyes on the surrounding area but it looked like he had picked a private enough place.

She leaned over and kissed the head while Stan played with her hair as she engaged his manhood in preparation to carry out its job.

TWENTY-NINE…

It grew, and grew while Amy's arousal soared and she could stand it no longer. She unbuttoned her shorts, and removed them along with her panties. At the same time Stan was taking off his jeans and undershorts, and there they were in a Starbucks parking lot in all their glory. Then he started massaging her with one hand, kissing her on the neck, and with the other hand exploring her breasts. She was moaning as he flicked each nipple with his tongue.

They each pleasured the other until neither could wait any longer. Amy was gasping and begging him to get on top of her but Stan knew what he was doing and continued. Then he decided it was enough and just in time as she thought she would orgasm if he kept going. He moved between her legs and entered her as the two of them gulped and panted, groaning with pleasure. Soon, Amy screamed, Stan cried out and it was all over.

Stan spoke first, "You are a very sexy woman, Amy, and you are also remarkably gorgeous. I would really like to see you again."

A shame, she thought, as she said, "I'd love to, Stan," and while still completely nude, she started to kiss his neck and shoulders as if she was interested in another go. She also grabbed his member with strokes of her hand to keep him occupied while she gently bit into his shoulder. This sent her venom throughout his body, which immediately made him tense up and feel like nitroglycerin was running through his bloodstream.

"What's happening?" he said with a chilling effect that this wasn't his body anymore and that he was helpless to do anything about what was happening to him. He sat there in a state of what seemed like paradise while the woman he had just made love to was doing something to him that he didn't understand. Her bites had started off just grazing his skin with her teeth then she sunk them in lightly, but now they were much deeper. Were those fangs?

And then Amy crunched down into Stan's shoulder and began to relieve him of his life-giving blood that quickly was assimilated into her system. As she continued to take from him she grabbed what was left of his erection and squeezed one last time. And then after a while she

124

began to feel full, not sure she could finish the job, unable to take on any more. She withdrew her fangs but the blood still flowed freely.

Amy stood in the Lincoln and bent over the seat to the front where she had thrown her clothes. She opened her purse and pulled out a couple of toilettes and wiped the blood from her mouth. With the other she made sure there was no more on her body and pulled out a plastic bag and put the dirty rags in. Then she put on her clothes, cleaning off surfaces she had touched, and took one final look at Stan. God, she didn't even know his last name.

At that point she headed for Starbucks realizing that she had let her immature enthusiasm get the best of her.

Karen was still sitting outside in the same chair and smiled as her friend walked over to her. "Where the hell is the beefcake?" she asked.

"He decided he was going to go home so we said goodbye." She took a quick look over at the Lincoln to make sure no one was around it. No one there. The parking lot was emptying and it was time for Starbucks to close.

Karen glanced at Stan's car, which hadn't moved yet. "Why isn't your friend leaving?" she questioned. "The car is still dark and doesn't look like any movement there."

"Don't know. Maybe he's just resting. He did all the work, you know," and she looked at her watch. "I have to get home to keep Walter happy," Amy said. "Talk to you tomorrow," and she leaned over and kissed Karen on the cheek.

Karen said she had to go to the restroom and when she came out her friend was gone. But she couldn't understand why the guy's car was still there so she decided to act on her curiosity and drive by it on the way out. When she pulled alongside, there was no sign of anyone in the car. Strange. She parked, got out of her car and walked over to the Lincoln. It was dark and from what streetlight there was, Karen saw a figure in the back seat.

She tried the door and it opened with the overhead light coming on. Muffling a scream with her arm, in plain view was Stan's body slumped over, completely nude with a gash in his shoulder and blood that had run down his body and was pooled on the seat. Karen had to

125

steady herself as she put her hand on the top of the car and then leaned forward and vomited on the ground. What in God's name had Amy done to this man and why had she done it?

She steadied herself then returned to her car and pulled out into the street and started home. Karen was shaking all over. "I guess I don't really know Amy Rogers," she said out loud, "but I'm going to find out what the hell's going on," and she pulled into another strip mall up the street from Starbucks. She took out her cellphone and dialed Amy. When she picked up it was obvious she was still in the car. "What the hell are you, a fucking vampire?"

"Yes" was the instant reply, and it befuddled Karen to the point that she couldn't speak. "I had a feeling you were curious when I left so I was just waiting for your call." A long pause. "Karen, are you still there?"

Finally, "I don't know what to say. I just found out my best friend is a monster. How are you supposed to react to that?"

"Okay, we need to talk right now, where are you?"

"I'm on my way to the I-10 but I passed an all-night McDonalds on Northern just before I turned south, on the north side. I'm turning around now. Can you meet me there?"

"Hell yes," was the answer, and Karen turned around and started back west on Northern.

Amy got there first and waited in her car for Karen and when she arrived the two of them went inside without a word said. They bought more coffee and found a corner seat away from everyone. Karen just looked at her friend and it wasn't an accusing look at all. It was one of…anticipation? Like "I want in on what's going on" kind of expression. Amy was taken aback by this and it had an effect on how she started.

"I expected you to be challenging me now for why you shouldn't call 911 and report this to the cops. Actually, I thought you might do it earlier when I figured you were sure to go looking for Stan. What's going on, Karen? You have the air of confidence on your face like you plan to win the lottery."

"How did you guess, Amy? Now why don't you tell me what's going on here. And I do want to hear everything or I just might have to dial 911."

She didn't like the threat but this was her best friend, although Amy had had mixed feelings lately about being too close to anyone with her particular situation, being what it was. But she owed it to Karen for leaving her in the Starbucks' parking lot with a murder she had just committed and no explanation. "Okay, here's the whole story," and she related everything from the Superstitions to Bernice O'Ryan to Dan Thornton and ending with tonight's scenario.

All Karen could say for a long while was "Holy shit," then she sat there with a look on her face again that was puzzling to Amy. After two or three minutes, "You're going to turn me into a vampire."

Her friend blurted out quite loud, "What?" and it drew looks from several other customers in the restaurant.

Karen had read the romantic stories of the life of those who feed on blood. "You're going to make me a vampire because you can't afford to have me as an enemy. And you can't kill me cause the cops know we're closely connected and would suspect you immediately. C'mon Amy, do this for me and you won't have anything to worry about. I'll even watch your back."

God, what have I done, she thought? "Karen, why would you possibly want to turn yourself into a vampire? It wasn't voluntary for me and it came with extra baggage that is, well, demanding."

"I want to live dangerously, Amy. My life is so boring I'll be certifiable soon if something doesn't change, and this could do it."

THIRTY…

"Just what do you plan to do with this new power?" Amy asked.

"I can lure men into my web and have my way with them just like you did Stan tonight. And Thornton before that. Even make it with women like you did with Bernice O'Ryan. I read where they can't trace the DNA of a vampire so I won't get you into trouble. We've been friends for a long time and this would just make us closer. Please?"

Amy was weighing both sides carefully. Although they had not met face to face, her mentor made it perfectly clear what her mission was telepathically. The Keeper would view this as a huge mistake on her part. It could eliminate her without a trace probably, but then there was all the work of developing someone in her place. On the other hand she could not alienate Karen for obvious reasons and Amy felt sure she could keep her in check.

"Okay Karen, I'll do it but you have to promise me you won't go out on your own without checking with me first."

"I promise."

"Agreed, now we have to make arrangements on how we are going to do this so I can be sure I get it right, and you don't suffer any after-effects. Deal?"

"I'm in," and they hugged and said goodnight.

*   *   *   *   *

The keeper was not happy over what it had just perceived but the mind was a malleable thing and this one could be put to good use.

Next there was Chew Quanah to take care of and that was a job for the vampire. It would schedule Quanah for the next few days. The question was how to arrange for a meeting between the two that would be appropriate for the blood-letting. The man was not married but did not frequent the kinds of places like Dan Thornton so it would have to be a special thing to get them together.

The other option was to get him in his home when he was alone with no witnesses.

* * * * *

The Maricopa County Sheriff's deputies were all over the strip mall parking lot. Sheriff Trask Ammadon stood beside the Lincoln looking inside the back seat. This had to happen in my county, he thought, obviously anticipating it would put a crimp on his immigration sweeps. He and his big belly sauntered up to the car and looked around at his men for an answer. "From what we can tell, Sheriff, the victim has some kind of gash on his shoulder and he bled to death."

They mentioned him being nude but Ammadon didn't inquire why. "Has forensics been here yet? Soon as they do, bag him up and take the car in. Assume you checked his plates for a name?"

"Yes sir, name is Stan Black and he lives in Peoria," Sergeant Brian Kinsey responded this time. "Sheriff, he's naked," and before the deputy could say anything, the mighty Trask Ammadon said, "I can see that. Probably gay, having sex with his boyfriend, and the guy knifed him." Well, he wasn't known for the country's most obtuse sheriff for nothing.

The Sergeant decided not to pursue his point of whether or not this had anything to do with the vampire murders in Phoenix. The man had made up his mind and there was probably nothing you could do about it. At least he didn't blame it on a Hispanic, or did he think Black was the name of a Latino?

"Have a report on my desk by tomorrow morning," and the Sheriff got back in his squad car and left. At that point the forensics people were pulling in.

Sergeant Kinsey released all but one deputy for regular duties. To him the vic looked as pale as if he was either an albino or had been relieved of all his blood. He suspected the latter, probably connected to the Phoenix killings, and then forensics confirmed his body was bone-dry. "Looks like another vampire killing to me, similar to Phoenix, but this time the freak must've gotten full before emptying the body. Blood is all over the chest and legs and pooled on the seat."

He would write this all up in his report and let the investigation take its course. In the meantime he'd secretly release what happened to a reporter friend so there could be no internal cover up of what had really happened.

*　*　*　*　*

Lani had just walked out of the shower. "Boo!" She jerked around and said, "Holy crap, you scared me to death, McKenna," and then they embraced and kissed and he fondled. "Watch it cowboy. I just took a shower. Did you wash your hands?" They both laughed and walked into the bedroom. "You're home early," she offered, "but I'm glad. Are you going to fill me in on the Governor's death or is this real hush, hush?"

She looked at Deke and saw that strained look on his face again, even though he had been frisky earlier. She started dressing.

"It's the wolfman again and it tore out Anita Butts' heart and in all likelihood ate it."

"That's gross," Lani replied.

"We figure it's just another step in wiping out Arizona politicians."

"Sorry but I can't resist, is that so bad?" Then she slapped her mouth with both hands and said, "Bad girl."

"Clever, and many would agree, but we don't know yet if it's limited to just politicians and government people. Hell, Ruben works for city government and I wouldn't want to see anything happen to him."

"Me neither and I'm sorry I even brought it up." McKenna broke into a grin and the whole thing was past tense. She had finished dressing.

"Sit down, let me fix us coffee, and I'll go over the whole incident in detail." He did and she found herself gasping over some of the particulars. "Lani, they've gone over the crime scene and the field where the demon took the heart and supposedly consumed it. This thing isn't leaving any solid clues and we can't seem to figure out the few leads we have. Either that or we are misinterpreting them. Damn."

Deke's cell phone was ringing and the ID showed it was McIntyre. "Hello Ruben."

"Can you get over here right away? This is too much for the telephone."

"Sure, I'm on my way."

McKenna sat down across from the Chief as someone was bringing in coffee. Once they had left, McIntyre looked at his friend and said, "At this point, when they write the story about these killings, I can't decide whether it will be a comedy or a tragedy."

Completely confused, Deke McKenna just stared at the Chief with the look of "what the hell does that mean?"

"Randy Clovis just left me an updated report on the Thornton case." "You remember the body was completely drained of blood, and although we suspected the vampire, Randy still couldn't find the teeth-marks. Well he finally found them and they're on the penis. That's right, Deke, it drained him of his blood through his dick. Now whether that's supposed to be making a statement or not, I don't know. But it indicates to me our vampire does have a sense of humor."

"It also most likely tells us our vampire is a female," McKenna added.

"You're probably right, no, I think you *are* right. This is beginning to sound like these modern day vampire stories where they mix blood, sex and murder."

THIRTY-ONE...

Amy was beginning to feel powerful with this ability she possessed. She thought she had researched enough and grabbed her cell phone and dialed Karen. It was nine o'clock in the morning.

"What's up," her friend answered.

"If you're sure about this thing we've talked about, I'm ready when you are."

"How about right now?" was the reply.

"We'll do it at your place since I don't want you driving for a while."

"Any special preparations?"

"Yes, take off all your clothes."

"Okay, and what else are you going to do to me?"

"Never mind, that comes later when we're both, uh, compatible."

"You're the boss. Will you be nude too?"

"Of course, I have to caress you passionately or my elixir won't work."

"Already I think I'm on the verge of having a wet dream and I'm not even asleep."

"Karen, you're impossible. See you in a half hour."

Amy pulled up in Karen's driveway, got out of her car and locked it. She was wearing a slinky velvet dress that was tight and red as a fire engine. She wore nothing underneath and had on a pair of red high heels. She rang the doorbell.

The door opened and there was Karen, completely naked but also in high heels. "Welcome to my den of iniquity and you look fabulous."

"God, honey you're beyond fabulous. You'll be the sexiest vampire in town."

"Nope, second sexiest, and you aren't wearing anything under that dress, are you?"

"Nada, figured it didn't make sense since I was going to chuck it once I got here."

"Then do it," Karen said in anxious anticipation.

Amy pushed the straps off each shoulder and let the dress fall to the floor. She looked at Karen and then they both embraced in a camaraderie of understanding of what was about to take place. "Let's get down to work," she said, but first let me explain just what I am about to do." They sat next to each other on the couch and Amy began to lay out the process and results of the transformation.

When she was finished, she looked at Karen very seriously and said, "Are you still sure you want to do this?"

"Absolutely," she replied, and her friend could see she meant it.

"Okay, first get an old sheet or anything large enough to put under us, just in case your blood is spilled. Probably won't happen but just in case." Amy's fangs were beginning to grow with the expectancy of tasting blood.

"Jesus, your eyes are turning red and they're glowing," Karen said with a startled look on her face. She went to get the sheet.

"Don't worry, that's normal when a vampire smells new blood. And I promise only to drink a little, just enough to whet my appetite, and then start immediately on the transformation."

"Now, close your eyes, Karen, and fantasize about making love. I want your sexual desires at their peak when I bite into your shoulder and fill you with the venom that will make you eternal." Amy didn't realize how dramatic she could be as she moved behind Karen and flicked her tongue across one shoulder then the other. She touched her arms and slid her hands up and down in a very light motion that was already sending ecstasy throughout Karen's body.

She kissed her on the neck, dancing her tongue around, driving her friend crazy as she was gasping for some kind of relief. Amy moved her hands under Karen's arms and cupped both her breasts in her hands. She rolled the nipples between her fingers drawing a desperate cry for fulfillment as she started to moan and rub against Amy. She moved down the belly until she touched the pubic area, making Karen shake with intoxication and almost reach orgasm.

133

It was time, Amy decided, and she gently sank her fangs into her friend releasing the kinky venom that would turn her into a vampire. There was a sigh, followed by a soft cry of contentment. Her body trembled but it must have been a good feeling since she had a blissful look on her face. As Amy drank her blood, she too swooned with joy and the two of them were momentarily in their own world. Then Karen crumpled into Amy's arms.

It was now eleven o'clock and Amy was positioning Karen on the floor so she would be comfortable, but not on her back until she was sure there was no bleeding. So far the wound was only a couple of pricks the size of a pen hole with only a couple drops of blood. Then she went to get her friend a pillow for her head. Amy put her dress on and sat on the couch and waited. Karen was breathing normally and she had a look on her face that was pure happiness.

Amy just hoped it would be.

It was now three in the afternoon when Karen finally woke out of the trance. "Wha...wha...what happened," she said in a faint voice.

Amy was right there and gently stroked her forehead. "Everything is fine and it's all over. You are officially a vampire unless my special elixir didn't work and I doubt that. It's only three. When is Robert due home?"

"Five-thirty, maybe six," as her voice grew stronger.

"Stay there at least another half-hour to be sure you're okay. Where are your clothes? I'll get them."

"In the bedroom on the bed. Can I at least sit up?"

"Sure, just don't try to stand up until I am there to help you." Amy went into the bedroom and came back with the clothes. She sat on the couch and looked at her friend while she contemplated their next move. The call had been very strong from the Keeper regarding her next assignment and she planned to include Karen in the task, so it was necessary to observe her very closely to make sure she was up to it.

It was now four o'clock and Karen was dressed and back to normal. Amy would begin the briefing into her part in the next blood-letting. She started from the beginning, covered all the past events, moving on to their next mission. "Because you didn't receive your shape-shifting from a harbinger"—she had earlier explained who the

Harbinger was and that shape-shifting was her changeover to a vampire—"you must follow my instructions to the 'T.'"

"You're the boss," her friend said, but as she spoke the words, Amy could see trouble written all over her face. She still thought she could deal with it.

"Get a good night's rest and we'll tackle our assignment this weekend." It was Wednesday.

Now it was Friday evening and Amy was calling Karen. "I have the details on our new venture and I'll pick you up at one-thirty tomorrow. Dress accordingly, if you know what I mean."

"Precisely," her friend answered, "and by the way, I feel like a million dollars."

"Good," Amy responded, then, "are you ready for this?"

"Never been readier for anything," and they hung up.

* * * * *

Amy was pulling up in front of Karen's house and didn't even have to honk. She came out of the house looking fantastic, as usual, and when she got in the car complimented her comrade. Amy came right to the point, "Our target is Chew Quanah, a state legislator and a Comanche Indian." She didn't know exactly why he was to be killed but thought it had something to do with the Apache Nation. Amy had done her homework on Quanah.

Having checked online for constituent meetings, Amy found that Quanah had one scheduled on Thursday. She had parked at the meeting and went inside briefly to see what the man looked like, making sure no one really got a good look at her. She dressed in grubby clothes and wore sunglasses and a baseball cap for disguise. Returning to her car she waited for the man to come out and followed him home. She made a mental note of the location.

Amy explained all this to Karen as they drove toward Quanah's neighborhood, as well as the fact that he observed a Native American ritual called "vision seeking" in which the man went to a remote spot in the desert to seek the vision of a powerful spirit. And Quanah did this on Saturday afternoons. She parked a block up the street next to a playground.

It wasn't long until Quanah's garage door opened and he pulled out in the street and headed for them. But he took the first left. Amy knew exactly where he was going. He had been doing this every Saturday for several years and it had been written up in the local press a few years ago. The coverage included where he did the ceremony, indicating there was only one road that led to the site.

Amy had lucked up and found this information online. She had actually drawn herself a map and as they watched Quanah's car drive away, she pulled the map from her purse and started to go over it with Karen. Living on the edge of the Yavapai Nation Indian Community, he would take state highway 87 north to Payson and from there take a trail into the Mazatzal Wilderness and drive about a mile. That was his destination. It was only a roughly graded dirt road.

Karen was looking at the map and said, "How can you be so sure that's where he's going?"

"Because that's the way he's done it for six years. At least that's how old the article I read was and then there was another piece published about a year ago stating that he was still making the trek and going to the same place. Quanah claims there is something very spiritual about the place."

THIRTY-TWO…

Her friend was new to all this mysterious planning and execution, and the deviousness of it was overwhelming. But she was learning fast. Karen couldn't wait to taste the blood of another human being, although just the thought of something like this a few days ago would have made her heave. "How long do we wait before we follow him?"

"We're going to leave now and make sure he's headed there and when we confirm that, I'm going to stop at a truck stop on highway 87 and we can have some coffee and wait. Can't afford to get too close since it's a dirt road and the car kicks up dust."

"Hey, won't you be leaving tire tracks all over the place that the cops can trace?"

"Just bought a new set with tires that have full treads and no identifying characteristics like those caused by nails and gravel. I've thought of everything, Hon. Just leave it up to Amy."

"Okay, you've thought of everything but you haven't told me exactly what I'm supposed to do. It's easy to read how all the blood has been drained from someone's body but just how does one go about doing that?"

Her friend grinned at the thought of the two of them working on this one poor guy but it could turn out to be an experience for both. They would be billed as the vampire twins. Amy looked over at Karen. "Here are the basics. As you get nearer to the victim, your canines will sprout and become the fangs you will use to suck out and drink the blood. Your eyes will blaze red with anticipation. Once you get started, you won't be able to resist your uncontrollable desire for blood.

"The attack is on the back of the shoulder just under the neck. Let me make the first bite since my venom is more mature than yours. It is this special toxin that stuns our prey and renders them helpless to fight against us." She stopped and let her friend absorb what she had told her. "You will become exhilarated during and after your intake of blood and your strength will heighten.

"Any questions so far?"

"Amy," she hesitated, "I'm scared that I won't do it right."

"Don't worry, Karen, just watch me and duplicate what I do. Take your time because even though Quanah may know what's going on, and he might even still be talking, he is incapable of fighting back." They had arrived at the coffee place.

After each had downed a couple cups of coffee Amy said, "It's show time." They grabbed their purses and left. In the car she asked Karen if there was anything last minute that she needed to know and the answer was no. Her friend still looked anxious but calmer than before.

They headed toward Payson, found the road and turned left. Karen said, "You said about a mile, right?"

"Right," Amy answered as the tenseness in the car grew.

Chew Quanah was dressed only in a loin cloth, moccasins and his native headdress. He was kneeling away from the road and in such deep concentration in his ritual that he didn't notice Amy and Karen approach. The two of them had rehearsed this scenario over and over so they had it down perfect. Amy jumped out of the car first.

"Thank God you're here," Amy said to Quanah, "we thought we would never find our way out of this place. We've been lost for over an hour driving around the desert."

Quanah was taken aback but quickly regained his composure and stood up. "You startled me…didn't think anyone else was out here."

"I'm sorry," Amy replied, "we were panic-stricken and desperate for help."

By now Karen had gotten out of the car and moved to where they were talking. Quanah noticed at once how they were dressed. Both had tight fitting dresses on that barely covered the unmentionables, with high heels that accentuated legs long and curved in just the right places.

Noting the baffled look on his face and knowing what caused it, Karen said, "We're on the way to a wedding in Payson and must've taken the wrong turn." They both approached Quanah and as they drew closer Amy shuffled off to his left side and began to maneuver behind him.

Karen spoke up again as she showed him the hand-drawn map she had in her hand, "Here's the map they gave us. Maybe you can figure out what we did wrong."

Now Quanah was moving closer to Karen but his eyes weren't on the map. Her cleavage had been engineered with precision, pushing up the breasts to their full-blown size and leaving bare enough skin that led right up to the nipples. As he made his move, Amy navigated behind him when it was obvious where his complete interest was directed. And then Karen made her move, "They're real," she said, pulling her dress down to reveal everything.

"Hey," he said, "your eyes look funny," moving his eyes up, "are they bloodshot or what?"

Amy caressed him from behind, kissing his neck and shoulders while Quanah tried to figure out what was going on. It was all so suspicious but their combined actions were muddling his thinking. And then he felt a slight sting on the back of his left shoulder, almost like a pinch.

That produced a dizzying effect and he knew something was not right.

At that moment Karen's eyes were exploding red and her fangs were elongated so that they protruded from her mouth. She leaned down and gripped Quanah's right shoulder with the force of an amateur that wasn't sure just how much pressure to use. Blood gushed at first but then she settled into a rhythm that was more consistent and she began to feel comfortable in the feeding.

Meanwhile their victim was reeling from having been hit by two vampire venoms, much more than he could handle.

First the Indian headdress fell to the ground as he convulsed in the combination of their magic potions that ran undeterred throughout his body. He was wavering around and would have lost his balance if he had not been wedged between their two bodies. He began to lose consciousness. His legs still held him up, although he knew it was just a matter of time when they would collapse under him.

They continued to drink the blood of their prize but after several minutes Amy backed off and when she did, Quanah's legs folded and he fell to the ground on his back. "Finish him, Karen," as she watched her friend fulfill her new insatiable desire for this life-giving fluid. When done she looked up at her teacher with blood running from her mouth and falling onto her chest, her dress still pulled down. "Don't let the blood get on your clothes," Amy said.

Then they just stared at their victim.

Mission accomplished, Amy thought, and Karen had done remarkably well in her first outing as a vampire. The fangs and red eyes were gone and now it was time to clean up, then decide what to do next.

Amy looked at her friend who looked approvingly and said, "You did great, nothing to worry about. How do you feel?"

"Exhilarated more than I can describe," was the answer. "And I feel as strong as a horse."

"Natural," was the reply, "but now you will have to replenish your supply of blood on a regular basis, but the way the Keeper has kept me busy, don't think that's a problem."

"When do I get to meet the Keeper?"

"No one meets the Keeper as far as I know. It communicates with me telepathically, letting me know what my assignment is and I carry it out.

"Is the Keeper a man or woman?"

"Probably neither, or if it is I don't know which."

Karen mulled all this over and decided she had done the right thing. Once completely on her own she could satisfy her fantasy desires and no one would ever know. She would be like the black widow spider; kill and eat her mate following copulation.

THIRTY-THREE...

     Deke was sitting in Lani's outer office while she finished a reading in the back room. He thought about the case and how it was affecting his life and everyone he was associated with. Particularly Lani. They had just gotten to the point where it was time to start discussing the future when all hell broke loose. He was serious about her and she had told him she was serious about him. And that's as far as they had gotten.

     In the meantime he would stick with Ruben McIntyre and help him solve the supernatural murders, which was sure to demand statewide attention. Hell, maybe the Chief would be so popular that someone would want him to run for Governor. Deke could be one of his campaign managers and maybe Ruben would make him a special advisor. Together they could shake up this state and finally put it on the right track. And then his fantasy was interrupted.

     The people Lani was reading for were leaving, nodded, and went to their car. She was right behind them and noticed the concerned look on Deke's face and mouthed, "What's up?"

     He had just received a call from the Chief and put his hand over the phone and said, "Tell you in a minute," and finished listening to what McIntyre was saying.

     "With a new Mayor and a new Governor, this state is going to be in chaos real soon if anything else like this happens. McKenna, we need to have a brainstorming session, and soon. When are you available?"

     "I think right now but let me check with Lani." He quickly told her what had happened and that he was going to have a conference with Ruben.

     "Go, we can talk later," she said, and he told the Chief he was on his way.

* * * * *

     McIntyre was looking at the report of Deputy Sergeant Brian Kinsey from MCSO on the killing of Stan Black in Peoria. It was obviously connected to the Phoenix paranormal murders and Kinsey had

141

nailed it from the start. But the Chief had heard through the grapevine that Sheriff Ammadon had decided at the scene that Black was probably gay, having sex with his boyfriend, and the guy knifed him. Typical for this Sheriff who thrived on publicity.

But the nude condition of the body definitely indicated there was something sexual going on. He said to McKenna, "We are definitely dealing with an X-rated vampire." What they had to do now was concentrate on this report in front of them, and it sounded like the vampire was branching out of Phoenix. Just what did that mean?

The beast was making it real hard for McIntyre to come up with a solid MO. The only pattern so far was a focus on politicians, and Stan Black didn't meet that criteria. Kinsey's report said that Black was an independent builder of homes who lived in Peoria. Maybe there were connections with local or state government but these monsters seemed to be interested only in civil servants of the Arizona kind. "Deke, I'm going to get Bly Gouyen in here."

He called her into his office, she acknowledged Deke, and he asked her to sit down. "Bly, you've read this MCSO report on Stan Black. What do you think? Why the deviation?"

It was obvious that she wasn't sure of her answer but she replied anyway. "Ruben, this whole case has been so erratic in its progression that you have to wonder if someone from outside of Arizona is trying to purposely destroy the politics of this state. Perhaps a liberal that has some reason to do it for self-gratification?"

McIntyre thought this over, looked at McKenna, and they had never considered the out-of-state angle. Interesting, though, that Bly Gouyen had brought this up.

It was the morning after Stan Black's murder, and Sheriff Ammadon was reading Sergeant Kinsey's report that also was accompanied by a forensics account confirming everything Kinsey said. The Sergeant's report simply laid the facts out that determined this was another vampire murder, which sent the Sheriff postal. Just as he was about to bellow for Kinsey, a deputy knocked and entered with the morning paper.

The headline screamed: "Another vampire murder in the county. No word from Sheriff Ammadon."

He sputtered, coughed and almost choked before telling the deputy to get Kinsey "now!"

"What the hell do you think you're doing, Kinsey, you trying to make me look bad?"

"Not sure what you're talking about Sheriff."

"You know damn good and well what I'm talking about, this report that makes you out the one who cracked this Stan Black case." He was stammering and wheezing and red-faced to the point of bursting a blood vessel.

"But Sheriff, you left the scene declaring it was a gay murder and told me to follow up with forensics, which I did, and you told me to have a report on your desk this morning, which I did. Not sure what I did wrong."

Ammadon looked at the Sergeant with that smirk he used regularly with the press to let everyone know he was in charge. The media had somehow gotten this report, and the limelight was on Kinsey.

"I want this report revised to include me in the investigation that determined the killing was this supernatural fiasco, and that I was the one that made the decision."

"But that's not true, Sheriff."

"I don't give a shit, just do it or else."

"Or else what, Trask?"

Ammadon almost had a coronary. He knew Kinsey had no doubt made a copy of the report for himself, and since it was done on the computer, a copy had automatically been sent to the archives. The Sheriff could delete that but then there was a record of the deletion of a report that was securely in the hands of the Sergeant. Maybe more. It was a Mexican stand-off and for the time Ammadon wasn't winning.

"I won't forget this Kinsey."

"Thank you, Sheriff, and neither will I," and he turned around and walked out.

When the Sergeant returned to his office, he walked by several deputies with smiles on their faces who had seen the report.

Kinsey sat down. Had he just made his mark or had he pretty much tanked his career with the Maricopa County Sheriff's Office? He wondered about it for a few minutes when the forensics technician walked into his office. "Phoenix PD is asking for a copy of your report on the Stan Black murder. Should I release it to them or should I ask the Sheriff?"

Without hesitation he said, "Release it."

THIRTY-FOUR...

"Chief, we're wrapping up the Butts' case," Bly Gouyen was catching up. "A car was left in the Desert Ridge parking lot, close to where the Governor was speaking and stayed there for several days unattended. Shortly after there was a missing persons report on a Bill Yarnell who lives in Scottsdale and he was linked to the car. Then a body was discovered in a dirt mound on Pinnacle Peak Road just west of Scottsdale Road, which turned out to be Yarnell.

"Looks like it could have been a part of the Butts' case. ME says his neck was snapped, no other signs of trauma. Maybe he just got in the way of our werewolf as it approached the Governor. Whatever happened, there seems to be no connection with Butts herself, nor her office in general. Talked to Sam Parks, Butts' Communications Director and he has never heard of him. Guy was in the wrong place at the wrong time. But his family has been calling, Ruben."

"Better let me talk to them. Have to be careful with the innocent victims in this case since the rest of it is so bizarre." She gave him the telephone number.

"Bly, sit down, I want to talk to you." Once she was seated, "Considering your heritage, and I know that your people consider the Superstitions sacred ground, how do you feel about the fact that Dcke McKenna has targeted those mountains as the source of our problems with the paranormal beings? You realize that Deke does not mean disrespect to the Apache people, I hope?"

Officer Gouyen sat very quietly for a few moments looking down, enough that McIntyre wasn't sure now whether he had opened a can of worms, and when she looked up her eyes were closed. First she made the Apache hand sign for "kill," then the sign for "white man." With each she actually uttered the words out loud and when done opened her eyes and stared defiantly at the Chief. "The white man has persecuted my people for years and continues to do so." And then she sat quiet.

"Bly, you have always been an excellent police officer and I appreciate your dedication and loyalty. That is the reason I promoted you to my special assistant Sergeant in charge of investigations. But if you feel there is a conflict here, please say so, and I will put someone else in charge."

"Ruben, you asked a question about Deke McKenna and disrespect of the Apaches. I answered you honestly from my heart. I do not blame him, and I do not blame you, but there are those who continue to heap torment on my people and I cannot deny that this troubles me greatly. But it does not prevent me from doing my job, which I hope is obvious in my work. However, if you still think there is a problem, please feel free to replace me in this investigation."

The Chief felt both taken aback and impressed by her answer. There was no mistaking the contempt in her eyes over what the Apaches had gone through, and he was not sure just how he should read this, but he was totally impressed by her dedication to her people and the Phoenix PD. "Bly, if you don't have a problem I don't have a problem. I just wanted to make it perfectly clear that both Deke and I sympathize with you and are on your side."

"Thank you Ruben," and she got up and left his office.

*   *   *   *   *

McKenna was in his favorite Cave Creek coffee shop and was talking to one of his friends from the state legislature. "Just left the Capitol and word is around that Chew Quanah didn't show up for work this morning. Never missed a day in his life. Someone went to his home and there was no answer. Not like him at all. He was devoted to his job and his legislative duties."

"Chew is Comanche, right?" Deke asked.

"Yep, and he's the sponsor of that bill that wants to take benefits away from the San Carlos Apache Indian Reservation."

This sent McKenna recalling all the past conversations about the Apaches and the Superstitions, and since they suspected that the preternatural beings were materializing from portals in the mountains, that was reason now to believe that this might be an Apache vendetta. But where was it coming from? Who or what was behind this? He had speculated over and over but there was no one to point a finger at.

146

He and McIntyre had discussed this before, but what they hadn't talked about was the higher power that sometime controlled the Harbinger and the Enforcer. He hadn't even been sure about this himself until the recent events had prompted more research with findings that indicated a human element could be involved. This seemed only natural, since it was a new way to inflict pain and suffering on others and that always attracted certain human beings.

"Thanks for the information, man. Gotta go," and he headed out to his car. When he was inside, he pulled out his cell phone and called McIntyre. "Ruben, we're looking for a human. Find that person and we'll get our paranormal creatures."

"McKenna, what the hell are you talking about?"

"Not over the phone. I'm on the way to your office."

The Chief had cleared his desk and was waiting for Deke when he walked in and told him to shut the door. "Is this the kind of breakthrough we've been waiting for?"

"Maybe," and he started conveying to his friend what the legislator had told him at the coffee shop and what his research had produced. Neither said anything for several seconds while McIntyre tried to assimilate what McKenna was saying.

"Apache vendetta? Are you kidding me? Does this mean we have a new Indian war starting? God, I have a full-breed Apache working right here in the office and Bly doesn't look like she's on the warpath to me."

"Of course not, and this does not look like a tribal uprising, rather the work of an individual or some small group with an axe to grind. Probably a bit far-fetched, Ruben, but right now we have nothing else even borderline to work with."

The Chief was staring straight ahead at the door, probably thinking about Officer Gouyen and whether she might have some input to this. As if he understood this line of thought and agreed. Then, "Maybe we should get Bly's feelings on this. What do you think?"

"Yeah, I'm with you on that. She must have plenty of friends in the Apache nation and they always have their ears to the ground."

McIntyre was on the phone to Bly Gouyen and asked her to come into his office. When she arrived, she acknowledged both men and sat down in a chair next to Deke. She looked a little bit uneasy so her boss tried to relieve any strain she might have. "We need your help Bly," and he explained what this was all about. "But McKenna has the real story and I'll let him take it from here."

When he had covered the same ground with her that he had with the Chief, he sat back and asked the question. "Obviously we don't think there's an Apache war developing against the white man, so what we're looking for is whether or not any of your people have heard any rumors of someone in state government setting all this up and using the Apaches for the fall guy?" They both looked at her hopefully.

"I know of nothing like you speak but I will be glad to contact some of my Apache friends and see if there is anything in the grapevine."

McIntyre responded, "I would think they would be happy to help us catch who's behind this as much as any of us since the Superstitions are involved. There's enough bad that comes from those mountains without adding more fuel to the fire. We appreciate your help, Bly."

She knew he meant well but there would be no "bad," as he put it in their mountains if it hadn't been for those whose greed for gold was stronger than their scruples. It was Apache gold that started all this but it would be the Apache people who would settle it. "No problem, Chief. I'll get back to you when I hear something," and she went back to her office.

THIRTY-FIVE...

Deke McKenna was still in Chief McIntyre's office. "There is something else, Ruben, just a hunch, but a strong one. I think you should follow up on the fact that Chew Quanah didn't show up for work today. Doesn't sound like there is anyone to file a missing persons report on him and I have a clear suspicion something might have happened to him."

"I trust your intuition and I am thinking with that Apache legislation that he authored—he's a Comanche right?—that he must have some enemies. Maybe even Bly will come up with something but I'm going to put out an APB on him right away." He called in an officer on desk duty and gave him Quanah's name, instructing him to dig up all the information he could on the man then post the bulletin. It would be on the wire to all police stations within the hour.

"Now what's that hunch you feel so powerful about?"

"Well, just look back at what's happened. I can't explain the Cynthia Haskins, Bernice O'Ryan or Stan Black murders, but consider what Clarence Talbot was into in relation to the Apache people. The White Mountain Tribe wanted to open a culture center and museum in Phoenix, even bought land close to the Desert Ridge Shopping Center. But Talbot nixed it in favor of more parking for the area.

"Dan Thornton was next. Cyrus Dean, the Governor's Chief of Staff, fought them tooth and nail when the San Carlos Tribe wanted to expand their gambling casino. They lost. Thornton was his aide and the one who stood before the commission to seek denial of the expansion.

"Anita Butts, now there's the classic example. She was the key figure in the fight to take away Native American water rights in Arizona. Not just the Apaches, but the entire American Indian Nation would probably have liked to string her up. And now Chew Quanah appears to be missing. Am I making any sense here, Ruben, or am I hallucinating?"

"Hell no, Deke, if anything you might just have put everything in perspective. You said we're looking for a human that is controlling all these murders and it seems at least a likelihood that it is Apache related."

McKenna labored with the whole thing and finally answered, "Ruben, I just don't know. What we are sure of is that we have seven murders, possibly eight, connected to supernatural beings. If it isn't some greedy politician, is there a new Cochise or Geronimo here in Arizona that has somehow uncovered the secrets of the Superstitions and found a way to avenge his people? If so, based on what's happened so far, he won't need to start a tribal war.

"Maybe it's not quite as bad as we think, Ruben. The string of murders I just mentioned do have a correlation in that the victims have been involved in activities negative to the Apache nation. And if this is the driving force behind the killings, we're back to the human element, most likely an unhappy individual or group with an axe to grind on the issue. I realize that this is over simplified, but I do believe it is on target.

"What we must find out is who is our person or persons."

"I'm still waiting on the APB for Chew Quanah, and I certainly don't wish the man any harm, but if he is deceased, killed like the others, this could further cinch your theory. So are we leaning toward the Apache angle?"

"Chief, based on the paranormal mode of execution, the serial type format, and the focus on anti-Apache politicians who have been the victims, I think we would be negligent not to pursue this full-blast. But the short answer is yes. We just have to find the Apache connection."

McIntyre said, "There's yet even another option that we haven't talked about. You remember Charlie Manson from the Sharon Tate and Leno and Rosemary LaBianca murders. Could we have a potential Helter Skelter here? Pitting Whites against the Apaches? Charlie's intent was to start an apocalyptic race war, which was supposed to line up the Blacks against the Whites.

"It didn't happen but in the process there were killings done in the name of the conspiracy."

They both mulled that over for a while until Deke said, "Ruben, we have to consider every angle possible and you've brought up another way to initiate an Apache vendetta. Either way, it could result in a race war based on the facts we're currently working with. And with no solid leads for a suspect we have to decide now where to focus our energies.

Since in either case it is an out-of-this-world event, what would you have me do?"

The Chief had been considering this for some time and had a quick answer. "We need to identify everyone in this state that has served as an Apache activist that could be considered a suspect. The first person that comes to mind, actually the only one I can think of right now, is a fellow named Sammy Hobai, who lives on the Fort Apache Indian Reservation and is a member of the Apache Tribe of Arizona Tribal Council.

"He's been involved in several protests in the past but kinda quiet lately."

"I know him, met him at the casino out in Pinetop." This was one of the largest Indian run gambling halls in the state located just outside the White Mountains town of Pinetop. "Didn't seem to me like the kind that would do this sort of thing, but you never know. When it comes down to your heritage and it's threatened, sometimes you'll do anything. He the only one you can think of?"

"Right now," the Chief replied. "Do you think he's worth checking out?"

"Ruben, right now my mother would be worth checking out. Not to worry, I'll get back to you when I'm done," and he left.

"Thanks," McIntyre called after him.

* * * * *

Chew Quanah worked for the Arizona Commission of Indian Affairs and his boss was Neville Bolden. It had been two days now and Quanah had not shown up for work or for a legislative session. When checking his personnel record, Bolden found that Quanah had no close relative listed nor did he provide a next of kin. Really strange that personnel would let that get by, but it left him no other choice.

It would be up to Bolden to file a missing persons report in lieu of no family. He called Phoenix PD.

The officer that took the call went immediately to Chief McIntyre's office to let him know of the report and the caller. "Said he was Quanah's boss and have his number if you want to call him."

151

"Thanks," and he took the piece of paper. Deke hadn't gotten back to him yet on the subject's background so he would wait on this before calling Bolden. And then he decided to go over the evidence again to see if they had missed anything. From Cynthia Haskins to the Governor. The phone rang.

"It's Deke, Ruben, and there's more to Sammy Hobai than you might imagine. What nationality do you think the name Hobai is?"

"Figured it was probably some Apache name. Am I wrong?"

"Same as I thought and we're both dead wrong. It's Romanian. His father is from Brasov, Transylvania in Romania. His mother is a full-bred Apache from the White Mountain Tribe. Like you said, he lives on the Fort Apache Reservation and is a member of the Apache Tribe of Arizona Tribal Council."

"Isn't Romania, particularly Transylvania, where all this werewolf and vampire folklore originates?"

"One and the same. Sammy isn't as active in his Indian advocacy now as he was a few years ago but it's worth a look to see if there is any connection, especially if he has been to Romania recently. Things keep getting weirder by the day and right now I'm not taking anything for granted."

THIRTY-SIX...

"I'll get someone on this right away," and they both hung up. After assigning the follow up to one of his officers, McIntyre decided it was time to call Chew Quanah's boss, Neville Bolden. He pulled the piece of paper with his telephone number on it from the case file and dialed.

"Bolden here."

"Mr. Bolden, this is Chief Ruben McIntyre from the Phoenix Police Department and I have some questions regarding Chew Quanah."

"Oh yes, was expecting a call from you. What can I tell you?"

"First of all, I initiated an APB on my own but thanks for your diligence. We're concerned over his disappearance since it may have a relationship to another case we are working on."

"Wouldn't be those werewolf and vampire murders would it? Never thought Chew was into the supernatural."

"Sorry, can't comment on that but what can you tell me about the man?"

"Great worker and dedicated to his Comanche tradition. Never missed a day of work since he's been with me, and I know he would sooner walk on hot coals than miss a meeting of the legislature. I tell you, this is not like him, Chief."

"Okay, what about his personal life, any close male friends or girlfriends? And I understand he has no immediate family in the area or even close, prompting you to file the missing persons report?"

"First, he does have a lady friend here in the office. Don't know how close the relationship is, but her name is Betty Delano. Here's her number and I'll tell her you're going to call." McIntyre wrote down the number. "Next, regarding his family, I must apologize for the fact that our personnel department here filed Quanah's application for employment without a next-of-kin. That's why I called in the fact that he was missing. But maybe Betty can shed some light on this."

The chief thanked Bolden and hung up. Then he waited a few minutes shuffling papers to give him time to alert Delano to his call. Then he dialed.

"Hello, this is Betty Delano."

153

"Ms. Delano, this is Chief Ruben McIntyre of the Phoenix Police Department. I just talked with Neville Bolden and he said you might be able to help me with some personal background on Chew Quanah. I'm assuming you knew he was missing."

"Yes, and I'm very anxious over his well-being. We're just good friends but close enough that I started to worry when I called him on Sunday and there was no answer. And I called him back a couple more times."

"Do you always call him on Sunday?"

"Yes, to see how his Saturday "vision seeking" ritual went. It's an old Native American custom. He goes to the Mazatzal Wilderness close to Payson dressed in a loin cloth, moccasins and his native headdress to seek the vision of a powerful spirit. It is very important to him and there is no way he would miss going."

"Does anyone accompany him?"

"Not that I know of."

"Do you know exactly where he goes? In other words, does he go to the same place every time?"

"I know he takes highway 87 north and turns left just before Payson and drives about a mile into the area. It's a very private place for him, like sacred ground."

"Can you narrow down where he turns left, like some kind of landmark or business?"

"I believe he said there was a Shell gas station on the opposite side of the road. He almost ran out of gas once."

"And just one more question, do you know anything about Mr. Quanah's family? Mr. Bolden says he doesn't know of any in the area."

"Chew has no family members in Arizona. We didn't talk about it much but once he mentioned an uncle somewhere in southwest Oklahoma. Sorry, but that's all I know."

McIntyre was taking fast notes and put a notation on this detail for follow up to try and contact that uncle and let him know his nephew was missing.

"Thank you very much Ms. Delano. You've been very helpful," and he hung up.

154

He quickly punched the key for Deke McKenna on his cell phone and he answered on two rings. "Think I know where Chew Quanah might be. Just talked to a close friend and she said he goes to do some kind of ritual in the Mazatzal Wilderness close to Payson. Have some pretty good directions and thought you might want to join Bly and me."

"Meet you at your office in twenty minutes."

The three of them headed out toward Payson. They were traveling north on 87 and reached the Shell gas station and on the left was the dirt road headed west into the Mazatzal Wilderness. It wasn't marked but, based on what Betty Delano had said in her directions, it fit the description. They turned left and headed in. The Chief said, "Supposed to be about a mile."

As they reached the mile mark there was an opening and there they found Chew Quanah waiting for them, extremely pale and somewhat decomposed but not significantly. With the other vampire deaths the ME had found that the venom injected had a tendency to slow down decay. He was leaning against a bolder in a loin cloth with moccasins and a full headdress.

The Mazatzal Wilderness was in two counties, Yavapai and Gila, under the control if the U.S. Forest Service. The Chief got on the phone and called the Phoenix office of the Tonto National Forest, which the Mazatzal Wilderness was a part of. He reported the body and requested their approval to investigate the crime scene, which he received. Then he supplied directions to the site and assured them they would stand by until someone from the service arrived.

Then they started their examination.

"Ruben, either our perp decided to take two shots at the victim or we have another beast to look for. There are two bites, one in front and one in back, and each looks distinctly different to me in the way the flesh is torn." McKenna had moved the body away from the rock and was inspecting each shoulder. "The Medical Examiner will have to confirm this but it's pretty obvious the tearing is different. The one in front looks more aggressive, like more force was used."

A truck pulled up and a uniform got out. "Hi, I'm Officer Brantley of the Forest Service."

"I'm Phoenix Police Chief Ruben McIntyre, this is officer Bly Gouyen and special assistant in our investigation, Deke McKenna. You've no doubt heard of the supernatural events going on in Phoenix, and this discovery is the result of a lead in the investigation. We are reasonably sure the victim is Chew Quanah, a Comanche Indian who works for Indian Affairs in Phoenix and is also a state legislator. He comes here regularly to perform a tribal ritual."

He continued and brought Brantley up to date on what had happened in Phoenix. "We're not sure why Quanah was chosen but we are fairly certain it is connected to the other paranormal murders." He paused for the Forest Ranger to comment.

"I'm just here to observe and to turn it over to the rightful jurisdiction. Let me call my boss for instructions on how to handle this. Sounds like you should be the choice, but I'm sure he'll have to clear it with Gila and Yavapai counties." The Ranger took out his phone and walked away for privacy.

While he was talking, the three looked around for additional clues. There were tire tracks other than theirs, and these would be preserved for casts by forensics. But on careful entry when they first arrived, they had observed no additional footprints; looked like the place had been swept clean by someone. The crime scene folks would conduct a full investigation of the area but like in the other killings, it appeared the demon—or demons—had done its work without leaving a trace.

It took about ten minutes but Officer Brantley came back over to them and said to the Chief, "I reported the status here and my supervisor checked with Gila and Yavapai county authorities, and they concede jurisdiction to Phoenix PD. Good luck. Looks like you're going to need it." The Ranger left and McIntyre was on the phone to the Maricopa County ME and forensics.

Officer Gouyen, notably, had no comment.

THIRTY-SEVEN...

Arnie was fidgety tonight, had been restless all week. He tried to read the newspaper and finally turned on the TV but all the news coverage was about the murders that were going on in the valley. Never in his life had he thought it would be fulfilling to kill someone but now it had become an obsession that had to be obeyed. And then the contractions started in his body and Barber jumped up.

Suddenly it started full-blast. His hands mutated into claws and the canines started protruding from his gums. His body shuddered all over and then there was uncontrollable trembling. His whole head throbbed and he began to sweat around his neck. The nose enlarged and extended from his face and turned into a wrinkled snout while his ears began to grow. The shoulders took on a grotesque form as they became larger and squared off to finish the profile.

Arnie was once again an animal.

It jumped from the couch and snarled at the surroundings, which were no longer familiar. Getting out of here was the goal at the moment but intrinsically, it knew it had to return to this place for its safe haven. It wailed and awkwardly tried to open the door and the knob turned easily, so now it was on the front porch. After a low growl the brute surveyed the area and seeing no one in sight, and with stealthy footsteps, moved out into the night to find its prey.

The mutant headed up Cave Creek Road. It crossed over to the east side without drawing any attention and proceeded north, quickly darting between brush, cars, businesses and whatever was available for a shield. Since werewolves are able to outrun a motorcycle, it took only a short time to make it to a well-lit area where cars were parked around a large building. It was a twenty-four hour Walmart and customers were scurrying in and out of the super store.

There was no real cover here other than the cars, so it had to carefully move between them, working closer to the building where the people were. Then the thing thought it had been spotted but it was only a gang of kids whose antics it really didn't understand. They continued walking and then all was quiet for a moment until a woman pushed a cart past, full of items she'd purchased with a toddler sitting in the baby's seat. She popped the lid of her trunk.

The child was the first to see it and just pointed and giggled.

The woman turned to get something from the cart and although the light wasn't very good, she could sense it was an aggressor, so she reached for her pepper spray. She fired a blast at her assaulter but at too far a distance. It was just enough to enrage the monster and it attacked with a heightened vengeance, using its claws to annihilate her face with a force that also ripped off part of her throat. As the body collapsed, the child began to sob.

The demon proceeded to separate the extremities from the body one by one laboring fervently with a precision that seemed to be crudely therapeutic. First the left arm, then the right arm and finally the legs. The brute laid the woman across the trunk opening on her back and began to grab the opening to her blouse, yanking it off and shredding her bra. It was then that it thrust its claws into her chest extracting the heart, making a quick meal of it in only seconds.

The savage was not yet satiated and it looked at the baby. It was crying now and had its hands over its eyes. Moving closer to the cart it put its claws on the toddler. How easy to devour the child's as it had the mother's heart, but something made it hesitate and at that point a family was making its way into the parking area. It fled.

With its work completed, the wolf began to take the human form again as it left the Walmart area and headed for Cave Creek Road. Covered with blood, as had been the case on similar occasions, fortunately the transformation process eliminated all traces of this and Arnie's nude body was now completely clean as he stood in the bushes by the road. He looked back into the parking lot in a kind of unexplained confusion that consumed him. Then he headed home.

*   *   *   *   *

The Keeper wasn't concerned that the werewolf had done its own thing again. It was careful enough and this would only hone its powers to make it more experienced to complete its next mission. Still, this one bore close scrutiny. Nothing must upset the plan now.

Deke McKenna was on his cellphone with Chief McIntyre. "Got the information on Sammy Hobai. Got time to talk about it now?" They had decided between the two of them that none of this was information they wanted to chance on a cell call that could be picked off by a good hacker.

"Absolutely," was the reply, "come right over."

When he entered the office, McKenna had some papers with him and placed them on the desk. "We already discussed some of this. Sammy Hobai is part Romanian. His father is from Brasov, Transylvania, in Romania. His mother is a full-bred Apache from the White Mountain Tribe. He is a member of the Apache Tribe of the Arizona Tribal Council and at one time was an outspoken advocate for Apache causes. But Sammy has been very quiet for several years.

"Hobai hasn't been to Romania at any time according to what I found and, as a matter of fact, since he went to Washington, DC for a demonstration in the '90s, he hasn't been out of Arizona. He works closely with the Tribal Council to help his people but really has been playing the behind-the-scenes role for years. Unless he's one hell of an actor and has the covert ability of the CIA, my contacts say he lives a normal life. Looks like a dead end here, Ruben."

"So if the assumption of an Apache connection is still viable where do we find it?" It was a serious question but McIntyre really didn't expect an answer. It looked like the only way to solve this case would be to capture one of the creatures and make it talk.

McKenna had the same troubled look on his face as the Chief but was always thinking ahead. "We need to double back on all the evidence and see if there are any loose ends." There was a large bulletin board in McIntyre's office with each phase of the investigation documented with pictures, starting with Cynthia Haskins through Chew Quanah. MCSO deputy Brian Kinsey's report on the Stan Black murder, out of their jurisdiction, was thumbtacked on the board.

They approached the display and Chief McIntyre took the lead. "Cynthia Haskins was murdered by a werewolf in north Phoenix just south of Cave Creek in a new apartment complex. The only eyewitness was her roommate who confirmed it was some kind of animal that attacked Haskins, which was later confirmed by forensics from hair at the scene and flesh from under the victim's fingernails.

"The woman had no connection to politics or state government. So what was the motive?"

Deke was next and approached Bernice O'Ryan's material. "She was at the Cardinals' game with her husband and went to the restroom where, after the power went out in the stadium, she was killed by the vampire. No eyewitnesses, but one of the fans reported a woman restless next to him who jumped up just after kickoff and left the stands. Just after the lights came back on she returned with blood on her mouth and clothes, then immediately left the stadium."

"Where is the report on this fan's interview?" he asked the Chief.

He received a puzzled look back.

THIRTY-EIGHT...

McIntyre opened the paper file and went through it page by page. Nothing. Then he went online and looked through the file in the Phoenix PD database just to make sure it wasn't there but not printed out. Nothing. He looked up at McKenna, "Holy shit. No one took a statement from him. We may not even know who he is. Not possible." He called in Bly Gouyen and questioned her.

She seemed hesitant at first, not sure of an answer, then went to her computer and did a search finding nothing and then she returned to the office. "Chief, I screwed up. I let it slip right through the cracks and I'll follow up on it immediately." She went to her desk.

"This investigation has been so bizarre I'm surprised we all haven't had more surprises," he said to Deke. "We have to locate the guy and get him in here for an interview. Now. Maybe this is a turning point."

"Wow," said McKenna, "not like her, is it? She seems a bit preoccupied over something, Ruben, did you notice?"

"Naa, just overwhelmed with everything that's on her plate. How likely is it that the person sitting next to this guy could be a vampire? I mean if she had blood on her mouth and shirt and she had just returned to her seat after O'Ryan's murder, seems just too coincidental to me."

"If this guy can be found quickly and help us identify the woman at the Cardinals' game I won't need to answer your question, Ruben. However, as I've said before, a paranormal presence can walk among us as normal human beings until the transformation takes place. And in many cases that metamorphosis, or shape change, as it is sometimes known, can take place in an instant...in either direction.

"The woman in the stands could have easily changed both ways in the restroom during the blackout."

Officer Gouyen had just gotten off the phone, setting everything in motion to locate the potential witness to the bloodied woman at the Cardinals' game. She was picking up the phone to make another call when the desk sergeant walked up to her desk and said, "There's another body consisting of just parts and a missing heart outside a

161

Walmart on Cave Creek Road. Just north of the Cynthia Haskins incident. I sent a squad car."

She jumped up and flew into the Chief's office. "Ruben, there's a new body. Looks like the werewolf this time, considering the condition the body's in," and she gave him the rest of the specifics.

Having just returned to the board and their recap, they both put everything away and headed out to the squad car. Bly Gouyen was right behind them.

It took close to twenty minutes to get there, even with sirens screaming, and as they pulled into the Walmart parking lot, it was obvious the officers had everything under control. Apparently the body had remained there overnight and into the morning until the lot started filling up again and someone discovered it.

The blanketed infant wasn't even noticed in the cart until the noise woke it up and it started to cry.

The officers at the scene had called Arizona Child Protective Services to care for the baby until the father could be located. The plates were traced to her home address and more officers were dispatched to talk to the neighbors, where they found out how to reach the husband. Traveling on a business trip, he hadn't called in a missing person's report the night before. He returned home immediately and police questioned him. No political or government affiliations.

"Is this another example of the escalation taking place in these creatures, Deke?" McIntyre asked.

"Yep, and since there is no connection to the proposed motive, we have to assume this brute has decided it likes killing so we can expect more of it. It's the hybrid nature of our paranormal creations. Same thing for the Stan Black killing. That one has no doubt combined its lustful nature with an insatiable desire for blood, well beyond the normal vampire needs. And although the werewolf has no control, the vampire can delay its permanent transformation forever."

"Meaning what?"

"Meaning, the werewolf will eventually evolve into the wolf for good, but our vampire can transform from human to demon and back as long as it desires."

Officer Gouyen said, "There's not much more we can do here. CPS has taken custody of the child until the father returns. We've confirmed the fact that there is no political or government connection with the husband, nor the deceased. I had them arrange a covering around the cart right away to prevent any photographs and particularly for the removing of the body parts. They're doing that now since forensics has done their thing. Anything else, Chief?"

"No, Bly, just wrap it up and have the car towed in. By the way, heard anything on our Cardinals' witness yet?"

"Not yet, but have more follow up to do when I return to the office."

"Good, let's get moving," and all three headed to the squad car.

As they drove back, McIntyre said, "Bet we have no forensics evidence on this one either." He was right

* * * * *

Karen Briggs was feeling the need and feeling it strong. But Amy had also warned her not to do anything without checking with her first. She picked up the phone. "Hey girl, I'm having a terrible time here fighting off the urge. You have to help me or I can't be responsible for what I do."

"Watch what you say over the phone, hon, where are you?"

"At home. What do I do?"

"I'm on the way over," and they hung up.

Amy pulled into Karen's driveway and the front door was open with her friend waiting anxiously. Karen's skin was pale and the reddening in her eyes was advanced as she shielded them from the brightness of the sunlight. She had a Twinkie in her hand and there were two empty wrappers on the table along with another empty container from a large Hershey bar. The desperation in her face was very real, requiring immediate action.

The two of them went inside and closed the door. "Karen, you need a fix and you need it fast."

163

"I know, and what if something like this happened while Bob was here?"

"Did you bring this on through anticipation or did it just creep up on you?"

There was a sheepish grin and Karen said, "I was fantasizing over how I could get even with an old friend, how I would drain the bastard of all his blood for dumping me in a relationship."

"Okay, that's what caused this and you mustn't do it again. I might not be around to help you. Any ideas for a possible victim?"

Her eyes were now a glaring red and canines had formed and were pushing through. She said, "There's a single guy down three houses, a paramedic, I think, who's hit on me before and he might be at home now. We can go down the back alley to keep from being seen. I have a couple of baseball caps for a disguise and we can wear sunglasses. I really don't know my neighbors that well anyway."

"Good, that's perfect, we can tell him you need medical attention," and they left through the back door. Fortunately there was no one in the alley or in their backyards and they made it to the man's back door without incident.

He opened the door and Karen placed her hand over her mouth while Amy introduced herself and told him her friend, his neighbor, had swallowed something and had been choking. He first eyed the two dressed in tight blouses and short shorts but then turned his attention to Karen. "What did she swallow?" he asked.

At that point he pulled her hand away from her mouth and cried, "Oh my God, what are you?..." but before he could say anymore Karen lunged at his neck and bit down fiercely with her fangs and sent the debilitating serum into his body. He thrashed around, tried to back off from the assault, but she held tight, continuing to relieve him of his blood. He finally fell on his back and lay on the kitchen floor until Karen had emptied him. Amy watched but did not participate.

The vampire, sated now, leaned back on its knees and looked at its friend but said nothing. They both were quiet for several moments when Amy said, "We have to get out of here but first check and make sure we've left no evidence of our being here. Use the tissue on the sink to clean the blood from your mouth and chin, and use another one to dab the bloody spots on your blouse, which you must burn. You have a backyard barbecue where we can do it. Now, let's go."

As they walked back to Karen's house, Amy said, "Karen, you mustn't let this happen again," but on the way neither noticed the neighborhood busy-body lurking through the curtains.

THIRTY NINE…

Bly Gouyen was at her desk again, following up on the Cardinals game witness. She rummaged through the files for statements given just after Bernice O'Ryan had been killed. Nothing. One of the officers must have taken the report, since it was common knowledge in the investigation that this woman, who was restless and had blood on her, was definitely in the stands. So why hadn't it been followed up on and why wasn't something in the files?

She searched for the officers present at the crime scene, called them one by one until she got a hit. Officer Chris Herndon admitted that he was the one that took the man's statement on the mystery woman and had failed to enter it into the investigative report. Gouyen noted that he had been on the force only two weeks and chastised him, but also let him know he had some very valuable information and he should gather his notes and come to her office immediately.

When Herndon showed up he was red-faced and looked very contrite. "Let's see what you have," she said.

He produced his notebook and started reading all the notes and finally got to the name and telephone number, which the sergeant wrote down.

"Thank you Officer Herndon, but you must never let this happen again."

Herndon left and then she dialed the number, and a woman answered. "This is Sergeant Bly Gouyen from the Phoenix Police Department and I'm looking for a Mr. Paul Goddard."

"This is his wife, can I tell him what this is about?"

"No ma'am, could I please speak with him if he is there?"

"Just a moment." There was crackling on the phone and he came on.

"This is Paul Goddard. What can I do for you?"

"Mr. Goddard, this is Sergeant Bly Gouyen of the Phoenix Police Department, and I would like to talk to you about the woman you sat next to at a recent Cardinals' game. She was quite antsy, leaving her seat and then returning with blood on her mouth and clothes."

"Oh yes, wondered when someone was going to get in touch with me. What can I do to help?"

"Well, it would be great if you could come in and look at some pictures to see if you can identify this individual. We'd be glad to send a squad car for you."

"No car necessary. When do you want me there?"

"Actually, as soon as you are available. Sometime today?"

"I'm retired so I can come in anytime this afternoon. You name the time and I'll be there."

"How about three o'clock?"

"Good, I'll be there. Okay to bring my wife?"

"Of course. But according to the report she wasn't at the game with you."

"That's right. Went with a couple of old buddies."

"See you at three." Bly hung up and made a note to get the names of Goddard's buddies. Then she knocked and walked into McIntyre's office.

"Chief, the Cardinals' game witness is a retiree by the name of Paul Goddard who will be here for an interview with his wife at three PM. I made the appointment so fast, didn't check to make sure you're free."

"I'd make myself free for that. No, it's fine. I'll let McKenna know. What pictures are we going to show him?"

"Just our regular gallery, but I've copied shots of Amy Rogers and Karen Briggs from their Facebook sites to intermingle with the others. Other than them we have no other real suspects."

"I know. Good job, Bly. What interrogation room are we going to use?"

"Number three."

"Sounds like a plan. Who was the officer that took the report from Goddard and buried it?"

"A two-week rookie, Ruben," and she explained what had happened. When she finished McIntyre was satisfied.

He asked, "Should we have him join us in the interview?"

"Don't think so. Too inexperienced, and this is too important for any mistakes. I will have Herndon go over the report when we're finished to see if he sees anything of interest."

"See you at three," he said.

"Chief, Mr. Goddard and his wife are here. I took them to Room 3 and they are waiting." Deke McKenna was there and they both got up and followed Bly Gouyen to the examination room.

Inside, she made all the introductions and the three of them sat down.

"First of all, I want to thank you both for cooperating in this investigation. The case has been so bizarre that it may be hard for you to comprehend what is going on," McIntyre said. Where do you live Mr. Goddard?"

"Fountain Hills. Retired there about ten years ago."

"I understand you weren't with your husband at the game, Mrs. Goddard?"

"No, not much of a football fan."

"So let's start back at the Cardinals' game when you noticed something unusual about the fan sitting next to you."

Paul Goddard explained in detail what had happened and as he spoke, Officer Gouyen followed the timeline in the written report of Officer Herndon and it was so close it was impossible to tell the difference. Since she and the Chief had set this up beforehand, he looked at her and she nodded approval. That was one indication that they had a solid witness. Another would be if he maintained a consistency throughout their questioning process.

Deke McKenna was first.

"Mr. Goddard, you say this person was restless, fidgety in her seat beside you. And you said that she was with a man. Did this man seem concerned over her agitated nature?"

"No, as a matter of fact, he seemed preoccupied, not really interested in the game."

"How is that?"

"Well, he didn't even watch the kickoff and he didn't follow the new guy Tyrann Mathieu return the ball. He seemed to be more interested in all the technical equipment in the stadium, particularly the retractable roof. He just didn't look like a football fan to me."

Chief McIntyre asked, "Can you approximate the amount of time between when this woman left her seat and when she returned? Also, about how long they sat there before leaving the game."

"She left right before the lights went out and returned just after they turned back on. I'd say between ten and fifteen minutes. And when the guy with her called her attention to the blood, they were gone within seconds."

Bly Gouyen was next. "You said that you thought the woman may have cut her lip and it bled on her shirt. Do you still believe that's a possibility? Did you actually see a scratch or cut?"

"No I didn't, and I heard what happened in the restroom to that poor woman, but the lady sitting next to me didn't look anything like a vampire. Aren't they supposed to have fangs? And this gal was drop-dead gorgeous." He flushed as he looked at his wife.

"Any more questions?" the Chief asked. When no one said anything, he opened the portfolio in front of him, turned it around and pushed it to Goddard's side of the table. "Mr. Goddard, I'm going to ask you to look at the pictures of the people on each page, carefully, one by one. They consist of felons, everything from petty theft to murder and rape, as well as police officers on our staff and some others who are people of interest.

"Take your time and let me know if you recognize any of them."

Goddard looked at the first page and started across and then down the rows at some pretty unpleasant looking characters. He continued until he had finished the book with no success. "Sorry."

"We're not through just yet. There are two more portfolios," and the Chief opened and moved the second one over to Goddard.

Page after page he studied each picture carefully...nothing. "So far there have been very few women that are even close, much less the one you're looking for. You say you have another one?" He took it and started through more pictures, realizing this was all there was to look at. Some of these people looked like the dregs of the earth and others very normal. As Goddard turned the pages it suddenly occurred to him just how important what he was doing was.

And then he saw her, and he was so sure that he looked right up at McIntyre and said, "That's her, I'm positive."

The three gathered behind him to look where his finger was pointing. It was Amy Rogers.

FORTY…

"Mr. Goddard," the Chief said, "due to the enormous importance of what you are doing, I have to ask you to look at the picture once more and be absolutely sure of what you are saying."

"I couldn't be more sure."

"Okay Mr. and Mrs. Goddard, I thank you for your time, and Officer Gouyen has some paperwork for you to sign if you would follow her to her office," and then everyone shook hands and the three left.

McIntyre looked at McKenna and said, "There's nothing in the police manual about arresting a vampire. Deke, would you join me in a briefing on just what kind of reaction we might expect?

"Sure, just let me know when you want to do it."

* * * * *

Chief McIntyre had assembled a task force to apprehend Amy Rogers, consisting of ten of his best male and female officers. They were sitting in the meeting room and the Chief and Deke McKenna were at the lectern ready to brief them on what to expect. McIntyre gave the introductions and indicated that he would be in charge of the task force team, when normally that would be the job of Sergeant Gouyen, then turned it over to McKenna.

"What to expect? My best advice is to expect the unexpected. But down to specifics. Don't think you can kill a vampire by shooting it. Only intensifies its ferociousness. You'll slow it down but its recuperative powers are without parallel, and when you think you have it in checkmate, it will be on top of you. Our alleged vampire's name is Amy Rogers, a housewife, and when she determines that we are there to arrest her, she will start her transformation into a vampire.

"The skin turns pale, the eyes change to blazing red, anticipating any move you make, and its strength is beyond human. All the other, combined with sprouting fangs, means you must always maintain a distance until you are ready to take the beast down. When threatened, it will hiss like a cat to intimidate its attackers, but if you do get too close when this is happening and the saliva from its mouth gets on a wound, you could catch a deadly infection.

"Many vampires have ESP and the ability to read your mind, which means they can anticipate the moves you are about to make. Depending on their maturity, they are also adept at telekinesis and pyrokinesis. The latter you must be prepared for, because that is the ability to set objects or people on fire through the concentration of psychic power. These are the major threats that you must expect in dealing with Amy Rogers in her shapeshifting state."

You could see the uneasiness of the task force team and this was also portrayed in the eyes of Chief McIntyre but he knew what had to be done. "Each of you has his or her assignment. As Deke McKenna cautioned, we won't even try to take our perp down with gunfire. As a matter of fact, since Ms. Rogers expressed an interest in Deke during an earlier interview, he has volunteered to go in first and try to negotiate with her using his knowledge of the supernatural, if necessary.

"Okay, let's go."

The ten officers piled into three squad cars, Officer Gouyen took her own, and McKenna rode with the Chief. Using the department's specialized GPS system, McIntyre headed toward Buckeye. They had already cleared the operation with the local police who would be waiting at a rendezvous point and would serve simply as a backup. Everything had been planned with the greatest of precision but there was no way to predict how it would actually come down.

* * * * *

Phoenix Police squad cars were coming in from both directions on Amy Rogers' street. Following at both ends were the Buckeye police. The Chief and Deke McKenna got out and walked casually to the front door. The team broke into two parts, one in front of the house and one covering the back.

The Chief knocked on the front door and Amy Rogers answered within seconds. "Well, hello Chief McIntyre and Deke McKenna. I'm honored, but why all the armament?"

Typical for this woman, thought McKenna, cool down to the bitter end.

McIntyre spoke, "We're here to arrest you for the vampire murders of Bernice O'Ryan and Dan Thornton. You are also a suspect in the deaths of Stan Black and Chew Quanah."

"Jesus, I've been busy," she replied.

McKenna observed her closely for physical signs of change and any indications her demeanor was being altered. Nothing. The Chief forged ahead with the Miranda and then told her an officer would have to handcuff her. She showed no opposition although it was obvious to all this was not an admittance of guilt but rather a stern defiance of the charge that was made as she said, "I killed nobody and you cannot prove that I did. Where's your evidence, Chief McIntyre?"

With that they walked to the squad car and Amy was carefully seated in the backseat.

Both McIntyre and McKenna shook their heads. It didn't make sense; this woman had superhuman powers she could have unleashed but chose to be taken into custody with virtually no resistance. Was she depending on some kind of higher power to rescue her, perhaps from a Superstitions portal? This was what each was thinking.

"As I recall, there were no fingerprints at the Bernice O'Ryan or Dan Thornton murders. Don't know about Stan Black or Chew Quanah, but I'm thinking there would be some mention in the news if there were. And we all know that I have a rock-solid alibi with Dan Thornton. All you have to do is confirm what Karen Briggs and Rudy Brown said, with my husband, Walter. Should I get him on the phone for you?"

She was mocking them and doing a damn good job. The Chief knew their case was circumstantial and if they couldn't break the alibi, Amy Rogers would walk. But the two remained silent and there was no more conversation in the squad car.

In police headquarters now, Officer Gouyen took the cuffs off and put Amy Rogers in a holding cell. "Ms. Rogers, if you have a cell phone you are allowed one call and then an officer will search you and take your personal property. Do you have a phone?"

"Yes I do," and she took it out of her purse as Gouyen left the cell. "Walter, this is Amy and I am in the Phoenix jail. They arrested me

for the vampire killings of Bernice O'Ryan and Dan Thornton."
Complete silence. "Are you there, Walter?"

First nothing, and then he began to stammer through "What the hell happened?" until he finally got it out.

"I told you I was afraid they suspected me but thought my alibi from the night with Dan Thornton convinced them I couldn't have done it. Apparently not. I want you to get me the best attorney there is in Phoenix. My gut tells me John Roberts will be very helpful."

Walter had regained his composure and was a bit perplexed over Amy's quick analysis of her situation. But he still couldn't imagine his wife as a vampire doing what they had accused her of. "I'll go in to see John right now."

"Walter, I do not want to stay in this jail another minute. I'm depending on you, and you tell John I'm depending on him too."

He didn't waste any time calling but rushed right over to John Roberts' office and told his secretary it was urgent that he see her boss. She checked with Mr. Roberts, who told Walter to come right in. "What's so urgent today, Walter?"

"John, they've arrested Amy, claim she's the vampire that killed Bernice O'Ryan and Dan Thornton. According to Amy the evidence is weak but they're holding her at Phoenix headquarters on Washington Street. She wants out, John, and she wants out *now*. She is convinced you can get her the best attorney in town and I agree." Walter was staring right into the eyes of John Roberts with a look that said Walter knew all about the Christmas party.

FORTY-ONE...

Roberts hesitated, trying not to be over anxious, then said, "I'll call Jerry Monaghan, at Hillcrest & Monaghan. He's the top defense attorney in town and he owes me a big favor." He got on the phone and was put through to the man.

"John, you lecherous old son of a gun, how are you?"

Roberts had no intention of letting his friend go there. "I'm fine, and you Jerry?"

"Couldn't be better. What can I do for you?"

"You've obviously been reading about the werewolf and vampire murders." He paused for any answer.

"Hell yes, ridiculous this sort of thing could happen in Phoenix and equally absurd that they haven't caught someone."

"Well they have, Jerry, and how would you like to represent her?"

"You're kidding me, John."

"Nope, she is the wife of one of my top CPAs here at the firm, Walter Rogers. Her name is Amy and she's being held at Phoenix PD headquarters on what she claims is a trumped up charge. Jerry, would appreciate it very much if you could help out here." The attorney agreed to listen to more, "Okay I'm putting her husband on the phone to bring you up to speed." Walter got on and started at the beginning continuing through recent events, including her alibi.

"Wow, looks like you've got a handful, Walter, but from what you've told me they're holding her on strictly circumstantial evidence, so I shouldn't have any trouble with bail. I'll fax you over a quick contract for representation that will allow me to get her out of jail. Does that work for you?"

"Absolutely, Jerry, and I do appreciate this very much."

"Thank John, I owe him one. Meet me at Phoenix PD in a half hour." and they hung up. Monaghan looked out his window onto the Camelback corridor and wondered if this time John Roberts had dipped his pen just a little too deep in the company inkwell.

Walter Rogers got there before Jerry Monaghan. He arrived and together they were ushered in by the Chief to the holding cell where Amy was being held.

Monaghan turned to McIntyre and asked, "Ruben, exactly what are we looking at here?"

"Amy Rogers was arrested today for the murders of Bernice O'Ryan and Dan Thornton; she is also a suspect in the killings of Stan Black and Chew Quanah."

"Aren't you just a little out of your jurisdiction on some of these, Chief?"

"Since the first supernatural event occurred in Phoenix, and because of the expert assistance of Deke McKenna, whom you know, all jurisdictions are waiving control when we know it is a paranormal occurrence. Sheriff Ammadon is being a hard-ass on Stan Black but the State Attorney has just ruled in favor of our handling the case."

The two men were good friends but now due to their jobs, they were also adversaries.

"What evidence are you holding Amy Rogers on?"

McIntyre said, "She was seen having several drinks with Dan Thornton and his friend, Rudy Brown, at The Big Place and is known to have left with Thornton. This was confirmed by both Brown and the married woman he was with, Karen Briggs. Dan Thornton did end up at home, but he was found dead in his car, minus all his blood. Ms. Rogers said they split in the parking lot of the bar, and a timed phone call seems to account for where she was."

"So why have you brought my client in on these terrible charges when she obviously has an alibi?"

"First of all, it looked tenuous when she first told us; Ms. Rogers said she made the call to Karen Briggs as she neared her home driving straight there from The Big Place. That could have put her there at about the time of the murder. But what if she committed the murder, then made the phone call to Ms. Briggs. No one actually saw her leave The Big Place parking lot in her own car. And even if she did, she could have followed Thornton home."

"Ruben, aren't you forgetting the fact that her husband clocked her in at 10:20 PM, making it impossible for Amy Rogers to commit such a heinous act and get home at that time? He's a CPA and he works with details all day."

"We're aware of that but the case turned a corner when we received confirmation that the woman seen at the Cardinals' game with blood all over her mouth and shirt just following the murder of Bernice O'Ryan was Amy Rogers."

Monaghan looked at Amy and received the semi-seductive look she had planned for him since she learned he was her attorney. He didn't respond. Then he turned to Chief McIntyre, "Who's the witness?"

"Paul Goddard, a Cardinals fan who was sitting right next to her."

"It is my understanding that Ms. Rogers explained that was due to being struck by the rest room door on the way out when she was returning to her seat. There was a slight cut inside her mouth and you know how that kind of wound bleeds."

McIntyre looked at Walter Rogers and asked, "Did you see a cut, Mr. Rogers?"

"Obviously not," Monaghan answered for him, "the cut was on the inside of her mouth."

"You wouldn't happen to still have that shirt you wore that day, would you Ms. Rogers?"

"Sorry, it's near impossible to remove blood from a white shirt. Had to throw it into the trash."

"Of course," the Chief answered.

"Come on Ruben, you don't really have enough to hold her. No witnesses, no fingerprints or other forensic evidence. I don't want to be the bad guy here but the media would love to get their hands on this."

McIntyre looked at McKenna, then at Bly Gouyen, and it was pretty apparent that Jerry Monaghan had moved them into a checkmate. "Give us fifteen minutes and I'll give you my decision," the Chief told the attorney, and the three of them left the room.

Amy was doing her best to act out the innocent, tortured woman that she supposedly was. So far, Jerry Monaghan had not responded to her seductive ways and she didn't think she could count on him to take her to bed and then be in her debt. But John Roberts was Monaghan's friend, and he owed Roberts a favor, according to Walter. Amy felt like she was sitting on top of the world with all these high-powered people working on her behalf.

Chief McIntyre returned, followed by Deke McKenna and Officer Gouyen. "I have decided that we do not have enough solid evidence to keep Amy Rogers in custody. I am releasing her but, Ms. Rogers, you must notify Phoenix Police if you plan to leave the state. Otherwise, you are free to go."

Amy got up, going right to Jerry Monaghan and hugged him full-front, to make sure he got the complete effect of her boobs, holding on for several seconds. This was simply backup just in case this guy might take the bait.

"Thank you," she said to her attorney, and it was clear in his look that there was some confusion in his mind over this whole scenario. She pretty much ignored Chief McIntyre and the other two and walked out of the room.

They were headed toward their cars when Jerry Monaghan turned to Amy and said, "You know you are the perfect profile for a female vampire; beautiful, alluring and very smart."

Back in the office McIntyre said to Bly Gouyen and McKenna, "Maybe we should set up a lie detector test?"

"Forget it, doesn't works on vampires," Deke responded.

The Keeper was not happy with Amy Rogers. It had created her and it could destroy her as well but that would most likely become very complicated. At least she had handled the Dan Thornton killing capably. And she did respond to the telepathic dispatches sent by the Keeper to take care of Chew Quanah but she had done Stan Black on her own.

The werewolf was no more stable than the vampire. Arnold Barber killing his wife was probably a necessity but his attack on the woman in the Walmart parking lot was not. It would be watching, but it felt that Amy Rogers was going to be a major problem.

FORTY-TWO...

The Chief was looking at the bulletin board with all the investigative findings for the case and when he got to MCSO Deputy Sergeant Brian Kinsey's report, he took it from the board and looked at it closely. He noted that fingerprints had been taken by the Sheriff's office but no follow-up report on identifications. This was Bly Gouyen's responsibility, so he called her on the phone to inquire.

"Hello, Gouyen here."

"Bly, this is Ruben, I'm looking at the MCSO report on the Stan Black murder and see that their forensics took fingerprints but there is no subsequent report if there were any identifications."

Silence, then, "Had so much on my plate haven't followed up yet. I'll get on it right now."

McIntyre sat back in his chair with a worried look on his face. A couple of slipups, he thought, and now he was concerned. He thought of Deke McKenna's comment, "My gut tells me she's first an Apache and second a cop." But there was no way he could comprehend Sergeant Bly Gouyen mixed up in a supernatural plot of this sort. He would check her records but he could not even remember her involved in any Apache advocacy in her past.

Still sitting at her desk, Officer Gouyen looked at the phone as she contemplated calling MCSO. The Chief hadn't sounded upset but this was her second screw-up and she knew that was not good in McIntyre's book. She made the call to Brian Kinsey. He picked up on the third ring.

"Brian Kinsey here."

"Sergeant Kinsey, this is Bly Gouyen at Phoenix PD. Thanks again for your report on the Stan Black murder, and I see forensics found prints on the car in a couple of places, not Black's"

"Right, We ran 'em but no one notorious came up, so guess nobody figured you'd want them."

"Could you tell me who it was?"

He quickly grabbed the file. "Sure, it was a woman, name Karen Briggs, figured she was just a girlfriend or something, since her prints

179

came up from her Arizona Fingerprint Clearance Card. Probably applying for a state job."

"Sergeant Kinsey, we definitely need the forensics findings. Karen Briggs is a person of interest in this case. Could you get them over ASAP?"

"Within minutes, Sergeant. And we have some vomit that was also recovered at the scene, right by the back door. That could be Karen Briggs too. Want me to send that over? "

"Absolutely, and thanks."

Deke McKenna was still there as Officer Gouyen knocked on the door and walked into the Chief's office. "The prints on the car are Karen Brigg's, Ruben. MCSO thought they weren't important since they didn't show up in any of the bad guy databases. When you arrested Amy Rogers, they just thought you had your vampire. I know I should have followed up on the forensics."

"When do you expect to have the fingerprint report and Briggs' upchuck?"

"It's on the way in a squad car, should be here any minute."

"The DNA people are going to love us. When you have the specimen get it over to them and say we need it yesterday."

"Right, Chief."

The MCSO deputy arrived with the evidence, Officer Gouyen signed for it, and she was on her way to DNA Forensics.

*   *   *   *   *

The Keeper decided it was time to eliminate Deke McKenna as its adversary and pondered over whether it should dispose of him or his girlfriend, Elaine Baker, or both. Killing Baker would no doubt infuriate McKenna to the point of desperation. No, it had to be the man, himself, and this had to be carefully planned and done by the werewolf. Amy Rogers was out of the picture and Karen Briggs could no longer be depended upon, and being under suspicion made her dangerous.

* * * * *

The desk sergeant opened Gouyen's door and said there was an officer from Glendale PD on the phone for her. She took the call from a Detective Barr, and when the female officer described another death she said their Medical Examiner had concluded that the victim, a male, had been drained of its blood. And when they knocked on doors, found an elderly woman who saw two, what looked like females, walking down the alley in back of the houses the day of the murder.

"Is this your perp?" she asked.

"Most likely," answered Gouyen, "can you fax me over the essential info on your case so we can determine if it's the same MO? And would your Chief waive jurisdiction for us to take over the investigation if it's our vampire?"

"God, that seems weird talking about 'your' vampire, and, yes, I've already cleared the waiver if you confirm the connection."

"Great, I'll be waiting, and thanks." She decided to hold off reporting this to the Chief until she could be sure it was authentic.

Everything was happening all at once, and Bly Gouyen knew that Ruben McIntyre was depending on her and she must not let him down. Not only was she loyal to the man, but her career depended on it. Making Detective was her goal and so far, she had an unblemished record, except for those two small mishaps. Someday her Apache ancestors would look down on her with renewed affection and appreciation.

* * * * *

It had been two days since the police had released Amy and dropped all charges against her. The media had run with it at first, then, when she had been exonerated it had immediately come over to her side, suddenly exhibiting sympathy and understanding because she had been so wrongly judged. But what bothered her most was the fact that she had not had a word from Karen. She must have heard, seen or read something.

And then her phone rang, a restricted number. "Hello."

181

"Amy, this is Karen," and there was loud traffic noise in the background. "Is your phone being tapped? I'm calling from a payphone."

"No, Karen, at least not as far as I know but I would rather talk to you in person."

"I don't know, is it safe?"

"Karen, cut the clandestine stuff and meet me at our favorite Starbucks."

"Okay, half an hour?"

"Good for me."

Amy arrived first and was already at the counter ordering for both of them. Karen entered with a floppy hat and dark glasses looking something like Mata Hari. She didn't walk up to Amy but took a chair over in the corner and waited. Her friend brought the coffee over and sat down. "How long is this going to go on?"

"Well, you can't be too careful. After all, they did arrest you. I could be next. Look around, people are already looking at you. Shouldn't you at least wear shades? Or are you enjoying all the attention?"

Amy thought about it and decided that maybe she was. But she couldn't let Karen know that. "Hey, what's done is done and there is nothing I can do about it. I'm going to live my life as normally as I can."

"But what about…you know…you have to have new, well, you know."

"I'll have to find a simple way to satisfy this need when the Keeper doesn't need me. You'd better figure out what you're going to do, Karen, now that you're a part of this."

They sat there in silence for a long time not speaking to each other but realizing the dilemma they were in. Karen was already beginning to feel the need for the life-sustaining ambrosia.

FORTY-THREE...

Forensics head Randy Clovis stopped at Officer Gouyen's door and said, "Want to follow me to the Chief's office?" waving papers that were no doubt results they were waiting for. The two proceeded and Clovis knocked. They entered and McIntyre and McKenna were waiting. Clovis stood, Bly sat down.

"The good news is that we have a DNA ident on the vomit at the Stan Black killing. The bad news is, or maybe it's also good depending on how you look at it, it is Karen Briggs. I had them re-run the prints again just to make sure and those are definitely from Briggs. What the hell's going on, Ruben?"

"Believe me, if I knew I would tell you." Turning toward McKenna, "Deke, I thought vampire DNA samples were scrambled, I mean, like they have been with Bernice O'Ryan and Dan Thornton? Of course we don't have Chew Quanah's yet. But what the hell does this mean if we are to assume Karen Briggs might be our vampire?"

"What is certain is the fact that had Briggs been the vampire at the scene of Stan Black's murder, you would have fingerprints but you would not have been able to read the DNA as hers."

"So if she wasn't our vampire, and Amy Rogers has been ruled out, somewhere in the progression of this case it's possible we've missed a potential suspect?"

"Perhaps, but also consider there are two options, one that Karen Briggs is not a vampire and just happened along that night and got curious. Or, two, she could have left those prints and the vomit before becoming a vampire, if in fact she is one now."

"Oh my God, then what was she doing at the Stan Black killing?"

"Well I do have a potential scenario. It's possible Karen Briggs was not a vampire when Black was killed, but became one later. Let's not forget that she is a good friend of Amy Rogers, and I'm still not convinced Rogers isn't our main vampire."

"Shit," said the Chief, "Bly, start the wheels rolling to bring Briggs in but don't serve the warrant until I give the word." He looked at Clovis, "Would you take one more look at the DNA evidence to confirm its findings, but more so to see if there is anything else unusual there?" They both acknowledged and left.

"Talk to me, Deke," he said, and McKenna knew what his friend needed, another refresher course in vampires.

"Ruben, as far as I'm concerned Amy Rogers is still our best suspect for the vampire. Don't care about the alibi, those can be rigged as you well know. And if she is, plus the fact that Rogers and Briggs are such close friends, it is possible that the former turned the latter into another freak of nature just for company. Hell, I know it's far-fetched but not too long ago werewolves and vampires were not common in Arizona's population."

"You're saying Amy Rogers did Stan Black with Karen Briggs there, who left her prints all over the Lincoln and then threw up in the parking lot. If so, where are Roger's prints, and if she saw her friend touch the car, why didn't she tell her to wipe it clean? Too many 'ifs' here, Deke, but at this point I'm willing to accept any potential scenario.

"But it's that easy for one vampire to transform another into their likeness? What does she do, just bite her friend?"

"Unfortunately, it is very simple, but that is offset normally by the fact that very few people *want* to become a vampire, and unless it's involuntary there are few transformations."

"So what does it take?"

"Basically, if someone is willing, the first step is to bite the shoulder of the aspirant and drink enough blood, leading to the next step. Then inject the venom that initiates transformation, accompanied by sexual stimulation. This is followed by drinking another modest amount of blood, after which the victim would crumble in the vampire's arms. The new vampire must rest for several hours but then is free to live the normal life of part human, part beast.

"If the vampire elected to kill its prey it would continue sucking out the individual's blood until death, like Bernice O'Ryan and Dan Thornton. Or, if it became gorged and could not take in any more blood, it would leave its mark to bleed to death, like Stan Black. This is not a complicated process, Ruben, rather the culmination over the years of the stories made famous by Bram Stoker's *Dracula*."

184

Karen was at home and the urge was getting greater by the minute. What had she gotten herself into?

"I'll try meditating," she said out loud, and was walking to the family room when there was a knock on the front door. "Who could that be? she said.

Opening the door, two uniformed Phoenix police officers confronted her, saying, "Are you Karen Briggs?"

"Yes," she answered.

"Please open the door," a screen, which she did. "Karen Briggs, you are under arrest for the murder of Stan Black. Please place your arms behind you," and she was read her rights. On the way out one of the cops picked up her purse and they went to the squad car.

Karen was so dumbfounded she said nothing until she was in the backseat of the car. "What are you doing?" she finally spoke, "I haven't killed anybody. Who is Stan Black?"

With no answer, she sat back in the seat and concentrated on staying a human while mixed thoughts thrust her toward becoming a vampire. It worked, no change, and she believed she might get through this ordeal if she could figure out who Stan Black was. Then it hit her, the cool guy with the Lincoln when she met Amy for coffee. The guy her friend humped in the backseat and she later discovered dead. This is what started everything, why she decided to become a vampire.

No problem here, she thought, Amy and I just alibi for each other and they have to drop the charges on me. Piece of cake, but how would she get to Amy? She would have to use her one call to Robert, her husband. He would call their attorney. But we don't actually have a lawyer, never really needed one.

She was hustled into Phoenix PD and they were met by Sergeant Gouyen, whom Karen already knew. The arresting officers did their thing and then Gouyen said, "Sorry you are back under these circumstances, please follow me." It turned out to be the same room as before and Karen started to feel at home. But she couldn't let her guard down, since she was here on a murder charge, no matter how solid her alibi. "When do I get my call? She asked.

"If you have your phone with you, right now. I'll let you do it in private and then come back and collect your personal effects." Officer Gouyen let Briggs retrieve her phone from her purse and left the room.

Karen dialed Robert and found her demeanor changing to that of exasperation, finally realizing she was here for murder. No matter what your excuse, the other side was being told that the police had enough evidence against you to arrest you for killing someone. Robert worked for the Arizona Sports and Tourism authority, the owners and operators of the Cardinals' football stadium, and answered on the first ring.

"Hello, Briggs here."

"Hi, honey, I have a little bit of a problem."

"How bad is it? Have an important meeting coming up in ten minutes."

"Kinda bad," she should probably tell him to take his usual dispassionate attitude over listening to her problems and shove it but this was her only call. "I've been arrested for the murder of a guy I don't even know. They think I'm the vampire that's doing all these murders."

"Jesus Christ, Karen, what have you done now? I told you trolling all those bars would get you in trouble. Where are you?"

"At Phoenix police headquarters. Do we have an attorney?"

"No, and this meeting really is urgent. I'll have to find someone to cover for me then make some calls," and he hung up.

"Holy crap," she said aloud, "He's more concerned about his fucking meeting than the fact that I'm in jail for murder." She sat still seething but refused to cry. That was because she had a new persona and that gave her strength she hadn't had before.

FORTY-FOUR…

Arnold Barber went to the refrigerator to get some ice cream before he went to bed and that's when the resolve hit him and the shape-shifting began.

First, he put down the ice cream and then Arnold Barber started disrobing, knowing the plan by now. Soon his body would go into the contortions that would turn him into a werewolf. He was receiving signals from the Keeper and it was instructing him that his next target would be Deke McKenna. Barber knew who the man was but was not clear about where the attack should take place. He would soon find out.

The transformation was moving at a faster rate than normal, no doubt due to his maturity as a hybrid lycanthrope, and soon he would lose all human reasoning for the instincts of an animal. Barber trusted he would soon know where to go, so he simply rode out the pain until the monster was fully converted, but he had remembered to leave the front door ajar this time and turned all the lights out in that part of the house. The beast walked into the night.

By impulse it knew to be cautious from here on, spending time behind several businesses before reaching its destination. Deke McKenna's favorite coffee house. It was on the south side of Cave Creek Road and stayed open until nine PM and McKenna had parked all the way at the south end. There was plenty of cover for the animal to hide and through sheer coincidence, there were only a couple feet from there to the Hummer. It waited.

After a half hour McKenna approached his truck and had an eerie feeling of pending danger. All his senses were activated as he unlocked the door, scanned the area completely, and started to get into the vehicle. The thing came up from behind and grabbed him by the neck as he spun around in anticipation of the attack. Deke slammed a fist into its face but was rewarded with slashes bone-deep on his knuckles.

The creature wasn't even stunned and thrashed back with a renewed vengeance that opened a wound in McKenna's chest that you could almost put your hand into. This slowed McKenna, but he fought on with a continuing vitality that marked his endurance. Even so, he was no match for a werewolf and its brute force was finally just too much for him. It attempted to rip off his right arm but managed only to sever it at the elbow.

During all this action, Deke had been screaming for help and finally the three pals he had been talking to heard the noise. They headed toward the Hummer, guns drawn, when they saw the freak of nature with their friend's arm. All three emptied their weapons with direct hits. One had a flashlight and turned it on and stood there dumbfounded. The fiend shielded its eyes from the light, was obviously disabled, and threw the arm at them and ran.

Nobody wanted to give chase to something like this so they focused on helping McKenna, first with a tourniquet around the stub to stop bleeding. One of them took off his shirt, pressing it on the chest wound to control the blood flow. The third called 911 and reported the incident. With the flashlight now centered on Deke, it was obvious he was not doing well. The guy making the 911 call knew McKenna's connection to the supernatural murders and called Phoenix PD.

The mutant moved through the chaparral behind the buildings on its way back to its lair as the re-transformation to Arnold Barber started taking place. During the process the gunshot wounds were rapidly healing. Then human reasoning took control, with no actual memory of what had just happened. But something told him to go back, then he heard sirens approaching rapidly so he continued his trek home. As usual, not a trace of evidence had been left.

Chief McIntyre had called Deke's girlfriend, Lani, before heading up to Cave Creek with Officer Gouyen. She was already there when they arrived and working with the paramedics to try and communicate with McKenna. So far he wasn't responding, and while McIntyre waited he decided to talk to the three buddies who had been with him. But since they had gotten there at the end of the attack there was little they could add. Except…it definitely was a werewolf.

The Chief could see now that they were loading Deke into the wagon and went over to talk to Lani. She was holding up okay, he thought, but then she would, knowing she must be strong for her man now.

"It doesn't look good Ruben. He has a large tear in his chest but the thing didn't damage the heart, fortunately. They've stabilized the arm and elbow stump as well as possible, hoping emergency can reattach it. He's a survivor, so we can only hope. But he's still unconscious and that isn't good." As she finished, the paramedics were pulling away with sirens screeching. They both followed them to Scottsdale Thompson Peak, the nearest ER.

* * * * *

The Keeper looked on this episode as a failure on the part of the werewolf. Agreed, Deke McKenna was a high-profile target and more able to defend himself, but there was no room for defeat at any level. The question was how to complete the task in the disposing of McKenna. He was the primary obstacle to eliminating more politicians. It would certainly be impossible to slip the werewolf into the hospital, but how about a vampire, very late at night?

* * * * *

Robert Briggs called in his assistant to conduct the meeting for him and then picked up the phone and called a friend. "Ron, this is Robert Briggs and I need the name of a good trial defense attorney."

"I told you betting on those bowl games was going to get you in trouble," followed by a chuckle.

"No, nothing like that, it's for, well, can't really discuss that now but it's definitely far out. You got anything for me?"

"Sure, Anthony Arcuri, Arcuri & Associates. Has a private practice and I've seen him operate, he's good in the courtroom and he's hungry. Robert, he's been known to bend the rules and he can be crass, but maybe that's what you need. Here's his number and tell him I recommended you."

189

"Thanks Ron, expect some tickets in the mail."

"Thanks man."

Robert made the call and explained the grisly details to Anthony Arcuri, who listened but did not comment on the weird particulars of the situation. When Karen's husband put it all in perspective with more background from all the media coverage, Arcuri began to understand the plight and the potential of this new client.

It was near impossible to rationalize how an ordinary Phoenix housewife could be accused of being a vampire. And there was nothing in the law books that he studied that would tell him how to represent a supernatural creature. Would the prosecutor go after a paranormal being or a human being? How would you ever get an impartial jury? What if the defendant suddenly turned into a bat on the stand? All absurdities, but he couldn't resist taking the case.

"Mr. Briggs, I would like to meet with your wife. I don't know how long that will take but it should be as soon as possible. I'm going to get right back on the phone now and arrange this. Assume you will join me at the police station."

"Well, uh, have to wrap up some business here first and then I'll be right down," and then he hung up.

Arcuri just stared at the phone in disbelief over how a man could put his job before his wife's well-being, especially when she was being accused of murder. Takes all kinds, he thought.

Anthony Arcuri stood waiting at Phoenix PD to see his client, Karen Briggs. He thought of how this could be the kind of case that would make him a star in the legal community, especially if he could get her out of this ridiculous accusation that she was the vampire committing these murders. He had studied the media coverage before making the trip here, and although the facts were pretty compelling, there was still just the slightest apprehension on his part.

Then Arcuri was ushered back to a room where he could interview Karen Briggs and within minutes, she was brought in and seated across from him.

190

"Really, are these handcuffs necessary?" and the jailer left the room and returned within seconds to remove the cuffs.

Already, Karen liked this man. "Thanks," she said, and a relationship was born that would go down in Arizona history as one of the most outrageous cases ever.

FORTY-FIVE…

"I'm Tony Arcuri, and your husband Robert has asked me to talk with you regarding your representation in the case the police have against you. We should decide here today if you are in agreement with me handling the case, and, if so, discuss how to proceed and then I will get together with Robert to sign the necessary papers. First of all, he hasn't arrived yet; he must be a pretty busy man considering the seriousness of your charge."

"If that's a question, the answer is a definite yes. It always seems to be work before family." The sarcasm in her voice was obvious, duly noted by her attorney.

"Okay, let's start with the question, did you do the killing?" They were talking softly and Tony made sure no one could lip read.

"Yes," said Karen looking straight into the lawyer's eyes, "at least one of them."

Tony Arcuri was so stunned he could say nothing for several seconds. "Excuse me, you're saying you are guilty of murdering someone but not the person they've accused you of killing?"

"Right."

Still in shock, there was another pause then, "Who *did* you kill?"

"The guy in the Arizona legislature, you know, his name is something Quanah. He's Indian, I think."

Arcuri had heard that Chew Quanah was found in full warrior headdress at one of his rituals deplete of all his blood. But he also knew that Amy Rogers had been arrested in connection with that murder but released for lack of evidence. Wow, he thought, this couldn't get more complicated. Before he could speak…

"I also killed my neighbor, an EMT, you know, emergency medical technician?"

It just got more complicated. He thought for a moment then said, "I'll take the case if you're still sure."

"Absolutely.".

"Now, let's hear the full story right from the beginning, and don't leave out any details…"

"And that's the tale of the last few weeks of my life. But you mustn't involve Amy Rogers. She's my alibi and I'm hers."

"Okay, we have to make a deal."

"What kind of deal?"

He whispered directly at her, "You sign a contract with me for a book and guarantee me access to you and Amy Rogers for all my sexual needs and I will not only take your case pro bono, but I will do anything necessary to win, even if I have to buy an alibi."

Karen thought for a moment about what a scuz this guy must be, but she wasn't exactly looking at a lot of options.

"You understand this has to be kept between you, Amy Rogers and me. I'll contact Ms. Rogers and work out a deal with her but give me a phone number." She did from memory.

Then Karen exclaimed, "I don't really have a choice in the matter. Let's go for it. It's a deal." Now the man knew she was a vampire but he was not alarmed…at least not yet. They were done and Robert still hadn't arrived.

*   *   *   *   *

Bly Gouyen had finally been able to piece the evidence together on the Glendale murder of the EMT. Glendale PD had turned over all the files to Phoenix and she wondered if it was just a coincidence that Karen Briggs lived in the same town. Maybe, but based on two flubs on her part already, it was necessary to check everything to the nth detail. She grabbed the Briggs folder and started comparing.

She looked at Karen Briggs' address and bingo, she lived three doors down from the victim. Gouyen literally ran to the Chief's office with the information only to find that he was at the hospital with Deke McKenna. She called McIntyre and had to leave a message, which she did.

It was only minutes and her phone rang. "Ruben, I have uncovered some new information that can assist in the case against Karen Briggs. There was a murder in Glendale that looked very similar to our vampire killings, and their PD called me to get our reaction. After

193

their description, I said it was our perp and to send the file over. They did, and something looked suspicious so I compared it with the Briggs' file.

"The victim was an emergency medical technician and he lived three doors down from Karen Briggs. The neighborhood busy-body saw what she thought were two women walking down the alley from his house at about the time of the murder. They had on baseball caps and dark glasses so she wasn't sure. When the Glendale detective, a female named Barr, first called, I asked if they would release the case to Phoenix and they have."

"Well done Bly, that's what I call good police work. Yep, this was a helluva job Officer Gouyen." The sergeant was beaming.

"Now, let me give you an update on Deke McKenna," McIntyre continued. "He's barely hanging on to life but they were able to reattach his arm and are waiting to see if his body will accept it. Apparently no real damage was done to the chest cavity. That's all I have for now."

"I'll keep you in the loop on this Glendale thing," she said, and they hung up.

* * * * *

At the least, Tony Arcuri was feeling just a little bit sleazy. Hell, he thought, this is downright obscene, and you know it. Arcuri had run his practice almost by the rules—although he had bent a few—and it hadn't landed him the Jaguar convertible he craved, and he still lived in a condo in Scottsdale. It had been the right decision, he was sure.

He dialed Amy Rogers' telephone number.

"Hello."

"Ms. Rogers, this is Tony Arcuri, and I am representing Karen Briggs on the charge of murdering Stan Black." He paused for reaction.

"Holy shit, when did this happen?"

"She was just recently arrested and I had a lengthy conversation with her in jail about her situation which, by the way, included you, and that's the reason I am calling." Another pause.

194

Oh my God, Amy thought, Karen knows I killed Stan Black. Has she turned me in to save herself? She decided to wait for him to continue.

She's cool, Arcuri thought, and that would make his job just that much easier. "We need to get together and talk. It isn't appropriate to speak about this on the phone so could you come to my office?"

Now Amy hesitated since she had been arrested herself and released due to lack of evidence on two murders. But what if something is going on that could drag me back into this, she wondered. It would probably be best to at least talk to this guy. "Sure, anything to help my friend. When do we do it?"

"My office is in Scottsdale," and he gave her the address. "Four-thirty this afternoon?"

"I'll be there," and they hung up.

She opened Tony Arcuri's door and there was a small outer area but no one manning the desk. His door was open and he came out to meet her. "Hello Ms. Rogers, please come into my office." There were two simple chairs as well as a leather—probably naugahyde—couch in the similarly small room. "Have a seat," and he pointed to one of the chairs.

She did and displayed the best pair of legs this attorney had ever seen. "I hope this is something we can work out, as far as Karen's situation, I mean."

"All right, let's get down to business.

"I think I should start by relating to you my conversation with Karen Briggs, which she has authorized me to do." He covered the fact of her involvement and the sex-for-representation in detail so Amy would understand her obligation but left out the book deal.

Once he had finished, he thought she was going to leave his office because she stood up. "Well, it looks like Karen has already worked out the particulars with you. I see no reason to change the terms. Would you like to first explore your sexual needs before we continue?" she said with her hands on her hips.

FORTY-SIX...

"Let me secure the office," Tony said. When he returned Amy was lying on the couch, nude. Arcuri began to remove his clothes and she wagged a finger at him to come closer, which he did. She caressed his erection and he worked faster.

After a range of pleasuring from the toes to her ears, he went inside her. They both moved to each other in a steady rhythm that was driving Amy crazy. And then she began to clench inside and tingle all over just before they both had a huge climax. During this she bit Arcuri passionately several times, releasing the immortal elixir.

"Get me a tissue, hon." Part of her pleasure came from knowing that now Tony Arcuri could not back out of their deal. She cleaned herself and put the dirty tissue in her purse and then she left.

* * * * *

Chief McIntyre had to question Amy Rogers. Since she couldn't talk to her friend, who was in jail, they would not have the chance to come up with the same alibi. He still felt that both of these women were somehow involved in the vampire murders, either individually or collectively. He dialed Amy Rogers' number.

"Hello."

"Hello Ms. Rogers, This is Chief McIntyre at Phoenix PD. I have some more questions I would like to ask you if you wouldn't mind taking the time to come in to my office."

"May I ask what this is about? I've already been cleared of those murders, so what could you possibly have to talk to me about?"

"This is a different murder, Ms. Rogers."

"So why are you calling me? Will I be a suspect for every killing that takes place in Phoenix now? I'll call my attorney and let him talk to you," and she hung up."

Well, the bluff hadn't worked, so he would have to talk to her through her lawyer anyway.

"Shit," Amy said to herself, "Which one? They ruled me out on Bernice O'Ryan and Dan Thornton. Karen's the suspect for Stan Black. It's gotta be either that Quanah guy again or Karen's neighbor."

"Hello, Mr. Monaghan's office."

"This is Amy Rogers and I need to talk to Jerry."

"I'll see if Mr. Monaghan is available." 'Mr. Monaghan,' Amy thought. She'd like to slap this woman cross eyed.

"Hi Amy, this is Jerry Monaghan. What can I do for you?"

She told him about her conversation with Chief McIntyre. "Don't do anything. I'll take care of it."

McIntyre picked up his phone knowing Monaghan was on the other end, "That didn't take long."

"If you expected a call from me, why didn't you just call me first?"

"Different investigation. Didn't know you were on a retainer with Amy Rogers."

"Not, but anything you have on this series of murders, call me."

"Will do. I am starting a probe on a new murder, one of Karen Briggs' neighbors, and need to ask Ms. Rogers some questions."

"Why would you suspect my client if it's Karen Briggs' neighbor?"

"Because just following the murder, two women were seen walking from the victim's house down an alley toward Ms. Briggs' house."

"So one of them had to be Amy Rogers?"

"Didn't have to be but she's the suspect's closest friend and the crime scene was only three houses away. A little too much coincidence, don't you think, counselor?"

"My business is full of coincidences, Ruben, but don't you think you're grasping here?"

"Not at all. When can you have her here?"

"I'll try to set something up for tomorrow. Early morning okay?"

"Sure, just let me know." They hung up.

Monaghan called back within an hour and confirmed the meeting the next day at 10:30. He also told Jane, his paralegal, to find out who was representing Karen Briggs.

Jane called him back in fifteen minutes and said, "Tony Arcuri is handling the Karen Briggs case." She gave him the telephone number.

"Tony Arcuri speaking."

"Jerry Monaghan here. I'm representing Amy Rogers and I need to talk to you about something confidential that can't be done over the phone. When can we meet?"

Arcuri choked momentarily, then said, "Sure, when and where?"

"My office this afternoon?"

"That's fine, where are you?"

"In the Camelback corridor," and he gave him the address.

"I'll be there in a half hour." And he hung up.

"Oh my God, did Amy Rogers rat on me?" he blurted out. "This guy could have me disbarred."

He found the building with no trouble and took the elevator to Monaghan's floor, where he announced himself to the receptionist. After a while he was ushered to the office. Jerry said, "Come in and sit down."

They looked at each other, neither trusting what they saw. It was more intense than Arcuri liked, as if the other guy was seeing something he couldn't hide.

Then Monaghan's hand shot out and he said, "Good to meet you." It was so abrupt that Tony was caught off guard.

"Yes, guess it was time that we meet," Arcuri said.

"What would you like to drink, Tony?"

"Regular coffee's fine, black."

Monaghan gave the beverage orders to his secretary. Arcuri's hands were damp and he wrung them repeatedly. It did not go unnoticed by the other man. As he sat there fidgeting he also found that he was perspiring more than normal, and he was just a little short of breath.

"So, what's the big secret you had me come here for?" he asked.

"The Phoenix PD is investigating one or more new vampire murders and my client, Amy Rogers, and I will be meeting with Chef McIntyre tomorrow morning." He had Tony's complete attention now and his body seemed to cool down with the knowledge it wasn't about his transgressions with Rogers.

"I know your client, Karen Briggs, is suspected in the Stan Black killing, but McIntyre thinks she may have had something to do with yet another murder being blamed on the vampire. His name was Taylor Robbins and he is a neighbor of Ms. Briggs. Did you know anything about this?"

The tension continued to drain from Arcuri's body and was replaced by some of his street-smart confidence. "No, nothing, but did you say a neighbor?" He knew this but it was a good cover.

"Yes, just three doors down. You should ask her if she knows him."

Monaghan filled him in on what he knew minus anything privy to his client. Tony told him only that Karen Briggs had been with Amy Rogers the night of Stan Black's death, and they may have had coffee at the same Starbucks where he was killed but other than that, she was completely innocent.

But Tony still had the foreboding feeling that Jerry Monaghan could see further into his psyche than he wanted him to.

FORTY-SEVEN…

It was the next day and Chief McIntyre, with Officer Gouyen, was waiting for Jerry Monaghan and Amy Rogers to arrive. "Bly, between Amy Rogers and Karen Briggs, who do you think is our most likely suspect? Or do you think they are in this together?"

Gouyen took considerable time before answering. "If Ms. Rogers is completely cleared of the O'Ryan and Thornton murders, and Ms. Briggs is the accused for Stan Black, I would think that the conversations upcoming with both of them could be a deciding factor." She was restless as she spoke. "If we can't connect the Taylor Robbins or Chew Quanah killings with either or both of them, Ruben, we're probably at the point of starting over."

McIntyre looked at her and knew she was right. "The two spent a lot of time together and could have set up a mutual alibi. We have no eye witnesses, there has been no connecting forensics, and their DNA is inconclusive, except for Karen Briggs' prints and DNA at the Stan Black crime scene. But both of these were outside the car and there is nothing to prove she was ever inside the car. Any good attorney could turn that around.

The desk Sergeant looked in the Chief's door and said, "Mr. Monaghan and Ms. Rogers are here."

"Send them in."

After a couple of minutes, Amy Rogers walked in, imposing as ever, wearing a tight fitting dress that left absolutely nothing to the imagination. McIntyre wondered how Monaghan handled this, being the straight-shooter he was. Hell, you couldn't ignore it. He was just glad that it didn't seem to bother him that much. The lawyer followed her through the door with his eyes straight ahead. "Hello Jerry, and thank you for coming in, Ms. Rogers."

"Hello Ruben. Could we get this going as soon as possible? Amy has plans and I have court this afternoon."

"Sure, Jerry, anything for you. My purpose in calling you in here today, Ms. Rogers, was to see if you know anything about the death of Taylor Robbins who died in a similar manner as others in this series of killings, completely drained of his blood." The Chief went on to cover the rest of the evidence, including the person who had seen two people walking down the alley toward Karen Briggs' house.

After he was finished Amy looked as relaxed as someone listening to their favorite music. Not a sign of concern on her face and her demeanor was completely unruffled. "Can you account for your whereabouts on that day, Ms. Rogers?" and he gave her the day and time.

"I will allow my client to answer your question but first tell me why you suspect Amy."

"Two women in the alley heading toward Briggs' house, Ms. Rogers a close friend of Ms. Briggs. More coincidence, but the strength is that it was only three doors from Karen Briggs."

"First, you said two *people*, Ruben, not women. Second, yes, another coincidence, and this is beginning to get into a pattern of harassment that bothers both me and my client. Now, having put that on the record, Amy, you may answer the question."

"Give me that date again," she asked while she took out something that looked like an appointment book. When he repeated the date, Amy said, "I was having coffee with Karen at a Starbucks, something we do on a regular basis to stay connected."

"Could you tell me which Starbucks Ms. Rogers?"

"Yes, the one on Bell Rd. just west of the 101. Kind of in between where we live."

"Ms. Briggs will confirm this, of course," McIntyre said with a doubtful look.

"Of course," was the answer, and she knew the Chief didn't believe her, but she and Karen had worked out their alibis carefully just in anticipation of this kind of situation. With no other corroborating evidence, they had to accept them. The biggest problem left now was Karen's fingerprints on Stan Black's car and her upchuck on the ground. She sat back satisfied and stared at McIntyre and Gouyen with a fearless expression on her face.

The Chief looked at Monaghan, who also looked complacent, and said, "Guess we're through here," and then added, "at least for now."

The two took it as a veiled threat, as it was meant to be, but without a word, got up and left the office. When they were in the parking lot standing between their cars, Monaghan said, "He's not going to give up, Amy, and I hope your appointment book will continue to support your alibis, even though that is somewhat thin in its significance. Your best asset is the fact that they have nothing else certifiable to connect you."

"Thanks, Jerry. Don't worry, I'll be a good girl." She looked at him and knew he didn't believe that. They both got in their cars and drove away.

As Amy drove home she was troubled over Chief McIntyre's persistency, although she knew how carefully she had covered her tracks. Deke McKenna was out of the way, at least for now, but McIntyre had to be dealt with. However, killing him would unleash the entire Arizona law enforcement community on this case and that was not good. There had to be another way, and she put her devious mind to work solving the problem. She was thinking outside the Keeper.

McIntyre looked at Gouyen and said, "Amy Rogers is as slick a suspect as I have ever seen, and she knows it. Bly, am I just chasing windmills with her or do you agree with me that there's a good chance she's our vampire?"

Gouyen was her usual poker face and replied with little enthusiasm, "Every time we've brought her in she's had an answer for the charge. The coffee incident may be weak but the Dan Thornton alibi seems rock solid, and if she didn't commit that crime, who did? Karen Briggs was with Rudy Brown during the murder so she couldn't have done it." She paused and carefully worded her next question. "Are you ready to admit there's another player in this?"

McIntyre looked exhausted but knew he had to keep moving. "How fast can you get Karen Briggs here for more interrogation?"

"Let me see, probably no more than an hour."

"Good, let's do it."

202

It was less than an hour and Karen Briggs was brought into one of the interrogation rooms. It was kinda crazy. She thought, because if she were to summon up her vampire strength, she could end all this right now. McIntyre was already in the room and seated. "Hello, Ms. Briggs," the Chief addressed her.

"Hello, and to what do I owe the honor of your visit?"

God, said McIntyre to himself, Amy Rogers had definitely rubbed off on her. "Yes, Ms. Briggs, we have some questions regarding another death."

"Do I really have a choice? But you can't talk to me without my attorney."

"I know; he was notified an hour ago and said he would be here as soon as possible." Before he finished the sentence, Tony Arcuri was led into the room.

"Assume you didn't start without me." It wasn't a question.

"Of course not, Mr. Arcuri, now please have a seat and let's get started."

The attorney said, "Could I have a brief moment with my client, Chief?"

"Sure," and the two walked over into a corner.

"Tony whispered, "I ran the deal by Amy Rogers and she approved everything."

Karen simply held a thumbs up and they returned to the table.

"Okay, Ms. Briggs, this interview is regarding another vampire murder that took place in your neighborhood, actually only three houses down from yours. We have a witness"—and this almost sent Karen ballistic, no one had seen them kill the EMT, at least she thought—"that saw two people walking down the alley from that house headed toward yours." Immediate relief, just the old busybody two doors down. "Where were you on … ?" and he read the time and date.

First Karen looked at her lawyer then thought for a moment. She and Amy had their standard alibi set up but it was necessary to connect the right coffee place with the right killing. "I was having coffee with Amy Rogers, at, I believe, a Starbucks on Bell Rd. Then we went back to her house."

"And just what makes you so sure of that, Ms. Briggs?"

"Because that's the day of the month Amy and I do our buddy self- check for breast cancer. Actually we do each other, you know, feel for lumps." That would lighten things up she figured and she saw Tony Arcuri squirming in his chair.

"Um, we'll take your word for it," and McIntyre knew the interview was over.

FORTY-EIGHT...

The Chief called Lani Baker to meet with him, Officer Gouyen and two detectives that had been working on the case from the beginning. They sat around the conference table in his office, the investigation evidence board behind them. McIntyre stood, looked at the board, then back at the others. "Unless we've missed details somewhere, which would be hard to understand at this point, we have the wrong suspects. But I don't think so," he said.

Four faces reflected what looked like agreement and he continued. "We're here today to start from the beginning and analyze each death individually until we come up with something. I'd like to hope that when we leave this room we will have uncovered a fact we've missed that will help solve this case." He saw less than real optimism in their eyes but was determined to move along if only to re-examine everything and prove they had missed nothing.

He walked closer to the board. "Cynthia Haskins was killed by a werewolf with no connection to the purported motive of killing certain Arizona politicians. The same goes for Bernice O'Ryan, Stan Black, the Walmart victim and Taylor Robbins. Governor Butts' limo driver and the guy from the rally parking lot appear to be innocent victims." The Chief let that sink in and looked at his audience. "Any questions regarding these?" There were none.

"John and Mack," referring to the two detectives, "have been looking into the backgrounds of the presumed innocent ones and have come up with nothing. I've gone over the results with both of them along with Bly, and we fully concur with their findings." He turned his attention to Lani, "You are our best chance now to tie these two women to the vampire murders."

She thought about it and then said, "Since I've given you everything I have, plus what Deke had in his files on the paranormal, my next contribution would be to conduct a fixated tarot reading and call in Loretta Popescu for another divination."

"How quickly could you set those up?"

"I can do the Tarot anytime but let me call Loretta and see when she's available. I'll have her come to Phoenix."

"Great, call me when you have it set up. Appreciate your stepping in for McKenna like this."

John said, "Chief, I know how important the vampire angle is but Mack and I have been thinking about the fact that we have no suspect yet for the werewolf. I know you addressed it in earlier meetings and the two of us have followed up on each death but we are completely without leads."

"I know, John, and that does need more attention but we thought we were close to nailing Amy Rogers, then Karen Briggs, so we went with the evidence." He kind of grimaced. "Unfortunately, our resources only go so far with the cutbacks and that's limited the coverage. Maybe now's the time, since we've run into a stone wall with the vampire."

* * * * *

Lani was back in her office and she had an idea. If she could get Amy Rogers together with Loretta Popescu somehow, assuming Lo would agree, her friend might be able to find out from Rogers who was controlling these monsters. Lo may have to bait her in a sexual encounter but she just might be willing to do that to help solve this case. Her friend was a great looking woman and Amy Rogers was apparently into about any kind of sex that came along.

First she had to clear it with the Chief, so she got him on the phone. "Ruben, I have a crazy notion of something that might uncover who's behind these savage killings," and she told him her thoughts.

"Lani, I'm willing to try anything at this point, but isn't that putting your friend in a terrible predicament? I mean, even if she is amenable to the sexual possibilities, it could get dangerous."

"Lo and I are close enough to tell me if it's asking too much. But she's always lived on the edge. Remember, she's a Romanian gypsy and one of her favorite sayings is, 'The dog that digs deepest finds the bones.' That's her mantra when it comes to approaching a project. Think about it if you have to."

"Nope, don't have to as long as I can come up with a strategy to protect her. Talk to her and if she agrees, make arrangements for her to come to Phoenix; we'll pay for a nice hotel that will give her a base to operate from."

"Great, I'll get back to you shortly." Lani thought to herself, hope this isn't a mistake and wondered what Deke would say.

When Loretta Popescu answered the phone she immediately asked about McKenna. "How's your man, honey?"

"He's still unconscious but they did reattach the arm. It and the chest wound now seem to be healing. Everyone's amazed, especially the doctors." Lani had called Loretta when it happened.

"Sending positive thoughts your way. Is there something else, like there's apprehension in your voice?"

"There is, Lo, and it bothers me to come to you with this. Do you have a minute?"

"I have all the time in the world for you, doll. What is it that's bothering you?"

Lani told her the plan and then related what she had discussed with McIntyre. "We would set up some kind of sting operation to lure Amy Rogers to your hotel. Like you're writing a book about this case and you're interested in her take on it. She swallowed hard and continued. "Lo, if she really is a vampire she could be dangerous and I wouldn't put your life in jeopardy, except Chief McIntyre is reasonably assured he can come up with adequate protection."

They both stopped for a breather and Popescu spoke first. "Lani, this is right down my alley; you know I've always taken chances. Of course I'll do it, anything for Deke. Could you send me some pictures of her?"

"Hold on. I'm sending several photographs from her Facebook page. They're pretty revealing. There, they're gone."

Within seconds her friend had them and blurted out, "Holy Aunt Martha, she can come to my hotel room any day. She's a born exhibitionist and the woman is way beyond gorgeous. When do I start?"

"Cool it, Lo, if she's all we think she is Amy Rogers could eat you alive."

"What a way to go. Seriously, Lani, I can handle this and if she's not the demon you think she is, I'm going to have some fun along the way"

"Okay, here's what I had in mind. You call Rogers and tell her who you are; so far your participation in the investigation isn't public, and our friendship isn't widely known so there should be no connection." Lani hoped she was right about this. "Make a date to interview her here in Phoenix at the Westward Bend Resort on Scottsdale Road. We'll make the arrangements. We're ready to go so you let me know when you are ready."

"Have to clean up some details on a project I'm working on, should take no more than the rest of the day. Call you later but figure on me being there tomorrow, late morning."

"Great, Lo, we all appreciate this very much. Give me a call when you get close to Phoenix and I'll meet you at the Westward Bend with Chief McIntyre and his people."

"Talk to you tomorrow, Hon."

*   *   *   *   *

Amy Rogers was talking to an old boyfriend, Kenny Boyd, who had just come to Phoenix for a convention. He was staying at the Westward Bend Resort and even though she told him she was married now, he still wanted to see her. Why not, she thought, it was obvious what he wanted and her extra-curricular activities had been limited lately, with Karen still in jail. He must be doing well, considering where he was staying. "What did you have in mind, Kenny?"

"Have meetings tomorrow until noon but have the whole afternoon off. Hoped we could get together here then. Late lunch, maybe in my room, then let the afternoon do its thing."

"Sounds great to me. What's the plan?"

"My room 12:30, number 203. We'll order lunch first."

"I'll be there." They hung up.

She needed a blood fix anyway and Kenny would never be the wiser.

FORTY NINE…

The next day Lani Baker was sitting in the lobby of the Westward Bend when Loretta Popescu came flowing through the doors followed by a bellman with two large bags. How long was she planning to stay, she thought? "Hi Lo, you're looking as beautiful as ever." She was wearing a long, red ochre peasant style dress that clung to her small, slender frame and sported very smart desert sandals. Loretta was big-busted to the point she had to wear special bras.

"Go with me to check in, honey, and we'll talk." They approached the desk and Loretta gave her name. It was 12:20. Once she had checked in, the bellman took her bags to the room and she and Lani went over to a corner to sit. "We're waiting for the Phoenix PD, I take it."

"Right, Chief McIntyre wanted to give us time to go over the plan again and make sure you were comfortable with what you're going to do."

"Say no more, I know what has to be done and I'm in this until you're satisfied you have what you need." It was 12:30.

Just at that moment Amy Rogers walked into the lobby and with her heightened senses spotted Lani Baker immediately. The large sunglasses shielded her eyes and a floppy hat covered part of her face so she wasn't afraid of being recognized. Besides, Baker had her attention on a very attractive woman. Amy loved the dress the other woman was wearing and guessed it covered up an equally alluring body. She proceeded on to room 203.

Chief McIntyre walked in with Officer Gouyen and the two detectives, John and Mack. "Hello, are we interrupting anything?"

"Not at all, Chief, let me introduce everyone to Loretta Popescu," and she did. "We've recovered everything with all the dangers involved and she's still solidly with us."

"Ms. Popescu, I want to thank you for agreeing to do this, considering there are definite hazards that I understand Lani explained."

"It will be my pleasure to help catch the creature that put Deke McKenna in the hospital. And don't worry, Chief, I'm aware of the uncertainty of the situation. But I've always been able to take care of myself; don't forget, I'm Romanian and a psychic, and that's a magic combination."

"Well, it seems that we're all on the same page. Why don't we move into the restaurant for lunch and continue this." When they were seated and had ordered, McIntyre asked, "Bly, do you have any questions?"

"No Chief."

"How about you two guys?" referring to the detectives.

John spoke up, "I know the strategy is to get Amy Rogers into some kind of, ah, romantic encounter, but can you give us a synopsis of what you plan to do?"

"You're already aware of the fact that I am gay and that Amy Rogers is a switch-hitter, so in the course of interviewing her for my bogus book, I will try to lure her with sexual innuendos. And I plan to dress accordingly since based on what I've heard, Amy Rogers is probably the most provocative dresser around these parts."

"I'm not trying to be seductive here but I feel we need to learn at least the basic specifics of your plans to evaluate how we can support you. Can you be more definitive about how far the innuendos will go and what you will do if she takes the bait?"

"I completely understand," Loretta said, "If Amy Rogers should begin to get amorous, I'm willing to go to whatever length necessary to get the information I want. I will be attempting to determine through Rogers' mindset just who is in command of these monsters."

Mack said, "Chief, you said you're planning to put a bug in the room, right?"

"Yep, already done. One on each end under the coffee table."

They all had finished eating by now and were having coffee and tea. "Now's the time if anyone has anything to add to this scenario. Bly, you haven't had much to say; know you're involved more in the logistics, but anything you want to contribute?" Nothing.

McIntyre continued, "Ms. Popescu, we have to be extremely careful putting a citizen in harm's way like this. You should not venture any further than you are absolutely certain of your safety. You realize that if Phoenix PD weren't at the end of our ropes we'd never try anything like this," he reiterated.

"We've taken up enough of your time now." It was 3:10. "I know you and Lani have some last minute details to cover so we'll leave you two alone."

"Thanks for the lunch, Chief McIntyre," Lani said, "and I appreciate everyone coming today. It's been very helpful." She and Loretta went out to the lobby and the others left.

They talked briefly. Lani said, "When are you going to make the call?"

"As soon as I get back to my room."

"Thanks again Lo, and my positive thoughts go with you."

"Thank you, Hon, and don't worry, we'll get this done for Deke." It was 3:30.

Amy knocked on the door of room 203 and it was opened almost immediately. "Hi Kenny, it's been a long time. You're looking great." It was 12:35.

"Amy, Amy, just as gorgeous as ever." He looked at her and thought only Amy Rogers could make a sheath dress sexy. It was sleeveless, tightly fitted, very short and made her breasts look like they were struggling to escape. This woman had come for action and he began to feel a twinge in his crotch. "Come in and let's have some lunch."

When they had finished, Kenny got up and pushed the table out of the way and invited Amy over to the couch. They sat down, had small talk, and the two moved closer together. They swapped tongues deliciously for minutes and then she straddled him and pushed her boobs in his face. It was 1:45.

Kenny immediately attacked the buttons in front and revealed two enormous breasts bridled by a pink lace bra that barely covered the nipples. It was strapless so he pulled it down and went to work, feeling his erection growing with rapid speed. Amy felt it too and started her version of a lap dance that produced dry thrusts from him to try and

211

keep up with her. Finally she stood, unbuttoned the rest of the dress and dropped it on the coffee table.

No panties, and that drove him crazier. She was also shaved. He stood and began to disrobe as fast as he could and as he uncovered his member, she got to it instantly and soon it was ready for engagement. He pulled Amy up to him and kissed her again passionately as he pushed toward the bed. She fell back, her high heels still on, and welcomed him on top of her. As Kenny made his entry, she delicately sunk her fangs into him and slowly drank.

As usual, the nectar of her bite produced a euphoria that lasted for several minutes. When he finally rolled off of her, she looked at the tiny marks in his neck and was satisfied they would go away before he got home. "Shit," he said breathlessly, barely getting the words out.

It was 3:25. Amy turned over and grabbed a tissue from the side table and cleaned herself. Suddenly she was getting a message from the Keeper. It was warning her of danger ahead. She went over to pick up her dress and then into the bathroom to finish dressing. The feeling passed.

Kenny was still lying on the bed and he was scratching his neck. Amy decided to take another look and leaned over with a quick kiss as she surveyed the area. Everything looked great; you could barely see the pricks. "I'm on my way now. Enjoy your conference and don't get into any more trouble." Sure, she thought.

"Will I see you again? I'll be here two more days."

"Afraid not Kenny," and she walked out and closed the door behind her. It was 3:40.

FIFTY…

At approximately 3:35 Loretta Popescu entered her room and decided this was a great place to have an affair. She was on the twelfth floor, room 1214.

She sat in the chair for a while, collecting her thoughts and planning what to say. It was actually very simple. In this call she would only make a date to interview Amy for her book. It was their meeting—which she hoped to set up for tomorrow—that would require a strategy, since the real reason Loretta was here must not be obvious. She got up and walked over to her purse and withdrew Amy Rogers's phone number. It was 3:45.

Loretta dialed the number and it rang, one, two, three, four, five times and went to voice mail. "Hello, you reached Amy. Not able to answer but I do want to talk to you. Please leave me a message at the tone."

"Hi, Ms. Rogers, this is Loretta Popescu and I am writing a book on the supernatural murders taking place in Phoenix. I'm at the Westward Bend Resort and would like to interview you on your involvement. Could you call me at …" then gave her the number.

* * * * *

Arnold Barber was in front of the mirror without his clothes because the hair and fur of the animal had not gone away from the Cave Creek episode. His canines seemed to be permanent now, and he could no longer wear shoes because of the size of his feet, or rather paws. His fingers were elongated and claw-like, with the face developing a full snout. With eyebrows fully conjoined, his eyes were ablaze in a yellow glow. He had been this way for three days.

Stepping away from the mirror, there was a guttural sound coming from his throat that turned into a fiendish growl. Barber, or perhaps "it" now, walked into the great room. The part that was still the human fought to maintain control, lest it might again shapeshift to wolf form and this time it might be for good. The animal engaged, but less aggressively, since its instinct told it that time was on its side. Arnold Barber sat on the couch vacillating between two worlds.

*　*　*　*　*

They had removed Karen from the holding cell and put her in another lockup of those waiting for transfer. Arcuri had been responsible for getting her out of the hell-hole. Now she was in with three other women.

It was time to replenish her blood supply, although not yet critical, but in this arrangement probably the best chance she'd have. Two of her cell mates looked like they weren't interested, or at least anti-social. The other girl appeared to be amenable to getting acquainted so Karen approached her at her bottom bunk bed under her own.

"Hi, my name's Karen, what's yours?"

Uh oh, she looked frightened and didn't say anything. Why shouldn't she be, the word was around that Karen was the vampire murderer. Better turn on my charm, she thought. "Honey, don't believe that stuff they're saying about me. It's crap. Can I sit down? Think we both need a friend."

The other two were looking at her suspiciously but the girl moved over to allow Karen to sit. "Here, see any fangs?" The girl giggled and the other two stared intently as if to make sure.

Finally, "My name is Felicia. I'm in here on a drug charge. I just smoked pot, that was all," and tears began to fill her eyes.

"I'm Karen and marijuana is no big deal. It should be legalized, and you know why I'm here."

"But you really aren't a vampire?"

"Of course not. Just happened to be in the wrong place at the wrong time."

"Sure," the other two said almost in unison.

It was late and pretty soon the lights were turned out. The other two went to bed and Karen was sure they would sleep with one eye open. But she and Felicia continued to talk, and the young girl seemed to want to pour out her heart with boyfriend problems and parents that were convinced she was wasting her life. It all came out in a combination of sniffles and gulps to catch her breath, she was talking so fast. It was getting late but they both stayed where they were.

In a few minutes a guard made her rounds, knocked on the bars and said, "In your beds beauty queens."

They both stood and as they did Felicia put her arms around Karen and hugged her long. Just long enough for a set of fangs to make a delectable puncture wound and release the blissful fluid that would disarm the young girl with an ecstasy designed to allow the slow drinking of her blood. She started to moan, and one of the other girls turned over in her bed to see what was going on. She turned back over. Karen finished the job, and got in the top bed.

The girl sat down, remained in a sitting position until the guard came back by and used her flashlight to look in the cell. "You okay in there?" she asked. The girl didn't reply. Again, "You alright?"

"She's upset over her boyfriend and family," Karen said. "Can I get down and help her to get in bed?"

"Yeah, do it quick while I stand here."

She shuffled down and hastily helped the girl undress and get in bed. Then she headed back up to hers. The guard left. Hopefully the bite marks would be gone by morning, at least that was what Amy had told her. How many times would she have to do this before she got out of this place?

* * * * *

Amy took the elevator down to the Westward Bend lobby and noted that Elaine Baker and her friend were not there. She proceeded out to her car and got in, placing her purse in the passenger seat. It was 3:45 and she failed to notice her phone vibrating in the bag. She headed home to Buckeye, which would take at least an hour. It seemed so easy to entice a donor with sex and there would no doubt be an unlimited supply for that.

Pulling into her driveway, the garage door opened and she entered, then continued into the house. Placing her purse on a table, Amy removed her phone and suddenly realized she hadn't taken it off vibrator. After changing it back there was an immediate indication that

215

there was a message. She dialed in and listened to a call from a Loretta Popescu, whom she didn't know. It said the person was writing a book about the recent murders and wanted to interview her.

At the Westward Bend. Wasn't that a coincidence? Why not? After all, she had been the center of attention as the vampire suspect until they gave up on her. But they still weren't convinced and Amy knew that. Damn, who better than her to play the part of a falsely accused ordinary housewife for the woman's book? She dialed Popescu's number.

"Hello, this is Loretta Popescu," a female throaty sound that was sexy as hell.

"Yes, this is Amy Rogers. You called me about an hour ago."

"Sure did. I would like to interview you for my book on the recent vampire and werewolf murders, if you might be willing to discuss your involvement."

"Not sure what you mean by involvement; I was exonerated on two of the vampire deaths."

"That's it, how you were wrongly accused, and how you think you might have become mixed up in these events."

"That sounds reasonable. When?"

"How about tomorrow, around noon? Room 1214. I'll order up lunch. Cobb salad okay with you?

"Fine," Amy replied, remembering her recent room lunch tryst, "I'll be there." They both hung up.

Loretta thought: God, there was sex dripping from every word this woman spoke and knowing what she looked like, she had to contain herself because there was a job to be done here. After she had found out what she wanted, and confirmed this woman was no vampire, maybe then the games could begin.

FIFTY-ONE...

Lani picked up her Tarot cards and held the whole deck to her heart, hoping something, anything, would give her a sign of what to do next. This had given her visions in the past and was what she was hoping for now. Something that would provide the right answer. The spiritual world could be so mystical and it was easy to miss something, even as trained as she was. Hopefully, Loretta would help in finding who was behind these monsters.

Suddenly there was an aura coming from the Tarot cards she had placed on the table in front of her. She saw the sign of death over a building she could not identify because it was shrouded in a murky haze that only showed a montage of windows. There was a person in the arrangement who wasn't recognizable that seemed to be fading in and out of the illusion. And then just as abruptly it was gone.

Lani looked at the cards again. God, she wished Deke was here to answer all her questions. She compared what she had just seen with the tarot card readings she had done twice regarding this case. The first, when the killings had just gotten started, there were six main cards out of the ten that decidedly pointed to violence and death. The second reading was so terrifying that she had gone into a spell that produced an almost devastating reaction.

When relating this to Loretta Popescu, she had described it as "seeing the end of the world," an "apocalypse." Lani wondered how this applied to Phoenix but most of these murders had a political angle that was even harder to analyze.

"Hello, Ruben, I just had a vision of more death and it had to do with a building, and an individual was involved. I could not identify this person nor the structure, just that it represented a fatality. It could be predicting the next incident or it might not even be connected to the killings. Sorry I don't have more but I'm trying."

"Thank you Lani. We're all trying our best and you may figure this out yet."

217

Lani arrived at Phoenix police headquarters later and was taken right in to the Chief's office where Bly Gouyen was seated.

"Heard anything new on McKenna?" he asked.

"It's really incredible, Ruben, his chest wound and the arm are still healing rapidly. The doctors are calling it a miracle. But he is still unconscious."

"The last time I called the hospital they said he still wasn't ready for visitors."

"Yes, I can only stay in the room for fifteen minutes but I have a feeling he knows we're all pulling for him."

"Any more thoughts on your vision?"

"Keep in mind I cannot evaluate things like McKenna, and I'm sure you know that. But I have compared the results of my recent two tarot sessions with the apparition I witnessed." She looked at McIntyre and Gouyen, "But I still don't have an answer."

"Yes, I remember the experience in your office but we never discussed the results. Nor do I know about the other episode," the Chief said.

"Okay here're the facts on both. The first was when the killings just started; six main cards out of the ten decisively pointed to violence and death." She paused for emphasis to separate the two. "The second reading was so terrifying that I went into a spell producing the devastating reaction you observed. I saw an apocalypse…the end of the world."

McIntyre spoke up again, "Are you saying that what we have going on here could cause Armageddon?"

"I firmly believe that if something isn't done to stop these two miscreants, they are likely to go on a killing spree in the city, slaughtering hundreds or even thousands. And then if they turn their attention to each other, they might open another portal in the Superstitions that could generate an unending supply of supernatural atrocities."

Lani sat back almost out of breath, but at least she had put all the cards on the table.

The Chief was quiet for a few moments and then looked at Bly Gouyen for some reaction. She was straight in her chair, hands in her lap with the look of the Apache warrior, not a police officer. It was the appearance of one going into battle with only war paint necessary to complete the picture. She commenced a war chant in her native Apache language, and the Chief quickly beckoned Lani to come with him and he shut the door behind them.

Outside he said, "I've been worried about Bly for some time. I don't know if it is the pressure of this case or whether it's just an inordinate amount of concern for the shabby way she feels her people are being treated."

The surprised look on Lani's face said it all for her. "Ruben, I have to tell you I didn't know what to expect in there. I've been to festivals where Indians do war dances and conduct rituals for the public, but this looked like the real thing."

McIntyre put his hand on her shoulder, "Just a minute," and stuck his head back in the door to observe. The chant continued but now she was down on her knees in worship and had piled up the chairs in the room as if building some kind of shrine. He closed the door and said, "Lani, think we've done enough for now. I need to take care of this situation, and thank you for all your input. Obviously we are going to have to become more aggressive."

She looked at the Chief with concern over the way he had aged in the last several weeks. "You know you can depend on me for anything," and she left.

McIntyre went back inside his office again. Officer Gouyen was on her feet now, making an appeal to her Gods to kill the white plunderers of her people. She danced around the enshrinement of furniture she had arranged, not once acknowledging her boss. This went on for some ten minutes until he tried to grab her arm and she flew at him in a rage, exclaiming that she would take him and everyone else in this building to their deaths.

Outside, the Chief summoned two police officers, partially explained the circumstances, and went with them to get Officer Gouyen and escort her to the holding room for people who needed medical attention. There was a cot and one chair, and they moved her to the edge of the small bed, where she sat down. She looked up at the Chief with a far-away look that wracked his emotions. This was a woman that he had worked close with and admired. He felt her pain.

FIFTY-TWO…

Amy Rogers stepped on the elevator of the Westward Bend Resort and pushed the button for the twelfth floor. When it arrived she got off and looked for directions to room 1214. To the right. As she knocked on the door, she had a creepy feeling and it just got worse when she saw Popescu.

"Come in," she said, "I'm Loretta Popescu."

"Good to meet you," Amy answered, and after shutting the door they headed to the couch.

"Maybe we can start by getting to know each other and then order lunch."

"Fine with me."

"I hardly ever get down to Phoenix, so this is a treat for me."

"The werewolf and vampire killings are on everyone's mind, so you sure have a hot subject." Amy was trying not to tip her hand.

"Yes, and it's so tragic about that man, believe his name is Deke McKenna, just barely hanging on to life."

"Sure is, and of course you'll be interviewing his girlfriend, Lani Baker, who has taken his place in the investigation."

"I certainly will, and I am looking forward to meeting this woman."

Amy's blood started to boil. Meet her, she thought, she was just kibitzing with Baker like two old friends yesterday. That's what the Keeper's message was about when she was in Kenny Boyd's room at this very resort. She had been set up for a sting. The room was probably bugged.

"Do you mind if I record our conversation for accuracy?"

"Not at all," God, she thinks I'm gullible, but now at least we're on the same page. She had researched Loretta Popescu on the Internet and knew she was a psychic. This woman was scheming to get next to her and mess with her mind, hoping to reveal her secret.

Popescu arranged everything on the coffee table in front of the couch, on which there was also a book of matches with the Romani Bar on the cover, and invited her guest to sit down beside her.

221

"In case you're not familiar with who I am, I am Romanian, live in Sedona, and have been a psychic advisor for several years. Have a couple of books to my credit, one comparing psychic reading with a paranormal event. I've become very interested in the supernatural murders and have a book planned to chronicle the deaths, following this case to its conclusion."

Popescu looked at Amy and there was a suspicious stare coming back that she didn't understand, nor did she like it. The woman continued, "I have one quick question for you to kind of size things up. Are you a vampire?" Amy was surprised and had some trouble breaking the hypnotic beam that was focused on her eyes.

But then she was able to shake off the spell and gave Popescu a defiant look when she answered, "Yes, now where do we go from there? By the way, vampires can't be hypnotized."

Obviously startled by the reply, Loretta Popescu was quickly confronted with what to do. Then Amy' eyes became a fiery red and canines were pushing through. Now Popescu was the one mesmerized by the demon.

The vampire moved closer to its prey, which was spellbound and unable to move. "Thought you could outsmart me, huh?" It could detect a fear within its victim creating a paralysis making what it had to do much easier. With an innate sense, the fiend used its telekinetic power, ordered Popescu to the window, willed her to open it and remove the screen. Then, commanded her push an ottoman in front of the window and get on it, which she did.

At this point, Loretta Popescu leaned toward the open window and did a swan dive without making a sound. Amy, now in control, grabbed the recorder, the Romani Bar matchbook, and made sure she was leaving no evidence of her being here and hurried out of the room. She headed down the hall and took the stairs at the other end of the corridor, carefully cleaning the door handles. There was a back entrance to the hotel, which she took to her car.

Alibi, she thought, and then she looked at the matches in her hand as she entered her car. The Romani Bar, and in checking the address it was just east of the Squaw Peak Freeway on McDowell Road. Hooker haven and drug addicts' paradise. It was then that she heard the sirens pulling up into the resort, a combination of ambulance, EMTs and police squad cars. She turned onto Scottsdale Road and headed for the 51 freeway.

At the off ramp to McDowell, Amy exited and took a left. The bar was on the right and she pulled into the parking lot; only one car at this early hour. It was one PM. The entrance was on the side where she parked and there was Romani carving in the door. It opened into a dark interior where a jukebox was playing Gypsy music made up of an accordion, mandolins and guitars with a man singing a soulful folk tune that was very plaintive.

She moved over to the bar and there was someone behind it, but she was not yet accustomed to the darkened room. Eventually she could see that it was a man with dark features and a mustache wearing typical Romani garb. After parking herself on a stool, Amy said hi and ordered a scotch and water. When it was delivered she said, "My name's Amy, what's yours?"

"Luca. You're not from this area and you're certainly not Roma. It's," he looked at his watch, "five past one and you don't look like a heavy drinker to me. Are you a cop?"

"Hell no," she answered, "you heard about that vampire on the loose, well, that's me." She could afford to be cavalier about this for, if necessary, she could take this guy out in a heartbeat.

The bartender grinned and put both hands on the bar. "You know anyone could walk in here and say that." He had the kind of sleazy look on his face that told her he would easily succumb to her sexual overtures.

"I have some pictures from the newspaper when I was arrested. They had to let me go because I had an alibi." She showed him the pictures.

Still somewhat skeptical, he asked, "So what do you want?"

"Another alibi," was the answer. "I just offed someone at the Westward Bend Resort and I need you to say that I've been here since noon."

"And why should I do that for you?"

"Because I'll make it worth your while for as long as you want."

"What does that mean?" and she knew she had his attention.

"Let me come behind the bar and I'll show you."

She did and went right for his zipper. He didn't seem that shocked so she went right to work. Slow and pleasurable until Luca, with his back to the bar gasped and let out a loud, "Yieeeeeee." He was done.

Amy stood up and wiped off her mouth. "There's more of that if you tell the cops, that is if they even call, that I was here since noon. Can I count on you?"

He thought to himself, if she actually is the vampire, she can do to me what she's done to her other victims. And she can do it anytime. On the other hand, all I have to do is verify that she was here and my sexual fantasies are fulfilled for as long as I want. Hardly worth even thinking about. "Of course you can count on me."

"Okay," she said, "but I have to have some reason for coming here."

"No problem, my mother is a psychic dealing in the supernatural and you came here to see her."

"Perfect," she replied, "and can I meet her now? Anyway, I have some questions I would like to ask her. I'll be glad to pay whatever she wants."

"Don't see why not, we have living quarters behind the bar. Let me ask her," and he left. Still, there wasn't anyone else in the bar.

Luca returned with his mother, reminding Amy of the old gypsy woman in the Wolfman movie. She wore big earrings, a bandana around her head and she had a fleshy nose. Her eyes were penetrating, and it was obvious at once that this woman could see right into Amy's inner being. "This is my mother, Vadoma. It means, the knowing one."

FIFTY-THREE...

The half-breed Arnold Barber padded into the kitchen and the human side opened the refrigerator and rummaged through week-old groceries, since Barber had not had the inclination recently to order anything online. There was some cheese and salami and a partial loaf of bread, so he made a dry sandwich and devoured it like an animal. Nothing satisfied him but he knew he had to maintain his stamina, at least until the transformation was permanent.

Suddenly the conversion began and the pain was much worse than before. The snout pushed forward to its fullest extent, the claws began to splay, and the feet spread out as hair and fur began to engulf the entire body. The suffering was excruciating as Barber realized he was probably experiencing this for the last time. And then it let out a terrifying scream.

The creature jumped off the couch snarling and headed to the door. It yanked on the knob tearing it completely off. It sensed a departure route there, rearing back and charging with its shoulder, splintering the door into hundreds of pieces. It had taken this route before so it knew how to get out of the neighborhood. A neighbor across the street screamed when she saw the animal.

With its enhanced speed it headed down the street toward Cave Creek Road and advanced toward the downtown, staying concealed as much as possible on the side of the road. At one point when it was out in the open, a car slammed on the brakes and the driver just sat there, gaping at what he was seeing. The mutant arrived at the west end of Cave Creek and took the same route it had for the Deke McKenna attack, the south side of the storefronts.

Passing the area of the confrontation, it continued on until reaching a complex where there were a few retail outlets, a restaurant and a beer garden. It was a few days before Halloween and there was a party going on in a tented area adjacent to the beer garden. The fiend could no longer contain itself and ripped through the tent into the gathering, howling and gnashing its teeth. The crowd looked on with amazement.

225

Everyone else was in costume, so the werewolf blended in, and no one suspected what was really going on. It looked around amongst people laughing and shouting, "Who are you?" and settled on someone dressed in a vampire costume and started toward her.

With a cagey look she confronted what she thought to be the greatest costume at the party and said, "Come on, a vampire beats a werewolf any day."

The monster didn't understand the invitation but made its move on sheer instinct that it must kill its enemy, shoving people out of its way as it moved forward. Some wondered about this unusual use of force but quickly knew it was for real when the woman was grabbed around the neck by two massive paws and everyone heard the sickening crack of her neck. This was followed by screams and a husband trying to save his wife.

But it was too late, and the wolf grabbed him with a freed paw and crushed his head between its appendages. The party turned into a cacophony of screaming people running to exit the tent and trampling anyone who stood in their way. The savage carried its vampire outside where there was a platform in the middle of the courtyard, and mounted the stairs. There the brute stood, dug its claws into her chest, pulled out her heart and ate it in full view of everyone.

* * * * *

Chief McIntyre stood in the cactus bed where Loretta Popescu had fallen, barely missing a cholla. He had been called by an officer stationed outside who saw her fall. McIntyre called up to the two detectives in the room next door to 1214. He asked John, "What the hell happened? She's down here in the flower bed, dead. You guys were supposed to be monitoring every move they made."

"Everything sounded normal, Chief, until Amy Rogers admitted being a vampire and the conversation became a bit muffled. But still, there was no sign of anything going wrong."

"She actually said she was a vampire?"

"Yes, Chief."

Startled, McIntyre turned to Lani who was leaning against the building looking at her friend with her hands around her head and sobbing, "This is my fault, Ruben, I talked her into this and now she's dead." Then she looked at him and said, "I saw this in a vision and should have known," explaining the trance she'd had.

"Do not blame yourself, Lani, Loretta knew what she was doing and she wanted to do it. And it's obvious now why she willingly took a leap out her window. At least we know what and who we're dealing with." The Chief immediately got on the phone and made contact with his special-forces unit and updated them on the developments

The detectives arrived and were looking up at the open window of room 1214 as they approached the scene. "We've set up a perimeter but there's no sign of Amy Rogers. I thought they secured their windows at these high rise hotels to prevent this sort of thing," Mack said.

"Normally they do but the Westward Bend has been going through a renovation and some of the rooms hadn't been finished, this being one of them. This was according to the maintenance guy," McIntyre said. "Okay, let's go up and see where this all started. Lani, do you want to come?"

"Sure, Ruben, I want to help you any way I can. Is anyone contacting her family?"

"I have someone on it. They're probably heading up to Sedona as we speak."

The Chief had already been contacted by Scottsdale PD and they had gladly turned the situation over to Phoenix. The door to room 1214 was open and there was a hotel maid there plus the assistant manager being interviewed by one of the officers. "She was in here cleaning up when we got here and barely speaks English, so we called the manager and he sent up his assistant," he said.

McIntyre looked right at the Assistant Manager and said, "A dead guest isn't important enough for your boss, huh?"

The man looked embarrassed and didn't seem to know what to say.

"Call him and tell him to get his butt up here now. And don't use that phone over there," meaning the room phone.

The poor guy was befuddled and decided to just go down and get the Manager.

The manager sauntered in and demanded, "Who's in charge?"

"I am, Chief McIntyre of the Phoenix Police Department, and who are you?"

"I'm William Rankin, the manager of this resort and I want to know why I was ordered up here like this?"

"Then I'll tell you, Mr. William Rankin, manager of this resort." The man was taken aback and looked insulted. "One of your guests just took a jump out of one of your windows which I understand is supposed to be safeguarded to prevent something like this from happening." This got his attention. "It looks like we're investigating a murder and it may be connected to the vampire and werewolf occurrences. It might be necessary to shut your resort down."

William Rankin sputtered before he was able to say, "You can't do that."

"Try me, and if you don't get real cooperative real soon you'll find out what I *can* do."

This shut William Rankin up and he moved over to stand by his assistant who had a grin on his face.

"I want the surveillance tapes from the lobby, the hallways and the elevators, if you have them there, and I want them before I leave here." The manager didn't complain. "I want to question any employee who has been at the front desk or anywhere around there and all your bellmen. Find me a vacant room."

William Rankin looked at his assistant manager and said, "You getting all this?" The guy looked scared to death but hadn't taken a note.

Forensics arrived and did their job, which took almost two hours, then left. During this time the Chief and one of his officers were interrogating employees with Lani observing. Showing one of them a picture of Amy Rogers, she confirmed that she had come into the resort today. McIntyre released everyone but told the manager not to rent this room nor let anyone in there until he released it. Yellow tape was placed on the door.

In the squad car Ruben McIntyre turned to Lani, "All we need is for the surveillance tapes to confirm it was Amy Rogers going up to

228

Loretta Popescu's room and maybe we can close half of this case down."

FIFTY-FOUR...

Amy had been sitting in a booth in a cove at the back of the bar when the old woman came to join her. Luca had said there was privacy and they wouldn't be interrupted there. Vadoma was still sizing up her patron when she said, "Luca tells me you are a vampire." There wasn't an inkling of surprise or any alarm. "You have some questions for me?"

"Yes I do," she said, "I've heard vampires have special powers but I don't know how to use all of them."

"My," the woman said, "who is your mentor?"

"I don't have one. I was mutated by an Indian maiden in the Superstition Mountains and my movements are controlled by a Keeper, which directs me to do things, but I don't seem to fully understand our connection."

"They call it mind compulsion, and your Keeper, as you call it, is your mentor or master. You have been called up for the purpose of killing politicians in this state and the Keeper is the one who commands you and the werewolf into action."

Vadoma saw the disbelief in Amy's eyes and said, "You think I read about this in the newspaper or saw it on TV and am just repeating what I have observed."

She was right, and the gypsy went on to describe in detail what had happened in all the murders, including things that weren't in the media. "We don't get a newspaper and we don't have a TV. Besides, what I know is only shared by you, Arnold Barber, the werewolf, and police officer Bly Gouyen, who is the Keeper."

Amy gasped, "Bly Gouyen is the Keeper? And I've never heard of Arnold Barber!"

"Right again," said the Romanian woman, "and you will meet Arnold Barber soon, who actually exists no more, except in the form of a werewolf. But let me give warning, you must kill the werewolf if you are to survive. Now, what were your questions?"

"Actually, I only have one question that probably includes many answers. As I indicated, I know I have powers but do not know how to use most of them. I'm hoping you can show me how."

"You were altered for a purpose and that was to eliminate all the politicians in Arizona that have done harm to the Apache Nation." Vadoma had a stern look on her face. "Bly Gouyen went into the Superstitions and summoned the powers through supernatural portals to do her bidding. That produced you and Arnold Barber."

"I've met Bly Gouyen and she doesn't seem capable of doing something like this."

"The Apache have much to hate the white man for, and Gouyen took it upon herself to requite this retribution. It eventually became too much for her and now she has suffered a mental breakdown."

Amy knew she was running out of time, "Please, will you tell me what my special powers are."

The old woman looked at her with eyes that were clearly cognizant of the destruction that Amy planned to wreak on those who would pursue her. These same eyes were also aware of what might happen to her but she knew she had no choice. "Listen carefully, for I can only tell you once.

"In your vampire state, and through deep concentration, you are able to read minds, mentally hear and see things from a distance and you are capable of both telekinesis and pyrokinesis.

"Your strength is super human with great agility and speed with the ability to fly, your senses are superior, and you are able to transform at will. You are practically invincible due to the speed with which you heal and you ceased aging the moment you became a vampire. Many of these powers you command with your mind.

"You can levitate and move at the speed of sound. You are able to impel people to do your bidding, and this power extends to the werewolf that you can call, and it will succumb to your demands." She reached for Amy's right hand, removing something from the pouch next to her and placing it on the back of her hand. She kept it covered with her two hands and began to chant something.

All of a sudden Amy whimpered and drew her hand back quickly. The old woman opened her hands, and a bat flew away. "That was a Mexican vampire bat you felt, which enables you to change into a bat at will." And when you change others to one of your kind they will also be able to convert to a bat.

231

Vadoma looked at her and said, "Now that you know what you can do, you are going to kill me, but you won't kill Luca. And there is something I haven't told you that I will take to the death." Amy was struck by both statements

She had already decided that Luca wasn't needed for an alibi. Her eyes began to glow while she called up the power she needed to do what must be done. First she grabbed the gypsy around her neck and squeezed until she heard the sound certifying that the neck was broken. The body fell to the floor. She thought, what else could she possibly know that would hurt me?

Acting in her most provocative way she headed out to the bar and approached Luca. Amy was kissing him on the ear and then down the neck until she reached his shoulder and was about to make the decisive bite when she heard the sirens. She looked at Luca and knew immediately that he had betrayed her and called the police.

A hasty exit would be necessary but first decided to use her pyrokinesis capability for the first time; she had already used telekinesis on Loretta Popescu. Amy headed for the door, turning around and sending flames toward Luca and Vadoma. That should take care of both of them, she thought. The sirens were still a few blocks away when she reached her car and drove off.

*   *   *   *   *

Chief McIntyre was standing next to the platform in the courtyard adjacent to the beer garden in Cave Creek where the werewolf had killed its latest victim. With him were detectives John and Mack, who had separated the party's participants into two groups and with additional officers interviewing each person one by one. They were having little luck other than confirmation that this was another werewolf murder.

It was dusk and hard to see, but many of the party-goers that witnessed the killing say the animal jumped from the platform and was last seen running west on Cave Creek Road. After the police examined the body of the woman, it was clear the heart had been taken. And her husband's head had been brutally crushed, as onlookers reported, between the fiend's fingers, or whatever that was on a wolf.

There were reports called in from a driver on Cave Creek road south of Carefree Highway that he had seen the beast earlier. And most interesting was a call from someone who thinks the animal is her neighbor. She supposedly saw it exiting the house across the street. McIntyre had sent officers to take her statement. If it isn't another victim, maybe we can now narrow down who the werewolf is and be closer to closing this case down, he thought.

The monster moved west on Cave Creek Road with the cover of darkness and when it heard loud sobbing sounds and saw lights flashing in the distance, it made its way north on Spur Cross Road. It no longer had the instinct to return to Arnold Barber's house. It was definitely on its own now and the predator inclination had taken over for good. It did not have to eat regularly to survive, just to satisfy the lust for the kill.

It crouched as it heard prey and went into the attack position until the victim came into sight. It was a young child, no more than eight or nine, pitifully crying. Then there were lights flashing, coming over the hill and a police car came closer. The officer on the passenger side jumped out of the car and walked up to the bawling child. "Little girl, what are you doing out here on this road at night all alone?"

"I...I...I," she was really blubbering now, "my momma left me at her drinking place back there," she pointed at Cave Creek behind her, "I'm trying to get home."

"Okay," and the officer picked her up and took her back to the car, "we'll get you home," and he put her in the back seat and got in with her. The cop turned the car around and headed back south again.

The werewolf watched everything from its vantage point, cocking its head first to one side and then to the other as if trying to determine what just happened.

FIFTY-FIVE...

Chief McIntyre sat in his office thinking only of the results he was waiting for regarding Amy Rogers and the werewolf. The surveillance tapes would tell them if Amy Rogers was at the Westward Bend Resort when Loretta Popescu was killed, and they would find out who lived in the house where the werewolf had exited earlier. This could very well be it, he thought, and then John and Mack came rushing into his office.

"We hit the jackpot, Chief. The tape confirms Amy Rogers was at the Westward Bend and it is an Arnold Barber who lives at the house, identified by the neighbor.

"Good job. We know where Rogers lives but do we know who this guy Barber is?"

Mack spoke up, "We interviewed all his neighbors and they say he and his wife, Agnes, were snowbirds from Chicago who came here for the winter." She hasn't been seen leaving the house for some time, the husband only once lately."

Then John, "But the clincher is the fact that forensics found shredded clothes in the house and hair that matches all the other werewolf attacks. Looks like this is our perp, Chief."

"Yes, but where the hell is he or it? We've covered Cave Creek in a twenty-five mile radius from that Halloween party and found nothing. We need Lani's input." He called her and she agreed to come to his office right away.

Lani arrived and was taken right in to see McIntyre. "Lani, we're pushed for time. We've just confirmed it was Amy Rogers that visited Loretta Popescu and who could be her murderer. John, Mack and I will lead a swat team to pick up Rogers and we need to know just what to expect. McKenna filled us in before but we need a refresher."

"Ruben, I can give you what I know, most of it learned from Deke, but I sure wish he was here."

"We all do, and he will be soon, but afraid this won't wait. And that's not all. We need your input on how we might track and capture this werewolf that has apparently reached maturity and is loose on the streets of Cave Creek."

"Whew. Okay, starting with the vampire's powers, their speed and strength are extraordinary to the point of being superhuman. The same applies to the acceleration in their ability to heal." She thought for a moment. "Oh yes, they have the capabilities of levitation, telekinesis and pyrokinesis."

Mack chimed in, "Isn't telekinesis about making someone do something with just your mind?"

"Right," Lani replied.

"Then that's probably how Rogers got Popescu to fly," Mack again.

"Obviously Lo wouldn't have taken that dive without help. But that's not all." She rustled some papers until she found what she wanted. "A hybrid vampire, which Amy Rogers is, according to McKenna, possesses the power to summon a werewolf and force it to do what it commands."

"What's the likelihood of that, Lani?" the Chief asked.

"Depends on just how desperate she is. Ruben, you must be extremely careful in capturing this…thing. Although the vampire is able to only execute one pyrotechnic assault in a given period of time, which I am not sure what that is, it most certainly would kill the target."

"Whoa," McIntyre reacted, "John and Mack, be sure to have protective shields for everyone on the swat team." They both gave a thumbs up. "Now, any idea how we can catch this werewolf?"

"God, wish we had Lo's psychic powers, but since we don't, the only thing I know of to do is you must use human bait. From what we have seen so far, this beast will attack by order, as is the case with the politicians, or just to satisfy its desire to kill for the human heart." She could see that this shot fear through all three of her listeners.

"I'm not putting anyone else in harm's way after losing Loretta Popescu," the Chief stated firmly, "it would almost be guaranteed the person would suffer potential life threatening injuries. No way."

"I'll volunteer Chief," Mack said.

Everyone looked at him with both concern and appreciation. "Can't let you do it."

"I'm volunteering, Chief. Just think about it, I was a Navy Seal and can take care of myself."

McIntyre looked at him, then at his partner John. "Hey, if he wants to do it. I've seen him take guys down twice his size." John was married with two kids, Mack was single.

"I'll take it under consideration, but first we have to take Amy Rogers into custody."

The Chief called Tony Arcuri to let him know that, based on pretty conclusive evidence that Amy Rogers was their vampire murderer, they were releasing Karen Briggs and had called her husband to pick her up. Apparently Briggs would have to wait; her husband was in a meeting and couldn't be disturbed.

*   *   *   *   *

Amy was sitting on the sofa in her bikini and high heels. The hardest part was the waiting, she thought, since she knew they had her on resort surveillance tapes and would be coming soon. She hadn't meant to kill Loretta Popescu, but the gall of the police and this woman had pissed her off so much that she had to make the Romanian psychic pay. With this getup on she would fluster whoever came in the door first and then be able to use her pyrokinetic powers.

She had left Walter a note to try and explain all of what had happened, beginning with her transformation in the Superstitions. She told him, although she was immortal, she had no idea what would happen if the police were able to arrest her and apologized for any embarrassment she caused him. Amy made it a point to let him know how many times she had slept with his boss and urged her husband to use that for future raises.

*   *   *   *   *

There were five doctors beside Deke McKenna's bed with Lani at the head, holding his hand. They were all marveling at how well he was healing when suddenly the monitor measuring his cardiac function fluctuated violently with warning sounds loudly reporting the problem. Nurses came rushing into the room and deferred to the doctors present.

They had McKenna's gown open to the chest wound and were observing it and the repaired arm.

In an instant they all witnessed a miraculous healing process taking place right in front of their eyes, none of which anyone could believe. In a series of ripples in the skin the incisions that had closed the gaping wound in his upper torso disappeared and left McKenna's chest as if there had never been any trauma. And then the injured arm began to thrash around shaking some of the attached lines loose. A doctor grabbed it, and it was completely healed.

Deke barely uttered, "Amy Rogers." Looking around at the people there, not even acknowledging Lani, the shapeshifting began. Hair started to grow all over his body, which slowly became a heavy blanket of fur. The nose was gradually remodeled into a projected snout and his ears grew long and pointed.

Claws ripped through the fingernails and his shoulders grew and filled out with muscles protruding. Feet were evolving into hind paws with animal-like toes forming. The body had grown measurably taller and by now all the IV connections to the body had been pulled free. Lani screamed, as did the nurses.

Deke McKenna was no longer. The brute there before them bounded out of the bed and shoved aside everyone in its way and went through the door, racing down the corridor, looking for an escape route. It noticed someone coming out of a door at the end of the hall and headed in that direction. The nurse just exiting the stairwell slammed against the wall and screamed when she saw the creature. It was down the stairs and out another door within seconds.

The area was unknown, but it knew where it was going and what it had to do. Although non-human instincts were in control, the McKenna wolf had a mission that had come to it from the subconscious of the human and demanded to be fulfilled. It precluded the animosity McKenna felt for its werewolf creator. It wasn't even interested, because its focal point now was the vampire.

Lani knew where it was going. Shaking uncontrollably, she dialed McIntyre and got his voicemail. "Ruben, Deke has shapeshifted to a werewolf and is headed to Amy Roger's house." Hanging up, she nearly dropped the phone and stared vacantly at the doctors.

FIFTY-SIX…

Chief McIntyre had his swat team assembled in the ready room and was checking every aspect of the operation. Everyone would carry a heat shield and each officer would be armed with assault-style weapons and revolvers. Three officers would be equipped with flamethrowers that looked like something out of a Martian movie. They would travel in two armored vehicles and approach the house from opposite directions.

McIntyre called for attention and asked if there were any questions. One of the officers with a flamethrower said, "Is this supposed to be able to kill a vampire?"

"Probably not," the Chief answered, "but hopefully it will slow her down. The idea is to fight fire with fire. Any more questions?"

Another hand up, "Aren't you worried the evacuation of the neighborhood will tip off the…thing?"

"She knows we're coming. Amy Rogers is highly intelligent and her vampire form is a thousand times smarter. I suspect we'll first encounter her in the human form, then the transformation will take place."

"Okay, if there are no more questions, let's reassemble outside at the designated vehicle. Good luck guys."

The Chief's phone had rung on vibrate but he decided there wasn't time to check the message now. Time was of the essence, since he was sure Rogers' intuition was telling her the police were soon to arrive. He joined the rest of the team outside and did a last minute check to insure readiness and was satisfied. Then he made a thorough examination of both vehicles to make sure they were in good shape, including both GPS systems. "We're ready to roll," he said.

* * * * *

The McKenna wolf had taken only minutes to reach its target and as it stood in front of Amy Roger's house one neighbor was pulling into their driveway next door and was so stunned he ran into the rising garage door. The animal knew that the door would provide entry to the house, so it pounded fiercely until it shattered to the inside. At first Amy

238

thought it was a police ramrod, but then she saw the werewolf. That's all it took to commence the transformation.

Her eyes blazed red in an instant and the fangs shot from the gums in readiness for the confrontation. The werewolf first looked at the bikini-clad body then began to charge at the vampire.

It sidestepped and began to levitate, moving around the room, more to distract its adversary than anything else while deciding the next move. The McKenna wolf was snarling and on the attack again, but the Amy vamp was also rushing forward and the two collided in the middle of the room. Reaching for the heart, the bra top was ripped off, which enraged the she-monster, and she hissed and floated backwards as a precaution.

The werewolf bellowed and advanced once more, barely missing the deadly fangs of the vampire that were poised to strike. They wrestled, but the vampire being slightly more developed, grabbed the arm of the wolf and attempted to bring it up to her mouth to inject the poisonous venom. The wolf in a flash wrested its arm away and grabbed the arm of the vampire, ripping it off at the shoulder.

There was more hissing, and the bloodthirsty creature looked somewhat bewildered at the severed arm but quickly regained its composure, grabbed the arm from the werewolf and thrust it back into its socket. It fused instantly. The battle resumed, with the wolf pinning the vampire on the couch on top of it with a fist in the face, raring back to take another shot at claiming the heart.

And once again the she-devil displayed the most strength and agility by forcing the slasher back off it and whirling over to the floor where it jumped to its feet once again in the ready position. The werewolf bounced back and made ready for the next encounter, which was a crashing blow to its chest by the vampire with fangs ready to plant in the shoulder. But the beast was too cagey as it came down hard with two fists on top of the head.

The female Dracula was temporarily stunned, but this passed within moments and it was ready again for what looked like a fight to the death. The werewolf decided to make an attempt to decapitate the vampire, which could kill it. They circled the room with arms outstretched like wrestlers contemplating their next move, when the vampire turned toward its opponent deciding it must use its pyrokinetic power.

The McKenna wolf shrieked with the pain but fortunately had turned sideways at the instant the flame was delivered, thus taking just a glancing blow. It was then that blaring sirens sounded out front that startled them both. The two armored trucks were head to head and Chief McIntyre was the first to hit the street and head for the open door, followed by all the swat team officers.

McIntyre couldn't believe what he was looking at. It was definitely a wolf of some kind and a female vampire with only the bottom of a bikini on. They were probably as surprised as he was and when the woman turned around to look at him, there was no doubt she was the vampire. He barked, "Freeze, police," but before he or his men could do anything the wolf thing grabbed the vampire's head, twisted it grotesquely until it snapped off and threw it backward.

"Holy shit," said John, the detective, and then something began to happen that was even more bizarre than the beheading. The werewolf began to change back into human form, and there was Deke McKenna in all his glory without a stitch of clothes on. One of the officers grabbed an afghan off the back of the sofa and handed it to him. He stood there for several minutes until the shapechange was complete. At first dazed, he finally cleared the cobwebs.

"Where the hell am I?" McKenna finally said and looked around at the room full of astonished police.

McIntyre spoke, "Deke, not sure how to break this to you but you just changed back into yourself from being a werewolf, after wrenching off the head of the vampire who was Amy Rogers. Don't you remember anything?"

"Werewolf? Impossible, no way, no way. Ruben, you know me, and you can't believe this is true."

"I wouldn't normally, but all of us here saw you change from an animal into a human being. And everyone saw you twist the head off the half-nude body of Amy Rogers. Look for yourself."

But instead of seeing the head detached from the body, the vampire stood where both had lain and dashed behind McKenna with an arm around his neck and sunk its fangs into his shoulder, releasing poisonous venom into his body that would eventually kill the man and the beast. However, Deke was able to break loose so that he received only a minimum amount of the poison. And then the vampire levitated again, turned into a bat, and flew away.

Deke McKenna was swaying back and forth and two of the officers got on each side of him to help stabilize his body. He was glassy eyed and the Chief, knowing he was bitten by the vampire, asked him what that meant. "It's a death sentence, Ruben. There are few ways to counteract her venom, and it takes a commitment from the antidote maker that could cause one to lose their life. I don't want that on my conscience, so just lock me up."

John and Mack escorted McKenna out to the car and McIntyre took out his phone and called Walter Rogers. After relating the entire incident, he thought he heard a sigh of relief and wasn't sure if it was over concern for his wife or just relief that it was all out in the open now. Rogers said, "Do you have any idea where Amy is now?"

"No, after the encounter with Deke McKenna, uh, the werewolf, as I explained, she just—now I know this sounds ludicrous—turned into a bat and flew away. It was so spontaneous none of us knew what was happening." There was a pause as he noticed two uniforms approaching. "I'm sorry about this, Mr. Rogers, but you realize now that we do have to apprehend your wife and I will have to protect my police officers. I'll be in touch with you again tomorrow.

His two men were holding a paper they had been looking at and one said, "Chief, you aren't going to like this," and thrust it into his hands.

McIntyre read it out loud, "Chief McIntyre, I thought you should know that Sergeant Bly Gouyen is my Keeper. It is she that has directed all my actions in the vampire murders. She is the one that controls the portals in the Superstitions where the supernatural beings have come from. Signed, Amy Rogers."

FIFTY-SEVEN…

Deke McKenna was sitting in one of the interrogation rooms with Chief McIntyre, John and Mack. "What happened, Deke?" the Chief asked.

"The werewolf attack, I finally figured it out. The injuries don't always cause a conversion but apparently I'm the lucky one. Have you talked to Lani?"

"Yes, she's on the way over here but I can't let her talk to you yet. Have to discuss your circumstances with the DA's office and see what, if anything, to charge you with." He scrutinized Mckenna for any signs of the wolf.

Mack asked Deke, "Can you explain how the decapitated vampire became whole again? I mean, we saw you jerk Amy Roger's head off and sling it aside, at least six feet from where the torso fell."

"A typical way to kill a vampire is to behead it, but this can be counteracted if it is able to reattach the head within a short period of time. The creature obviously did this."

An officer knocked and opened the door, "Chief, the Assistant DA is on the phone." McIntyre went to his office to take the call.

"Ruben McIntyre. Thanks for getting back to me, Eric. Have you decided anything?" He listened while the DA explained their predicament. When finished McIntyre said thanks and affirmed that he would follow up.

"Deke, I'm afraid I'm going to have to detain you for a while to allow the DA's office to run this through federal channels. Frankly, they're baffled over what to do."

"I understand, Ruben. Anyway, I'd rather be locked up until I find out if my alter-ego will show itself again."

Mack said, "Why shouldn't it if you are a valid werewolf?"

"Without a mentor, I'm on my own. In the case of Amy Rogers I believe I instigated the shapeshifting only because of what I felt needed to be done."

"Speaking of a mentor," the Chief said, "the Keeper of the other werewolf and Amy Roger's vampire is Bly Gouyen. We've taken her into custody, and she is being held on multiple murder charges."

"Not totally surprised," McKenna commented.

"The question is," John spoke up, "without someone to guide them, what can we expect now from the two mutants?"

"The answer to that is, anything," Deke replied.

* * * * *

The Barber werewolf felt the telepathic decree to head south out of Cave Creek, a command that it could not ignore. It didn't know where it was going but the paranormal GPS system guiding it did. The route was down Scottsdale Road just past McDowell and then it was directed to turn west. With its speed, it could be there in minutes.

It surveyed its destination and found a place to enter that was secluded. The creature moved through the brush and quickly demolished a wire structure that stood in its path.

And although the freak didn't know it, it was standing in the Mexican Wolves cage of the Phoenix Zoo surrounded by what it thought to be…its brothers. But they were not returning the warm feeling. One of the zoo patrons standing on the other side of the enclosure pointed in the direction of what they thought was a very unusual wolf.

When the monster discovered the humans that had seen it, there was a horrific howl: "Aieeeeeeeee," with a couple of yips as it scampered toward the crowd. It easily hurdled a moat that had been designed to keep the zoo animals in. It hit the ground with a thud, and the concentration of people dispersed, yelling for help, men shielding their wives and children. It then plunged into the gathering and began to wreak havoc.

The brute first approached a woman with a baby in a stroller who was frozen in the spot where she stood, looking at what was charging at her. It first grabbed the carriage by the handle and hurled it back into the wolf pen. The child looked unharmed until one of the wolves attacked it and began to tear it apart. And then the thing grabbed the woman and viciously bit into her neck, all but decapitating her.

Now people were screaming and running in all directions to get away from the terror, but there was nowhere to go. It passed the bobcats and there was another confrontation, this time with an off-duty Phoenix police officer working security, who pulled his gun and carefully aimed at the approaching menace. Three shots hit their target, barely slowing it down. And then claw fingers wrapped around the cop's head and with a ghastly sound, squashed his skull.

Nobody knew what to do. If bullets wouldn't stop it, what would? A caretaker from the zoo came rushing up, and as soon as she saw the demon grabbed her walkie-talkie and shouted to someone at the other end. The Barber werewolf started for her, then heard sirens filtering through all the bedlam and recognized that as trouble from earlier and looked around for refuge. Then it saw the coyote cage, an enemy, but submissive to the wolf.

Vaulting across the wall, there were plenty of hiding places, but a boulder arrangement was chosen to provide cover as well as a possible escape route. The sirens were louder now, but the coyotes were more interested in the intruder than the noise. The trespasser backed deeper into the breach in the rocks and prepared to take its stand against whatever threatened it.

* * * * *

Amy had used her presence as a bat to enter an open space in a window to the attic of her house and roost there overnight. The next morning she entered the back door in her human form, still clothed only in a bikini bottom. As she stood there thinking about what had happened and what was about to happen, there were no doubts in her mind about what she had to do. The werewolves must be eliminated for her to establish supernatural domination.

Amy looked around, probably for the last time, she thought. Sitting down at the desk, it was time to tell Walter goodbye for good and let him know she had felt that they had had a good marriage. Until now, of course. Once finished she put the short note in an envelope with his name on it.

Again in the form of a bat, it set its directional to the path of the Phoenix Zoo and was there within minutes. The police were everywhere, and it quickly located its target that it had beckoned,

244

crouched between two large boulders. Landing on top of one of the huge rocks, it immediately changed into the vampire mode. Still bare chested.

The Barber werewolf saw it and growled first then let out a challenging howl that was heard throughout the area, alerting the police. Jumping from the boulder onto the werewolf, it made one fast attempt to go for the shoulder to inject the poisonous venom that would kill it. Thwarted by a blow from the animal, it fell back against the rock and the wolf took advantage of the situation and charged. It was able to claw at the exposed breasts and blood flew everywhere.

The clash continued as the two moved out from between the boulders, and now the public and police were able to see the combat. Women screamed and grabbed their children, which caught the attention of the creatures and they temporarily paused their battle. It gave police time to get inside the coyote enclosure and move toward the fighting mutants who now focused on them. Instincts willed self-preservation and together they attacked.

FIFTY-EIGHT...

The 911 calls from the Zoo had said there were bizarre-looking freaks fighting in the coyote pen but not much more, and a lot of the communication was incoherent due to the frightened posture of the callers. Dispatch had sent three units close to the area and a Sergeant to check out the situation. Although Chief McIntyre had briefed the entire force on the vampire and werewolf episodes, the four officers were still not prepared for what they saw.

The two demons lunged at the police, the werewolf with its claws advanced, the vampire in readiness to discharge its pyrotechnic assault, which it did. The front two cops were hit and cried out in pain until the flames had burned their bodies beyond all functions. In the background the coyotes began to howl and moved toward the conflict with aggressive snarls aimed at the remaining police. One officer was in front, then the Sergeant moved beside him.

As the wolf marched up to the two it took round after round of 9mm semi-automatic slugs, causing slight tears to the savage's skin but barely slowing it down, due to the maturing of the monster. With their weapons emptied, one officer went for a Taser, the Sergeant his pepper spray but it was way too late. Using its super human strength, the werewolf grabbed one in each hand and launched both in the air, each landing outside right in the middle of the crowd that was quickly dispersing.

They were dead on impact, and since none had had the opportunity to call for more backup and classify the incident as pertaining to the other supernatural events, there were no more sirens to be heard. People were fleeing again to escape the monsters, who had turned their attention back to each other. The vampire had no firepower now, so the only way to overcome the wolf was with its poisonous venom in a close confrontation.

The spectators noticed the new focal point and temporarily halted their flight but looked ready to bolt again in an instant. Cameras were out and being held over the heads of others to record the battle of the preternaturals, and they wouldn't be disappointed. Both came storming at each other.

In close encounter the vampire stabbed the werewolf with its fangs but wasn't given the time to release the venom because of a shove to the face. Then the werewolf made another attempt at clutching its head, which also failed. The coyotes had already fed on the cops but now sensed another kill that could provide dessert. The combatants continued to clash, with the wolf shoving the vampire against one of the boulders and attempting to gain a shoulder lock on its opponent.

There was a brief pause, and the vampire used this to overpower its foe in a move of superior strength that threw the animal over its shoulder and all the way out of the coyote's pen. It landed on the walk adjacent to the giraffe exhibit and just missed hitting a family of five. The werewolf jumped to its feet immediately, unhurt, and surveyed the area for the vampire. Within seconds it arrived and the freak show started again.

Then there was the noise of multiple sirens, indicating a large number of law enforcement vehicles approaching. One of the Zoo patrons had called 911 and reported that what was going on there was definitely connected to the supernatural killings. The werewolf, most affected by the sirens, was distracted for the moment and in that instant the vampire sprung forward and burrowed into its shoulder, releasing all of its deadly venom through its fangs.

Stunned momentarily, it stood there looking at its adversary, for it wasn't sure what had just happened but it knew that it had to attend to the vampire. Mustering all the power that was left to the werewolf, it darted at its drained, temporarily off-guard target, and with a modicum of surprise in its favor, grabbed the head and twisted it from the body. Then with its final lunge of force, threw it across the Zoo where it landed in Monkey Village. The werewolf stumbled, then looked around for an escape.

When Chief McIntyre saw the devastation between the death of four of his officers and all the Zoo attendants and customers, he cursed to himself and wondered again if this would ever end. He had ordered the gates closed; no one was to leave until he gave the approval. John and Mack broke the attending officers into two groups and they went about taking statements.

The vampire's headless body was still close to the coyote area. The officer assigned to guard the body told the Chief that most all of the animals had come over to the edge of the moat as if curious to what happened to the invaders of their lair. But then one by one, they started their typical sing-song and mysteriously backed away. The cop said it was eerie as hell.

McIntyre asked, "Where's the werewolf? All the witnesses said the vampire bit into its shoulder and then it faltered just before ripping off its attacker's head. It was obviously wounded as it headed in the direction of the Oryx."

Mack answered, "It went into their corral and hasn't been seen since."

"Was there any noise indicating the Oryx were unhappy with their trespasser?"

"No, nothing. And so far none of their keepers are willing to venture into the area to find out what's going on."

"Can't say I blame them," but the Chief knew something had to be done to locate the beast.

On the other side of the Zoo a child was giggling and pulling at his dad's arm pointing to a monkey holding something. When the father looked closer, he noticed with horror that the object was a human, vampire-looking head and searched for someone to report it to. A Zoo keeper was standing talking to a police officer and observed the man waving his hands. Walking over he said, "Can I help you sir?"

"Yes, one of your monkeys over there," pointing, "is holding what looks like someone's head."

Both the keeper and the cop jerked their heads in the direction of the pointing. "Oh my God," was the keeper's reaction. The officer started running and high jumped the fence, landing in the moat, then scampered up the side onto the grounds.

This startled the monkeys, and they formed a circle around the one with the head. As the lawman closed in on the primates and approached the one with the skull, they began to toss it between themselves as if playing a game. The cop didn't know what to do, but by then the keeper was inside the enclosure giving signals to the monkeys that resulted in them turning over the head. He turned around and motioned for the cop.

The officer took it, exited the pen and was met by another cop who said it looked like the vampire's head, from the coyote area. When he arrived there, there was still the one officer guarding the body. He observed what the other was holding and waved him over. He walked over to where the rest of the vampire lay and placed its head alongside it.

There was a minor shudder to Amy Roger's body; it had transformed back to human form after the decapitation. She sensed rejuvenated life and began to slowly move toward her head. The two cops were talking and didn't notice what was happening until she stood, whole again, returning to her vampire shape, hissing at the pair. They both drew their weapons and started firing but to no avail, and then as a bat again it soared off to only it knew where.

Chief McIntyre was called and on the scene in minutes. When he heard what had happened he was at first furious with his two officers but became more calm when he thought of the complexity of this whole case and how they probably didn't know or had just been distracted by what was happening. The question was, where had the vampire gone?

But that wasn't the primary concern right now. The major challenge at the moment was locating the werewolf and doing what they could to subdue the monster and kill it, if that was possible. Chief McIntyre knew from the meeting with Lani, and what Deke had said after he was bitten, that if the werewolf were bitten by the vampire and if it released its deadly venom, that it could kill the beast.

There was only one way to find out what happened. Locate the werewolf. McIntyre said, "I need volunteers for a dangerous mission and I prefer those who are single."

FIFTY-NINE

The werewolf felt the injury of the vampire's bite, but not being mature enough in its kind to understand the probability of what could happen, it crept off as fast as it could to find shelter. Most of the visitors were rushing off the walkways into a central area around the refreshment stands so it had no one to challenge it. As it rounded a corner there were keepers and police officers at a checkpoint, so the beast took a quick left into an exhibit.

The wolf was swaying now but even with its impaired vision was still able to spot a clump of brush and trees. The Arabian Oryx just stood in place and watched the intruder head toward a hedgerow. The werewolf moved into the shrubs where it stumbled and almost fell, which it finally did on a small sandy area. By now the sky was reeling as were the trees around it, and as the vertigo grew, all of a sudden there was only darkness.

* * * * *

The bat landed on a patio chair at the back of the house. After a quick transformation she grabbed the key and once again entered her back door in only a bikini bottom. Amy Rogers was having trouble doing the things she normally did and all she could think of right now was to find a place to lie down and rest. She would eventually have to replenish her blood supply but all she needed right now was some peace and quiet, time to rejuvenate.

Walking through the house there was a creepy feeling about what was going to happen to her next. With no blood available right now, she could only rest and regenerate her body.

She moved slowly through the house until reaching the door to their bedroom and there she crawled onto the bed.

* * * * *

The Chief and his volunteers were headed toward the Oryx enclosure armed with everything from revolvers to assault rifles.

McIntyre led the way and the five officers followed. They climbed the fence into the pen and began to examine the open expanse. "Spread out to the fences," the Chief ordered, "and move slowly, since we don't know what shape this thing is in."

They proceeded across the field spotted with rocks, brush and small trees. It was interesting that they hadn't yet run into any Oryx although their keepers indicated that there were twenty-two here in the herd. They agreed this was strange, because the animals were usually out and around, socializing for the spectators to see.

One of the officers on the right flank shouted, "I see something. Straight ahead."

Then a keeper in that area confirmed, "Looks like the whole herd. He held up a hand to caution everyone before continuing. Let me go first."

The keeper approached the collection of Oryx and barked a command that sent them spreading out but not completely abandoning their focus of attention. The more they scattered the better the view of what they had been crowded around. Everyone moved toward the scene until they could see into the clearing. The keepers drew a sharp breath at the sight but the cops immediately drew their guns. It was the werewolf, and it was perfectly still.

The Chief pointed to one of his men and said, "Back me up, the rest of you stand by." He moved ahead. The creature did not move but that could be a trick. He motioned his other men to join the two of them and leaned down and waved a hand over the wolf's eyes. Nothing. He put an evidence glove on and nudged the shoulder of the animal but there was no reaction. He stood back up and looked at everyone, "I believe one-half of our puzzle is solved."

Forensics was called, and when they arrived there were several opinions of how the investigation should be conducted. Randy Clovis, Phoenix PD's head of the department was in charge and decided to start the examination where the body lay, just in case this held some kind of clue to the death

* * * * *

251

Lani was at police headquarters waiting to see Deke. Chief McIntyre had cleared the way through the D.A. with the bizarre explanation of how she was the only one who could save McKenna's life, adding there was potential evil influence and possible physical injury. The District Attorney had added, "Ruben, if something goes wrong here, yours and my butt will be on the carpet, maybe out the door." The Chief assured him that Lani was reasonably sure she could make it work.

McIntyre took her to the cell where McKenna was being held but would not let her go inside. There was privacy, with no one else in this cell block. "Hi Hon," she said.

"Hi sweetheart," he answered, "Hell of a mess, huh?"

"We'll get through this," she replied. "Let me explain what I plan to do to save your life. I've used your research and done a ton of my own and am convinced that the answer to saving your life is in Sedona."

Deke cut in immediately, "Not going to let you do it. Way too dangerous. I know what you're thinking, and the risk to you is way too costly."

"Sorry, Hon, it's the only way out of this, and I'm not going to let you die."

"Lani, you know you could die yourself doing this and then there'd be two deaths. Not worth it. There must be some other way."

"You're the expert on the supernatural, so what is it?"

He was holding on to the bars and trying to rationalize how this whole thing could be carried out without harm to Lani. "There is no other way but I can't let you do it."

"McKenna, right now you know you have no other choice. Just hear me out before you make up your mind." She looked at her notes, "Through a friend of Lo Popescu I was introduced to a witch priestess in Sedona who performs spells that afford liberation from supernatural curses."

She continued. "The priestess' name is Fatin. It's Arabic. Through a friend she instructed me to come to Sedona to her place, which, by the way, is located close to the center of the Airport Vortex." She took a breath, "I am to come armed only with a cutting from your right hand thumbnail adorned with a drop of your blood and the Magician's card from my Tarot deck."

He looked drained, downcast, at the point of breaking, but with his unusual physical strength he wouldn't, which was one of the reasons why he hadn't already died from the vampire's venom. Resigned, he said, "Go on."

"I checked Fatin out with a friend of mine who owns a New Age bookstore in Sedona, and she says the witch comes into her place often for new books on the supernatural. Has quite a following."

"How about results?"

"Apparently she doesn't talk about her achievements but some of her clientele have, and they rave about her abilities. My friend knew of one case where the witch cured a woman who had stage-four breast cancer." She waited to see how this would sink in. "And another case involved a newborn baby with hemolytic disease the doctors couldn't cure. The witch cured the child in one night." Lani felt she was winning the battle.

"What exactly will she do?" Deke was warming to the idea.

"She will mix some herbs along with everyday household items, and then light a series of candles selected for their shades of black to represent the curse we need to expel, and white to represent the positive outcome we want." Lani knew Deke understood this and continued. "And there is a chant she will use to seal the deal and then the rest is up to you."

"What does that mean?"

"Then I'll return to Phoenix for another ritual between you and myself. It has to be done in the Superstitions at Weavers Needle and during a full moon." Now there was angst in his face. "With the Magician's Tarot Card in my hand, you must face it head-on and attempt to turn yourself into a werewolf.

"McKenna, this is our only hope. I've talked with Ruben and he will provide protection for me. He and several officers, plus detectives John and Mack, will go with us to insure that nothing goes wrong." He still looked skeptical but guardedly interested. "I will not be at risk of you harming me."

What she didn't tell him was that if the spell didn't abolish the curse, it could backfire on Lani and she would likely end up turning into a werewolf.

SIXTY…

The werewolf had been taken to the Maricopa County Morgue, and it was a first for Randy Clovis, Director of Forensics. Randy had contacted medical examiners he knew throughout the country and invited them to Phoenix to assist him in the examination. There were ten, and they were as bewildered over what they were looking at as Clovis. Gathered around the autopsy table, each ME had an assistant taking notes of the findings.

"Here is a chart on the anatomy of our specimen." He passed around a copy for each doctor.

"You're pretty much looking at the physical structure of a typical wolf with the extended snout, but with hands and feet closer to a human. The front paws extended to accommodate claws and the back wide, like a clown's shoe would fit." He hesitated for effect. "There is a tail, however, and rather than the all-fours position, the werewolf walks on its back paws."

The room was buzzing and one of the MEs broke in, "If it's so much like a normal wolf why are we doing the autopsy?"

"Great question, Gerald." He was from California, "The only thing we are interested in, at least speaking for myself, is the nature of what killed the beast. Paranormal mythology has a number of possibilities, but with no trauma to the body, my gut tells me it was the venom from the vampire's bite."

Once again, everyone was talking among themselves and Clovis let the dialogue proceed without interruption. Finally, another doctor spoke up, "So, we aren't going to do any dissections?"

"Contrary, we are going to incise several areas of the animal's body to take small tissue segments to study. The blood has been taken and is already in the lab for analysis." He looked around and saw approval from all his guests. "I have a chart here for ten cuts, one for each of you, which I will attach to the bulletin board next to the autopsy table." He did and they gathered around. The plan had been marked for each section by doctor.

"Ladies and gentlemen, it's time to take up your scalpels and go to work."

Chief McIntyre was in the room with John and Mack, and Clovis made his way over to him. "Not that I'm too lazy to do the work but this will give us objective case studies to analyze, extracted by some of the best pathologist minds in the country."

"When do you think we can look at the results of the blood test and this work?"

"Less than a week, I suspect." And they left the array of doctors to do their work.

*   *   *   *   *

Even though his wife was a felon and a monster, Walter Rogers still wanted to help her. He just hadn't decided yet exactly how to do that. There were several things he could do, but whatever he decided on, it had to prevent Amy from doing any more harm. He didn't even remember how many murders she had committed. But that wasn't the real Amy, it was a creature she was turned into while in the Superstition Mountains.

Rogers was in his office and it was after five o'clock. Most of the staff was gone and there was nothing really keeping him here so he headed to his car. As he started for the elevators, his boss, John Roberts, approached. Riding down alone, Roberts asked him about Amy, and Walter told him, minus the gory details. His boss was asking if there was anything he could do when Walter said, "Need to talk to you about a raise soon." John Roberts looked very anxious.

Walter rarely talked to himself while driving, but today he had a regular conversation and didn't care if other drivers saw him. He contemplated what he might do with or to Amy, considering the circumstances.

And the decision was, he wasn't sure. Maybe he should turn her over to the police if she did come home. That would be iffy since she would certainly react fiercely and possibly take it out on him. She was not the Amy he knew, and he saw no way there was a future for them; maybe he should consider even more drastic measures. He had had

256

ideas but dreaded even thinking about them. He pulled into the driveway, still uncertain.

*   *   *   *   *

Karen Briggs was antsy again, needing blood to keep her going and not sure where to find it. Oh, she knew that hustling some guy would provide the perfect opportunity, but her husband had clamped down on her movements since she got out of jail. And then she didn't have to worry. Her cell phone rang and it was Tony Arcuri reminding her of their agreement involving sex for getting her out of jail. He hadn't really done much, but now she needed him.

"Sure, Tony, are you available now?"

"Hell, yes. Want to come over to my office?"

"Why not? Be there in a half hour."

Karen knocked on his door "Hi Tony," as high spirited as she could.

"Hello beautiful," he countered with a lascivious look. "Ready to go to work?" Equally as crude, she thought.

"I hope you're not planning on doing it on this desk." It was the only piece of furniture in the outer room.

"Nope, nothing but the best for you. Come into my office, Babe, you're gonna be done on Tony's famous couch." She didn't know what it was famous for, but it certainly wasn't for its looks.

They entered together as Arcuri immediately put his hand on Karen's butt and pushed it along with the rest of her to the upholstery-ragged sofa. Then he went back and locked the outer door, followed by the one to his office and started to take off his clothes. She began to remove her blouse and skirt. They were both in their underwear when her eyes began to blaze and the fangs started to protrude, and she turned her head away.

"Tony dear, would you please close the blinds. I like sex better in the dark when everything is a surprise." There would be a surprise but it wouldn't be hers. "Now that's much better," and she went to Arcuri and commenced kissing his neck and right shoulder, using her tongue to please her prey. As she found the right position she sunk her

257

fangs in, lightly releasing her essence of ecstasy. And then she began to draw blood.

But in her effort to gratify her overanxious need for blood, an inexperienced Karen went too far and unknowingly released her toxic liquid into Tony, which immediately gave him a crawly feeling that he didn't understand. The rest was all over within minutes. But in the lovemaking Tony Arcuri was not performing up to his level of expectations and he didn't know why.

Thinking about it later, he hadn't felt like himself since that prick on his shoulder earlier

But Karen had breathed new life into her blood supply; had taken more than normal, not knowing when her next opportunity would present itself. Arcuri sat on the couch as limp as a washrag, feeling very alien. Good, she thought, he wasn't that good a lover anyway.

Karen was on the way home, seriously deliberating over the danger of her attorney knowing her secret. Probably all that would be necessary for him to spill the whole thing would be for some female undercover cop who suspected he might know something offer to hop in the rack with him. The question is whether he would weaken, with the threat that she would reveal the deal he had made with her and Amy. No, better safe than sorry.

SIXTY-ONE

Randy Clovis explained the ten tissue samples taken from the body of the beast and how they were examined to confirm or disprove the DNA results. The blood used had been separated into three different portions, with two used and one held in reserve. The two blood studies were done just to make sure there had been no error. Since this was history in the making, there was no room for a mistake. Both tissue and blood models all arrived at the same results.

"Our combined determination is that the specimen is the mutation between a wolf and a human. Because the chromosomes are all jumbled up, we cannot identify who the human was. We do know that there were forty-six human chromosomes, and seventy-eight from a wolf." He pointed to a chart. "Interestingly, there were three baffling chromosomes that we cannot identify. From my research into supernatural lore, we have ourselves a werewolf."

"You're saying it matches all the other werewolf murders," McIntyre asked.

"Precisely, Ruben, but I cannot tell you it was the same animal."

"And officially, the cause of death was the vampire venom."

"We're still focused on Arnold Barber, and the evidence so far would confirm this," the Chief retorted. "But we still can't locate his wife, so if he's our culprit and she's dead, he probably killed her."

*   *   *   *   *

Lani was on her way to Sedona to see Fatin to conjure the spell. The witch had given Lani general directions to an area adjacent to the vortex where she had a small shack hidden by juniper trees and brush. It was a gravel road to the left, just before reaching the airport. Trashy as her place was, Fatin was tolerated by Sedonans.

Fortunately, Lani had worn her hiking shoes so she was able to negotiate the hillside and rock formations she had to pass in order to reach Fatin. Finally, there it was and not too shabby at all, painted a dull orange with a black door and trim. Before proceeding she took the Tarot Magician's card from her purse and immediately felt more secure.

Lani knocked on the door and heard a voice say, "Please enter my sanctuary, you are welcome, whoever you are."

Lani entered the one room dwelling with only one window, and Fatin was sitting in a plush red velvet chair with an identical one across from her. "Sit there," she said. Once Lani was seated, the old woman closed her eyes and crossed her hands over her heart and launched into an incantation.

It took a few minutes and when it was over, the witch explained that she was imploring the spirits to charm the spell they were about to enter into. She noticed the Magician's card and instructed Lani to hold this over her heart from now until they were finished, no matter what force was attempting to take it away. At that point, she asked for McKenna's thumbnail and checked for the drop of blood. When satisfied, Fatin dropped it into a large metal vessel on the floor.

The old woman lit incense in a container on a miniature table at her right hand and Lani inhaled the fragrance, feeling more serene every minute. There was also a petite bell on the table sitting on an embroidered white napkin. An ornately carved wooden box sat close by, which Lani would find out later held the witch's ingredients for the spell. Finally there were black and white candles with odors she couldn't identify, but which were compatible with the incense.

The witch began by asking Lani, "Why have you come to me today?"

"I wish to rid my loving companion of the curse of the werewolf."

"Are you willing to risk your own life to do so?"

"Yes, I am."

"What is the name of this person?"

"It is Deke McKenna."

"And where is he now?"

"In jail in Phoenix."

"Why is he there?"

"Because he is a werewolf."

"How did he become a werewolf?"

"He was bitten by another werewolf."

"Is he a good person?"

"Yes, he is the best person I know."

"And do you believe you can make him pure again?"

"Yes, I do, with your help."

The old woman pulled the wooden box from the table and placed it in her lap. At the same time, she moved the cauldron closer to her feet and then opened the box. First, she removed a vial of oil and placed three drops of the liquid on the thumbnail with a dropper. Next came a container of powder that she opened, dropping two pinches on the same spot. That was followed by a collection of herbs and the crushed root of dittany bark.

Fatin then lit a sage stick and waved the smoke around the kettle for several minutes, finally dropping it in the pot on top of the other ingredients. It ignited, and Lani gasped as if it she felt the pain of the fire on her but remained focused on the ritual. And then the chanting began in language only the speaker could understand. She continued for several minutes, looking straight at her guest and began to hum in a monotonous tone.

Then she spoke, "Are you ready to lift this curse of your man friend by the name of Deke McKenna?"

"Yes, I am, with your help."

The old woman pointed with one hand to the vat full of her sorcery, directing the other up to the heavens and started another chant.

> "The cauldron is full
> A soul needs a cure
> Reverse this spell
> So he may be pure."

She kept repeating the verse over and over. Lani began to feel a trembling in her body that she could not control but held the Magician's card close to her heart. She felt like she was caught up in vertigo, or was it the vortex? The confusion continued as the sound of wind commenced then got louder and louder while the witch continued the same chant over and over...

> "The cauldron is full
> A soul needs a cure
> Reverse this spell
> So he may be pure."

"The cauldron is full
A soul needs a cure
Reverse this spell
So he may be pure."

"The cauldron is full
A soul needs a cure
Reverse this spell
So he may be pure."

...until Lani thought she would scream...and all of a sudden there was a bright light coming through the window with almost the brilliance of a laser, so she was afraid to look right into it and closed her eyes. Then she began to see primitive images through her eyelids that looked like ancient, larger than life wolves she recognized from Deke's research.

The trembling now escalated to tremors all over her body that made it impossible to sit normally in the chair so she wiggled around attempting to shake off what was happening to her. The creatures continued to dance around behind closed eyes with the light getting brighter to the extent she thought it would burn right through her eyelids. All during this, the witch continued the chant and Lani pressed the Magician's card to her heart.

Suddenly, the light exploded with a cryptic sound that resembled thousands of voices all articulating different incantations, some in foreign tongues. Then she felt an overwhelming tug on the arm holding the Tarot card. With all the strength she had, Lani tried to pull away but it seemed a losing situation. She was an agnostic but prayed hard to repel the force. Just as unexpectedly, it stopped with another bang that returned everything to normal.

At that point the old woman picked up the bell and gently rang it. She bolted back in what looked like a seizure, the bell falling from her hand onto the floor, along with the carved box from her lap with all the ingredients spilling out. There was a thunderous roar that propelled her chair across the floor and up against the wall with a jolt that should have broken Fatin's back. But she abruptly stood up, plucked out both of her eyes, and fell to the floor in a heap.

SIXTY-TWO…

Lani was too stunned to scream or do anything but stand there and look at the carnage that had taken place right before her eyes. She stared at the two orbs that began to move closer to the head of the witch as if they had legs, locating the empty sockets and repositioning. It was then that a murky haze arose from the body like steam, which seemed to envelop it until there was another shattering clap of thunder and the old woman just vaporized. The Magician's card was still over her heart.

With all her nerves at the point of fracturing, Lani slowly got up from the chair and backed off toward the door just in case there were any more surprises. The room remained quiet and the vapors had cleared with only the bell and the box, less its ingredients on the floor. What the hell happened? she asked herself. After curiosity drew her back to where the action had taken place, she felt a calming feeling that maybe everything was okay now.

She called the Sedona police and they knew exactly where the shack was. It took only a few minutes until they were there and questioning Lani about what had happened. She told the detective in charge that her visit to Fatin was associated with the vampire and werewolf deaths in Phoenix, and he checked everything out with Chief McIntyre. His comment was, "We all wondered just when this would happen." Lani was released.

*　*　*　*　*

Deke McKenna was up at his cell bars as the Chief explained Lani's results in Sedona and the fact that she was on her way back to Phoenix and headed straight here. "Is she okay, Ruben?" he asked.

"Says she's fine but boy, does she have a story to tell us."

McKenna drew in a long breath and sat down on his bunk. Color returned to his face and a slight grin crossed his lips.

"What?" McIntyre questioned.

"Oh nothing really, except, I'm beginning to think she enjoys being on the edge. Maybe you should put her to work."

"My guess is she'll be glad to get back to her Tarot card readings and leave the crime solving to you and me. By the way, have you had any urges to do the transformation thing lately?"

"None, but I've been careful not to think about it so that I don't get any involuntary compulsions."

"Lani told me she is also prepared to complete the lifting of the curse on you as soon as she gets back. I have contacted the DA again for permission to transport you to the Superstitions."

* * * * *

As Walter Rogers got out of his car and closed the garage door, he looked over at Amy's car, which had been in its parking place since the last rash of incidents started. She didn't need it anyway, he thought, since she could apparently fly. But turn into a bat? Walking into the living room, Walter decided to sit for a few minutes and think about the future. Without Amy? Maybe I should just let her turn me into a vampire; they're supposed to live forever.

Where was Amy now? he thought. They claimed she had killed the werewolf, so wasn't that something in her favor? He wanted so much to exonerate his wife in this whole mess but knew that would never be possible. According to Chief McIntyre, she, as the vampire, and the werewolf, had been on a mission to kill Arizona politicians.

Walter stood up and started for the kitchen to fix something for dinner, and then decided he would change into some comfortable clothes first. It was dark in the bedroom and he walked straight through to the bathroom where there was a night light burning. And then he turned around, could swear he heard heavy breathing. "Walter, I'm here waiting for you. I need you Walter. You must come to me now, Walter."

He quickly flipped on the light and was startled by the sight of Amy lying in the bed, still in only her bikini bottom. "Jeez, you scared the crap out of me. What're you doing here?" Walter hesitated to move closer. "The last I heard, you wreaked havoc at the Phoenix Zoo and you killed the werewolf they're looking for. Amy, you realize that I have to call the police and tell them you are here."

"Walter I'm your wife and I need your help. Please help me."

265

"You may still be my wife but you're also a vampire and you have killed several people. Anyway, it's only a matter of time until the police check the house for you."

"But Walter, I need your blood. I promise it won't hurt and it won't turn you into a vampire. Just enough to rejuvenate me to my maximum capacity."

He inched over and noticed her eyes were a soft pink and her fangs slightly protruding. What the hell do I do now, he thought.

"Please Walter, I need you. I need blood to complete my mission."

He knew what that meant, that she would kill again, maybe even him. Maybe even right now, so he had to make his move. And then he decided what he had to do.

He lurched back and looked directly at Amy. "No, I won't do it," he said, and that invoked a breathy snarl stronger than before. The eyes turned vicious while still pleading and she contemplated using her mind control to make him do her bidding.

She sat up on the side of the bed and looked like she was coming for him, but then turned on the sex. "You know what I can give you if you help me, Walter. Anything you want," and then she hesitated to see what he would do.

"Okay, but first I have to do something." He turned around, flipping off the light, and walked as fast as he could to his tool shed in the backyard. Inside he soon found what he was looking for and rushed back into the house. Walter knew he had to get this done before he lost his nerve and didn't know how much longer that would take.

Amy wasn't sure, but she felt her husband still loved her, and her human instincts told her that he would help her and that when he returned she would get her needed blood and things would be restored to normal, whatever that was right now.

As he entered the bedroom Amy managed a mewl, and then she saw what he had in his hands from the night light. Her eyes erupted into a red terror that understood the meaning of the garden stake and a rubber mallet Walter was holding. He quickly approached the bed with the vampire instrument of death as his wife began the shapeshifting. As he tried to position it the half demon fought him with new strength.

It was just before the final transformation that Amy realized what Vadoma had meant when she said she knew something about her she would take to her death.

But Walter Rogers was determined while she was still off balance and finally was able to seat the stake just over the left breast. He raised the mallet and let it fall with all the strength he could muster to make sure it pierced her heart. There was a grisly scream, then just gurgling, while blood spurted out in a solid stream that landed on her bare chest. He drove it deeper, just to be sure, producing some serious quivering with blood rippling from her mouth.

After that she was silent with her eyes still wide open, no longer the crimson red they had been. The vampire was dead, or was it just Amy? Was this murder, Walter wondered, or would it be considered justified homicide? He stood next to his wife and actually mourned over what had happened to her and how they had gotten to today's devastation. For once in his life, Walter sobbed. The police would have to be called, but first he would contact Amy's attorney.

SIXTY-THREE...

Bly Gouyen sat on the bunk in her cell considering what her options were. She might be crazy, or at least that is what they had labeled her, but she knew there was one last goal she must achieve. It was the only thing that would bring back honor to herself and her people. She looked at the wall where the symbols of her mission hung. There was an owl, which was the symbol of death and a sorcerer's mask, representing her last connection to the supernatural world.

Gouyen had requested the objects from Chief McIntyre as her religious relics and he had accommodated her in getting them. She didn't know exactly how she would fulfill her objective but the sorcerer told her the opportunity would definitely present itself. Time wasn't important to her now, for she recognized her inevitable fate and all that mattered was the pursuit of the prey. There had been accomplishment; four politicians dead wasn't such a bad record.

But there was still one left, and he was right here in this building, if only she could figure out how to get to him. As she concentrated on the owl and the sorcerer's mask, a vision began to appear on the wall between them that was first a blur then the back of a woman began to take shape. Gouyen fixated on the image but the figure did not turn around. What it did do was throw up its hands, and there was a large eruption from the heavens.

The light was blinding, and the image suddenly dropped both hands toward the ground, and a building in the background began to collapse as if it had been detonated with dynamite. Chunks of concrete flew in all directions in a three-dimensional effect followed by clouds of smoke and other debris. It was so realistic she recoiled on the bed as if she might be hit. And then everything cleared away in an instant, and there was only wall again.

The sergeant had drawn her hand up over her face for protection, lowering it when the vision went away. What was that? she thought, and then realized she had just seen what could be the answer to her problem. It all made sense now; it would be her Armageddon. It would be a special satanic ritual, one that she had uncovered earlier and kept, just in case. At that moment, an officer delivered her meal through the bars.

Lani was sitting in one of the interrogation rooms with Chief McIntyre and Deke McKenna. "I'm still not convinced," McKenna spoke up first, "there's just too much that can go wrong. I don't like it."

McIntyre spoke right up, "Do you want to talk to Lani like this the rest of your life?" he gestured to the hardware he was wearing.

"Okay, now that we understand each other, let's get on with the nuts and bolts of how this all will come down," Lani retorted.

"Give me just a minute," the Chief said, and he went out the door and came back with detectives John and Mac. "They will direct the support team for your protection in the Superstitions under my command. Now we can go ahead."

"There will be a full moon tomorrow night, and we must be situated at Weavers Needle in the mountains ready to go no later than nine PM," Lani said, looking at a chart in front of her on the table, "How many men do you plan to use, Ruben?"

"John and Mack plus a swat team of ten officers."

"By the way, they mustn't form a complete circle around Deke and me. That would prevent the spirits from entering and participating in the ritual. Just make sure there are four openings."

Then she went into a brief explanation of what the ceremony would consist of. "The final objective is to confront McKenna with my Magician's Tarot card, and he must face it head-on. Then he must try to turn himself into a werewolf."

Mack said, "And what if the whole thing doesn't work and he actually becomes the creature?"

All eyes were on Lani who chose her words very carefully. "Since this is our only option left, it must be up to Deke what to do if it doesn't work. Or maybe that decision is in the hands of Chief McIntyre."

The group was strained at this point with everyone's eyes on McKenna. He spoke, "I'll make it easy for Ruben, you must use whatever means you have to kill me."

"What are those options?" the Chief asked Lani.

"Got any silver bullets on you?" No one even smiled.

"You're serious about this?" he responded.

"Yes, completely."

"Okay, that means we have to cast a supply of silver bullets for tomorrow. John, Mack, could you get started on that right away, unless Lani has more for you." A shake of her head indicated no. "We have our strategy planned to surround the two of you, and we'll have one more session tomorrow before heading for the Superstitions."

Lani's head dropped and the dread on her face was obvious, but inside she knew she had to stay strong for the task she had to complete.

Deke finally broke the silence, "Hey, do we have confidence in Lani or not? You two look like you're planning to meet the end of the world."

McIntyre smiled, "Hell yes we do, so what are we worried about?"

Lani was buoyed somewhat, but still carried baggage that she was afraid to share with the others, especially McKenna. Maybe she never would.

*　*　*　*　*

Karen contemplated how to get rid of Tony Arcuri. She could rest a little easier now that Amy had established herself as the vampire of record and no one but Arcuri knew of Karen's circumstances. Yes, Tony could be her nemesis but she wasn't about to let that happen. It all came down to how to kill the man without being caught, something she hadn't figured out yet. She could shoot him using Robert's gun but that would eventually lead back to her.

She could always hire a hit man with the same come-on she used with Arcuri, but she would have to kill him too. Maybe she would just use a disguise. That was it, she thought, a wig, some special makeup, and clothes she hadn't worn in years. Tell Tony when she got to his office it was a cover up to fool the media that had been harassing her. She could park a couple of blocks away and walk to his building and no one would know.

Amy would take the blame since she was still on the loose, probably at the end of her rope anyway. The cops knew of her connection with Arcuri, and because she had been judged innocent, Karen thought, there's no way they could pin it on her. Had she just come up with the perfect murder? She wouldn't call Tony and leave tracks, just show up, and then she searched her closet for the right clothes. Pretty soon she would be able to sleep again.

Arcuri was surprised that now she was standing in his office. Karen explained the way she was dressed but that she needed him, and the disguise was just in case. They both were in the process of disrobing when there was a knock on the outer-office door. He looked at his watch and said, "Oh shit, it's my appointment I forgot all about. Give me a minute and I'll be right back." He hurried to the door, still nude, and asked, "Who is it?"

"Why it's Elizabeth Taylor, of course, who the hell do you think it is Tony, it's Gloria? What's going on in there?"

"Hon, I'm in a very important conference right now, could you come back in an hour?"

"Yeah, but why can't you even open the door?"

"Because my clients don't want to be identified so please find a coffee shop and give me at least an hour."

"Okay, but you're going to have to make up for this."

"I will, I will, see you later," then he came back to Karen sitting on the couch. "Just a woman I'm working with on her case," he said. "Now, where were we?"

She got up from the couch and said, "No way am I going to have sex with you with another one of your girlfriends hanging around until we are through." She put her clothes back on.

"Don't worry, she's gone and won't bother us."

"Nothing doing. We can do it another time." Karen was anxious but couldn't afford a slip up.

She thought there was a red tint in his eyes as he said, "You're not backing out of our deal, are you?"

"No, Tony, we just have to be careful. You know that. Today's just not the right time." She finished dressing and promised to call him soon. But on the way home she couldn't get over that crimson tinge in his eyes.

SIXTY-FOUR...

Walter Rogers called Jerry Monaghan and told him what he had just done, asking him if he would represent him if necessary. Monaghan had told him he didn't want anything to do with it but recommended another attorney. Rogers tried him, but he was out of the office. He decided he'd better call the police. "Police headquarters, Desk Sergeant Johnson speaking."

"This is Walter Rogers speaking, husband of Amy Rogers, the vampire you're looking for. Please let me speak with Chief McIntyre."

"One moment, Mr. Rogers," and the sergeant headed for McIntyre's office and knocked on the door.

"Come in," and he stuck his head in the door and gave the message.

"Mr. Rogers, sorry but I still don't have anything to report."

"No, but I do. I just killed my wife."

After a hesitation, "Are you okay?" he asked.

"I'm fine but you'd better send someone out right away. She's lying in our bed with a stake in her heart."

"I'll be right there with some men. Don't go anywhere or make any phone calls." The Chief called for John and Mack, and they were on their way.

At the house they knocked on the door and Walter Rogers answered right away. McIntyre had called for Lani to meet him here and she was also pulling up. "Mr. Rogers, I'm not going to handcuff you but please stay within our sight until we decide what to do." He nodded, with a bleak look on his face. "Where is the bedroom?" He pointed, and the five of them made their way in.

To say it was a ghastly scene would be accurate but not because of the blood and gore, which were plentiful, but just the stark realization of the destruction of a once very beautiful woman. She lay there, a stake in her heart with a small pool of blood around it, but the tragedy was in her wasted body blanched of much of its color, lips turned a bluish gray, a terrible contorted look on her face reflecting her violent demise. Her eyes were still open.

Mack had gone back to the front door to wait for the Medical Examiner and now directed Randy Clovis into the bedroom. As he viewed the body he wore the same clinical look he always displayed when tending to corpses. "Mr. Rogers, how did you know where to place the stake?" Clovis asked.

"I looked it up online," he answered.

"Okay folks, we need room here to do our job, so everyone is excused but my staff."

"Uh, Randy, you do know not to pull the stake out, right?" Lani asked.

"I do, but thanks for reminding me," was the answer, with a sheepish grin on his face.

They reassembled in the living room and the Chief motioned for all to sit down. He looked at Rogers, "I'm going to have to take you in and hold you until I get some word from the District Attorney on how to handle this. What exactly was your wife when you put the stake in, vampire or human?"

"All I can tell you is that her eyes were turning a reddish color, her fangs were growing and she was hissing."

"How does that jibe with your supernatural experience, Lani?"

"Assuming Mr. Rogers' description is accurate, she was at least in transition to a vampire status."

"Any questions, guys?" referring to John and Mack.

John said, "How long have you known your wife was a vampire?"

"For sure, not until today."

"But you suspected?"

"I just knew something was wrong about her and there were some weird things going on. But I didn't know what. Amy was independent and I let her have her space."

"You guys take Mr. Rogers in and book him. Sir, they'll have to handcuff you, but you can cover it with your jacket. Lani, could I bum a ride to the DA's office and have you join me to talk to him?"

"Of course," and after McIntyre checked with the ME, they all left.

* * * * *

They were sitting in the DA's office waiting for Donald Acker when the door opened and he walked in with two assistant DAs. "Ruben, what is this mess you brought me?"

"At least we solved all the cases for you. All you have to do is decide what to do with Amy Rogers' husband. As far as I'm concerned, he did us a favor, Don." Acker was looking over his glasses at the Chief. "It's up to you, but from what we know, he killed a vampire, not a human being."

"I've been looking at the Arizona statutes and there is nothing pertinent to vampires or werewolves. I can possibly let him out on parole with justifiable homicide. Depends on the media."

"You mean you're going to base this man's future on what the news people say? Think that's a big mistake, Don. Bound to backfire."

There was a look of defeat on Acker's face. Damned if he did, damned if he didn't. "We still have one more hurdle to go with Deke McKenna. You've been right so far, Ruben, I'm releasing him but don't want him leaving the area."

The meeting was over, but the DA's comment reminded Lani of what they had to do next.

Back in Chief McIntyre's office, they discussed the quest to rid Deke McKenna of the werewolf curse. The meeting included the Chief, John and Mack, Lani and McKenna. She had checked every source available, and tomorrow was definitely scheduled for a full moon, the main requirement for the ritual. "What time do we head for the Superstitions?" McIntyre asked her.

"The full moon rises at 9:26 PM and we should be established in our camp by then. There's no specific time required but I think we all want to get it over with, especially you, Hon," referring to Deke.

"I want to do it the safest way for you," he responded.

And then the chief spread a map of Weavers Needle on the table and pointed out the positioning of the extra officers for all to see. "These guys are volunteers and have been thoroughly briefed on their

275

responsibilities, including the fact that something could go wrong. But since we don't know exactly what that might be, I had McKenna fill them in on the paranormal in general." He looked at Lani, "Where will you and Deke be, since that determines where John, Mack and myself are?"

"Have to place ourselves as close to the Needle as possible without cutting off the view of the moon. I figure somewhere around here," pointing to the spot.

"Okay, John will be here, Mack there," pointing to the locations. "I'll be right behind McKenna so I can see your face. How does that sound?"

"Looks good to me, Ruben." Lani sounded confident but everyone noticed the anxious look on her face.

"Something bothering you, Hon?" Deke asked.

"Only that we do this perfect," was her reply.

"Fine, looks like it's a go. We'll meet here at six tomorrow evening," McIntyre said, and the meeting was over.

Walter Rogers was reliving the driving of that stake when…

"Mr. Rogers," and he was jerked out of his thoughts, "can I talk to you for a moment?" Chief McIntyre was asking.

"Sure, I'm not going anywhere."

"Well, maybe you are if we can just iron out some particulars."

"Whatever you need to get me out of here, you've got it."

"I have some papers here you will need to sign regarding the disposition of your wife's body. In effect, Mr. Rogers, you are turning over the ownership of the remains of Amy Rogers to the city of Phoenix."

Walter Rogers was surprised but not shocked since this was such a weird case anyway. "Does that mean she can never be interred?"

"I'm afraid so, at least until we can complete further investigations into the issue."

"I'm sure that's best. I'll sign the release." A jailer opened the cell and the Chief went in with the papers. "After these are processed and I get the OK from the DA, you'll be a free man."

"Thanks, Chief McIntyre, I know you must have had something to do with getting me out of here."

"Just trying to do what's right, Mr. Rogers. But please keep in touch, and you must not leave the area."

"Don't worry, we probably haven't seen the last of this anyway."

"Why do you say that? Sounds like you know something we don't."

"No, nothing concrete. Just a feeling I have."

SIXTY-FIVE...

Tony's girlfriend had dropped him because of the incident in his office, and at the bar he frequented the girls had shied away from him recently for some reason he couldn't understand. There was always Karen for an office "quickie." He'd call Karen now.

After Arcuri had talked to her, it lifted his spirits somewhat when hearing her enthusiasm to see him. And it was also encouraging that she had agreed to do it at his condo in Scottsdale and maybe he could talk her into staying over. It was set for this afternoon and he planned to leave early to stock up on booze and something to nibble on. Karen said she drank vodka and seven, so he bought some cheap booze and 7-UP.

Tony lived in South Scottsdale, where he could afford his condo and still say he lived in Scottsdale. There was a market close by where he had shopped and now he was in his place unloading the plastic bags. He had an almost empty bottle of Absolut vodka someone had given him several years ago. He opened the cheap brand he had just purchased and poured it in with the expensive stuff. Now that should impress Karen Briggs.

The doorbell rang and he almost knocked over the bottle of vodka. Opening the door, Arcuri was surprised to see Karen Briggs dressed in similar clothes as the last time at his office and had on the same wig and dark glasses. "Come in, come in, still going incognito I see."

"Yep, can't be too careful," she responded and moved through the doorway. She was still taking great care to keep Arcuri's death from being connected to her. The place was furnished with early Salvation Army but somehow he had made it look comfortable. She stood and waited for Tony to fix two drinks while deliberating over how to achieve her mission. He brought them and they sat on the sofa, another relic like the one in his office.

"Here's to great sex forever," he toasted. Karen touched his glass and they both took a swallow. They quickly finished their cocktails and began to undress. "Let's have another," Tony said, and headed for the bar, naked, not waiting for an answer. But she wasn't

278

resisting since this would be his last drink. With that in mind, it was time to set her plan in motion as her eyes began to shift to pink.

Arcuri sat down beside Karen, half undressed, and she noticed his eyes were shaded a blush color, probably just hungover. Karen sipped her drink and anticipated the next move, when a hand started moving up her leg toward her crotch, and she knew it was time for action. In an instant her eyes blazed red and a set of fangs were jutting into position as a snarl caught Tony completely off guard. And then he was reminded this woman was a vampire.

At that moment a strange thing happened to Arcuri, when he felt enormous pain in his gums and knew something was happening in his mouth. As he looked at Karen, she had sprouted vicious looking canines and her eyes were glowing a robust cardinal color as she lunged at Tony, zeroing in on his left shoulder. The transformation in his body made him shudder and tremble for a moment. And, although he didn't completely understand, he was beginning to realize his new prowess and liked what he felt.

He grabbed her around the head as she closed in and ripped off a large portion of her scalp, exposing the skull, then threw her back against the sofa. Undaunted, she charged at him again and managed to chew off most of the right cheek from the nose down to the chin. Both mouths were weeping blood, Karen looking grotesque with her loose hair flopping around and the side of Arcuri's face unmasked and gaping.

Neither of the beasts realized their full power as neophytes, but being the most experienced of the two, Karen concentrated on her speed and strength and ran at Arcuri, surprising him as she grabbed his head by both hands and easily snapped it off. He was flailing around reaching for the body part that was no longer there. She threw the head at the body and looked pleased as she began to tend to her head wound that had begun to heal.

When trying to re-position the matted hair in front of the bathroom mirror, there was a shriek behind her and she turned to see Tony Arcuri…with a head.

Karen hissed and rushed at Arcuri, hitting him with an impact that forced him up against the wall, stunned, while she used her canines to scoop a large chunk of flesh out of his chest accompanied by vessels, muscle and a mass of bloody gore. He slapped his hands against the wall and pushed away, barreling at his foe and grabbing her arm and swinging her around. Tony stuck two fingers in her mouth and twisted her head around with a violent jerk to rend her vertebrae.

She fell to the floor and Arcuri thought he had at least gravely injured Karen, so he went to the kitchen to get a knife and finish the job. Yanking her husband's gun from her purse, she aimed it at him and emptied the clip as he walked back in. He dropped, but she didn't know if it would kill him.

The walls, the couch, the floor were all splashed with blood, turning the room into a canvas of brutality. Karen shuddered in confusion over what to do as she kept an eye on Arcuri. Then there was a knock on the door, and a female said, "This is the condo manager. Someone reported gunshots from this unit."

Moving closer to the door, she said, "Everything's okay, don't…" and before she could get the word 'worry' out, Tony had wedged an eight-inch kitchen knife in her back. Karen fell against the door as the manager continued pounding on the door, demanding to be let in.

Arcuri shoved her aside with the blade still in her back and cracked the door, forgetting the monstrous injury to his face. The woman took one look and screamed as she fled away from the door, crying for help.

Tony shut the door and touched the part of his face that had horrified the woman. All he could feel was bone and mushy flesh, which prompted him to run to the bathroom mirror.

After he was gone, Karen struggled on the floor to reach the knife in her back. Finally, she was able to wedge it between a table and a chair; she moved forward until it fell to the floor. And without warning it came to her, like mental telepathy from the unknown; she could feel it and now she knew what to do.

Arcuri came raging out of the bathroom screaming, "I'll kill you for doing this to me;" Tony wasn't a mature enough vampire yet to heal faster. But it wasn't clear how he planned to kill her, since there was no weapon in his hand and he wasn't yet aware of his powers.

Still at the front door, Karen stood and looked right into Tony's eyes as she raised her right arm and pointed to him. "Die you son of a bitch," she said, as a massive ball of fire hit him and ricocheted around the room, igniting all the walls, cheap furniture and drapes. It was an inferno within seconds and as Karen stood there in hysterical laughter watching Arcuri cringing in the holocaust, she burst into flames while continuing the diabolical cackling.

The manager was standing in front of the condo with the police while the fire department extinguished the blaze and made sure it didn't move to other units. Tony Arcuri's condo was a complete loss, even this early that was obvious, when the fire chief said it was one of the hottest and fastest blazes they had ever fought. There would, of course, be an investigation. But something that was yet to be discovered…they would find no distinguishable ignition source for the fire.

SIXTY-SIX...

The police were still at Tony Arcuri's condo, or rather what was left of it, waiting for the firemen to decide when the Medical Examiner could get in. They had been able to talk to the first-in firefighters, who indicated there were at least two severely burned bodies in the condo remains. Since there were still hot spots, it would be a while before the ME could enter. In the meantime, the two officers radioed headquarters for a check on who owned the unit.

Within minutes word came back that the condo was owned by a Tony Arcuri, an attorney who was single and living there alone. The cop making the check wasn't sitting far from the two detectives John and Mack, and when he repeated the name Tony Arcuri, Mack immediately went over and asked him what was going on. "The guy's house was just burned to the ground with two people in the fire. No description yet, ME can't get in."

Mack grabbed John and they headed for McIntyre's office. They all headed for South Scottsdale.

The first officer on the scene said, "Still too hot to go in but the ME is standing by. I told Doctor Clovis the place was owned by Arcuri, so he's placing a priority on it."

"Okay, Tony Arcuri was representing Karen Briggs, so we need to learn her whereabouts right now. Mack, send a squad car to her house." McIntyre looked at John, "You get on the phone and call her husband. If they tell you he's busy or in a meeting you tell them to get him on the phone immediately or I'll send officers after him." They both went to their tasks.

The squad car reported back within twenty minutes that no one was answering the door, should they force their way in? By then John had talked to Robert Briggs who knew nothing about where Karen was or was supposed to be. He was, however, able to tell them the next-door neighbor had a key to the house, and he called so she would release it to the officers. After a thorough search, there was no Karen Briggs, nor was her car in the garage.

Then McIntyre dispatched the two officers at the scene and two more they called in to do a check of cars parked on the street in a block

282

radius. The four returned with twenty-eight numbers. Mack took the plate digits to the patrol car and ran them through the computer. Bingo, Karen Briggs.

"Chief, it was Karen Briggs' car parked a block away on a side street. I called in an unmarked to watch it."

"Good work, guys. The other remains in the condo are probably hers. The question is why?"

*　*　*　*　*

It was early the next morning, day of the full moon, and McIntyre was at the fire and crime scene with the Medical Examiner, Randy Clovis. "We've got dentistry from both of them and some jewelry from one of the bodies that could be identified," the ME offered.

"Let's start with the one having the jewelry. Can you determine if it's male or female?"

"It included a watch and bracelets, and my crew agrees they are something a woman would wear."

"Okay, can we get them off the body and check the dentures as soon as possible? We'll run the jewelry by the husband, although he probably has no idea what she wore, and ask him who their dentist is. How long before I can have it?"

"Five minutes, tops," and he sent one of his assistants in to get the items.

There was a guy walking around in civilian clothes and McIntyre asked him who he was.

"I'm the fire inspector." He looked perturbed.

The Chief introduced himself and asked if he had any idea what started the fire.

"Beats the hell out of me, and that's my professional and off the cuff answer. Nothing shows up, and I have left nothing uncovered in that shell."

He continued. "Although I can't identify an ignition origination, I can tell you that whatever it was, it was gigantic."

"So what we have to go with now is that the source is unknown?" McIntyre was getting frustrated.

"That's it, Chief. Wish I could help more, but anything that comes up you'll be the first to know."

They did their cordialities and McIntyre headed for his squad car. Inside he said out loud, "What was it McKenna told us about vampires and pyrokenesis?"

Back at police headquarters, the chief picked up the phone and dialed Robert Briggs. "Mr. Briggs' office, this is Lauren."

This is Chief McIntyre, Phoenix police, please let me speak with Mr. Briggs."

"He's in a meeting right..."

"You get him out of his meeting, now, and on this phone within fifteen seconds." He heard the phone drop and the sound of movement.

It was exactly twelve seconds, "Chief, this was a very..."

"Shut up, you idiot. I have news about your wife's possible death. What kind of bottom-feeder are you?" Then he told Briggs to be at the police station within the hour to identify the jewelry. "Who is your dentist?"

Briggs told him but still didn't sound like a man who may have lost his wife.

"Get to my office in a half hour, or else."

It only took Briggs seconds to identify what was left of a silver watch he had given his wife. "Yes, that's my wife's; I don't know about the jewelry." He looked up with little emotion.

"Briggs, you are the most coldhearted bastard I have ever run into. Now if dentures prove the remains are Karen Briggs, the deceased will be held until this investigation is over. Any questions?"

"No." The man still showed a minimum of concern.

"Get out of my office," and Robert Briggs was on his way.

The Chief was still shaking his head when Lani answered her phone. "How soon can you get over here?" he asked.

"Long as it takes me to get there," she answered.

When Lani showed up McIntyre was in the same interrogation room again with John, Mack and Deke McKenna. "Gotta clarify this Karen Briggs incident before we head for the Superstitions, just in case there's a connection." He covered the fire and deaths of Briggs and Tony Arcuri, including the fact that there had been positive identification on both remains.

He continued, "Deke, I've talked to the fire inspector again—by the way, he called in an expert from Arizona Department of Public safety who confirmed his findings—and he says there is definitely no discernible ignition source."

McKenna asked, "Didn't you say the fire was one of very high intensity?"

"Yes, the fire inspector characterized the ignition source as 'gigantic.'"

Deke spoke immediately, "It was a pyrokinetic force generated by a vampire, most likely Karen Briggs, since there is no background to suggest Tony Arcuri had been transformed." He looked directly at McIntyre, "When you do an autopsy on Briggs, her DNA will reveal the elements of the chromosome makeup of vampirism."

John chimed in, "But she was cleared already."

"Not of participating in the supernatural, she was cleared of a murder charge. Big difference."

It was Mack's turn, "But I don't understand why she did this to Arcuri. He was her attorney and the one who got her freed."

"That's something we may never know," offered Lani. "Assuming Karen Briggs was a vampire, you remember McKenna's comments; sometimes these hybrids evolve completely out of control."

"The fact that her car was parked over a block away from Arcuri's home tells me that she didn't want anyone to know that she had been there," the Chief said. "It would also suggest that she might have been there to do him harm. Like Lani said, we may never know. It's time to head for the Superstitions. John and Mack, get your team ready, I'll take care of Deke. Lani, you ready?"

"Ready, Ruben, brought everything with me."

285

"Good. You, McKenna and I will ride together. The rest have their transportation. First, I have called a press conference in five minutes to bring the media up to date."

SIXTY-SEVEN...

Everyone was assembled in the Superstition Mountains. Deke McKenna, minus handcuffs and leg irons, but under heavy surveillance by the officers with their AR-15s loaded with silver bullets. They were under strict orders not to shoot unless given the command by Chief McIntyre. His men were lined up on four sides of Lani and Deke with breaks at each corner. The two stood looking at each other, ready to do battle with the spirits.

It was nine PM, just before a full moon, and the time was near. Lani had her Magician's Tarot card, which she held facing her chest. You could see Weavers Needle silhouetted in front of the white orb of night. The time was near, with everyone involved strained to the limit, ready for the whole thing to get under way. The two principals were situated where they could both see the moon. Deke was ready, Lani was ready, and then something happened.

There was a thunderous roar, and the sky lit up, revealing both white and black clouds with images of devils, gargoyles, witches and warlocks, ogres, and various other monstrosities. The police immediately aimed their assault weapons at the heavens while the Chief screamed, "Hold your fire." Lani and Deke cowered, as there was a rash of lightning strikes perfectly aimed to take out most of McIntyre's men at once.

The Chief, his two detectives and the two paranormal participants were unhurt, but stunned, so that Lani and McKenna didn't know what to do next and somehow the Magician's card was dropped in the assault. They didn't know whether to take cover or what, for the lightning was still striking all around them as if warning they shouldn't proceed with the ritual. The demons were still up above, and suddenly they began to descend.

The five formed a circle, and as they huddled together, Mack saw the Magician's card on the ground and quickly scooped it up and handed it to its owner. She had a cautious look on her face as she stared at the card, and then she was roused by something that prompted her to step out of the circle.

"What the hell are you doing?" Deke shouted, as he went toward her.

"Stay where you are McKenna, I know what I'm doing." He hesitated.

They were on the ground now surrounding the five, moving in harmony to close in on the prey, when the first archfiend charged at Lani. Instead of retreating, she rushed right at the invader and when she was within a couple feet, flashed the Magician's card in its face. There was another clap of thunder accompanied by a fire bolt that lit up the whole area as the beast was extinguished in flames.

The remaining demons recoiled at what happened to one of their own, but it was only momentary, when another malignant spirit attacked and once again Lani was on the defensive. She waited for the right moment and then flashed the Tarot card at her antagonist just as it was in her face, and the former incident repeated itself with the complete destruction of the incubus. Lani was breathing heavily and glancing wildly in all directions, expecting another onslaught.

At that moment, the satanic apparitions began to swirl in a pattern that came together right over Lani's head. At first there was a pause as if they planned to attempt more carnage, but then the churning astral bodies zoomed skyward with an ear-splitting shriek and eventually disappeared. Everyone looked around to make sure the predators had gone. Deke rushed out and caught Lani in his arms as she collapsed in exhaustion.

"That's it," he said, "no one else is going to die. Just shoot me now with one of the silver bullets and let's get this over with."

Lani was regaining consciousness and he re-directed his attention to her. "You okay?"

"Yeah, fine, the intensity of it all just takes a lot out of me." Now let's get back to the ritual."

"No way," McKenna said, but before he could continue...

"Don't argue with me, Deke, would you rather spend the rest of your life behind bars or take a silver bullet in the heart? Hell no, and you know it, so just cooperate with me and we'll get this done."

By now McIntyre and the two detectives had gone to check on the officers that had fallen and when they returned to where Lani and

McKenna stood, all three faces were crestfallen and there were tears in everyone's eyes. "This didn't have to be," Deke said, "it could have been avoided."

"Look," the Chief was admonishing him now, "these men realized what they signed on for, and all of them volunteered for this job. We'll miss them greatly, but you can't back out now on what they all died for."

McKenna was taken aback but promptly realized the truth in what Ruben had said and looked at Lani, "Okay, whenever you're ready."

They returned to the ceremonial spot, and this time McIntyre was on one side and the detectives on the other. Lani clutched the Magician's card over her heart in her right hand and placed her left hand on Deke's right shoulder. She looked straight into his eyes and started the special chant given her by Fatin, the Sedona Witch Priestess:

"With Magician's Card and all its verse
I turn around this wicked curse.
As these words of mine are spoken
Let this evil spell be broken."

His eyes began to take on a yellow cast and she knew she must hurry. Lani challenged him saying, "If you can, become the werewolf beast you have come to abhor...do it now McKenna, do it now."

His eyes were glowing yellow now and canines were beginning to show. Thick hair sprouted on his arms and face and around the portion of his neck they could see with his facial features contorting to the look of a...wolf. The Chief and his men took out their weapons and pointed them right at Deke but Lani waved them down. "It's time McKenna, if you choose to remain in the other world of the paranormals. Do it now. Become the wolf you hate."

His clothing exploded as the animal began to break through and grow while the shoes split to allow an expanded paw to emerge. Fingernails were now claws, and for the first time there was a snarl from the creature that brought up the guns again, with Lani once again rejecting their moves. "Hear me, McKenna," and she recited the chant once more...

"With Magician's Card and all its verse
I turn around this wicked curse.
As these words of mine are spoken
Let this evil spell be broken."

Unexpectedly, Weavers Needle gave rise to a great white light that glowed in the form of a bubble, hovering just off the ground. It moved toward the five, and the three brandished their weapons again, but Lani cried out, "give it room, let it in." They moved aside as the apparition maneuvered until it encircled Deke McKenna as he continued his transformation. The brightness grew even more brilliant as the mass began to revolve, accelerating by the second.

The four stood in awe of what was going on, knowing that Deke was inside; only Lani having any idea of what the outcome might be. The specter was now whirling at such speed that it seemed to be throwing off sparks of light that landed all around the area. The two detectives checked to see if the sparks left any lingering effects, when there was an enormous implosion of the mass. As the circle of light raced upward, McKenna was ejected and thrown to the ground.

Lani rushed over and cradled his head in her arms. His clothes were in tatters and his shoes split open to reveal his feet. He looked up at her with the realization that the spell had worked. No more of those urges he couldn't control or understand. She looked at him and said, "We did it, Hon," and he shook his head in agreement. And then as if on cue, the presence, still aglow, seemed suspended over Weavers Needle briefly and then it vanished.

* * * * *

The next day McIntyre had explained everything to Donald Acker, the Maricopa County District Attorney. There was a pause and then Ackerman spoke, "Ruben, I hope this doesn't come back to haunt us," then realizing what he had just said. "Let the man go, but at least watch him closely for a while." He hung up.

McIntyre put down the phone and looked at Deke, "You're free," which drew a cry of relief from Lani and looks of approval from

John and Mack. "We'll get you two out of here to your place in an unmarked while I'm holding a press conference."

McKenna was mellowing already as he lay back on the seat and looked at Lani. She was equally relaxed as she nuzzled into his shoulder and said, "There for a while I wasn't sure we would ever get back to talk about our future. Still want me to hang around?"

"Are you kidding? I've never been more sure than I am right now."

"What's the first thing you think we should do?" she asked.

"Ever had sex with a werewolf?" was his reply.

SIXTY-EIGHT…

The three of them were sitting at an outside table of Deke McKenna's favorite coffee shop in Cave Creek. McIntyre looked first at Lani, then Deke, and said, "Here's to the successful end of the most bizarre case I have ever dealt with." They clicked cups and each took a sip, with only Lani expressing a look of apprehension bordering on premonition. She wasn't even sure what the feeling was all about and it did not go unnoticed.

"What's the matter, Hon?" Deke said, "You look doubtful."

"Don't know, just a gnawing feeling I've had since we got back from the Superstitions. Probably nothing, don't let me dampen the spirits."

Both McKenna and McIntyre knew Lani's dubiousness was not to be ignored but collectively hoped this time it was just left over from the trauma in the mountains. The Chief spoke next.

"Deke, since our two major adversaries are dead, as well as those they begat, what happened to the Armageddon Lani anticipated?"

"The only explanation I can come up with is the immaturity of the creatures in our scenario. They didn't have time to develop. The beasts weren't aware of the fullest extent of their powers. Even Amy Rogers, although she was maturing at a much faster rate than the others."

"Not to belabor this, but are we certain that the stake in Amy Rogers is going to remain there, secure, and no one will try to remove it?" Lani asked.

"As far as I know," replied the Chief, "but will check with Randy Clovis again."

* * * * *

Bly Gouyen sat quietly in her cell contemplating her final action to save face in the Apache nation. It wasn't ritually pure, because it would be necessary to deviate from ancestral ceremonials and consult the devil to complete her mission. But was that wrong, she thought; would her forebears look at this with aversion and revulsion? No matter.

She would proceed, regardless. All that was necessary now was to have the right people here in the building.

Chief McIntyre was in his office on the phone talking to Donald Acker, the Maricopa County District Attorney, about Bly Gouyen. The action had been so concentrated lately he hadn't pursued her fate and still was not having much luck. The Chief was looking for some degree of leniency and Acker was having none of it. "I know where you're coming from, Donald, but she's been such a good cop all these years."

"Doesn't make up for what she did, Ruben. And you know we'd be run out of town on a rail if we give her any kind of charity. Absolutely not."

Succumbing to reality, the Chief decided that he couldn't put this off any longer. He called Deke and asked him to contact Lani, and would both of them like to help in the prosecutorial plans for Bly Gouyen? He agreed, assuring McIntyre that Lani would also; then, the Chief called in detectives John and Mack.

At last the stage was set.

The jail grapevine was swift and Bly Gouyen knew exactly when her prey were assembled in McIntyre's office. First, she focused on the owl of death, then the sorcerer's mask that gave her the power for her ritual. She raised her head and began the chant.

"Before an almighty God Satan including all Demons of Hell, I, Bly Gouyen, renounce any prior loyalty.

I renounce the Christian God Jehova, I renounce his son Jesus Christ, I renounce his holy spirit.

I affirm Satan as my one and only God, and to honor him absolutely.

I request in return, his unyielding support in the carrying out of my aspirations."

She waited, still staring upward, when a vision appeared, first blinding her then becoming clear so that she could recognize what the image was. It was the Phoenix Headquarters building, and at that moment she raised her hands in the air. The blinding light returned, she closed her eyes and began another incantation.

"Angel of darkness, I call upon you,
Destroy this building and all those within.
Leave nothing in place nor soul endure,
Let pain and suffering abound to be sure."

She waited then chanted it one more time.

"Angel of darkness, I call upon you,
Destroy this building and all those within.
Leave nothing in place nor soul endure,
Let pain and suffering abound to be sure."

And then she lowered her arms commandingly and opened her eyes. At first there was a haunting silence followed by an eerie wailing sound with muffled moaning in the background that grew louder. Suddenly there was a shrill blood-curdling scream, and a figure in black appeared between the owl and the sorcerer's mask. It had horns, pointed ears, wings that were bright red and a tail with a spear on the end. Satan's eyes exploded with evil.

The five were gathered in the records room now to help determine how Sergeant Bly Gouyen should be charged. McKenna and Lani were there for their usual input of the paranormal impact on this case. John and Mack were offering their notes to the discussion. "Chief, are we even sure how many counts of murder we can charge Bly with?" John asked.

"No, but we can move ahead with the deaths we are sure she is responsible for," and he looked up as there was a creaking sound overhead and the ceiling began to crack.

Police Headquarters was a four-story building, and it couldn't have been more perfect if there had been a controlled demolition explosion by experts. People walking outside on West Washington

Street scrambled out into traffic that had stopped when seeing the building fall right before their eyes. It started imploding from the middle, moving to the outer walls, with all the debris falling inward. The dust cloud billowed upward as if an atomic bomb had exploded.

Within a matter of minutes, emergency vehicles were converging on the devastation. The Fire Department was in charge, since most of the police infrastructure had been destroyed. The Fire Chief took command and ordered a tactical team to start surveying the wreckage for possible survivors and ways to enter the rubble. From the looks of the huge pile of concrete and steel, it was unlikely anyone could be alive in these ruins.

"What the hell's happening?" Mark bellowed, as a thunderous roar could be heard from above.

Everything went dark and emergency lights quickly flashed on. McIntyre looked up and saw the ceiling beginning to buckle and hollered, "This way," pointing to a metal sliding door on the east side of the room. He punched a code in and it slid open just in time for the group to charge in as the overhead in the room came crashing down. "Faster, faster," he urged them into the tunnel for safety. With emergency lights here too, they could see the chaos behind them.

The passage ended several hundred feet away from the building in steps leading up to a squatty brick building that opened onto the lot next to what used to be the Phoenix Police Department building. Now only destruction, as the five of them suddenly realized that they were the only ones who could have possibly survived the blast. Deke said, "What in God's name did this?"

John said, "That tunnel saved our lives. What was it there for, Chief?"

"Just that," was the reply, "it was built in case there was a terrorist attack. Guess you might call this something like that."

"No Ruben," Lani spoke up, "it was not a terrorist attack. It was the blackest of Magick. Look at the dust cloud over the devastation."

There was an image hovering in the haze of Satan with a scythe in its hand covered with blood and Bly Gouyen worshipping at its feet.

They were all stunned, but it was clear now, at least to these survivors, just what happened. It would be learned later that no one else had seen the vision but the five.

*　*　*　*　*

"Did you hear what happened at police headquarters?" an orderly came rushing into the morgue body storage area of Phoenix Police forensics.

"No, we've been here most of the day, what?"

The intruder gave them an explanation of what he knew and told them orders were to evacuate the building, just in case.

One of the two technicians was in training and they had been looking at Amy Rogers' corpse, as much for erotic gratification as for education. "I'll be right there," as they were leaving the room. "I left the vault open," and he went back to close it. When attempting to slide the compartment shut, the stake in her heart was for some reason higher than before and lodged when closing. The trainee said, "Oh hell, she doesn't need this anymore," and yanked it out.

www.ingramcontent.com/pod-product-compliance
Lightning Source LLC
Chambersburg PA
CBHW051411170626
46809CB00006B/2116